D0359912

Strange but True

ALSO BY JOHN SEARLES

Boy Still Missing

WILLIAM MORROW

An Imprint of HarperCollins*Publishers*

Strange
but True

JOHN SEARLES

Grateful acknowledgment is made to reprint the following:

Last stanza from "A Curse Against Elegies," from *All My Pretty Ones* by Anne Sexton. Copyright © 1962 by Anne Sexton, renewed 1990 by Linda G. Sexton. Reprinted by permission of Houghton Mifflin Company. All rights reserved.

Excerpt from "Suicide Note," from *Live or Die* by Anne Sexton. Copyright © 1966 by Anne Sexton, renewed 1994 by Linda G. Sexton. Reprinted by permission of Houghton Mifflin Company. All rights reserved.

Excerpt from *Charlotte's Web* by E. B. White. Copyright 1952 by E. B. White. Renewed © 1980 by E. B. White. Used by permission of HarperCollins Publishers.

HarperCollins books may be purchased for educational, business, or sales promotional use. For information please write: Special Markets Department, HarperCollins Publishers Inc., 10 East 53rd Street, New York, NY 10022.

FIRST EDITION

Designed by Mia Risberg

Printed on acid-free paper

Library of Congress Cataloging-in-Publication Data

Searles, John.
  Strange but true / John Searles. — 1st ed.
    p. cm.
  ISBN 0-688-17571-6 (alk. paper)
    I. Title.
  PS3569.E1788S73 2004
  813'.6—dc22

                                                              2004044980

04 05 06 07 08 WBC/RRD 10 9 8 7 6 5 4 3 2 1

This story is for Thomas Caruso

Strange but True

chapter 1

ALMOST FIVE YEARS AFTER RONNIE CHASE'S DEATH, THE PHONE
rings late one windy February evening. Ronnie's older brother, Philip,
is asleep on the foldout sofa, because the family room has served as
his bedroom ever since he moved home from New York City. Tangled
in the sheets—among his aluminum crutch, balled-up Kleenexes, TV
Guides, three remote controls, and a dog-eared copy of an Anne Sexton
biography—is the cordless phone. Philip's hand fumbles in the dark until
he dredges it up by the stubby antenna and presses the On button. "Hello."

A faint, vaguely familiar female voice says, "Philip? Is that you?"

Philip opens his mouth to ask who's calling, then stops when he realizes who it is: Melissa Moody, his brother's high school girlfriend. His
mind fills with the single image of her on prom night, blood splattered on
the front of her white dress. The memory is enough to make his mouth
drop open farther. It is an expression all of the Chases will find themselves
wearing on their faces in the coming days, beginning with this very phone
call. "Missy?"

"Sorry, it's late. Did I wake you?"

Philip stares up at the antique schoolhouse clock on the wall, which has ticked and ticked and ticked in this rambling old colonial for as long as he can remember, though it never keeps the proper time. Both hands point to midnight, when it's only ten-thirty. Back in New York City, people are just finishing dinner or hailing cabs, but here in the Pennsylvania suburbs, the world goes dead after eight. "I'm wide awake," Philip lies. "It's been a long time. How are you?"

"Okay, I guess."

He hears the steady whoosh of cars speeding by in the background. There is a thinly veiled tremble in her voice that tells him she is anything but okay. "Is something the matter?"

"I need to talk to you and your parents."

If she wants to talk to his father, she'll have to track him down in Florida where he lives with his new wife, Holly—the woman his mother refers to simply as The Slut. But Philip doesn't bother to explain all that, because there is too much to explain already. "What do you want to talk about?"

Before Missy can answer, his mother's heavy footsteps thunder down the stairs. A moment later, she is standing at the edge of the foldout bed, her worn-out white nightgown pressed obscenely against her doughy body. A few nights before, Philip had caught the second half of *About Schmidt* on cable. Now he thinks of the scene where Kathy Bates bares all before getting in the hot tub—this moment easily rivals that one. He shifts his gaze to his mother's curly gray hair springing from her head in all directions like a madwoman—which is fitting, because to Philip, she *is* a madwoman. "Who is it?"

"Hold on," Philip says into the phone, then to his mother, "it's Missy."

"Melissa? Ronnie's girlfriend?"

Philip nods.

And then there is that expression: her eyebrows arch upward, her mouth drops into an O, as though she too has been spooked by the horrible memory of Melissa's prom dress splattered with Ronnie's blood. "What does she want?"

He gives an exaggerated shrug, then returns his attention to Melissa. "Sorry. My mom just woke up and wanted to know who was on the phone."

"That's okay. How is she anyway?"

All the possible answers to that question rattle around in his mind. There is the everyday fact of his father's absence, his mother's binge eating and ever-increasing weight, her countless pills for blood pressure, cholesterol, anxiety, and depression. But all he says is, "She's fine. So what do you want to talk to us about?"

"I'd rather tell you in person. Can I come by sometime?"

"Sure."

"When would be good?"

Philip thinks of his life in New York, the way he asked perfect strangers over to his camper-size studio in the East Village at all hours. The buzzer was broken, so he had to instruct each one to yell from the street. "How about now?" he hears himself say into the phone.

"Now?" Melissa says.

He waits for her to tell him that it's too late, too dark, too cold. But she takes him by surprise.

"Actually, I've waited too long to tell you this. So now sounds good to me."

After they say good-bye, Philip presses the Off button and tosses the cordless back into the rumpled mess of the bed. The skin beneath his cast itches, and he jams two fingers into the narrow pocket of space just above his kneecap, scratching as hard as he can. His mother stares down at him as an onslaught of questions spill from her mouth like she's regurgitating something and she cannot stop: "Aren't you going to tell me what's going on? I mean, why the hell would that girl call here after all this time? What, she doesn't know how rude it is to phone someone so late? For Christ's sake, aren't you going to answer me?"

Philip quits scratching and pulls his fingers free from the cast, which looks more like an elongated ski boot with an opening for his bruised toes at the bottom, instead of the plain white casts kids used to autograph when he was in high school only a decade ago. "If you shut up for a second, I'll answer you."

His mother crosses her arms in front of her lumpy breasts, making a dramatic show of her silence. The other night he'd watched *Inside the Actors Studio* and one of those actresses with three names (he could never keep track of who was who) had talked about playing her part for the back row of the theater. That's how his mother has gone through life these last five years, Philip thinks, her every move broad enough for the people in the cheap seats.

"She wants to talk to us," he says.

"About what?"

"I don't know. Whatever it is, she's going to tell us in person."

"When?"

"Now."

"Now? She can't come over now. It's the middle of the night."

"M," he says. The letter is a nickname Philip has used for her ever since he moved home one month ago. She's never questioned it, but he assumes she thinks it stands for *mother*. By now you might realize that it stands for that other M word: *madwoman*. His own private joke. He goes on, "Two A.M. is the middle of the night. Technically, it is still early evening. In New York, people are just finishing dinner."

At the mention of the city, she squeezes her lips into the shape of a volcano and shoots Philip a disgusted look. It makes him think of the only time she came to see him there, after the police called to tell her that he was in the hospital. She took Amtrak in. His father caught a JetBlue flight up from Florida. They had a Chase family reunion, right there on the tenth floor of St. Vincent's as Philip lay in bed, the wound on his neck buried beneath a mummy's share of gauzy bandages, his leg freshly set in its ski-boot cast, his body black and blue beneath the sheets.

"This is not New York," she says before turning and thundering back up the stairs, offering him a glimpse of her dimpled, jiggling ass through her threadbare gown.

A whole new meaning to the words *rear view*, Philip thinks.

When he hears the dull clamor of her opening drawers and slamming them shut, Philip reaches for his crutch and uses it to leverage his thin, aching body out of bed. The lights are off in the family room, but there are tiny ones everywhere: the red dot on the cable box, the flashing green numbers on the VCR, the blinking green light on the charger of his cell, the orange blur on all the dimmer switches. Together, they leave him with the vague impression that he is gazing out the window of an airplane at night. That image stays with Philip as he limps down the wide, echoing hallway. He takes the shortcut through the dining room no one ever uses, with its long mahogany table and Venetian glass chandelier, then crosses through the foyer into the bathroom beneath the stairs, which is about as small and confining as one on an airplane.

Philip's face in the mirror looks older than his twenty-seven years. There are no crow's-feet or creases in his brow or any of those obvious signs of aging. There is, however, a distinct pall of sorrow and worry in his eyes. It is the face of someone who has seen too much too soon. Then there is the matter of that wound—well on its way to becoming a fat red zipper of a scar across his throat that the doctors said would fade but never go away. Philip finds one of his baggy wool turtlenecks on top of the hamper, puts it on for camouflage, then combs his tangled brown hair and brushes his teeth. He's about to go back into the hallway when something makes him stop and open the medicine cabinet. The inside is still untouched, just like his brother's locked bedroom upstairs. He reaches in and pulls out the retainer. Ronnie's most obvious imperfection: an underbite.

"What are you doing?"

He turns to see his mother dressed in her librarian clothes, or rather the kind of clothes she wore when she was still a librarian. A beige cowlneck sweater and beige pants that she must have bought at the plus-size store at the King of Prussia Mall. She should have picked up a new nightgown while she was at it, Philip thinks. "I don't know," he tells her.

She steps inside, bringing with her a cloud of Right Guard for Women sprayed on upstairs in lieu of a shower. Her pill-swollen hand snatches the retainer from him and returns it to the exact shelf where he found it, between a dusty peroxide bottle and a tilted pile of cucumber soaps. When she closes the cabinet, her reflection in the mirror speeds by him in a dizzying flash, causing Philip to flinch. "I don't want you touching his things," she says.

It is an argument they've had before, and he won't allow himself to get caught up in it. Melissa will be here any minute, and the last thing he needs is to get his mother more worked up. He steps past her and heads down the hall to the kitchen, where he snaps on the lights. After making do with the camper-size kitchen in the studio he sublet in New York from that kook, Donnelly Fiume, Philip can't help but marvel at how sprawling this one is. It has dark wood cabinets, recessed lighting, and a porcelain-tiled floor that's made to look distressed, as though it belongs in a Tuscan monastery rather than a house on the Main Line of Philly. Most of their meals have been microwaved these last four weeks, but no one would ever guess, judging from the mountain of pots in the sink and bowls scattered across the granite countertop, all smeared with green. A few nights before, his mother had been possessed by one of her cravings. Pea soup, this time. Years ago, they had a cleaning woman who came twice a week for just this reason, her services paid for by his father's hefty salary as a heart surgeon at Bryn Mawr Hospital. Not anymore. Philip pulls open the refrigerator and takes out a paper sack of coffee to brew a pot the way he used to in the city when he was waiting for one of those strangers to shout up to him from the street.

"You're making coffee now?" his mother says from behind him.

This time, he doesn't turn around. He scoops two tablespoons into the filter for every cup, remembering how his heart used to beat hard and fast after he tossed his keys out the window and listened to the clomp-clomp-clomp on the crooked old stairway. "Yep."

"But won't you be up all night?"

"Nope."

They don't say anything after that. She gets a can of Diet Coke from her stash in the fridge and a bag of Doritos from the cabinet, then sits on the wooden stool by the chopping block and chews. Loudly. As Philip pours water into the machine, he thinks back to the last time Melissa Moody came for a visit. The summer after Ronnie died, she stopped by unannounced. His mother had been upstairs staring at her bedroom ceiling, his father puttering around his study, pretending to read one of his medical books. Philip had to put aside the assignment he was working on for his poetry class at the Community College of Philadelphia and drag them to the family room, where they sat, staring at this blond, broken-hearted girl covered in bandages until finally, his father walked her to the door and told her good-bye.

Now, as the coffee machine starts to gurgle and spit steam, white lights fill the room from the window. A car door slams in the driveway. Philip's heart begins to beat hard and fast, just like it used to those nights in New

York. He places his hand against his chest, then absently traces his fingers up to that wound beneath the turtleneck as he follows his mother to the foyer. To each side of the thick paneled door is a narrow slit of glass. She presses her face to the one on the right and broadcasts in a how-dare-she tone of voice, "She's pregnant. I can't believe it. The girl is pregnant."

Before Philip can remind her that Melissa has every right to be pregnant, she begins rambling again, keeping her face to the glass.

"Do you think that's what she's come to tell us? It better not be. That's all I have to say. The last thing I need to hear right now is how happy she is married to someone else when my son is rotting six feet beneath the ground."

"M," he says, "why don't we try something unconventional? Let's wait for her to tell us what she wants *before* you throw a fit."

She turns around and looks squarely at Philip, a pink smudge in the middle of her forehead from where she had pressed it to the glass. "I wasn't throwing a fit."

"Well, I can tell you're getting ready to. Besides, it's obvious you've never liked Melissa. But it's not her fault that Ronnie is gone."

"Maybe not," she says. "But you don't know everything."

"What don't I know?"

"I just told you. Everything."

"Whatever," Philip says, giving up on the discussion.

He puts his face to one of the narrow slits too, standing so close to his mother that he can smell the sweat beneath her Right Guard. As he gazes out at their snow-covered lawn, Philip inhales and holds it to keep from breathing in her odor. In the silvery winter moonlight, Melissa's body is a perfect silhouette, her stomach bulging before her as she navigates the icy, unshoveled walkway. When she gets closer, he sees that she is wearing nothing but a baggy Indian-print shirt that hangs down past her waist, and a loose pair of army green cargo pants. Before she reaches the front porch, his mother pulls open the door. Her lips part to say hello, but her mouth just hangs there.

"Hi," Melissa says from the shadows.

His mother is blocking the view, but Philip calls out, "Hi. Aren't you freezing?"

"It's not that cold."

Even as she says it, a gust of wind kicks up in the yard and blows into the house. Behind her, the branches of a tall oak tree make an angry scuttling sound in the darkness. Philip's mother is still locked in her strange, stunned silence, so he asks Melissa to come inside. Once the door is closed and she is standing in the bright light of the foyer, he realizes why his mother is so taken aback. Melissa is no longer the pretty blond girl his younger brother had taken to the prom five years before. Her once shiny, shoulder-length hair is now impossibly long and straggly, the color darkened to the same drab brown as Philip's. Her small ears, formerly bare and delicate, are now pierced with so many silver studs and hoops that it looks painful. The biggest change, though, is Melissa's face, which used to be so gentle and feminine, the kind of pure, all-American girl you might see in an ad for spring dresses in the department store circulars that come with the Sunday newspaper. Now that face, that smile, those eyes, are ruined by the scars from her last night with Ronnie. Philip would have assumed that she'd gone to a plastic surgeon, like the ones his father played golf with in Florida, but no. Imprinted on her left cheek is a crisscross of lines. Above her right eye is a mangled patch of skin that has somehow interfered with the hair meant to grow there, leaving her with half an eyebrow and a permanently lopsided appearance. She keeps her lips sealed in such a tight, unyielding way that it makes him think of a coin purse snapped shut. Only when she speaks does he get the briefest glimpse of the dark vacancy where her two front teeth used to be.

"What happened to you?" she asks Philip.

He is so preoccupied by her appearance that it takes him an extra second to remember his own physical state. "Oh," he says, realizing that it's best not to bring up what his mother calls "that business back in New York." He looks down at the hard gray plastic of his cast, the black bucklelike contraptions across the top of his foot. "I had an accident. A skiing accident."

"Are you okay?"

Philip wants to ask her the same thing, but it doesn't seem appropriate. "In another few weeks, I'll be good as new."

Melissa stuffs her hands into the pockets of her Indian-print shirt, causing the material to shift against her swollen stomach as she glances up the staircase. "Is Mr. Chase here?"

The question snaps his mother out of her trance. "No. Mr. Chase is not here."

Before she can go óff on the topic of his father—one of her favorite and most easily triggered rants—Philip says, "So you're pregnant."

Melissa looks at her belly, then turns her moss green eyes toward his. The tremble in her voice returns when she tells him, "Nine months."

"I guess you're due any day then?"

"I guess so," she says.

The moment feels tense, awkward suddenly, and Philip lets out a nervous laugh, trying to lighten the mood. "Well, don't go into labor on us or anything."

Melissa doesn't so much as smile. "Don't worry," she tells him. "I know when the baby will come."

And that's when his eyes trail down to her hand. He notices that she is not wearing a ring. In his mind, Philip hears his mother's voice saying, *The last thing I need to hear right now is how happy she is married to someone else when my son is rotting six feet beneath the ground.* Apparently, she doesn't have to worry about that. "Why don't we go into the kitchen so you can sit down?" he suggests, already leading the way.

Once they're inside, Melissa eases herself into one of the ladder-back chairs that Ronnie and his father used to complain were uncomfortable. His mother, who is keeping suspiciously quiet, resumes her position at the chopping block.

"M," Philip says, "why don't you join us over here?"

"I'm perfectly content where I am."

If Melissa notices his mother's peculiar behavior, she doesn't let on. Her face remains as still and vacant as a mannequin's, or a damaged mannequin anyway. Her mouth is sealed tight like that coin purse he'd imagined. Only those moss green eyes of hers move as she stares around the room—from the streaky pea-soup mess in the sink and on the counter, to the clutter of prescription slips held to the hulking refrigerator by a Liberty Bell magnet, to the wooden key rack hanging by the telephone, to the empty metal pot rack above his mother's head.

"Would you like something to drink?" Philip asks. "I just made a fresh pot of coffee."

"Thanks. But I can't have caffeine because of the baby."

This response relieves him, because he'd been wondering if someone so far along in a pregnancy should be driving, let alone walking around without a coat on such a frigid winter night. But Philip decides that maybe she knows what she's doing after all. Melissa tells him that she'd like water instead, so he pours her a glass from the Brita pitcher, then takes a mug from the cabinet for his coffee. It is one of his mother's from her days as the head librarian at Radnor Memorial Library, and the question *Can You Do the Dewey?* wraps around the side. Philip sits at the table and stirs while his mind busily churns up random details about Melissa that he'd all but forgotten: her father is a minister at the Lutheran church, and Ronnie used to complain about how strict he was; she has a twin sister named Tracy or Stacy; she had been accepted to Penn, just like Ronnie. "So I guess you're done with college by now," Philip says in an effort to get the conversation moving.

Melissa shakes her head. "I never went."

"But I thought you got into Penn?" He remembers specifically because he hadn't bothered to apply to any decent schools like that one, since he was too busy getting the crap beaten out of him in high school to earn the kind of grades he needed.

"I did get in," Melissa says. "I decided not to go."

"So where are you living these days?"

"Right here in Radnor."

"With your parents?"

She is about to answer when his mother leaves her stool and comes to the table. "Listen, you two can chat all night after I go to bed. But it's late. So if you don't mind, I'd like to skip the small talk. Why don't you tell us whatever it is you want to tell us?"

"M!" Philip shouts. "Don't be so rude!"

"It's okay," Melissa tells him, rubbing her hand on the exact center of her stomach where the Indian print comes together in a tangled cross. In her faint, shaky voice, she says to his mother, "Of course you want to know why I'm here."

"You're right. I do. So let's get on with it."

Philip doesn't bother to reprimand her again—not that it ever does any good anyway.

Melissa clears her throat and slowly picks up the glass from the table. When she takes a sip, her fingers are shaking so much that water sloshes over the rim and dribbles down her chin. She wipes it with her sleeve, then opens her mouth to speak, showcasing those unsightly black gaps front and center in her mouth. This is how she begins, this is how all the madness of the coming days begins: "I understand that it must seem strange for me to appear back in your life after all these years. But . . . well, I've thought about your family a lot as time has gone by. Especially you, Mrs. Chase. Because there can't be anything worse than a mother losing her child."

Philip glances at his mother and sees that her face has softened. For her, grieving has been a competition these past five years—the slightest acknowledgment that she is the winner makes her happy. With that last comment, Melissa may as well have draped a gold medal over her head.

Melissa goes on: "And I've never once stopped thinking about Ronnie either. That's why . . . well . . . I'm sorry I'm so nervous. It's just that I've thought about this moment for a long time. I wanted to come and tell you, months ago. But I was afraid."

"Afraid of what?" Philip asks.

"That you wouldn't believe me."

"Believe what?"

"Believe that—" She stops and swallows, making a lump in her throat that puts Philip in mind of the pet snake he took care of for Donnelly Fiume back in New York, the way it looked when it was digesting a mouse. "I'm sorry it's taking me a bit to get it out. But you know how you plan something in your mind, and then when the moment finally arrives, you forget exactly how you wanted to say things? That's how I feel sitting here right now. I guess . . . I guess I don't know where to begin. So maybe I'll just ask you first if you've ever watched that guy on TV, the one who talks to the dead?"

The question does something to his mother's face. Philip sees her blink three times in rapid succession; her upper lip twitches. But his face goes blank. His heart, which had been steadily picking up speed, feels as though it has just slammed into a wall. He has seen the guy Melissa is talking about plenty of times on late-night TV. Maybe you have too. A cherub-faced balding man with a thick Long Island accent who calls out random initials to people in the crowd as though he is summoning their beloved. When he hits the right initial and guesses a name, the guy spews details that the dearly departed is supposedly sending:

You once lost your engagement ring. . . .

You took a trip to an island. . . .

The two of you had a favorite song that you used to dance to. . . .

These bland bits of information cause people in the audience to weep, but Philip always finds himself wondering why they don't ask for more concrete details that might actually prove something, like a Social Security number or the name of a first-grade teacher. Instead of saying any of this, he stays quiet and listens to his mother and Melissa.

"Did you see this guy?" his mother asks, her lip still twitching as hope bubbles up in her voice.

"Not him. But there is a woman in Philadelphia named Chantrel who does the same thing. I went to see her."

"When?"

"Tonight."

"But I thought you said you've wanted to tell us this for months."

"This is all leading up to what I want to tell you."

"Well, what did this Chandra woman say?"

"Chantrel."

"Okay, Chantrel. What did she say?"

"Well . . ."

"Well, what?"

Melissa's eyes move to Philip, then to his mother again. "Ronnie communicated with me from the dead."

Philip's body language does nothing to hide his reaction. He leans back from the table and crosses his arms. At one time, he might have believed in this sort of thing, but there is a lot he used to believe that he doesn't anymore: God, love, fate, luck, and psychics who channel the dead, to name a few.

Meanwhile, his mother sits at the table and leans so close to Melissa that it looks as though she's going to take a bite out of her. "What did she say?"

"She told me that Ronnie is happy in heaven. He plays football all the time. He remembers the rose corsage he gave me on prom night."

As she talks, Philip has to fight the urge to limp back to the sofa bed and pick up his Anne Sexton biography or turn on Letterman, which is starting right about now. He hasn't done much this past month but read biographies of famous poets and watch TV. This moment reminds him why: his real life sucks. Melissa goes on to tell them that Ronnie misses his parents and that he visits the house a few times a year, especially on Christmas Eve. Philip is tempted to ask if he haunts them *before* or *after* Ebeneezer's house, but he refrains. When he can't stand keeping his mouth shut a second longer, he stands to get more coffee. That's when Melissa puts her hand on his. Her fingers feel as brittle as an old woman's, the pads chapped and warm.

"Philip," she says, looking at him with that eerily motionless face. "Ronnie had a message for you too."

Even though he knows better, even though it makes him cringe inside, even though he tells himself not to, Philip asks, "What did he say?"

Melissa reaches into her shirt pocket and pulls out a cassette. The blue writing on the label has the woman's name and today's date: CHANTREL: 2/3/04. "I think you should hear it for yourself."

"There's a tape?" his mother says. "Why didn't you tell us that sooner?"

"Like I said, I wasn't sure where to begin."

The only working stereo in the house is behind Ronnie's locked bedroom door, along with his maroon and white football uniform, the Canon AE-1 that he got for his last birthday to take pictures for the yearbook, his collection of beer T-shirts that say things like BEER: HELPING UGLY PEOPLE HAVE SEX FOR 2,000 YEARS, and a hundred other remnants of a teenage boy's life. The only difference, of course, is that this teenage boy is dead.

"We don't have a cassette player," Philip says.

"Yes, we do," his mother tells him. "In the family room."

"It doesn't work."

"Yes, it does."

"No, it doesn't."

"Yes, it does."

"No, M. It doesn't. No one but me listens to music in this house. So I should know. I've tried it."

"We could listen in my car," Melissa offers, realizing what must be obvious to anyone in their company: these two require a referee to reach even the smallest of decisions.

Philip's mother pushes away from the table, the legs of the ladder-back chair scraping against the tile floor. "Fine. That's what we'll do then."

"You two have fun," Philip tells them. "I'm not going."

As his mother stands, she makes that volcano mouth and shoots him another one of her disgusted looks. "What, your brother sends you a message after all this time and you're too good to hear it?"

"It's not that I'm too good to hear it. It's just that—" He stops. In both of their eyes, he sees how desperately they want—make that *need*—to believe this. As ridiculous as it is to Philip, he doesn't have the heart to take their foolish hope away. "It's just that it'll be too hard to fit in the car with my cast and all."

"No, it won't," Melissa says, rising slowly from the table. "You can squeeze in the back."

Outside, the walkway is slippery. Philip manages to steady himself with the help of his crutch. His mother, who is bundled in a black wool cloak that gives her the silhouette of a wide-winged navy jet, like the kind Philip once saw sweep over the city sky during Fleet Week, walks ahead with Melissa. Her attitude toward the girl has done a complete one-eighty. She has asked Melissa to drop the formal "Mrs. Chase" in favor of her first name, Charlene. She is even holding Melissa's hand in a way that looks like she is clinging to her, desperate for this unexpected connection to Ronnie. His mother's new tack makes Philip just as uncomfortable as he'd been with her rudeness earlier, because he knows how quickly she can change her mood and lash out—especially if she doesn't like what she hears on the tape.

The roof, hood, and trunk of Melissa's old Toyota Corolla are buried beneath a cake-layer of snow. A veneer of ice covers all the windows, except for a small patch cleared from the front windshield, as though she could only be bothered to do the bare minimum necessary to operate the car. When Melissa opens the back door for Philip, the smell of stale cigarette smoke and a faint undercurrent of rotting fruit or maybe old shoes instantly assaults him. Again, he has to wonder about a pregnant girl whose car smells like smoke. He wipes the seat clean of tapes, paperbacks, and a pair of gray sweatpants, then makes himself as comfortable as possible, considering the arctic feel of the air inside. It is not just cold—it is that certain kind of biting cold, particular to a car before it's been started on a bitter winter night. The seats feel hard and unyielding. The air stings the inside of his throat when he breathes it in. As he rubs his hands and waits for his mother and Missy to settle in up front, Philip looks at the dirty sweat socks, wrinkled jeans, T-shirts, and what he at first thinks are small black pebbles but then realizes are dead flies against the back window. His mother had cut Melissa off before she'd told him exactly where she lived in Radnor. Judging from the looks of things, he is beginning to suspect that it might very well be in this car. Philip turns to examine the seat pockets, stuffed with plastic grocery bags from Genuardi's and a math textbook with thick block letters on the spine that read: *ALGEBRA FOR YOUR FUTURE.* Finally, he glances at the floor and notices the labels on the cassettes that he pushed down there a moment before. He recognizes a few—Jewel: *Pieces of You,* Natalie Imbruglia: *Left of the Middle,* Hole: *Live Through This*—but the others look homemade and have the same handwriting as the one Melissa is about to put into the tape player, only with different names and dates:

Helene, 6/18/01
Davida, 12/23/99
Rasha, 3/17/02
Lyman, 6/18/03

To quell the uneasiness growing inside of him, Philip leans forward between the seats as Melissa starts the car then turns on the heat. That's when he sees a row of pictures taped to the cracked vinyl dashboard. From behind the yellowed, peeling tape, Ronnie smiles back at him with that infamous underbite. His sandy blond hair tousled, his eyes a dazzling Windex blue. In one shot, he is wearing his maroon and white football uniform and kneeling on an empty row of bleachers. In another, he is stretched back on a plaid blanket wearing a T-shirt from his collection: BEER: THE ONLY PROOF I NEED THAT GOD EXISTS. In another, he is dressed in a tuxedo and standing beside Melissa in front of a white brick fireplace. Her lacy dress is spotless, since the photo was taken before they piled into the limo to come home that night.

Philip wonders if his mother is beginning to realize how truly bizarre this visit has become. But then she taps her nail-bitten finger against Ronnie's senior class picture and says, "I have this one too. Only it's the eight by ten. I keep it on my dresser."

"I love that picture so much," Melissa says, pressing her hands flat against the vents to check on the hot air. "You can really see how blue his eyes are."

Were, Philip thinks and leans back in his seat.

The ice on the windows gives the car an igloo feeling that leaves him all the more cold and claustrophobic. Through a small opening, like a fishing hole in the ice, he stares out at their mammoth Pennsylvania flag-stone house with its wide sloping roof and tomato red shutters. One of his earliest memories is of the day they first came here when he was only four, just before Ronnie was born. They'd lived in an apartment on Spruce Street in Philly while his father finished his residency at Penn. Compared to those cramped quarters, this house felt palatial. Philip could still remember how happy he'd been when his mother—as pregnant as Melissa at the time—let him run up and down the empty hallways, his squeals of delight echoing around them as she trailed after him, teasing, *I'm gonna getcha . . . I'm gonna getcha . . . Mommy's gonna getcha, getcha, getcha. . . .*

"It might take me a minute to find the spot on the tape," Melissa says. "Because there were other people there tonight who she called on before me."

Philip looks away from the house and toward the front seat again. In the firefly glow of the dashboard, the scars on Melissa's face have faded. It is the slightest bit possible to glimpse the girl she used to be. He glances at his mother and tries to see her former self as well—the one who came to this house all those years ago and let her son run up and down the hallways, laughing as she followed him through the dining room and up the stairs.

"I think I found it," Melissa says.

When Chantrel begins speaking, her voice is not the heavily accented or cigarette-rattled sort Philip expects. It is smooth and calm. Articulate. The sound makes him think of the ER nurse at St. Vincent's who held his hand and spoke in soothing tones in his ear: *You've been through quite an ordeal. But you are going to be okay.*

"There is a young person speaking to me with the initial R," Chantrel says.

"Is his name Ronnie?" Melissa asks on the tape.

"Yes. It's Ronnie. He is telling me how much he misses you. He is showing me flowers. They look like they might be roses. Does that sound correct?"

"He gave me a rose corsage the night of our prom . . . the night he died."

That's all it takes for Chantrel to begin filling in the blanks. Each time Melissa provides another detail—the rented white limousine, Ronnie's love of sports and photography, her overwhelming grief—Chantrel runs with it. She tells her that Ronnie comes to visit his family a few times a year. She tells her that he likes to play football with other teenage boys who have died. The whole time, Philip wants to scream: What about his Social Security number? Or what about the name of his first-grade teacher? Or his beer T-shirt collection? Or the first time our father took us to play golf and I got in trouble for accidentally hitting Ronnie in the stomach when I swung? Or what about anything a little more fucking specific?

"I see someone writing a letter," Chantrel says. "Yes, someone is writing a letter. That is what Ronnie is showing me."

"Are you sure it's not a poem?" Melissa asks.

Philip remembers then that he had read one of his poems at the funeral. It was the first time he had admitted to his family that he liked to do something other than read and watch TV. The poem had been called "Sharp Crossing," and it was an extended metaphor about a young boy who climbed over a rusted barbed wire fence and cut himself on his way to the other side. Philip's poetry professor at the community college had loved it. But all the journals he'd submitted it to after he moved to New

York had sent back a polite form letter of rejection. Only one lousy editor took the time to scrawl something on the bottom, and even that wasn't encouraging: *Less metaphor, more meaning!* Philip used the letters to line the tank of that grotesque snake as well as the cage of the vicious mynah bird he took care of in the studio he sublet from Donnelly Fiume—*that* rejection went on top.

"Hold on," Chantrel says. "Indeed, it is a poem. Does someone connected to Ronnie like to write poetry?"

"His brother," Melissa says on the tape.

"Does his brother's name begin with a *B*?" There is a moment of silence during which Chantrel must realize she's gotten it wrong. Then she says, "I'm sorry. I heard him incorrectly. He is showing me what I think might be a *D* or a *T*." Another pause. "Does his name begin with a *T* or a *D*, or perhaps a *P*?"

Or an A, B, C, D, E, F, G? Philip thinks. Or maybe H, I, J, K, L, M, N, O, P?

"Philip," Melissa says to her. "It's his brother, Philip."

"Yes, that's it. Sorry, the connection was bad for a moment. Ronnie wants you to tell him that he loves his poetry."

"Did you hear that?" Melissa says now, looking at him in the rearview mirror.

Philip forces a smile, but it makes him feel like crying. He glances at his mother, who is making the volcano mouth again. When the tape stops, her voice erupts so loud and sudden that it startles Philip. "That's it? That's what you woke us up in the middle of the night for? To tell us that Ronnie likes Philip's poetry!" She says the last word with all the emphasis on the *p*, like she is spitting out something rotten—to her, Philip's poetry *is* something rotten.

"M," Philip says when he sees the look of surprise on Melissa's face. "Cut it out."

His mother stops to take a breath, but she is not done yet—far from it.

"How dare you waste my time with this bullshit? Do you know how hard it is for me? Do you? Every single day of my life I have to walk by his door. Every single day of my life I have to wake up and think my son is dead! You can just go on with your life, like Chantel or Chandra or whatever the fuck her name is said on the tape, but I will never go on! You can get knocked up by some guy without bothering to get married and live happily ever after, but this is it for me. Do you understand that? This is my life!"

"M!" Philip shouts again as tears well in Melissa's eyes and spill down her sad, ruined face. "Enough. Come on. Stop it."

But she won't stop. And she is wielding her finger now like a weapon, pointing directly at Melissa's face when she says the word *you* or *your*, then jabbing it into her own chest when she says something about herself. "*You* think *I'm* supposed to be impressed by those scars? Honey, *you* may look like that on the outside because *you* happened to be with him on the night he died. But *you* have no idea how disfigured and downright ugly *I* am on the inside because of what happened to *my* child. And if *you* could see it, *I* guarantee *you'd* run the other way. So do us both a favor, little girl, and back this shit box out of *my* driveway and don't *you* ever come back. *You* go have *your* bastard child and live *your* fucking life. But leave *me* alone."

"Mom!" Philip screams. "I said shut up! Shut! Up!"

And this time, she finally does shut up. She puts her finger against the cold glass, cooling it down, recharging for round two. The only sound that can be heard is Melissa crying as she buries her head in her hands. Her every breath is notched with small choking sounds, as though something long and knotted is being dredged up out of her throat. Philip is used to these violent eruptions, but this poor girl came here tonight without a clue as to the bottomless cauldron of vitriol that is his mother.

He waits for Melissa to stop crying and make the motions to leave. But it doesn't happen. He waits for his mother to tighten that black wool cloak around her neck and get out of the car. But that doesn't happen either. Instead, she stays in her seat, probably waiting for the opportunity to finish the girl off. She keeps her gaze on Melissa's shoulders as they heave up and down, like a cat spitting up a hairball or a clump of mowed grass.

Philip doesn't know what to do next. His eyes go briefly to those photos on the dashboard, where Melissa is smiling next to Ronnie. His brother was everything Philip wasn't—popular, outgoing, athletic, an honor student. The normal son his parents wanted and got right on the second try. Ronnie had even outdone him by dying, because he would never get the chance to mess up his life the way Philip had. All these years later, Philip still feels a phantom pang of jealousy just looking at his brother's picture, which only makes him feel more pathetic for being jealous of a dead person. Finally, he stops looking at the picture and puts his hand on Melissa's small shoulder. He tells her that he's sorry for what just happened, that there's no reason to cry, that everything is okay.

"Everything is not okay," she says, peeling her hands from her face and craning her neck to look at him. From this angle, the dashboard light illuminates a jigsaw portion of her face, setting her mangled patch of skin aglow. She looks lit from within, as though a fire has been stoked inside of her. "You don't understand. The tape is not done yet. I just have to flip it over so you can hear the rest."

"The rest?" Philip says.

And then she does exactly that—reaching down to press the Eject button, flipping the tape, and pushing it back in. Instantly, Chantrel's voice fills the car, this time more hushed than before. Melissa turns up the volume. "But none of that is why you've come here tonight, is it?" Chantrel whispers.

Outside, the wind blows so hard it shakes the car. The bare branches of the giant oak tree in the front yard make that angry scuttling sound.

"No," Melissa says on the tape, shaking her head now too.

"You have come about the baby, haven't you?"

Melissa nods, as though she is still in the presence of Chantrel. It is all so pitiful and sad that Philip has to turn his eyes away. He doesn't want to think about what his mother will do when the tape ends this time. Through that tiny fishing hole in the ice, he looks up at his brother's dark window and begins making a mental map of the room to put his mind on something else. Anything else. There is the single bed with the navy blue quilt; the nicked wooden desk with the electric pencil sharpener; the clutter of trophies, each with a small golden man on top, running, throwing, catching; a U2 poster on the back of the door of Bono strumming a guitar; an ancient set of oversize silver walkie-talkies on the bookshelf. When Philip can't remember anymore, he tries to recall those beer T-shirts instead:

I GAVE UP DRINKING: IT WAS THE WORST FIFTEEN MINUTES OF MY
    LIFE . . .

THE DIFFERENCE BETWEEN BEER AND JESUS: YOU DON'T HAVE TO WAIT
    2000 + YEARS FOR A SECOND BEER . . .

"All these years and you've never stopped loving him, have you?" Chantrel is saying as his mother starts tapping her fist against the door, warming up for what is sure to be an explosive finale. "First love is the most pure, because we give our entire heart and soul over to the person. You gave that to Ronnie, didn't you?"

"Yes," Melissa says in unison with her own voice on the tape.

His mother knocks her fist harder.

BEER, SO MUCH MORE THAN A BREAKFAST DRINK, Philip thinks.

CONSERVE WATER, DRINK BEER . . .

GREAT MINDS DRINK ALIKE . . .

"He is telling me that he hears you. He is telling me that he knows the pain you've felt since he passed to the other side. And that's why he has found a way to carry on in your life. That's why this baby is special. I think you know it is the gift that you have been praying for all these years. It has been blessed by Ronnie so that you can move on. It is . . . I'm sorry, dear, but the connection is cutting out. He says he has to leave now. He's gone. I've lost him."

This time the tape goes quiet for good.

Philip stares nervously at his mother, who has stopped her tapping. She looks like she is getting ready to scream again, but Melissa is crying harder now, her shoulders heaving, her hands shaking. He senses that even his mother doesn't know what to do.

"What is it?" Philip asks Melissa.

She is gasping so loudly that it takes her a moment to get out her next words. "Don't you get it? That's what I came here to tell you. What she said about the baby on the tape is true."

"What's true?" Philip says, without giving his mother a chance to speak.

"It is a gift from him." She stops talking and inhales a final deep breath before telling them, at long last, the reason she has come here tonight. "I've only been with one person in my life. Ronnie. On the night he died. It was our first and last time together. My first and last time with anyone. And now, all these years later, I'm pregnant and I don't know what to do. Because somehow, I don't know how, but a strange sort of miracle has happened. This baby inside me belongs to him."

chapter 2

FOUR YEARS, SEVEN MONTHS, FIFTEEN DAYS, AND FIVE HOURS BE-
fore Melissa Moody shows up at the Chases' house and delivers this unthinkable news, she is sitting on the cushioned seat by her bedroom
window, waiting and watching for the white limousine to round the corner with Ronnie inside. On this warm June evening, she is still a high
school senior, still an innocent teenager with the same kind of sweet, flaw-
less face as those girls in the department-store circulars that come with the
Sunday paper. Melissa doesn't know yet, of course, that this will be her last
night with that face. For now, she is happily dressed in her lacy, pearl-
colored Gunne Sax gown. It is a vintage dress that she bought for twenty-
nine dollars at The Rusty Zipper in Philadelphia, since she couldn't find
anything decent at the King of Prussia Mall given the fifty-dollar budget
set by her stingy parents. Melissa is so grateful that they consented to let
her and her sister go to the prom that she hasn't dared utter a single word
of complaint.

Down the hall, she hears the sounds of Stacy getting ready. A hair dryer
whirs on and off. A brush clanks against the vanity. The medicine cabinet

opens then slams shut. Stacy opted for an emerald green dress off the clearance rack at Filene's that their mother took in on the sewing machine. Melissa warned her that it was a mistake, but Stacy didn't listen. Now her sister is sorry because it looks, well, it looks like an emerald green dress off the clearance rack that their mother took in on the sewing machine.

"Missy!" Stacy yells in a nails-against-the-chalkboard voice. "Please come save me from this fashion nightmare!"

"I'll help you in a minute," Melissa calls back, gazing once more toward the end of the street and past the white clapboard church on the corner. The limo is nowhere in sight. All she sees is a group of young girls Rollerblading near the stop sign. They've built a makeshift ramp with scrap plywood and two large rocks borrowed from a neighbor's stone wall. So far none of them has made it over without crashing to the ground. I used to babysit for those girls back in junior high, Melissa thinks, now here I am going to my prom. For the first time in her life, she feels grownup and free—or close to free anyway—from the prison of her parents' rules. Much of that feeling has to do with Ronnie and the plans they've made for tonight, not to mention the plans they've made for their lives after graduation.

"Missy! Ronnie and Chaz will be here any second, and I look like a mermaid!"

Melissa can't help but laugh. "I'm sure Chaz will love you as a mermaid. It'll be like that movie they always show on TBS with Daryl What's-her-ass and Tom Hanks."

"Very funny," Stacy says, pushing open the bedroom door and holding the brush in front of her like a small sword. "I'm serious. I need your help."

"It's not like I didn't warn you."

"Okay, so you warned me. I admit it. You are hereby officially dubbed the all-knowing goddess of prom-dress wisdom. So can you come down from your throne and tell me what I should do?"

Stacy puts her hand against her hip, a hip that Melissa can't help but notice looks twice its normal size thanks to the dress. The thing fits her like the slipcovers their mother made for the donated chairs in the lounge of the church basement—tight in all the wrong places, baggy everywhere else. The color hurts to look at.

"Is there a dimmer switch on the back of that thing?" Melissa says, shielding her eyes with her hand.

Her sister lets out a huff. "Make fun of me all you want, but it's not like you just stepped out of the pages of *Seventeen* in that hundred-year-old doily."

"It's a twenty-year-old doily."

"Whatever. Look, are you going to help me or not?"

Melissa knows that she should stop teasing Stacy, but it is just too much fun. She goes to her dresser and pulls open the top drawer. Buried beneath her socks and underwear and what she thinks of as her decoy diary is a pair of sunglasses. Melissa takes them out and gives them to her sister.

"I don't get it," Stacy says.

"Tell Chaz to put them on to protect him from the UV rays when you guys are dancing."

"Fuck you!" Stacy screams, and throws the hairbrush and sunglasses at Melissa. They nearly hit her in the face before landing on the waxed wooden floor and sliding beneath the bed.

"Girls!" their father calls up the stairs in his deep, Sunday-sermon drawl.

Melissa and Stacy know what's coming next, and they mouth his words in unison when he says, "You know how I feel about profanity."

"Stacy, tell him you're sorry before he changes his mind about letting us go."

Her sister looks down at her green ruffles in all of their splendor. "At this point, he'd be doing me a favor."

"Come on, Stace. I'm not letting you screw up this night for me. Tell him you're sorry."

"If I do, will you stop ragging on me about the dress?"

"Deal."

"Sorry, Dad!" Stacy calls down the stairs. Then to her sister, she poses the same question she's been asking for weeks. "So should I wear my hair up or down?"

Melissa steals another glance out the window toward the stop sign near the church at the corner. One of the Rollerblading girls—Wendy Dugas is her name—attempts the jump and wipes out. The limo is still nowhere in sight. She turns her focus back toward the mirror that is her sister. Melissa used to love everything about having a twin, from the matching outfits their mother bought them growing up to the questions people would inevitably ask: *Have you ever had a psychic experience? Have you ever traded places for a day? How did your parents tell you apart when you were babies?* Just knowing there was a Xerox of herself in the world used to make Melissa feel special. Lately, though, that feeling has changed. When she looks at Stacy, Melissa finds herself focusing on their differences instead of their similarities. For starters, there is the way her sister's mouth is always set in a bratty pout, the way her face looks stretched and elastic when she laughs. Then there is the laugh itself, which is grating and so much louder than Melissa's. Ronnie was the first to point out the small differences while listing the reasons he was drawn to Melissa instead of Stacy. He was the first person to ever see her as a wholly separate being from her twin, which makes her love him all the more.

"Earth to Missy," Stacy is saying. "Hello. Are you in there?"

"I'm here."

"Well, what do you think of my hair?"

"Your hair? I thought it was the dress that needed help."

"It *is* the dress. But I'm focusing on the things I can fix in the next few minutes. So which is it: up or down?" Stacy demonstrates, as though for the first time, holding her hair on top of her head, then letting it fall to her shoulders.

"Down," Melissa tells her, because she is wearing hers up and she wants to look different from her sister tonight. Especially tonight.

Stacy is about to ask another question when her eyes go to the window. "Oh, my God! They're here!"

Melissa turns and sees the gleaming white limousine pass the evergreen at the corner of the yard then pull into the driveway. The last bits of fading sunlight glint off the long sleek hood; the glass is tinted black just like in the movies. They cross the room and watch as the car comes to a stop behind their parents' gold Geo. A door opens and out steps Chaz. At the age of seventeen, he already has the beginnings of a beer belly. His skin is the color of a cooked ham, his hair clipped so close to his scalp that it is impossible to tell the true color. Chaz is leaving for the air force one week after graduation. Even now, as he stands in their driveway dressed in his rented black tux, Melissa can picture him in uniform. He and Ronnie are friends because they're on the football, basketball, wrestling, and track teams together, but Melissa has to constantly reassure herself that they are nothing alike. For one thing, Chaz is forever groping her sister by the lockers at school—a major no-no if their parents ever found out. And in algebra class, he makes a habit of writing Melissa flirty little notes in the pages of her textbook—a major no-no if Stacy ever found out. Worst of all are the lame "minister's daughter" jokes he makes when the four of them are together:

She's a minister's daughter, but I wouldn't put anything pastor. . . .

She's a minister's daughter, but she sure knows how to fleece her flock. . . .

Melissa is always tempted to respond: You're not a minister's daughter, but you sure are an asshole.

"Where's Ronnie?" Stacy asks, because Chaz has been standing in the driveway for almost a minute, yawning and stretching, adjusting the crotch of his pants.

Another thing Melissa hates about Chaz: he is always adjusting the crotch of his pants.

She feels a stab of worry that something has gone wrong, that perhaps Ronnie has changed his mind about tonight. But just then, the sunroof slides open and his six-foot-tall, broad-shouldered frame sprouts out of the car like a beautiful blond sunflower. He looks toward the bedroom window, and when his eyes meet Melissa's, Ronnie lifts his camera and snaps a picture. Then he smiles and extends his arm in mock-drama. "Juliet. Juliet. Wherefore art thou, Juliet?"

Melissa pushes the window up all the way. "You dork! You have it backward! Juliet is supposed to say the 'wherefore art thou' part."

"Oh," Ronnie says. "Well, what does Romeo say?"

"I don't know. How about let down your hair, Rapunzel? I like that story better anyway."

"How about you two get your butts down here?" Chaz says.

Stacy puts her finger to her mouth and shushes him. Then she points to the front door, indicating that he should shut up before their parents hear.

"Sorry," Chaz says and makes the sign of the cross. "Well, are you guys coming down?"

"Not until you ring the doorbell and make a good impression on our mom and dad like proper gentlemen," Stacy tells him.

Chaz picks at his crotch. "A first time for everything."

With that, Ronnie drops back through the black rectangle of the sun-roof, momentarily vanishing before reemerging from the side door, holding his camera and a clear plastic box with Melissa's red corsage inside. As the guys approach the house, Stacy turns away and squats to look under the bed in an effort to retrieve her hairbrush. Meanwhile, Melissa keeps her eyes on Ronnie. She can hardly believe that she found someone like him among all the jerks like Chaz at their school. Melissa loves everything about him. Everything. The sweaty smell of his skin after practice. The way his ass looks so tight and pinchable in his football uniform. The brilliant blue of his eyes. His beefy shoulders. His slight underbite. The fast, excited way he jumps from topic to topic whenever they are talking. Melissa loves him because he is unafraid to act goofy, like he did with that "wherefore art thou?" routine. She loves the way he keeps his sandy hair parted, not quite in the middle but not on the side either. A few loose strands are forever hanging down over his forehead, which he constantly pushes back to no avail. Melissa even loves his habit of licking his lips when he talks, because it makes her think about kissing him whenever he is in her sight. He is doing it now, in fact, flicking back his hair and licking his lips as they walk toward the front door of the Moodys' small cape.

Right on cue, Melissa's thoughts go to all the times after school when they sneak into the darkroom off the photography class. Since Ronnie is the yearbook photographer, he is the one and only student with a key. He always lays a blanket on the floor, and they make out in there for hours, pressing their bodies against each other in the dim red light of that room, the smell of the developing chemicals making her high. How many times have we forced ourselves to stop from going all the way? she wonders. Too many to count. But Melissa is glad they waited, because it will make to-night all the more special.

When the doorbell rings downstairs, it is as though someone comes up from behind her and dunks her head in one of those developing tubs in the darkroom, because she feels plunged suddenly into an intense, poisonous kind of nervousness. Melissa puts a hand to her roiling stomach and walks to her white wicker nightstand to take a sip of water. She squeezes her eyes shut in an effort to force out all thoughts of those times with Ronnie and what they've planned for tonight, at least until she gets through the next few minutes with her parents. Melissa straightens her dress, then looks out the window once more. The Rollerbladers have dragged their makeshift jump to the side of the road and left it there until tomorrow, when they'll try again—only Melissa doesn't plan to be around to see if they finally make it over.

"Girls," their mother calls, in a voice so forced full of cheer that she sounds like a '50s mom on a Nick at Nite rerun. "Your dates are here."

"Let's go," Stacy says from over by the dresser mirror, where she is brushing her hair.

"I need to pee," Melissa tells her. "Go ahead. I'll be there in a second."

When her sister is gone, Melissa unzips the large purse she is taking with her despite Stacy's jabs over the last few days about its size. Melissa does one last check of its contents: a rolled-up pair of khakis, a plain white T-shirt, flip-flops, a change of underwear, and a toothbrush. Cushioned inside it all, is a red forty-watt lightbulb she bought at CVS a few days before as a small surprise for Ronnie. If she can manage to get through the night without breaking it, she plans to screw the bulb into the lamp beside the bed at the inn where they are going to stay, as a funny reminder of all those times in the darkroom. There is more she would like to take along, but that's all that will fit, and she doesn't want her parents or Stacy to become suspicious. Besides, she and Ronnie plan to be gone just a few days. Even though the trip will get her grounded for the entire summer and punished more than she can ever imagine, Melissa tells herself that it will be worth it. She wants their first time to be special. Unlike those slutty girls in her class who gave it up long ago in their bedrooms after school while their parents were at work, Melissa wants to remember this night forever.

Before leaving, she opens her top drawer and unlocks her diary to read over what she wrote inside a few hours ago. In a perfect girlie script she crafted just for this book, it says:

I am so excited for the prom tonight! Jesus has blessed me with the most amazing mother and father, and I am grateful to them for letting me have this special opportunity. I am also blessed to have found a good Christian boy like Ronnie, who shares my same beliefs about the Lord.

Melissa knows she is laying it on thicker than usual, but she doesn't want to take any chances. And for some superstitious reason, she kisses the page before closing and locking the book, then burying it back beneath her underwear and socks. When she leaves the bedroom and goes to the top of the stairs, Melissa pauses and looks down. Ronnie, Chaz, and Stacy are on the other side of the living room, so she can't see them from here. Only the full moon of her father's bald spot and the yellow puff of her mother's hair are in view. Something about their waxy, creaseless faces and neat clothing has been bugging Melissa lately. She wishes they'd get a few more wrinkles on their faces *and* their clothes, the way normal parents do. Her mother is quiet, like she always is around her father. His deep, dry voice drones on as he lectures about the rules of the evening while jangling the change in his pocket, fishing up the coins, then sifting them between his fingers.

At first, it is hard for her to make out the words. She hears him say the obvious things: "no alcohol . . . home before midnight. . . ." Then something, something, something, and the subject changes. ". . . track meets before graduation . . . you think you'll be able to break your shot put record?"

"I intend to, sir," Chaz says in response, pulling off the gentleman routine better than Melissa would have guessed.

"Chaz is the only one in the history of Radnor High School ever to throw more than nineteen meters," Stacy says.

Melissa knows Ronnie must be bored out of his skull by this discussion, since they've already been subjected to Stacy and Chaz's verbal diarrhea about his dumb shot put record. When Melissa descends the staircase to save him, Ronnie looks so good standing there in his tuxedo over by the white brick fireplace that a new kind of aching fills her. It feels as though someone has pumped too much blood into her body and it is seeping out her pores into the air, making everything around her glow red just like in the darkroom.

"You look lovely, dear," her mother says, lifting her disposable camera to snap a picture.

"Just gorgeous," her father tells her in the fake, jovial voice he puts on in front of company or in the reception area at church.

Melissa glances at the weapon of his thin brown belt, then looks away toward Ronnie to stop the roiling in her stomach. "So what do you think?" she asks, looking down at her dress. "Do you like it?"

Ronnie licks his lips and smiles. "Like it? I love it. You look beautiful."

Even though she tries not to, all Melissa can think about is kissing him, pressing her body to him, feeling him go hard in his pants as he pushes and pushes and pushes against her . . . until, for the first time tonight, he will push himself *inside* of her.

"Why don't you put the corsage on Missy before we take a picture of the two of you over by the fireplace?" her mother says.

Ronnie steps closer, bringing a wave of body heat as he does. His thick fingers pull the roses out of the plastic box, and she holds her wrist in front of her rapidly beating heart. As he slips the lace band over her hand, Melissa hears the sound of her father fishing up the contents of his pockets and sifting it through his fingers. Although she can't see it there among the quarters, dimes, nickels, and pennies, she knows he is carrying the spare silver key to her diary—the one that went missing months ago. She knows too that he will unlock it and read her most recent entry not long after they leave this house tonight. But by the time he begins to suspect that everything she has written inside is a lie, Melissa will be miles away from Radnor, on her way to someplace secret, where he won't be able to find her until she is ready to come home.

When Ronnie finishes securing the tight fist of roses to her wrist, he gives her hand a gentle squeeze and asks, "Are you ready?"

"I'm ready all right," she tells him. "Ready as I'll ever be."

chapter 3

"ARE YOU FUCKING CRAZY?" CHARLENE CHASE SHOUTS AT MELISSA from the passenger seat. "Is that it? Are you some kind of a nut job?"

Melissa knew Ronnie's family would have a hard time believing what she just told them. Even she had a hard time believing it . . . at first. But now that the baby has grown full-term inside of her, there is no denying that this is the miracle she has prayed for all these years. Night after night after night, on her knees, beside her bed, in the run-down cottage she rents from sweet old Mr. and Mrs. Erwin, Melissa has sent up an endless stream of desperate, drunken cries from her lips, as they say, to God's ears. *Please . . . If I could just have Ronnie back . . . If you could just give me another chance like I almost got that summer. . . .* And now, somehow, those prayers have been answered. Melissa's fate, which had been snatched away from her, has been returned. She sees herself as a modern-day rendering of those stories her father preached from the pulpit every Sunday morning throughout her childhood as she squished between Stacy and her mother, absently kicking the heels of her white buckle shoes against the front pew while she listened to him prattle on.

There was a woman in the crowd who had been hemorrhaging for twelve years. She had spent everything she had on doctors and still could find no cure. She came up behind Jesus and touched the fringe of his robe. Immediately, the bleeding stopped.

"Who touched me?" Jesus asked.

Everyone denied it, and Peter said, "Master, this whole crowd is pressing up against you."

But Jesus told him, "No, someone deliberately touched me, for I felt healing power go out from me."

When the woman realized that Jesus knew, she began to tremble and fell to her knees before him. The whole crowd heard her explain why she had touched him and that she had been immediately healed. "Daughter," he said to her, "your faith has made you well. Go in peace."

Melissa sees herself as that bleeding woman whose bleeding has finally stopped.

This baby is her healing. Ronnie's healing too.

Yes, of course, she is afraid. And yes, of course, she had expected shock from the Chases, along with all the rest: confusion, bewilderment, a never-ending parade of unanswerable questions. But somehow she had allowed herself to imagine an edge of excitement and anticipation beneath it all, because that is the way she feels. If anyone might share those feelings, it would be Ronnie's family—or so she thought before tonight. The last thing Melissa anticipated was this venomous reaction from his mother. As a result, she feels blindsided by her own disappointment, knocked off-kilter by Charlene's relentless verbal pummeling. Melissa tries hard to get hold of herself and stop crying as she fixes her eyes on the woman's creased, mole-speckled face, on the ringed flab of skin that shakes above the folds of her beige cowl-neck sweater while she rages on and on.

"How dare you come here in the middle of the night and deliver this line of horseshit! My son is dead, and you're fucking with my emotions! What is this, your idea of a joke? Well, let me tell you, it's a pretty sick joke at that."

"Calm down, M," Philip says from the backseat, for what must be the tenth time tonight. "Why don't you forget this ever happened and go on inside?"

"Don't tell me to calm down, and don't tell me to forget anything! My son is dead and this . . . this . . . this nobody who dated him for one lousy year of his life shows up in the middle of the night and claims she is carrying his baby." She thrusts her finger forward and this time does more than point; she jabs it with such force into Melissa's shoulder that it stings. "Don't you have anything to say for yourself? Huh? Don't you? Answer me!"

Any response Melissa can think to offer is certain to sound flimsy when faced with such fury, so she stays quiet. All this crying has left her eyes and nose running. She feels drained of energy as she joins her shaking hands together, prayerlike under the steering wheel, in an effort to still them.

"Say something!" Charlene screams. "Say something before I strangle your scrawny little neck!"

"Cut it out," Philip says. "Give her a chance."

A heavy silence falls over the car then. Nothing can be heard but the hiss of hot air from the dashboard vents. If it weren't for Charlene and Philip, Melissa wouldn't have bothered with the heat at all. As it is, her skin feels slick and slippery with sweat beneath her clothes. No matter what she has done these past nine months, Melissa has been unable to cool down. There have been ice-cold showers. There have been nights in bed with the covers kicked off and the windows wide open. Those efforts work for a short time, but sooner or later, the fever that burns inside of her returns. It is the baby, Melissa knows. It is all part of this strange miracle.

"Well?" Ronnie's mother prods.

Finally, Melissa opens her mouth and says the only thing she can think to say, "It's true."

Charlene is about to start screaming again, but Philip cuts her off, "Melissa, you know very well that it can't be true. It's not possible."

"You don't believe me now," she tells him, pressing her hands tighter together and trying to keep her voice from cracking. "But you will."

"I don't understand," he says. "Do you have some sort of blood test or something to show us?"

"No. I made the decision to stay away from doctors, because I know they won't understand either. That's why I was hoping Mr. Chase—"

Before she can finish, Charlene and Philip sputter over each another. "You're nine months pregnant and you haven't even gone to a friggin' doctor!" Charlene shouts at the same time Philip asks, "Then what proof could you possibly have that would make us believe?"

Melissa's mind is so muddled and fatigued that she hears a hybrid of these two things: *you're proof pregnant could possibly have a friggin' doctor believe.* It takes her a moment to disentangle and decipher each statement before she tells Charlene, "No. I haven't," and Philip, "You will believe when I have the baby."

"Why?" he asks.

"Because you will see its resemblance to Ronnie."

"That's it. I'm getting the hell out of this car!" Charlene yanks the door handle and steps outside, somehow managing to snag her arm in the seat belt. There are a few seconds of mad wrestling until she dislodges herself and shouts at Philip, "Are you coming or not?"

"In a second."

She lets out a guttural sound from the back of her throat that signals her absolute exasperation with him too. "Suit yourself, stupid," she says, then leans her flaccid, blinking face into the car and looks deep into Melissa's eyes. "You, young lady. You should be ashamed of yourself."

Melissa swallows hard and shakes her head from side to side. "I loved your son. And I have nothing to be ashamed of."

Charlene's only response is to slam the door.

Neither Melissa nor Philip says a word as they watch her stomp up the walkway, pound up the front stairs, then disappear into the house. When the porch light goes dark, Melissa feels disappointment scrape against her insides.

Maybe, she thinks, maybe if I hadn't told them so much at once, or maybe if I hadn't played the tape of Chantrel. Or maybe . . . maybe . . . maybe . . . Her mind spins out all the possibilities until finally settling on the fact that it is too late now.

What's done is done.

Behind her, Philip clears his throat. Maybe, she thinks, maybe he stayed behind because he wants to believe me after all. She glances at his pale, angular face in the rearview mirror. It seems odd to her how little he resembles his brother. Unlike Melissa and her sister, somehow Philip and Ronnie had managed to inherit the exact opposite genes from their parents. Ronnie had his mother's wide eyes, his father's broad shoulders and olive skin, whereas Philip has his father's squinty eyes, his mother's slumped posture and pasty complexion. Still, there is a kindness about him that reminds Melissa of Ronnie, a familiar compassion in his weary eyes.

"Sorry about her," Philip says in a gentle, reed-thin voice, which is yet another distinction from Ronnie, who sounds, or used to sound, like a DJ on drive-time radio.

A memory surges up in her mind then of Ronnie pleading with her in that rushed voice on prom night. *Come on, Missy. Don't be pissed. I didn't mean to mess up our plans.* As quickly as the memory comes, Melissa forces it back down. She doesn't want to think of all the time she wasted being angry at him in those final hours of his life, no thanks to Chaz. She removes her hands from beneath the steering wheel and rubs the spot on her shoulder where Charlene jabbed her. It feels as though she has been stung by a bee, or maybe an entire swarm. But she is used to pain—in fact, she has come to crave it. "I understand why your mother's upset. I know how difficult it must be to accept what I'm saying."

"Difficult is hardly the word. Melissa, it's—"

"Do you still have Ronnie's old Mercedes?" If he is going to tell her again that it's not possible, she doesn't want to hear it.

"I guess. I haven't been in the garage since I moved home. But I doubt my mother got rid of it. The woman treats his retainer like it's a museum relic. She keeps everything of Ronnie's. I mean, everything."

So do I, Melissa thinks as she stares straight ahead at the Chases' garage. On the other side of those three red doors, the 1979 cream-colored 300 DSL Ronnie bought with his father's credit card from a used-car lot rests quietly like a game-show prize waiting to be revealed. Melissa pictures Mrs. Chase going out there each week and starting the engine to keep it from dying the way she must have to do. She imagines her sitting in the leather seat where Ronnie used to sit, sliding Ronnie's silver key into the ignition, placing her foot on the pedal where Ronnie used to place his. It is just not fair, Melissa thinks. None of it is fair. "We were supposed to take that car to the prom instead of renting a limo," she says out loud without really meaning to. She has a habit of this, though normally no one is around to hear except Mr. and Mrs. Erwin, whom she spends so much time with that she thinks of them less as landlords and more like surrogate parents. Melissa doesn't know how she would get by without them.

"What did you say?" Philip asks.

"I said, we were supposed to take that car to the prom instead of renting a limo."

"So why didn't you?"

"It was Chaz's big idea."

"Chaz," Philip says, and Melissa thinks she detects a tone of disgust in his voice, which he quickly confirms. "I never understood why Ronnie hung out with that guy. I couldn't stand him."

"Yeah, well, me neither."

She stifles a yawn. This conversation, this night, these last nine months, have left her exhausted. She feels as though she could put her head against the steering wheel and sleep for years without waking. It is only a matter of time, she figures, until Philip brings the conversation back to the baby, so she braces herself for another round of accusations and questions. But he keeps right on blathering about Chaz. "I mean, what the hell kind of name is that anyway? His parents might as well have called him WASP idiot."

Melissa lets out a laugh, despite herself. Even that small effort depletes her energy more.

"Don't tell me. He went off to Princeton or some other Ivy League college. By now he's probably in law school somewhere, thanks to his parents who greased the wheels for him by making donations every step of the way. God forbid people in this town make something of their lives on their own."

"Actually, last I knew, he went into the air force."

"Oh. Well, whatever. It's still a stupid name."

Melissa glances at him in the rearview mirror again. Only this time, she stops thinking about Philip in relation to Ronnie. She finds herself wondering about the kind of person he has become these past five years.

Last she knew, he was waiting tables at the Olive Garden over in Wayne and taking classes at a community college in Philadelphia. "Where were you living before you moved home?"

"New York."

"Did you like it?"

"Mostly, I guess. It's crowded and expensive. But it's a lot more exciting than Pennsylvania."

She asks him how long he lived there, and he tells her about four and a half years. He goes on to say that one night, months after Ronnie died, he got fed up with his job as a waiter and his part-time classes. In the middle of his shift at the restaurant, with his midterm poetry portfolio due the next morning, he punched his time card and walked out the kitchen door. A short while later he was on his way into the city. "I realized pretty quickly that it wasn't the job or the classes that got to me. It was my mother. She was too—well, as you just witnessed, she can be pretty unbearable."

It's odd, Melissa thinks, because the way Charlene looked and acted from the moment she opened the door this evening was in direct contradiction to Melissa's memory of her. She wasn't thin, even back then, but she certainly wasn't as big as she is now. And she used to seem so spunky and full of life. "Why did you come back?" she asks Philip.

"Like I said, I had an accident."

"Oh, yeah. Skiing."

"Skiing," he says again, running his index finger around the rim of his turtleneck.

She can't say why exactly, but Melissa gets the feeling he is lying, or at least that he's not telling the whole story. Either way, she lets the conversation die, because it's none of her business and because she is distracted by her thirst. Despite the problem her swollen stomach presents, she manages to lean over and drag her hand along the cluttered floor, locating her bottle of Poland Spring. It's the kind with a pop-top, which is supposed to make it easier to drink from, but Melissa finds it more difficult, since the water has a way of spilling through the gap where her front teeth used to be. As she lifts the bottle to her mouth and takes a sip, Philip finally brings the discussion full circle.

"Missy, what you just told us doesn't make any sense. It's been too many years—"

She pulls the pop-top from her lips, inadvertently making a faint tsk sound as she does. "Want some water?"

"No. Did you hear what I just said?"

"I heard you."

"And?"

"And I told you already that I've only ever been with one person. Ronnie. On the night of our prom."

"Well, I don't know what to say then, if you're going to keep insisting on something so . . . so ludicrous."

"You can say that you believe me."

"But that's just it. I don't. And for that matter, I don't believe a word that woman said on the tape. People like her are just out to make a fast—" Philip cuts his sentence short. Melissa can almost hear the next bit of faulty logic forming in his mind, before he asks, "Is that what you want? Money?"

She takes another sip and wipes the dribble with her sleeve. "No."

"Are you sure?"

"I'm sure," she tells him.

The truth is, Melissa hasn't been able to work at either of her part-time jobs—answering phones at an insurance company and washing sheets at a motel in Conshohocken (both places where people don't have to look at her face). The jobs became too difficult for her, given the countless mornings she spent with her head over the toilet, vomiting, and the confusion and anguish she suffered when she first realized what was happening to her. As a result, she is more than six months behind on rent. Still, money was the last thing on her mind when she came here tonight. So when Philip persists with his questions about whether this is some crazy scheme she cooked up for cash, Melissa cranes her neck around and tells him, "Look. I don't want anything from you people, except for you to believe me. And if you don't, then that's your decision. I just thought you had a right to know, since Ronnie is going to be a father in a few more days." At this, Philip's mouth drops open the way it did earlier in the kitchen. But the expression does little to stop her. "So if you ever find yourself curious about your niece or nephew, I live right across town at 32 Monk's Hill Road. You're welcome to come see the baby for yourself."

When Melissa is finished, she feels breathless and bone tired. The compassion she'd seen, or thought she'd seen, in Philip's eyes is gone. Now that she has resigned herself to the fact that he is not going to believe her, she wants him gone as well. Philip must sense what she's thinking because he pulls on the door handle, bringing a rush of winter air into the car, washing over her hot skin like a salve. "I guess there's nothing left to say then. Except good night."

"Good night," she tells him.

There is his cast and crutch to contend with, so it takes Philip a full minute to slide across the seat and gain firm footing on the icy ground. Once he's finally standing, Philip looks back at her in the driver's seat. "Actually, I do have one more thing to say. Maybe it's not my place to tell you this, Missy. But I think you need some sort of professional help so you can get through this. Not just a doctor to deal with the pregnancy, but a counselor or someone you can talk to about grieving for Ronnie. It's like, I don't know, you're stuck or something. And now that you're having a baby, I think your mind is getting confused and all mixed-up about what's happening to you." Philip stops to take a breath. "The only thing I can think is that it's like this biography I'm reading about Anne Sexton. When she got pregnant, it really screwed with her head." Again, Philip pauses. When he speaks next, his voice drops lower. "Things only got worse for her instead of better. And I wouldn't want the same to happen to you."

"Are you done?" she asks.

"I'm done."

"Good. Well, thanks for the advice. Now close the door so I can leave."

Instead of the loud slam of an exit his mother made, Philip shuts the door so gently that there is nothing but the softest click. Melissa shifts the car into reverse, steps on the gas, and rolls out of the driveway so quickly that chunks of frozen gravel kick up from under her tires and spit at Philip as he hobbles toward the house. When he reaches the top step of the porch, he turns to wave, but Melissa looks away at the road before her, slams the car into drive, and takes off up the street.

"I'm not crazy," she says as the tears start again. "You believe what you want. But I know what is happening to me. I know."

By the time she reaches the stop sign on the corner, her skin, which was merely hot before, is on fire. She finds it difficult to breathe. Melissa turns off the heat and rolls down the window, letting more cold air fill the car. A rope of snot is coming from her nose, and she mops it up with her sleeve. If someone were to ask before tonight, she would have said that it wasn't possible for her to miss Ronnie any more than she already does. But as she picks up speed again and the bare trees and dark houses flash by outside her window, Melissa is overcome with a new kind of sorrow and loneliness, worse than anything she has ever felt.

I am all alone in this, she thinks, or maybe says, out loud.

That's when the kicking starts, harder than she has experienced before. She imagines the baby's feet pushing and poking against her womb, fighting to be let loose into the world.

"Not yet," she says, pressing her palm flat against her stomach as her face crumples in tears. "Not yet. Not yet. Not yet."

At the intersection of Matson Ford and King of Prussia Road, Melissa turns right, then makes a quick left onto Blatts Farm Hill. She is taking the long way home on purpose, driving faster now, doing forty-five in a thirty-five zone, then fifty. As she zips over the hill and snakes around the third sharp curve, she glances in the direction of the stump on the side of the road. Melissa has seen it there hundreds, maybe thousands, of times, but she stretches her neck in hope of catching another glimpse. The sky is so starless and black, though, that it's impossible to see it there in the shadows, skinned of so much bark that someone might mistake it for a boulder rather than the remains of an old tree.

The memory sweeps over Melissa anyway.

She and Ronnie are sticking their heads through the sunroof of the limousine, their mouths open wide, shrieking, howling into the night as they whip around turns and sail over the hills. Melissa's stomach drops, then drops again, as though she is riding the most thrilling and terrifying roller coaster of her life. Down below, Chaz and Stacy are tickling their legs. One of them—most likely Chaz—pinches her ass.

"Cut it out!" Melissa screams, but her voice is sucked into the night.

Ronnie leans his head down and shouts at them to knock it off. When he looks up again, Melissa tells him that she thinks she swallowed a bug. He asks her how it tasted, and this makes her laugh. Ronnie licks his lips and leans forward for a kiss, but the limo winds around another turn and they lose their balance. Melissa's hair comes completely undone and goes wild around them, thrashing and snapping at their faces. When they steady themselves, Ronnie gathers it behind her head and kisses her, slipping his tongue quickly in and out of her mouth. When he pulls away, he tells her, "You know I love you. Even if tonight didn't go as planned, I love you no matter what."

"I know," she tells him. "I love you too."

By the time Melissa comes to a stop in front of 32 Monk's Hill Road, most of the snow has blown off the hood, roof, and trunk of her Corolla. Her driveway, which is nothing more than a patch of dirt beside the road, has been cleared of snow too. Mr. Erwin must have shoveled it while she was in Philadelphia seeing Chantrel earlier tonight. Melissa parks the car and cuts the engine. Before going inside, she sits for a moment, gathering her strength as she stares out at the three tiny houses huddled together, caravan-style. Closest to the street is her cottage, which consists of nothing more than a ten-by-ten living room with a kitchenette along one wall, a bedroom barely big enough for her single bed, and a minuscule bathroom with a mildew-stained shower stall instead of a tub. To the left, and slightly back from her cottage, is the Erwins' place, large enough for a real kitchen with a table and chairs, plus a decent-size living room and bedroom. It even has a basement with a washer and dryer, instead of a crawl space like the one beneath her cottage. Farthest from the road, closest to the woods, is the vacant house that has never been winterized. All three used to be hunting cabins in the 1940s and were abandoned until the Erwins retired from the police department—she was a dispatcher, he was an officer—and bought the property as an investment.

Melissa leans forward and spots the soft yellow glow of the lamp beside their bed. She can picture them inside, snug beneath the covers, pillows fluffed behind their heads as Mr. Erwin reads one of those books of funny facts he loves so much and Mrs. Erwin turns the pages of a Mary Higgins Clark novel, trying to guess the killer. Even though Melissa is tempted to knock on their door the way she does when she needs to talk, she stops herself. She hasn't told them the truth about the baby. Instead, she made

up a story about a boy she was seeing who took off the moment she became pregnant. The lie would make it difficult to explain to them what's
bothering her tonight.

Finally, she rolls up the window and gets out of her car. When she
opens the front door of her cottage, the stubborn smell of stale cigarette
smoke lingers in the air, though she quit months before, when she first realized she was pregnant. Melissa steps inside and Mumu, her cow-spotted
cat, winds between her legs, purring. She scoops him up in her arms and
buries her scarred face in the animal's soft fur. Mumu is the pet her parents gave her as a sort of consolation prize for the way they treated her after Ronnie died. He is one of the few things that she took with her when
she left home. Melissa keeps on nuzzling until the cat has had enough
and leaps from her arms, then pads off into the bedroom. That's when she
turns on the light and looks around at the messy stack of newspapers on
the coffee table, the baskets of tapes and books by the ripped sofa, her
clothes strewn everywhere, a row of empty wine bottles on the floor by the
kitchenette.

With one hand on her queasy stomach, Melissa steps over a pair of
dirty black stretch pants and goes to the mantel of the stone fireplace,
where there are even more pictures of Ronnie. She picks up one that is
identical to a photo on her dashboard. He is on the plaid blanket they
used to keep stashed in the darkroom. As she stares down at his starry
smile and bright eyes, Melissa feels something slip inside of her. All the
books she has read about communicating with the other side, and all the
psychics she has visited, say the same thing: if you talk to the dead, they
will listen. So instead of allowing herself to buckle again, Melissa speaks to
Ronnie the way she often does late at night.

She tells him that she finally worked up the courage to go to his family.

She tells him how disappointed she was that his father wasn't there,
since she hoped to see him most of all.

She tells him that his brother was hurt in an accident.

She tells him about the way his mother screamed at her when she
broke the news.

She fills him in on every last detail of the night until her feet grow sore
from standing there so long. Melissa carries the picture to the sofa,

stretches her body out on the scratchy cushions, and rests the frame face-down on the mound of her stomach. "Your mother is so different now," she says into the empty room as she gazes up at the stain-blotched ceiling. "Do you remember how happy she used to seem?"

As Melissa loses herself in the memory of the first time she met Char-lene, her heavy eyes flutter shut. Her mumbling grows hoarse and incom-prehensible in the retelling. She and Ronnie had snuck out of school and gone to see his mother at the Radnor library for diesel money for the old Mercedes. His parents had taken away his credit card to punish him for buying the car on a Visa in the first place, so he was always in need of cash. Behind the counter stood a big-breasted librarian with two blond curls sweeping up from the top of her forehead. She reminded Melissa of one of those women from a Cross Your Heart bra commercial, her mam-moth breasts lifted and separated beneath a fuzzy blue sweater. When she looked up and smiled at Ronnie, Melissa assumed it was his mother. But then she pointed and told them in a harsh, unfamiliar accent that fused all her words into one, "Charleneisinthestacks." Melissa felt relieved, be-cause there was something unlikable about this lady, though she couldn't name what it was. She followed Ronnie through the maze of shelves, al-ternating between staring at the back of his faded Levi's and glancing up at the titles of obscure books, until they spotted his real mother, standing atop a metal stepladder with small holes like a cheese grater on the surface of each step. She was dressed in a pleated blue skirt and blazer, a gold frog pinned to her lapel. Before she noticed them, Ronnie took Melissa's hand and led her around to the other side, where he proceeded to push the book Charlene had just shelved back in her direction so that it fell to the floor. His mother climbed down the ladder, picked it up, and reshelved it, only to have Ronnie shove the book back out again. It was just the sort of prank that would infuriate her own humorless parents, but Charlene stuck her arm through the shelf and grabbed Ronnie by the wrist. "Ronald Chase, I hereby place you under library arrest!" she said, and the two of them started to laugh.

As the sound of their laughter echoes in Melissa's memory now, the image of that moment fades to a gauzy white nothing in her mind. She feels as though she is falling, like that book Ronnie pushed from the edge, only instead of dropping quickly to the floor, she is plummeting through a long tunnel, falling and falling and falling, until finally, she is asleep.

Melissa begins to snore, a habit that came with the pregnancy, and her arm inadvertently stretches out so that her hand comes to rest on the coffee table beside that messy pile of newspapers. Upon first glance, someone visiting this cottage might look at those papers and assume they are nothing more than leftovers from recent weeks, yet to make their way to the recycling bin. But if that someone—say it was you—were to look closer, you would notice that every single one of those papers has the same date at the top: June 19, 1999. What's more, you would see that they all have the same black-and-white photo on the front page of a limousine crushed into a thick oak tree on Blatts Farm Hill.

And now that you are looking, downright snooping in fact, do you see what's right next to those newspapers? It is the decoy diary Melissa used to fool her father five years before. And next to that? A newer, black leather diary with Melissa's name emblazoned in gold enamel on the front, a gift from her sister just before they stopped speaking. *For my sister and best friend,* the inscription reads. *Although it doesn't seem like it now, you will start over, and you will be happy again one day. I promise. Love, Stacy*

All of the pages are blank.

Across the room, there is that row of wine bottles in the kitchenette— their lips sticky with old wine, their bottoms filled with sediment and sludge—every one of them from more than nine months before, when Melissa spent lonely nights like this getting drunk and smoking cigarettes on the sofa before spewing prayer after endless prayer on the floor beside her bed.

Just to the right of those bottles is a small white refrigerator with a freezer compartment big enough for two empty ice trays, a sack of Starbucks coffee, and one more thing shoved way in the back. If you push aside those trays and that coffee and reach your hand deep inside, you'll pull out a red, freezer-burned clump that will be unidentifiable unless you hold it to the light. That's when you'll see that this thing in your hand is Melissa's rose corsage from prom night, which she keeps frozen inside like a heart that's stopped beating.

Don't drop it because you will wake her.

Put it back behind the ice trays and the coffee. Close the freezer.

There's one more thing you'll want to see, far more disturbing than anything so far, behind the bathroom door. But as Melissa said to the baby on the car ride home:

Not yet.

For now, leave it there as she sleeps and the world moves quietly around her. Mumu the cat is prowling in the kitchenette too, hunting for mice. Next door, Mr. Erwin switches off the bedside lamp and falls into a restless, fitful sleep beside his snowy-haired wife, who lies awake thinking of the way she spent her day, doing laundry, then cleaning the cluttered work area in their low-ceilinged basement, only to turn up an unexpected mess. Their refrigerator hums on and off, releasing the same pings and ticks as the engine of Melissa's car cooling in that makeshift driveway beside the road. The wind, which blew so hard earlier, has died off, leaving the woods around the three small houses in a perfect hush.

Across town—back up Monk's Hill Road and through the crisscross of streets to Blatts Farm Hill, down through the intersection of Matson Ford and King of Prussia Road, up Dilson Avenue and down to the Chases' large gray-stone colonial at 12 Turnber Lane—Philip tosses and turns on the foldout sofa in the family room while his mother sleeps soundly upstairs with the help of the pills she swallowed before bed. Again and again, he replays the conversation with Melissa, not yet considering that what she said could somehow be true, but wondering if he should have been nicer to the girl.

When it is clear to him that he is too preoccupied and troubled to sleep, Philip sits up and turns on his tiny book light, glancing at the antique clock on the wall. The hands point to four-thirty, though it is really somewhere around three. He opens his Anne Sexton biography. The pages smell musty, like a book bought at a tag sale, which it may as well have been, since he picked it up at a used bookstore on Broadway just a few weeks before he went over the edge of that fire escape and dropped to the alleyway below. Philip turns to a random page. Rather than plodding along sequentially through biographies, he much prefers to flip around to the various periods of the subject's life depending on his mood, mixing up the order of events, then putting it together afterward like a puzzle in his mind. When he looks down, he sees that the previous owner of the book had scratched a few lines of a poem in black pen in the margin:

The woman wonders why he murdered their love
But the killer in him has gotten loose
She knows she should run while there is still time
But she pauses here
Soon to be dragged into darkness

Philip doesn't know whether it is a copy of something Anne Sexton had written or an attempt to imitate her. Either way, the words have no particular resonance to him, so he turns to another section and begins rereading a chapter about Anne's parents, who died one after the other in March and June of 1959. After twenty minutes of reading, he finds himself lingering over a passage from a poem she wrote called "A Curse Against Elegies":

I refuse to remember the dead.
And the dead are bored with the whole thing.
But you—you go ahead,
go on, go on back down
into the graveyard,
lie down where you think their faces are;
talk back to your old bad dreams.

Philip's thoughts return to his brother, of course, and to Missy. Again, he begins to mull over all that happened tonight until finally he is just too tired to think or read anymore. His arms droop slowly like the heavy branches of the trees outside, and the book comes to rest on his chest. His eyes shut.

As the night passes, the starless winter sky over the small Main Line township of Radnor turns to an inky, fathomless black. The roads become empty and drained of all life. Even the highway on the outskirts of town is soundless, except for the occasional whoosh of a tractor trailer barreling past the exit ramp that leads to Radnor. And when it seems that it can't get any darker or quieter, the first bits of sunlight break on the horizon. The light comes slowly at first, then more quickly. Outside the cottage at 32 Monk's Hill Road, a family of crows perches on the dented gutters, twitching their necks and pecking at their oily black wings before flapping away in a sudden rush.

Melissa doesn't hear the footsteps approaching her small house, but she wakes to the shhhhhh sound by her front door. Lifting her stiff neck off the ratty arm of the couch, she squints her eyes and looks around to see if Mumu has caught another mouse. But the cat is asleep, purring loud and steady at her feet. Just as she's about to close her eyes again, she spots a small white envelope on the floor by the front door. She stands and stretches, putting a hand to the back of her neck while glancing out the window for some sign of the person who left it there. Whoever it was is gone. Her first thought is Philip. Perhaps he reconsidered and wrote her a note, or maybe even one of his poems, to let her know that he believed her after all. Mumu is awake now too and sniffing at the envelope. Melissa kneels down, brushing the cat away. She picks it up and pulls out the piece of unlined paper.

Dear Melissa,

I am terribly sorry to have to write this letter, but as of the first of this month, you are seven months behind on your rent. Mr. Erwin and I have been very patient and understanding due to your condition. However, we cannot allow you to occupy the cottage any longer if you are not going to pay the amount we agreed upon when you signed the lease. Please understand that we rely on this money as a main source of income during our retirement. And for that reason, we have no choice but to kindly ask you to vacate the premises as soon as possible. I know this may come as a surprise, but we hope you'll understand. We regret this more than you know.

Sincerely,
Mrs. Gail Erwin

chapter 4

WHEN CHARLENE OPENS HER EYES IN THE MORNING, THE FIRST thing she sees is a spider spinning a web in the corner of the skylight above her bed. Normally, she'd stand on the mattress and squash the little fucker with a towel, but she feels so listless and groggy from the three Tylenol PMs she gulped down the night before that she just lies there and watches its spindly legs moving in and out as it creates an ugly, hodgepodge sort of web. Charlene used to host a children's story hour at the library, and she liked to read from a picture-book edition of *Charlotte's Web*—that is, until one of the mothers complained that the spider's death on the last page was too sad for the kids to handle. "Inappropriate reading" were the exact words she used. Back then, Charlene had smiled politely at the woman and promptly removed the book from her reading list. But if she was working at the library nowadays and a parent dared pull that kind of nonsense, Charlene would tell her and her daughter where to go. After all, they might as well get used to the cold, hard fact that death is as much a part of life as waking up in the morning and brushing your teeth. Whether they like it or not, sooner or later it will wreak havoc on them too.

This kind of thinking has become one of Charlene's favorite pastimes. There is nothing she likes more than imagining what it would be like to tell off the countless people who walked all over her years ago. She loves conjuring up the look of surprise on each and every one of their faces as she lays into them. Her mind goes down this road so often that she keeps a running list in her head that she thinks of as her People I'd Like to Rip a New Asshole list, or P.I.L.T.R.A.N.A., for short. (Philip isn't the only one in this family with inside jokes.) Charlene's possible victims include that surly checkout girl at the specialty-food store in Radnor who once refused to let her use a debit card because her purchase was fifty cents short of the twenty-dollar minimum, even though Charlene had shopped there for years; that high-strung carpenter who messed up the light switch in the garage then never returned her calls to come and fix it; that bitch on the phone at the cable company who wouldn't credit her bill despite the fact that the repairman was a no-show for three appointments; and then the re-pairman himself, who finally did show, only to leave without fixing the re-ception when Charlene went into another room to answer the telephone.

And the list doesn't stop with people she knows either.

Some days, Charlene loses herself in thought for hours at a time just thinking of all the celebrities she'd like to tell off as well. There's that greedy Martha Stewart, that big-mouthed Dr. Laura Schlessinger, that pervert Howard Stern, that fake-saint know-it-all Dr. Phil. . . . And still there are others who she wouldn't even waste her breath telling off but who she thinks could benefit from a good old-fashioned bitch slapping: Michael Jackson, Björk, the Osbourne family (with the exception of Sharon, who Charlene has a soft spot for because of her battle with colon cancer), George and Laura Bush, Dick Cheney, Donald Rumsfeld. And in case anyone thinks she is partisan in her hatred, they needn't worry be-cause Charlene considers herself an equal-opportunity bitch slapper and would happily give Bill, Hillary, Tipper, and Al a smack or two as well.

At the very top of this list are the three people Charlene despises most in the world: Richard, Holly, and Pilia. Richard, her ex-husband, because he up and left her after Ronnie died. (Yes, Charlene knows she became impossible to live with in the aftermath, but what the hell did he expect?) Holly, who met Richard at a medical convention in Vegas, where she was working as a third-rate stand-up comedian with an apparent habit of hopping into bed with married men. And Pilia, the Polish ice princess of a librarian, who used to act so smug, with her Lana Turner sweaters stretched over her giant breasts. Ever since Pilia stepped foot in the library some seven years before, she had been after Charlene's position as head librarian—and now she has it. Someday, Charlene thinks as she stares up at that spider in the skylight and grinds her jaw, someday, I'll storm into that library, march right up to the front desk, and stick a pin in those mammoth tits of hers.

Last night.

In the middle of this daily regimen of hatred, the memory of the previous evening comes flooding back through the haze of sleeping pills: that girl with the scarred face and missing teeth returning to their lives again like an apparition, only to deliver such preposterous news.

This baby inside me belongs to him.

The mere echo of those words sends a wave of nausea sloshing through her stomach. Charlene moves her clammy mouth around and spits into the wastebasket beside her nightstand, which is overflowing with empty SnackWell's packages, Doritos bags, and other ghosts of junk food binges past. When the nausea passes, she lifts her worn-out body from the bed and goes to the bathroom. She pops open the *T* for Tuesday compartment of her plastic pillbox, drops two blood-pressure, one cholesterol, and an anxiety pill into her mouth, then puts her lips beneath the faucet for a gulp of water. The mirror is too scary to deal with this morning, so she turns and walks down the hall. On the way, she passes what she thinks of, quite literally, as the closed doors of her life—both her sons' bedrooms and her ex-husband's study. Then she passes the lopsided constellation of dusty pictures along the staircase. One of Richard and her standing in a white gazebo at their wedding. Another of Philip in a maroon cap and gown at his high school graduation. And a whole slew of pictures from when the boys were young on various family vacations: shoveling sand on a beach in Hilton Head, riding the teacups at Disney World, standing outside their favorite cheese steak joint in downtown Philly with both sets of their grandparents, who are no longer alive. Given Charlene's mood this particular morning—given her mood most mornings, in fact—the pictures are enough to break her heart, so she does her best not to look.

At the bottom of the stairs, she turns and cuts through the foyer into the dining room, then comes to a stop just outside the archway to the family room. The drapes have been pulled almost completely shut, so the inside is shrouded in shadows. Philip is sprawled out on the sofa bed, sound asleep. He looks to her like some poor shipwrecked soul washed ashore on a mattress with all of his worldly possessions—the phone, the remote controls, a blue box of tissues, that biography he's been reading spread open on his chest with his tiny book-light still lit. From where she's standing, Charlene can see his bruised toes sticking out of the bottom of his cast. She can also see the long, jagged slit on his throat since, for some reason, he has removed the bandages. It makes her stomach unsettled just to look at it. "Are you awake, Philip?"

Silence.

She knows she should leave him alone and let him rest, but she can't help herself. "Philip, are you awake?"

Without opening his eyes, he pushes the book aside then rolls over, burying his face in a pillow. In a muffled voice, he says, "I am now."

Charlene steps into the room, the wooden floorboards creaking beneath her bare feet. A single shaft of sunlight shines through the divide in the drapes, and she walks through it as she moves closer to the bed. "Do you always have to be so sarcastic?"

Philip lifts his head from the pillow and squints at her. His hair is sticking out in all directions the way it always is first thing in the morning. Back when he was in school, she used to tease him, naming his various bed-head looks over breakfast: *I see that today you're sporting The Don King . . . The Pat Benatar . . . The Pilia* (since her hair was forever swept up in two dramatic curls at the top of her forehead). Even then, Philip had been a grouch in the morning, so he never laughed at her jokes. "Me?" he says now. "Do you always have to—Never mind, it's too early for this."

He rolls over, giving her a more complete view of his neck. The sight of that wound—puckered and red like a set of diseased lips that have somehow slid down onto his throat—brings back the slosh of nausea she felt upstairs. "Why did you take off the bandages?"

"Dr. Kulvilkin said it would heal faster if I let it breathe."

She thinks of those lips again—sucking in air, then blowing it out. "I hate that doctor's name. He sounds like—"

"I know who he sounds like, M. You've mentioned the similarity every day for the last month. But it's Kulvilkin, not Kevorkian. And besides, you don't have to go to him. I do. So stop worrying about it."

"I wasn't worrying."

"Good," he says.

"Good," she says.

"Good," he says.

She tells herself to let it go, that she doesn't always have to get the last word, but it slips out anyway. "Good."

Philip groans and buries his face in his pillow. Charlene inches closer to the bed, then plops herself on the edge of the mattress. She looks down at her white legs sticking out of her white nightgown. There are dozens of purple explosions, a regular fireworks display going on beneath her cellulite, more than Charlene remembers noticing before. As laughable as it seems now, there once was a time when men complimented her about her legs. But unlike most people, she doesn't mind getting older. Charlene feels grateful that there's no more worrying about the way she looks, no more of those constant, silent comparisons between herself and other women. She is happy not to be like Holly, who at forty-three (only eight years younger than Charlene) exercises obsessively and eats nothing but a steady diet of vegetables and tofu in order to keep herself looking like a spandex-wearing skeleton. All that effort, and it doesn't make her look truly younger, or happier for that matter. In fact, Charlene thinks it makes her look sad, like she's trying too hard to be something she isn't anymore.

"Can I help you?" Philip asks, interrupting her thoughts.

Charlene looks up from those bursts of purple at her son's thin face and tired eyes. She wonders if all mothers see the same sort of time lapse when they stare at their child. In her mind, Philip is a pucker-faced newborn with his arms stretched toward the sky, and then he is a toddler with chocolate cake smeared on his face at a birthday party, and then he is a sulky, brooding junior high student standing apart from the other kids when she picks him up at school one afternoon, and then he is a waiter who takes classes on the side and comes home late at night, smelling of marinara sauce and garlic, and now here he is, this twenty-seven-year-old man with a broken leg lying in the sofa bed and asking if he can help her. "Help me? No. I just wanted to talk."

"Well, don't you think it's a little early for one of our wonderful mother-son chats?"

Charlene glances at the hands of the clock, automatically doing the math to determine the correct time. "It's quarter after nine," she says, then tries a joke to lighten the mood. "In New York, people may just be waking up, but here in Radnor, we've been awake for hours."

"Very funny," Philip tells her, running his hand over the wrinkled sheets until he locates the remote control.

When he presses the Power button, Judge Judy bursts to life on the screen, shouting from the bench, "Stop lying to me! You look me in the eyes and tell your story one more time. I want to know, did you, or did you not, mail the check?"

"Philip, can you turn that off?"

He doesn't answer.

"Philip, can you please turn that off?"

"Why?"

"Because I want to talk about last night. Besides, I hate that lady."

"Hate her?" Philip says. "You *are* her."

Charlene can't help but feel insulted by this comparison. As much as she wants to rage against all those people on her list, her behavior would be perfectly justified, whereas Judy Shienling, or Shinklin, or Shitface, whatever her name is, obviously bursts into those random tirades simply for higher ratings. With that thought, Charlene adds Judy's name to her list, right between Martha Stewart and Dr. Laura, surprised she never thought of it before.

"Listen to her," Philip says. "Yelling all the time. Doesn't she sound familiar?"

"I don't yell *all* the time," Charlene tells him, making her voice quiet and gentle to prove her point. "Now can you please turn off this nonsense so we can talk about last night?"

Philip pushes the Power button again and the room goes quiet. "What about it?"

"What do you mean, 'what about it'? That girl comes here and claims she is pregnant with Ronnie's baby five years after he died, and you have nothing to say?"

"I have something to say all right. You didn't need to freak out like that. She is obviously pretty messed up. And the last thing she needed was you screaming at her."

Charlene is about to raise her voice, but she stops herself. Count to ten, she thinks. When she gets to three, she says, "Well, what about me? What about what I need, huh? I mean, the nerve of her. She gets herself knocked up with some other guy, then comes stalking around pointing her finger at my dead son. As far as I'm concerned, I let her off easy. What does she expect us to believe, that she has the womb of a sea turtle?"

Philip cocks his head. "A what?"

"A sea turtle. I read once that they carry their babies for years and years before giving birth."

"M, I think that's a certain type of elephant. And it's not years and years. It's twenty-two months."

"Fine, an elephant. Whatever. Anyway, my point is that it's just not possible."

"Well, it's not totally *im*possible," he tells her.

Despite the fact that he stayed behind in the car last night, Charlene never thought for a second that Philip—Mr. I-Don't-Believe-in-God-Anymore—would buy Melissa's line of bull. "Don't tell me you are crazy enough to believe her."

"I'm not saying I believe her. But I thought about it a lot last night. And I realized there's a small, *very* small, possibility that what she said is true."

Charlene doesn't want to ask the question, but her mouth opens and out come the words: "And what would that be?"

"Well, if Ronnie's sperm had been frozen for some reason before, or even right after he died, then Melissa could have impregnated herself all these years later and that would make it his baby."

Charlene lets loose a high-pitched cackle that sends a message, loud and clear: you are being ridiculous. "I hardly think that was the scenario she was spelling out for us, Philip. For Christ's sake, the girl hasn't even been to a doctor in nine months. Besides, you know as well as I do that

Ronnie never would have thought to freeze his sperm. He was a teenager with his whole life ahead of him."

Philip is quiet a moment, and she wonders if he is going to turn on the TV again and put an end to this conversation. But then he asks in a soft voice, "What if someone took it from his body afterward?"

The only response Charlene can think of is, "You saw that limousine. You know what shape your brother's body was in when they pulled him out."

Philip closes his eyes, as though changing a channel in his mind and ridding himself of the image of that mangled wreck and Ronnie's body. When he opens them again, he tells her, "Well, I'm not saying it happened. I'm just saying that it's a remote possibility, however unlikely. I thought I should mention it, that's all."

"So you think Ronnie froze his sperm, and then what? Oh, wait, I get it. Melissa kept it in her freezer next to the Ben & Jerry's until she finally decided it was time to have a baby. Then she just defrosted a batch and shoved it up her hoo-hoo and presto, she got pregnant. That makes perfect sense, Philip. I'm surprised I didn't think of it sooner."

He stares at her without speaking until finally, he says, "You need to get a grip."

"No, you do. You're the one who believes her."

"You see, that's the problem with you, M. You exaggerate everything. Did you even hear what I just said? I do not—repeat, *do not*—believe her. I just wanted to tell you that these things happen in the world. I've read about it in the paper and seen it on TV."

Charlene has had enough of this twaddle, so she stands up from the bed. "Yeah, well, watching too much TV will make your brain rot."

"You should know," Philip says.

As she walks out of the room, Charlene says beneath her breath, "No, you should know."

"You should," he calls after her.

"You should," she says back, managing to get the last word as she cuts through the dining room and foyer again, then heads into the messy, pea-soup-smeared kitchen, where she grabs two Diet Cokes and a box of SnackWell's.

For the rest of the morning, Charlene lies upstairs in bed, flipping channels and staring at the television, letting her brain rot the way she had just warned Philip. From nine-thirty to ten-thirty, she loses herself in an infomercial that features a contraption called "Mister Magic Dicer," which chops vegetables into exactly ninety-nine different shapes and sizes. Charlene becomes so entranced by all the frantic dicing on the screen that the colors actually start to look pretty and the vegetables seem like works of art to her. She especially likes the bright orange carrots shaped like rosebuds, sitting atop a bed of shredded zucchini that resembles mowed grass. Finally, she picks up the phone and orders a Mister Magic Dicer with her American Express for $19.95, plus shipping and handling. When she hangs up, Charlene flips to the higher channels—88, 89, 90, 91—numbers that she thinks of as no-man's-land because she never knows what she'll find up here.

Today, she stumbles upon back-to-back reruns of *The Jenny Jones Show*. The first topic is "HELP! MY TEENAGE DAUGHTER IS A SLUT!" For half an hour, Charlene watches as a pack of young girls, dripping in makeup and jewelry, parade around in short skirts and skimpy tops. Every time they mouth off to their mothers, the audience erupts into a chorus of cheers and boos, which only encourages them more. By the end of the show, no one seems to have learned a thing from the experience. As much as Dr. Phil annoys Charlene, she decides that at least he tries to help people. So for that reason, she takes him off her list and puts Jenny Jones in his place instead.

The topic of the second show is "HELP! MY WOMAN IS A CHEATIN' HO!" Charlene finishes the last of her soda and cookies, tosses the empty containers onto the floor because the wastebasket is too full, then makes herself even more comfortable by folding an extra pillow beneath her neck as she watches. There is a white couple, a Hispanic couple, and a couple of mixed ethnicity. All three of the men recount stories of how they caught their girlfriend cheating—one in a public rest room, one in their very own home, and another at a motel. Finally, the skinny white guy with a shaved head announces that he suspects their baby is not even his. The audience shrieks, and Jenny says in a perky voice, "When we come back after this commercial break, we'll have the results from the paternity test, which will tell us if the baby belongs to Jared or to some other guy. So stay tuned."

Charlene presses the Mute button and wonders what has become of the world. Eventually, her thoughts return to Philip downstairs, who she figures is probably reading more of that damn biography right now. She doesn't understand why he is so interested in Anne Sexton anyway. The only reason the woman got so much attention was that she had the stupidity and courage to do herself in. The same goes for Sylvia Plath, who he also had been reading about. Take Robert Frost, on the other hand. Charlene considers that man to have been a poet through and through. He knew how to string a few words together, and he didn't have to fumigate himself in a sealed garage or stick his head in the oven to prove it.

She toys with the idea of sharing these thoughts with Philip but decides that it will only lead to another argument. It's been years since the two of them were even remotely close, but their bickering has been nonstop since he came home one month ago. Other than what the police officer told Charlene when he called to say that Philip was in St. Vincent's hospital, she doesn't know the details of how he ended up going over the edge of that fourth-floor fire escape. And she's not sure she wants to know either, since what little she has gathered leads her to believe that it's not the kind of thing a mother wants to hear about her son. As a result, there have been so many times during these last weeks when she finds herself staring at him, and after seeing that time lapse in her mind, wondering how someone so smart could get himself caught up in such a mess. She blames it on the fact that he moved to New York in the first place. She still remembers when he called, as sirens wailed behind him, to tell her he was in the city.

"But I thought you were working at the Olive Garden last night," Charlene remembers saying, "and then, I don't know, you didn't come home." They'd had another one of their arguments the day before. In the midst of it all, the most horrible statement possible had sprung from her mouth, and Philip grabbed his apron and tore out of the house for the restaurant.

"I was, Ma. But I hate that place. I hate my life in Pennsylvania. I hate living with you and fighting all the time. You're just too mean now. That's why . . . that's why I'm not coming back."

First Ronnie, then Richard, and now Philip, Charlene had thought as a line of dominoes toppled over in her mind. And since she didn't know what to say—the words she had shouted at him the day before were far too cruel for a simple apology, after all—Charlene just slammed down the phone. Over the years, they hardly spoke to each other until that officer called to tell her that Philip had been found in an alley, barely breathing but alive.

As soon as he gets better, she knows he will leave again too. He all but said so to Melissa last night: *in a few more weeks, I'll be good as new.* Some-day soon, she could walk downstairs and find him gone. Once more, this big old house will be empty, except for her. Charlene's life will continue its tiresome, lonesome routine of crafting and recrafting that vengeful list in her head, watching endless hours of television, going to the garage to start Ronnie's car, checking her bank account for Richard's monthly al-imony deposit, watching the mail for the eternal updates from her lawyers regarding the lawsuit that is still ongoing all these years after Ronnie's death, and whipping up the occasional pot of something or other to satisfy a sudden craving. The thought of going back to living a life unchecked by another person under the same roof frightens her. Having Philip home again has made her realize how much she has let things go. So despite all of their arguing, Charlene doesn't want him to leave. But there is nothing she can do about it.

On TV, the commercials are over and *Jenny Jones* is on again. Char-lene leaves the volume down, because she couldn't care less if the baby belongs to Jared or some other loser. As she watches their mouths move with no sound, she thinks about something else Philip said:

I'm just saying that it's a remote possibility. . . .

For the first time, she allows the thought to slip quietly into her mind, like the books used to do when dropped into the return bin at the library after she put a pillow at the bottom to soften the noise. It comes in the form of a question, this question: wouldn't it be nice? Her eyes go watery as she lingers over the answer. It would be more than nice; it would be wonderful, joyous, miraculous, just to have some small part of her son back after all these years.

A grandchild, Charlene thinks. *My* grandchild.

She knows she'll never get one from Philip, so she gave up hoping a long time ago. But if this did turn out to be a chance, however small, a chance . . .

Charlene stops herself.

She does her best to douse that flicker of hope, because no matter what

Philip has read in the paper or seen on TV, she knows deep down that it can't be true. It simply cannot be true. She feels embarrassed for even allowing herself to consider it.

Still, the feeling lingers as the credits roll on the screen and Jared and his hussy wife hug, kiss, and cry behind the scroll of titles and names: *lighting designer: Trip Hilkin, key grip: Bob Trinkis, assistant to Ms. Jones: Melanie Reinwink* . . . Charlene can't believe that any of these people actually want credit for this circus act. She looks away and stares up at the skylight. The spider is nowhere in sight, but as she gazes at the empty web, she thinks back to those story hours and remembers herself holding the book in front of the children as she read each page that she knew practically by heart:

> All winter Wilbur watched over Charlotte's egg sac as though he were guarding his own children. He had scooped out a special place in the manure for the sac, next to the board fence. On very cold nights he lay so that his breath would warm it. For Wilbur, nothing in life was so important as this small round object—nothing else mattered.

While Charlene read, Pilia stood behind the circulation desk stamping books so loudly she may as well have been taking a hammer to them. The commotion was all done in an effort to distract Charlene, since Pilia was jealous that she didn't get to run the library events. But Charlene didn't let it bother her. She maintained perfect focus as she turned the pages and read on, never once stumbling over the words:

> He walked drearily to the doorway, where Charlotte's web used to be. He was standing there, thinking of her, when he heard a small voice.
> "Salutations!" it said. "I'm up here."
> "So am I," said another tiny voice.
> "So am I," said a third voice. "Three of us are staying. We like this place, and we like you."
> Wilbur looked up. At the top of the doorway three small webs

were being constructed. On each web, working busily was one of Charlotte's daughters.

"Can I take this to mean," asked Wilbur, "that you have definitely decided to live here in the barn cellar, and that I am going to have *three* friends?"

"You can indeed," said the spiders.

After she finished the book, Charlene used to take out a fake spider's web made from white yarn and ask the children to tell her what words they imagined in it to describe themselves. The boys always saw adjectives like *fast, strong,* and *tough,* whereas the girls saw words like *sweet, pretty,* and *happy.*

Even though she feels silly about it, Charlene allows herself to play the same game now. She looks into the web above her bed and imagines that spider coming back from wherever it is to spin something that describes her too. At first, all she can envision are the same words from the book, *Some Pig.* Lying there among all those empty soda cans and junk-food packages in her bedroom, the truth of the statement causes her to laugh in spite of herself. Then she squints her eyes and does her best to imagine other possibilities. It's been so long, though, since she's pretended or played any sort of game that it doesn't go very well. All Charlene sees is:

Some Mother.

Some Wife.

Some Failure.

She looks away, releasing an enormous sigh and telling herself that it's a stupid game and she's too old for it anyway. On the TV screen, there is that grating commercial for a wide-eyed psychic with a purple scarf and clunky jewelry. The sound is still off, but Charlene has seen it enough times to know that she is promising a 100 percent accurate reading as she shuffles the tarot cards and the phone number flashes beneath her with the words CALL NOW! It makes Charlene think of Melissa Moody again and her cassette tape of the woman who claimed to speak to the dead, so she turns her gaze from the screen once more and looks at the ceiling. The image must still be etched in her vision, though, because for the briefest moment Charlene thinks she sees the same words up there in the web: CALL NOW!

And what she does next surprises even her.

Charlene reaches over to the nightstand and picks up the telephone. But instead of punching in the 900 number of that psychic on the screen, she calls the only person who might be able to answer the question Philip asked downstairs: what if someone took it from his body afterward? Charlene is calling her ex-husband, Richard, in Palm Beach. He's a doctor, after all. A doctor who happened to be working at Bryn Mawr Hospital that summer night five years before, when the EMTs brought in the mangled body of their younger son.

chapter 5

PHILIP IS PARKED OUTSIDE THE OLIVE GARDEN RESTAURANT, looking over his midterm poetry portfolio and killing time before his shift. As a rule, he never *ever* gets to work early. But he and his mother had another one of their blowouts this afternoon, their worst yet, so he tore out of the house and drove aimlessly around Radnor and Wayne before finally ending up here in the parking lot, trying to forget the last thing she said to him before he left home.

Spread out on the passenger seat among his Madonna tapes, spiral-bound notebooks, and a soiled waiter apron are the drafts of the poems he has been working and reworking all semester, each of them marked with tomorrow's due date: October 20, 1999. When he read over the revisions last night, Philip actually felt the slightest bit proud of his work. But as he scans the titles now—"Dark All Day," "Unfamiliar Family," "Don't Try This at Home"—it is all he can do not to use the car's cigarette lighter to set the pages on fire. He even contemplates tossing the entire portfolio into the Dumpster behind the restaurant, but a flock of dirty seagulls is hovering above, taking turns swooping down for scraps, and Philip has always had a phobia of birds.

At the very top of the pile is the poem he wrote last June for Ronnie, the one he worked up the courage to read at the funeral. Now he is mortified that he did.

"Sharp Crossing" by Philip Chase

You walked along a barbed wire fence
Between this field and the next
Ambling and happy, showing no sign of what was about to occur
You waited for the farmer to turn his tractor toward home
You waited for the horses to move to another patch of grass
That's when you climbed the fence
You thought no one was looking
But I was
I saw you slip over to the other side
Tear your clothes
Cut your skin
But what did that matter now?
You were limping toward a new home with new rules in that faraway field
As the farmer disappeared behind his barn
As the horses returned to smell your blood on the grass
You were the one who was hurt
But I am the one who is crying

Dr. Conorton, Philip's shaky-handed, bushy-browed poetry professor, had called Philip into his cramped office at the community college and told him that, in his opinion, "Sharp Crossing" was good enough to publish. He even scrawled the names and addresses of a half-dozen journals and reviews he thought might accept the poem for their summer issue. The news had been the first thing to remotely lift Philip's spirits in a long while. For weeks afterward, he walked around feeling puffed up with pride and (even though he would never admit it) a tad superior to the other students. During class, he took to looking around the circle of desks at the faces of his peers—the angry, divorced woman with the shaved head; the muttonchopped Italian guy with the pierced tongue and a leather vest he never seemed to take off; the plump, daffy hairdresser with overprocessed hair and extralong fake nails, each with a different swirling design and the occasional faux diamond chip near the tip—and Philip thought, Unlike you people, Conorton actually thinks I stand a chance of publishing my work. Someday, somebody besides the ten of us in this classroom might read my words.

All of that uncharacteristic arrogance and optimism is gone, though, as he sits in the restaurant parking lot, feeling less like an up-and-coming poet and more like a waiter with a pipe dream. He begins to wonder if Conorton had said those things simply out of pity, since at this very moment, his work reads like the same kind of self-indulgent crap that everyone else in the class writes. To prove it, Philip reaches for his backpack on the floor and pulls out his folder of other students' poetry. The first one he finds is by that divorced woman whose writing is always a free-verse metaphor for sex with her ex-husband:

"*Run Me Over, You Fucking Bastard*" by Jilda J. Horowitz

Go ahead, bastard
Shift your monster truck in reverse
And back over me again
Who's going to stop you anyway?
Certainly not me
I'm just a stupid animal
Lying naked and splayed
In the middle of the road
Full of desire for this sweat and sex
That is certain to kill me once more
Even though I'm already dead

Go ahead, bastard
Make me see the light
As you grind your tire tracks into my soul
Deep and grooved, the way a horny bitch like me wants it
Otherwise, how will I know you've been here?

So plow your pitiful path in the mud
Only it's my blood that will bear the marks you leave behind

Go ahead, bastard
Now that there's no doubt
I am dead, yet again
Spin those fat tires onward to the rally
Where you will drink and laugh
With other man-monsters just like you

Go ahead, bastard
Forget about me
Back on the highway
Where Animal Control has come to shovel up the carcass
    that was once your wife
I am no different than roadkill to you, bastard
A road pizza with the works
A raccoon
A possum
Somebody's once-cuddly pussycat

Philip groans and tosses the paper on the seat, trying his best to recall exactly what Conorton had told Jilda about this tirade she calls a poem in order to gauge the validity of his comments about "Sharp Crossing." He closes his eyes and replays the moment she read it aloud to the class as spit sprayed from her thin lips whenever she said the word *bastard,* and her voice rose and fell, rose and fell, until she finished and the room went silent. Everyone in the class stared down at the copy on their desks as though searching for a teleprompter to tell them what to say. When Philip couldn't stand the tension any longer, he cleared his throat and told Jilda that he liked her use of the truck rally as a metaphor to express her anger, leaving out the obvious fact that it was more than a little bit heavy-handed. The compliment softened the permanent frown on Jilda's face so much that Philip got carried away and went on to tell her that he thought "Run Me Over, You Fucking Bastard" was even better than her previous week's poem, "Attention Kmart Shoppers, My Vagina Is on Sale."

When the back door of the restaurant creaks open and slams shut, Philip gives up trying to remember exactly what Conorton had said to Jilda. He opens his eyes to see Gumaro, the five-foot-tall muscleman dishwasher from Mexico City. Even though the Olive Garden is an Italian restaurant, not a single Italian works in the kitchen. Mexico, Portugal, Brazil, the Dominican Republic, even Guam—but Italy, no. Philip watches Gumaro carry a bus bin to the Dumpster, where he stands on his toes and empties the contents over the edge, sending the seagulls into a tizzy of swooping and squawking, before he turns back toward the kitchen door. That's when he spots Philip sitting in his old Subaru across the lot and shouts, "*Oye, maricón. Como estás?*"

The guys in the kitchen call just about everyone who works at the Olive Garden a *maricón*—faggot—so Philip isn't insulted, though he makes sure to call him a name right back. "*Bien, pendejo. Y tú?*" I'm good, asshole. How are you?

Philip has learned more Spanish working this job than he did during all four years of high school. He'd be hopeless checking into a hotel or buying a train ticket in a Spanish-speaking country, but if he ever wants to tell someone off, he knows all the right words. And since the next thing Gumaro says is, "*Bien. Pero tu mamá no vino anoche a mamarme mi pinga como siempre,*" which means, I'm good, but your mother didn't show up to suck my dick last night the way she always does, Philip takes a breath and lets it rip: "*Qué pena, porque tu mamá, tu hermana, tu tía, tu abuela, y tu abuelo vinieron a mi casa para mamarme mi pinga y a doscientos de mis mejores amigos ayer. Y lo hicieron gratis esta vez. Fue excelente. Tengo el video si lo quieres rentar.*" Translation: That's too bad, because your mother, your sister, your aunt, your grandmother, *and* your grandfather showed up at my house last night to suck my dick and two hundred of my closest friends. They did it for free this time. It was great. I have the video if you want to rent it.

Gumaro drops the empty bus bin and makes a beeline toward the car. Even though it's a cool, cloudy autumn day, he is wearing nothing but a thin white T-shirt and the same kind of black-and-white checkered pants that all the guys in the kitchen wear, only his pair is cut off unevenly and frayed at the knees. When he reaches the car, Philip notices a thin layer of sweat glistening on his dark skin from the heat of kitchen. Gumaro grins, big and wide. "You are getting good, my friend," he says in a low voice, leaning one of his beefy arms on the roof of the car. "See what happens when you study with the best *profesor* in town?"

"*Gracias, profesor,*" Philip tells him.

Gumaro motions toward the passenger seat with his chin. "What's that?"

"Just some school stuff." Philip wishes he had thought to put his portfolio away, since he doesn't want to be teased about it from now into eternity.

"It looks like poetry," Gumaro says. "*Te gusta* poetry?"

Philip asks him how to say "You are a nosy bastard" in Spanish, but Gumaro doesn't answer. Finally, Philip surrenders to the moment and nods. Yes, he likes poetry. He braces himself for a crack about only *maricónes* going for that sort of thing. He even prepares a comeback about what Gumaro's mother likes to do with the sheep in the barn late at night while his father sleeps. But all Gumaro says is, "In my country, we have peoples who know how to paint the most beautiful pictures with words. Do you know José Emilio Pacheco?"

Philip shakes his head, grateful he's not being teased, but also embarrassed because he himself cannot paint a picture with words. Whenever he tries, for example, to make the sky bluer by describing it in writing, his poems end up reading like a combined listing from *Webster's Dictionary* and *Roget's Thesaurus* ("The azure, cerulean celestial regions as seen from earth . . ."). One more reason to believe that Conorton had probably said those things simply out of pity. "So how's it going inside the old Olive Pit today?" Philip asks to change the subject.

Gumaro casts his dark eyes toward the restaurant then back at Philip. "We got hit with an early rush. The boss is doing The Robot for almost one hour now."

The Robot is what the staff calls it whenever Walter—a self-proclaimed "top graduate" from hotel and restaurant management school—starts waving his arms around like the robot in those *Lost in Space* reruns used to do whenever there was danger. In this case, the danger is that Walter can't handle more than a few tables at a time if he's stuck on the floor alone. "There's no one on the floor to help him?"

Gumaro shakes his head. "He cut them loose because we were dead before. Big mistake."

Philip figures he should get in there and save him, not that Walter will act the least bit appreciative. He gathers up his poems and puts them in his backpack, then grabs his apron and gets out of the car. As he and Gumaro walk toward the back door of the restaurant, Philip looks beyond those birds still hovering above the Dumpster to where the sky is turning even more gray and cloudy. He thinks, for a moment, of a trip he and Ronnie took to Cape Cod with their grandparents when Philip was only twelve or maybe thirteen years old. When they first drove into town, the sun was shining and people were out on the streets in brightly colored T-shirts and shorts. But an hour after they checked into the hotel, it started to rain, and it kept on raining. Even though their grandparents came up with activities to occupy them (from Chinese checkers to regular checkers to Old Maid to a trip to the Pirates museum and endless shopping excursions), Philip and Ronnie did almost nothing but stare up at the sky for seven days, in hopes of spotting a glimpse of sun so they could go to the beach. It never came. And the small Cape town, which seemed so happy and full of life when they first arrived, took on a bleak, infectious kind of dreariness. The feeling Philip had on that trip seems like a childhood version of the way he feels mourning his brother—as though everything around him is damp and gloomy, as though there is only darkness where there should be light.

"So how is your beautiful wife?" he asks Gumaro.

"*Bien.*" He holds open the kitchen door and lets Philip go first. "Working hard. Always working hard. I don't know why you work this stinking job if you don't got to."

Philip shrugs and steps inside, passing through the maze of oversize pots and strainers hanging on the wall, shelves full of industrial-size containers of olive oil and minced garlic, into the heart of the kitchen. A few weeks before, Philip made the mistake of mentioning that his father was a doctor. Ever since, Gumaro insists on asking Philip why he works at the restaurant instead of living what he calls "the good life." Philip has already explained to him that he wants to make his own way in the world so that neither of his parents can have a say about how he lives his life. But Gumaro doesn't get it. As Philip scans the rack by the metal clock in search of his time card, he listens to the usual speech about all the other things he could be doing with his time.

"You could be hanging out on the beach in Miami or gambling in Vegas, my friend. *Que es lo que pasa contigo?*"

Philip is about to tell him that he is not interested in the MTV version
of the good life when The Robot bursts into the kitchen from the bar, his
arms full of empty glasses but waving frantically about nonetheless. He
takes one look at Philip and says, "You're late!"

Philip punches his card and glances down at the tiny blue stamp: four-
fifty-one. "Actually, I'm nine minutes early. But if you want, I'll come back
when I really am late."

Walter slams down the glasses with such force that they sound as
though they might shatter. If anyone else did that, he'd throw a fit. Gumaro moves in from behind and whisks them away with the speed of a magician, mouthing to Philip as he does, "*Que es lo que pasa contigo? Tu es
loco trabajas aquí.*"

What's the matter with you? You're crazy to work here.

"I don't have time to argue now," Walter says, wiping his hands against
the front of his pleated, overpressed khakis. He is one of those tall, wiry
men with a disproportionate gut. And the way he dresses doesn't help,
since his pastel shirts are always too tight and his khakis are forever bal-
looning out in front of him. "Just get your ass on the floor. It's like a fucking insurance salesmen convention descended on us out there."

Philip thinks about asking Walter if he learned such stellar motiva-
tional lingo in whatever Podunk hotel and restaurant management school
he earned his toilet paper certificate from, but he's already suffered
through one argument today. Don't think about it, he tells himself, pushing his mother's words out of his mind as he ties his apron around his waist
and steps onto the floor.

What Walter described as an insurance salesmen convention is really
just a mob of sloppy, drunk corporate-types still in their office getups—or
mostly in them anyway. The majority of men have peeled off their rumpled jackets and loosened their ties. The women have kept their blazers
on, but a few have kicked off their pumps beneath their chairs. Just one
look at them, seated at a long, pushed-together table for twenty near the
bar, and Philip knows—the way only a waiter can know—that they'll
linger here for hours. They'll keep right on drinking and ordering the oc-

casional appetizer, then act shocked when the check comes. After that, it'll take them a good fifteen minutes to divvy up the bill, then cough up five different credit cards and a mountain of rumpled tens, fives, and singles, only to screw him out of a decent tip in the end. Since there is nothing he can do about it, though, Philip takes a breath and heads toward the table.

On the stereo, Dean Martin is singing about the moon hitting someone's eye like a big pizza pie, and Philip overhears one of the women say, "Oh, I love this song. I just love it."

So did I, the first ten thousand times, he thinks as he makes his way, counterclockwise, around them, taking orders for a dozen drinks and two appetizers. After he enters it all into the computer at the service station and waits for the bartender to start pouring, Philip cleans the ketchup bottles and checks to make sure the rifle-size pepper mills are fully loaded while eavesdropping on their various conversations.

A tall, broad-shouldered woman, who has made the mistake of wearing shoulder pads when she shouldn't, is keeping the people around her enthralled with a deadly dull story about a proposal that she saved on her hard drive, only to find that it wasn't there when she got back from her business trip to Chicago. "I called the help desk, and it took two days for a technician to show up," she says in a horsey drawl. "They should rename it the slow desk."

They all burst into laughter, and Philip looks a few seats down to where a bald man is telling his friend, "I faxed Cathy the parameters of the deal first thing Monday morning. She had the nerve to request that I cc her on all correspondence with the main office from now on. I mean, does she need to get laid or what?"

At the seat closest to the bar, a tiny runt of a woman with shiny black hair and severe Cleopatra bangs is saying, "The doctor found a lump on her breast so she's been on a leave of absence for the last month. The thing is, I know this sounds awful, but I am already getting used to not having her around. Don't get me wrong. I don't wish anything bad on her. But maybe when she gets better she'll decide she doesn't want to come back to an office environment. That happens a lot to sick people when they recover. And if it does to her, then well, I'll finally get promoted."

The last comment is enough to make him stop listening. Since the bartender is taking his sweet time making the drinks, Philip turns and heads into the kitchen to check on the appetizers. They're not up yet, but when he opens the door, Deb Shishimanian is just clocking in. Her spiky highlighted hair is still damp and falling down in front of her eyes. Shish is the moodiest person on the waitstaff, so Philip tries to guess, from the expression on her broad face, which one of her personalities walked through the door tonight. "Hey, baby," she says, pulling her apron around her wide hips. "How you doing?"

Nice Shish, Philip thinks. "I've been better," he says.

"Yeah, well, whatever's wrong with you, it can't be worse than my week."

Sometimes Philip wonders if anyone in this place even remembers the fact that his brother died five months ago. At the time, they sent flowers and a few people from the staff—Gumaro and Shish included—showed up at the wake. But no one has mentioned it since. "What's the matter?" he asks as she sticks her time card back in the rack.

"I caught Beth in 'Women4Women' the other day."

"Where?"

"A chat room on AOL. Remember? It's the one where I met her in the first place."

"Oh, yeah," Philip says. "That's right. Sorry, I forgot."

Beth has been Shish's girlfriend for the past year, ever since they met online and Shish invited her to the Olive Garden one night during her shift. Since Shish has a habit of broadcasting her business to the entire staff—never bothering to hold back on the details of her period or her personal life—they all knew she was expecting a mystery guest that night. And when Beth arrived in leather pants and a tank top with tattooed arms and a pierced nose, every single one of the waiters and waitresses made a point of swinging by the table to check her out. Even Gumaro and the other kitchen guys spent a good part of the night staring through the kitchen window, trying to catch a glimpse. Walter was the only one who refused to take part in the fun.

"I had a feeling she was messing around on the Internet again," Shish is saying now as she shines up her thin lips with a wand of goo she pulled from her apron. "So I logged on under a fake name from the computer in Walter's office."

"He let you?"

"No. The turkey was at the bank doing payroll. Anyway, I started IM-ing her, real flirtatiouslike, you know, and she suggested that we meet up. I asked her if she was single, and she wrote back 'yup.' Just like that: '*y*-fucking-*u*-fucking-*p*.' Can you believe it?"

"I never trusted her," Philip says

The second the words leave his mouth, he realizes it was the wrong thing to say because Shish's broad face takes on an angry sneer. Her stumpy nose crinkles, and her shiny lips turn inward. "What do you mean, you never trusted her? You told me you liked her."

"I—"

"For your information, Philip, we made up. Beth explained the whole thing. She knew it was me, since I was using a screen name I used when we first started talking. Online, I mean. Anyway, I forgot about it until then."

Not only has Philip lost track of her story, but somehow, right before his eyes, nice Shish has morphed into evil Shish. And since he doesn't know what else to say, Philip tells her, "I'm sorry." Then he asks, "But if you made up, why was your week so bad?"

"Chicklet got hit by a car yesterday. She's dead."

Chicklet is—was—Shish's cat. "I'm sorry," Philip says again.

But Shish continues looking at him with that angry sneer, her stumpy nose still crinkled, her thin lips turned thinner. "You know, Philip," she says as the kitchen crew clangs pots and a pan hisses with the sound of something frying, "maybe if you came out of the closet and had a rela-tionship of your own, you'd stop being so judgmental."

Philip sucks in a breath. He is willing to tolerate Walter's crap, as well as the verbal thrashing from his mother today, but he refuses to put up with abuse from Deb Shishimanian, psycho lesbian waitress. "Just be-cause I don't broadcast every detail of my sex life to the staff of the Olive Garden does not mean I'm in the closet."

Shish adjusts her apron around her waist, lining up the tops of her pens like it's a holster, clearly unfazed by what he just said. "Oh, please, Philip," she tells him as she fishes through yet another pocket and produces a claw-shaped clip, which she uses to hold her damp hair away from her eyes. "What sex life do you have? I bet the fucking pope sees more action than you."

Philip opens his mouth to go back at her when the door flies open and the bartender points to the dining room, where Walter is doing The Robot once again. "Philip, your drinks are up. And someone better save our leader before he self-destructs."

"Shit," Shish says and walks out the door into the dining room.

"*Que es lo que pasa contigo? Se loco,*" Gumaro calls from over by the dishwasher.

"Where are my two Sampler Italianos?" Philip yells to the guys from Guam manning the grill and the Fryolater.

"They're coming, *maricón,*" one of them yells back.

He turns and goes to the bar, where he grabs a tray. Philip loads it up with all twelve drinks and turns to head for the table. At the same time, Walter storms by, arms waving madly, and smacks right into him. For a brief, slow motion moment, it looks as though Philip will be able save the glasses from toppling. But then a gin and tonic knocks into a Long Island iced tea, which knocks into two chardonnays, and down they all go, crashing to the floor so loudly that the pack of corporate imbeciles all stop talking and stare at Philip, bug-eyed. Only Dean Martin can be heard on the stereo. He's moved on to "Volare."

What are you people looking at? Philip wants to scream. Haven't you ever seen someone spill a tray of drinks before?

And then that black-haired, Cleopatra-banged runt of a woman, the one who had all but wished her coworker dead just so she could get a promotion, thinks she is being funny and starts to clap. The rest of the crowd quickly joins in the applause, and one of the bald guys even shouts, "Bravo!"

Philip tells himself to smile and take the joke, to bend down and pick up the broken glass. But he can't do any of those things. He feels frozen in place as he stares out at the people clapping, at Deb standing by the coffee machine with a smirk on her face, at the bartender who is already making a duplicate round of drinks, and at Walter, who is not yet saying anything but will definitely start screaming the second they're in the kitchen. That's when he hears Gumaro's weeks of questions rattle off in his mind:

Que es lo que pasa contigo? What's the matter with you?

Por qué tiene que trabajar aquí si no tiene qué trabajar? Why do you work here if you don't have to?

It is during this frozen moment that Philip's mind goes back to this time last year when his brother came home and announced that he had bought a used Mercedes on the credit card their father had given him. The card was intended for emergency use only, so their parents were furious. But after a lot of yelling and screaming, they let Ronnie keep the car. Philip has an identical Visa card in his wallet right now, though he has never once used it. All because he has this notion about making his own way in the world, a notion that seems ridiculous, downright idiotic for the first time this instant.

"Well, are you going to just stand there?" Walter asks when the applause dies down. "Or are you going to at least tell Gumbo back there to get the mop?"

Philip doesn't answer.

He turns and walks through the door into the kitchen, where he punches his time card and looks down at the tiny purple stamp: five-thirty-seven, the world's shortest shift. He heads back through the maze of shelves, loaded with olive oil and minced garlic, and the oversize pots and pans hanging on the wall, until he sees Gumaro. He doesn't mention the mop. Instead, he pats his bulky shoulder and says, "*Adios, amigo.*"

"*Adios,*" Gumaro says as he slides a dish rack into the machine and slams down the lever. His voice is so casual that it's obvious he doesn't get that this is good-bye for good.

Philip keeps going out the door anyway.

The moments that follow feel automatic:

He gets in his car.

He starts the engine.

He takes off out of the parking lot.

For the first five minutes, he drives along Lancaster Avenue with no particular destination in mind. What is surprising even to Philip is that he is not thinking about the restaurant or what he's just done. As odd as it may seem, his mind is focused again on that week at the Cape when he felt trapped by the same sort of endlessly gloomy aching he feels now. He remembers that every shop his grandparents took Philip and Ronnie into, they would ask the person behind the counter for the weather report. It became a kind of game to them, racing to the register to see who could blurt the question first. Everyone gave the same answer: rain for the rest of the week. Finally, their grandmother took them both by the arm and snapped, "Would you two stop this nonsense already? No one is going to tell you anything different. Face facts: the bad weather is here to stay. We'll just have to make the best of it." But neither Philip nor Ronnie wanted to make the best of it—if it wasn't going to get sunny, then they simply wanted to leave.

At the next red light, Philip turns on the radio and flips through the stations in an effort to distract himself from all the things he really should be thinking about. Nothing is on but talk radio and rap music, so he switches it off. When the light turns green, he begins moving again and soon finds himself on a commercial strip, which looks like the same congested stretch of road that can be found in most states these days. He passes a Home Depot with a crowded parking lot, a Wal*Mart, a TGI Fridays, a 7-Eleven, a Subway, a Dunkin' Donuts, a Target, a Burger King, a Wendy's, a Mailboxes Etc., and etc. and etc. and etc.

He keeps on driving, his thoughts returning to that day Jilda Horowitz read her truck poem to the class, as he resumes the mission to gauge the validity of Conorton's comments. After he complimented Jilda, Philip remembers that the hairdresser, who wrote mostly about rainbows and dolphins, said she liked the poem too. But then she added that it might be stronger if Jilda didn't use the word *bastard* so much.

"I feel like it's hitting me on the head. It's like I tell my clients when I'm giving them highlights," she said while doodling what looked to Philip like a unicorn at the top of the page. "Sometimes less is more."

Class rules forbid the writer to speak during the critique session following a reading, but Philip knew exactly what Jilda was thinking, that she'd like to run the hairdresser over with a monster truck and leave her carcass behind for Animal Control to shovel up.

And that's when Philip remembers that Conorton chimed in with this noncommittal assessment: "Jilda, I think it must be wonderfully cathartic for you to get your rage out on the page." He stopped and chuckled, coughed a hacking cough. "Listen to me. Rage out on the page. I guess I really am a poet. Rhyme schemes flow from my mouth like a fountain. Okay, next poem."

As Philip drives on, he wonders if Conorton really did mean what he said about "Sharp Crossing" after all. Finally, he decides to stop thinking about it, since at the moment he has more important things to worry about, like where he is going and what he is going to do now that he just walked out of his job. Since he doesn't want to go home yet and face his mother, he decides to wait until later when she's asleep and he can tiptoe up the stairs to his room. But then what? Tomorrow morning, he'll wake up and have to face her again.

When he focuses on the road ahead, Philip sees the entrance ramp to Route 476. Without signaling, he turns at the last possible second. After paying the toll, he tries to merge with the other cars on the highway. They are all moving faster than the speed limit, zipping by his old Subaru in a steady whoosh-whoosh-whoosh. Philip steps on the gas in an effort to keep up. Soon he is going sixty, then sixty-five, then seventy. Each time he glances down at the speedometer, the police report from his brother's accident flashes in his mind: *Based on the damage to the vehicle, it is estimated that the limousine was traveling at a speed of seventy miles per hour in a thirty-five-miles-per-hour zone at the moment of impact.* Normally, that memory makes him slow down. But he presses his foot harder on the gas, going faster still: seventy-one, seventy-two, seventy-three, seventy-four, seventy-five. . . . When the car reaches eighty, the steering wheel begins to shake in Philip's hands. He sees a sign for 276, which leads to the Jersey Turnpike, then on to New York City. This time, he signals before turning. Once he is on 276, Philip glances in the rearview mirror, where there is a car with piercing blue-tinted headlights, following too closely. He lets his mind wander, thinking of all the things he is leaving behind him:

There is Walter, barking, "You're late . . . Get your ass on the floor."

Gumaro, asking, *"Que es lo que pasa contigo?"*

Deb Shishimanian and her shiny lips, saying, "Maybe if you came out of the closet and had a relationship of your own, you'd stop being so judgmental."

And then there is gray-haired Dr. Conorton, seated at his wooden desk in his office crammed with too many books, telling Philip, "I think you stand a chance of publishing this piece, young man. I really do."

The faster he drives, the faster Philip's mind ricochets among all these memories and more, some as far back as high school. There is Jedd Kusam knocking Philip's books to the floor, slamming him up against a locker, and saying, "Repeat after me: My name is Dickless Fairy." There is his father, only a few months ago, standing before Philip in the family room, explaining, "I've already told your mother, so now I need to tell you. I've met someone else. Her name is Holly. She was working as a stand-up comedian, of all things, at the medical convention I attended in Vegas. I'm moving out right away. I'll give you my phone number, and you still have that emergency credit card if you need anything." There is that shoe salesman at the Payless store in the King of Prussia Mall whose eyes linger on Philip's longer than most men's do, a look that leads to them sitting in the man's Miata in a dark corner of the parking lot, both their pants down at their knees. There is Philip crinkling up his number afterward and tossing it out the window the way he has done so many times before.

Among this swirl of memories, there is one that keeps bubbling to the surface, no matter how much Philip struggles to force it down. He sees his mother standing at the top of the stairs in her nightgown earlier today. She is screaming at Philip, after having chased him from Ronnie's room, where he was looking for a clean T-shirt, since all of his were dirty. "No one does laundry in this house anymore, so what the hell do you expect?" Philip yells back at her. And then she silences him with a single statement. "Too bad the wrong son died!" she yells in a bloodcurdling voice as Philip steps out the front door of the house with his apron in hand. "Do you hear me? It's too bad the wrong son died!"

Philip feels as though he could drive on forever.

And still the memory of those words would not be far enough behind.

chapter 6

HOLLY IS IN THE MIDDLE OF HER MORNING WORKOUT WHEN THE phone rings. Normally, she wouldn't stop to answer it, but instead of her usual combination Pilates-yoga routine, today she is trying a DVD she borrowed from her friend Marley called *Facercises: Stretch Your Way to a Natural Face-lift*. On the screen, a baby-faced brunette who can't be a day older than eighteen is poking her tongue against the inside of her cheek, creating a bulge that looks positively obscene. For thirty minutes now, Holly has been struggling to follow along with the various moves, but she feels as though she is in training to become a pornographic mime rather than working off her wrinkles and sagging skin. Either way, she welcomes the interruption of the phone, at least until she presses the On button and hears the voice on the other end of the line.

"Hello."

"Salutations, Holly. Is your darling husband at home?"

Charlene. She has not called in weeks, but whenever she does, it never fails to put Richard in a bad mood. Holly once saw a Lifetime movie star-ring Meredith Baxter Birney as a jilted wife who left angry, ranting messages on her ex-husband's machine until she finally showed up during the night and shot him and his new wife while they were asleep. That's what Holly is thinking of when she musters her perkiest voice and says, "Uh, hi. Salutations to you too, Charlene. How are you?"

"Never better. Listen, it's been great catching up with you. Now put Richard on the phone."

On the television, the girl with the baby face is saying, "This next exercise works wonders to keep away my frown lines. Just open your mouth big and wide. Make it big. Make it wide. Bigger. Wider. Bigger. Wider. Bigger. Wider. Okay, now thrust out your tongue like you're trying to lick a melting ice-cream cone. Go on, ladies. Don't be shy. Lick it up!" Holly doesn't want to give Charlene any more ammo, so she grabs the remote and presses Pause, freezing that girl with her mouth open so wide it looks as though she is about to vomit. "He's asleep," she says.

"Still?"

"Yes, still. We were out late last night at a benefit for a hospital up near Vero Beach. Richard has been doing some consulting for them." Holly doesn't know why she feels the need to offer an explanation, but talking to Charlene always makes her nervous. She finds herself blurting things she wouldn't with anyone else.

"Oh, that's right," Charlene says. "How could I have possibly forgotten that I've just called the home of Mr. and Mrs. Palm Beach? Well, I'm sure going to all those glamorous black-tie events on Richard's arm must beat your days working on the Strip before you launched Operation: Steal Someone's Rich Husband."

Holly closes her eyes and sees the scene from that Lifetime movie, the dead couple in bed with a spray of bullet holes in their backs. As absurd as it sounds, that image has been one of the main things that's kept her from retaliating against Charlene's insults all these years. Today, though, for whatever reason, when she opens her eyes, Holly thinks, Fuck it. "I did not steal your husband, Charlene." Her voice is tentative at first but quickly becomes sterner. It is the tone she used to take with hecklers in the audience back in Vegas. Since it was always the men who got drunk and shouted at her, Holly used to stop her act midsentence and say in the same sort of deadly serious voice, "If you're such a big man in need of so much attention, why don't you get up here and show us all your big dick? Come on. Don't be afraid." Sometimes she'd even ask the person in the lighting booth to shine a spotlight on the idiot's crotch. That never failed to shut him up. Now, to Charlene, Holly says, "And you know what else? I don't have to sit here and take this crap from you. In fact, I don't know why I ever did. I'll have Richard call you when he wakes up. Good-bye."

Her thumb is a half second away from hitting the Off button when Charlene's voice comes roaring through the receiver. "Oh, no, you don't. Because I'm going to tell you what you'll do. You are going to wake up that poor excuse for a father. Get his sorry ass out of bed. Then put him on the phone. And you're going to do it this second. Understood?"

Now that Holly has finally begun to fight back, she can't stop herself. "Fuck you, Charlene. You can pull your crazy act on Richard and Philip. But like I said, I don't have to take it. I'm sure this month's deposit will post into your account at Main Line Bank any day now. And since that's all you seem to care about, then I think whatever it is you want can wait."

With that, she hangs up the phone and tosses it on the circular white carpet over by the sliding door that leads to the terrace. As she sits up on her exercise mat, Holly's shoulders feel lighter—so does her entire body, for that matter. Her only regret is that she didn't do it years ago. When she presses Play, the Facercise girl finishes making that vomit expression and says, "Next we're going to do an exercise that helps keep my lips pliant and prevents me from getting those skinny chicken lips that come with age. I'm sure everyone will be good at this one. All you have to do is pucker up like you're kissing someone. I'll leave it to you ladies to imagine who that someone is. Personally, I'll be thinking of Brad Pitt. So come on, show me those kissing lips. Kiss. Kiss. Kiss. Hold it. Kiss. Kiss. Kiss. Hold it. We're aiming for maximum tension here. Kiss. Kiss. Kiss. Hold it."

Holly keeps watching but doesn't follow along with the exercise, if you could call it that. After all, the girl on the screen—an "international beauty expert," as she's called on the case—is years away from getting frown lines or old-lady lips, so what does she know anyway? If Brad Pitt were to kiss her, the authorities would probably haul him off to prison for pedophilia. Holly's friend Marley had clearly lost her judgment on this one.

The phone rings again.

Holly looks over at it warily, as though it's a time bomb resting on the white carpet where she had thrown it a moment before. Since she has decided not to bother with this Facercise madness any longer, she pauses the DVD, then crawls over to the phone in her spandex and answers it, intent on giving Charlene another piece of her mind. "Hello."

"If you ever hang up on me again, you skinny bitch, I will be on the next plane to Palm Beach. And you know what I'll do? I'll buy an apartment in your building. Maybe even right next door. And I'll torture the two of you until your dying day. So I'm going to tell you again that I need to talk to the father of my children. Because I am not calling about money as you so rudely assumed. I am calling about Richard and my son."

Holly is about to hurl a litany of insults back at Charlene until she hears that last part. Ever since Philip was found in the alleyway behind his apartment building one month ago, Richard has been acting differently. It's nothing he's said exactly, but after he stepped off the plane from his visit to the hospital in New York, Holly has sensed a kind of heaviness about him. Especially when Philip's name comes up in conversation. What's more, he seems permanently distracted, changing his mind at the last moment, acting more indecisive and impulsive than ever before. Just last night, on the way to the event at the hospital, he announced that he didn't want to go, for no good reason at all, though Holly managed to finally convince him.

As she stands and makes her way through the condo, her bare manicured feet slapping against the marble tiles while she moves past the row of sliding glass doors, down through the hallway and on toward the bedroom, Holly drops the stern voice and asks Charlene, "Is Philip okay?"

"Not that it's any of your business, but this has to do with our other son. Ronnie. The dead one. I know you two never met, but I'm sure Richard might have mentioned him in passing over the years."

Holly doesn't know what to say anymore—her head hurts from this conversation, and her face hurts from all that absurd stretching—so she tells Charlene to hold on while she gets Richard. When she opens the door to the bedroom, he is lying on his stomach, snoring into his pillow. She watches his tanned, freckled back rise and fall and has to shake the image of that TV movie from her mind once more. Since Richard likes to keep the curtains open in order to feel the breeze off the ocean, the room is filled with light. Holly is an early riser so she never minds, but she doesn't understand how he can possibly sleep with so much sun pouring in. She puts her thumb on the Mute button and a hand on his arm. "Richard," she says in a quiet voice, gently shaking him. "Richard, honey, wake up."

"Huh," he says, lifting his head from the pillow. The part in his salt-and-pepper hair has formed a haphazard zigzag overnight, and Holly can't help but smile. It makes him look boyish in the midst of his grogginess. "What's wrong? What's the matter?"

There it is again: another sign of that heaviness about him. "Nothing is wrong. At least I don't think so. But Ms. Sunshine is on the phone."

He squints at the green numbers of the digital clock on the nightstand. Without his glasses, they are probably a blur to him. "Who?"

"Charlene. She insists on talking to you."

"What time is it?"

"Almost noon."

Richard points at the phone and mouths, "Can she hear me right now?"

Holly shakes her head.

"What does she want?"

"I don't know. She says it's about your son."

A flicker of something passes in his eyes then: worry, guilt, sadness, a combination of all three. "Philip?"

"No. She says it's about your other son. She says she needs to talk to you about Ronnie."

"Ronnie?" Richard shakes his head, completely awake now. He reaches for his silver wire-rimmed glasses and puts them on, then takes the phone and says hello.

Holly turns and goes back toward the hallway. Even though she's never been the type to listen in on other people's conversations (with the exception of those times she eavesdropped on her mother's calls to various boyfriends years ago in Santa Monica), she can't help but linger outside the door. Since Richard never tells her the details of his phone calls with his ex-wife, her curiosity is piqued—this time, more than usual.

She hears Richard say, "Of course I remember Melissa Moody."

Then, "What? What the hell kind of question is that, Charlene?"

Then, "I don't know where this is coming from."

Then, "Charlene, Charlene, wait a minute. Back up to the beginning. Start again."

After that, he says nothing for a long while as he listens to whatever it is she is carrying on about on the other end of the line. Holly is ready to give up and turn back toward the living room when she catches a glimpse of Richard's reflection in the mirror above their dresser. He gets out of bed, wearing nothing but his blue paisley boxers. At the age of fifty-five, he still looks more athletic than most men his age, with the exception of a slight potbelly that Holly thinks is cute.

"Hold on a second, Charlene," she hears him say as he carries the phone into the bathroom, not bothering to close the door. "I have to, well, I have to do something. Just give me thirty seconds. A half a minute." He pauses. "I'm not acting cagey! I have to piss, if you really want to know. I just woke up, for God's sake."

With that, she sees him put the phone on the sink and stand with his back to her. He starts splashing into the toilet, and when he is halfway through, Richard calls out her name. "Holly!"

"Yes," she says, trying her best to sound nonchalant, as though she was busy doing something down the hall and came only when he called.

"What the hell kind of cleaner did you put in this toilet? It reeks of chlorine. I feel like I'm pissing in the pool at the Y."

So the bad mood has begun already, Holly thinks, and he's not even off the phone. "I didn't put anything in there. The cleaning lady did."

"Well, tell her it's a toilet bowl, not a swimming pool. She doesn't have to use the industrial-strength stuff."

Richard rarely snaps like this—in fact, they rarely argue at all, *except* when his ex-wife calls. As tempting as it is to snap back, she doesn't bother because it will only give Charlene too much pleasure to overhear the exchange on the other end of the line. Instead, Holly turns and really does walk away this time.

Back in the living room, the pause time has elapsed on the DVD player, so the baby-faced girl is busy poking her tongue against the inside of her mouth once more. "I do this exercise wherever and whenever I can to prevent sagging cheeks," she says. "If I'm driving in my car down the freeway or stopped at a stoplight, I just take my tongue and poke-poke-poke the inside of my cheek, creating that little bulge right there. I don't care who sees me do it."

"I bet you don't," Holly says to the screen, "because I'm sure you get lots of interesting propositions from men in the next lane." With that, she presses eject. When the DVD slides out of the machine, Holly returns it to the case, stopping a moment to read the back:

> **Facercises: Stretch Your Way to a Natural Face-lift™** *is an easy-to-do exercise regimen guaranteed to shed years off your face. Since face muscles are smaller than most, these simple and fun exercises can produce dramatic results in no time. Plus, they will increase blood flow to the surface of the skin, giving you a healthy, glowing complexion, or your money back. . . .*

Holly lets out a sigh and wonders what she was thinking, trying something so pathetic in the first place. If her options are this limited in the battle against aging, she may as well get it over with and go under the knife like the thousands of other woman here in Palm Beach, or what she thinks of as The Face-lift Capital of the World. But she doesn't want to look like all the other Joan Rivers clones around here who have that I-just-stepped-out-of-a-wind-tunnel appearance.

Up until recently, none of this had been a concern to her, because Holly had been lucky enough to go through life looking younger than her age. When she was first trying her hand as an actress in L.A. in her thirties, every part she landed was as a teenager (in two straight-to-video movies, *Psycho Keg Party 2* and *Psycho Keg Party 3*, plus as Shannen Doherty's friend in five episodes of *Beverly Hills 90210*). Her young looks also came in handy when her agent got her the gig in Vegas doing after-hours stand-up at conventions. The casting call was for "a pretty, fresh-faced girl with a filthy mouth." Holly had the look, and delivering the material was easy, since it was written by a group of writers to fit the different crowds at each convention. Whether it was musicians, fashion editors, botanists, computer geeks, or a bunch of doctors like the ones at the convention where she met Richard, the jokes always matched. She was surprised at how easy it was for the writers to take the lingo from any profession and create a dirty joke around it. They had even given her one or two about plastic surgery that she still remembers.

Last month, I went to my plastic surgeon, who's a little hard of hearing. I told him I had a deviated septum, so he put me under and went to work. When I woke up and looked in the mirror, my nose was exactly the same. I asked him if he had touched my deviated septum at all. "Septum?" he said, "I thought you told me you had a deviated rectum." So now my asshole is twice as small as before. I've been on a juice diet ever since. My boyfriends love it, though. When they say I have a tight ass, I know they mean it. . . .

The things people will laugh at if they have a few cocktails in them, Holly thinks as she puts the DVD in a bag by the door so she'll remember to give it to Marley at lunch later today. Just the memory of that joke reminds her of how grateful she is to have those days behind her. It's enough to shake her out of her Charlene-induced bad mood. She decides to go to the kitchen and squeeze some fresh juice for Richard and herself. Even though he snapped at her about the toilet cleaner, Holly is determined not to let it ruin their day. After all, she can't say she blames him, having to deal with that lunatic of an ex-wife.

As she sets about slicing the oranges, the kitchen fills with the sweet smell of citrus, and she starts planning their afternoon. When he hangs up, she'll suggest a walk on the beach before lunch with Marley and Tom. Maybe later, they'll play tennis if they can get a court on such short notice. She is about to plug in the juicer when Richard's voice bellows down the hall. For a moment, she thinks he is calling for her again, but then she hears him yell, "Charlene, this conversation is going nowhere! I'm not going to keep answering the same question over and over until you get the answer you want to hear!"

Holly puts down the plug to the juicer and does something she hasn't since those days in Santa Monica when she lived with her mother. She leaves the kitchen and goes to Richard's office on the other side of the apartment, where she carefully and quietly picks up the receiver. She clasps her hand over the mouthpiece and listens.

"Charlene, do you want me to come there? Is that what you want?"

"No, I don't want you to come here! Why the hell would you even suggest such a thing? What I want is for you to stop acting so cagey."

"I'm not acting cagey. Stop saying that."

"I know you, Richard, and I can tell when you're hiding something. You know, at first I thought this girl was nuts, and believe me, I told her so. But then Philip said something that got me thinking. And it occurred to me that this is just the sort of freak stunt my husband—"

"Ex-husband."

"Ex-husband! I know that part. Believe me, I thank God for it every day. It occurred to me that this is just the sort of stunt my ex-husband would pull without telling me. And now we've been on the phone for what, fifteen minutes, and you are still hiding something from me. I know it. I was married to you for almost thirty years, so I know."

"Charlene, I'm a heart surgeon. Not a mad scientist. You are being ridiculous."

"If I'm being ridiculous, then why were you stuttering before, the way you always do when you lie?"

"What do you mean the way I always do? Like when?"

"Like when you first joined the Bimbo-of-the-Month club after our son died. Like when you first met your funny lady friend from Vegas and denied that something was going on."

"Charlene, I've told you. She's not from Vegas. She worked in Vegas."

"Whatever, she's still a slut."

"I am not having this conversation. If you keep talking like that, I am hanging up. That's your last warning."

Charlene is quiet a moment before she says, "You also stuttered when you neglected to tell me that you caved and let Ronnie keep the Mercedes even though we agreed he should sell it."

"Charlene, that was a long time ago. Besides, those were isolated incidents. You can't build a federal case around the fact that I stuttered after hearing what was admittedly some very strange news."

"Well, just tell me this: Is it possible?"

"I am not going to speculate—"

"Just answer, yes or no. As a doctor, is this sort of thing possible? To freeze someone's sperm?"

Richard hesitates. "Of course, it's possible, but—"

"Yes or no?"

"Well, then, it's yes, Charlene. Yes. It is possible. Are you happy?"

"Thank you. That's all I wanted to know."

Holly leans on Richard's wide wooden desk and stares out over the ocean, wondering what in the world all this is about. She hears Richard take a breath. Then, in a softer, collapsed sort of voice, he says, "Charlene, I have to go. Holly and I are supposed to have lunch with some friends in a little while." He pauses. "Are you still there? Did you hang up? Hello?"

For a moment, Holly thinks that Charlene did hang up, but then her voice comes through the line, quieter and gentler than she's ever heard her sound. "You know something, Richard? She kept asking for you. Twice anyway. Even at the time, I thought it was odd. When she first got here, she looked up the stairs and said, 'Is Mr. Chase here?' Then later in the car, she said she was hoping to talk with you. Don't you think that's strange?"

Richard is quiet for a moment. Finally, he says, "Well, the whole thing is strange, Charlene. She is a troubled young girl. Listen, I need to go. But tell me one more thing. How is Philip doing?"

"Fine. You know, a big grouch as always."

"Well, tell him to call me if he needs anything. He never calls me."

"The phone works both ways, Richard. You have the number here, and you have his cell number too. So you could get in touch if you really wanted."

"I know. It's just that— Well, tell him I said hello."

Since the conversation is winding down, Holly carefully places the phone in its cradle then scoots back to the kitchen. As she plugs in the juicer and starts the machine whirring, she feels a mix of emotions spinning inside her. First, there is the guilt about having done what she just did. Then there is the utter confusion as to what they were talking about— from Richard suggesting he go there, to freezing someone's sperm, to all the rest. Serves me right, she thinks and mashes half an orange onto the nose of the juicer while bits and pieces of the conversation ring in her head:

This is just the sort of freak stunt my ex-husband would pull. . . .

I'm a heart surgeon. Not a mad scientist. . . .

Just answer, yes or no. . . . Is this sort of thing possible?

She kept asking for you . . . Even at the time, I thought it was odd. . . .

By the time Holly finishes filling two glasses and scraping out the pulp from the machine, Richard comes padding down the hallway in his bare feet. He has put on a baggy yellow T-shirt with the faded words BRYN MAWR HOSPITAL on the front and has evened out the part in his hair. When he finds Holly in the kitchen, holding the glasses in her hands, Richard takes one look at her and says, "I'm sorry I acted like that about the toilet bowl. I just, I don't know, that phone call rattled me out of a sound sleep."

"It's okay," she tells him, his conversation with Charlene still echoing in her mind. "From now on, I'm just going to call you Mr. Ty-D-Bol."

Richard kisses her on the cheek—a cheek, she thinks, that is no firmer thanks to those ludicrous exercises. "You were funnier when other people wrote your jokes," he tells her.

"Sad but true," Holly says.

They fall into an uneasy silence, and Holly senses that heaviness about him again. "Is everything okay?" she asks.

The question causes a strained look to come over Richard's face. His eyes grow wide and worried. His mouth hangs open in the same haunted expression that Philip and Charlene had both worn the night before when Melissa Moody first entered their lives again. Richard doesn't answer so much as grunt.

"Should I take that as a yes?"

He stares down at the kitchen floor, absently running his tanned big toe along the grout between two tiles as he sips his juice, a fleck of pulp sticking to his top lip.

"Richard, are you all right? Look at me."

Slowly, he lifts his head to meet her gaze.

"What is it?" she asks. "What's wrong with you?"

"Holly," Richard says, and she can sense by the somber tone he uses just to say her name that whatever's about to come next is serious. "I've never told anyone this before. But I—Well, it's about my son Ronnie's high school girlfriend. Melissa Moody. The girl he took to the prom the last night he was alive. Something happened that summer after he died. Something I've kept secret all these years."

chapter 7

HALFWAY THROUGH THE BAND'S RENDITION OF WHITNEY HOUS-
ton's "Heartbreak Hotel," Stacy comes back from wherever she's been for
the last fifteen minutes and shouts into Melissa's ear. A mammoth black
speaker is vibrating so close to where Missy is sitting that she hears her sister's words all wrong: "Missy, I need to walk it's new!"

"What?" she shouts back over the steady throb of bass.

"What?" Stacy shouts at her.

"No, I'm asking you 'what?' What do you need to do?"

"I said, 'I need to talk to you!' Some place quiet and private!"

"Now?"

"No, I was hoping to make an appointment for some time next month!
Of course, now!"

Missy looks around their table. When they arrived an hour before, it
had been perfectly arranged with a pink floral centerpiece, white plates
flanked with shiny silverware, and glasses embossed with the words, *Radnor High School Senior Prom, Starry Night, June 18, 1999*. Hundreds of
tiny yellow lights twinkled against the lattice that stretches between the
beams of the inn's vaulted ceiling, giving the place a magical, enchanted

feeling that made Missy smile the moment she stepped inside. Now, though, the gold-painted chairs are empty and pushed haphazardly away from the table, the tablecloth is smeared with food stains, dishes of half-eaten pasta primavera and chicken cordon bleu are scattered about. Waiters are everywhere, busily rushing around in their ill-fitting black-and-white uniforms, but not one of them has been by this table in at least a half hour. And those twinkling lights on the lattice near the ceiling are lost in the frenzied bursts of the strobes blinking to the beat of the music. Melissa turns back to her sister, whose emerald green dress appears alternately softer then harsher, depending on the flashing light. "But Ronnie and Chaz are about to come back from taking pictures with the team! Then we're going to start dancing!"

"I don't care!" Stacy yells in her ear. "This can't wait! Let's go to the bathroom! Now!"

She grabs Melissa by the hand and yanks her out of the seat so fast that her purse falls to the floor. Melissa feels dizzy from all the champagne they drank in the limousine. As she watches it drop, she worries that the lightbulb inside will shatter, or worse, the clasp will pop open and her packed clothes will spill out in front of her sister. She scoops up the purse and feels the sides to be sure the bulb is still in one piece. As far as she can tell, it is. Melissa clutches the bag close to her waist as Stacy leads her by the hand toward the bathroom. On the way, they weave through a colorful sea of their classmates, all shouting to one another over the music. Most of them are red in the eyes from whatever booze they managed to sneak in or drink before they got here. A few reek of pot. Melissa checks out the dresses on the other girls, ranging from formal ball gowns to ghetto prom style. Seneca Lawson, for one, is wearing a glittery black dress held together on each side by a ladder of silver, tinsel-like strands. Her breasts are poised to pop out the top at any moment. In profile, she looks just about naked.

"What are you staring at?" Seneca asks Missy, flipping her long, pin-straight brown hair over one of her bare, bony shoulders.

A prostitute, Melissa thinks but doesn't say. Instead, she tells Seneca how pretty she looks and how much she loves her dress, since she doesn't want to start trouble tonight. Even though Melissa knows she should be enjoying herself—living in the moment, as people always say—all she really wants is to be away from this place, out of this dress, wearing the clothes packed inside her purse, sitting beside Ronnie in the front seat of his Mercedes, driving toward the B and B in Rehoboth, Delaware, where they booked a room for the weekend.

"Did you see that dress?" Melissa asks her sister. "Or should I say, half a dress?"

Stacy doesn't answer. She keeps weaving between people on their way to the glowing red EXIT sign. The motion of being pulled like a water-skier behind the speedboat of her sister makes Melissa's already woozy stomach woozier. Her nausea got worse on the ride over in the limousine and hasn't subsided since. Finally, they break from the crowd and walk down the hall, their heels sinking into the worn green carpet. When they reach the bathroom, a long row of wilted girls is waiting outside the door, their backs pressed against a mural that depicts the history of Radnor Township. "Shit," Stacy says. "There's a line. Follow me down this hall instead."

Melissa has had enough, so she tugs her hand free. "I'm not following you anywhere else unless you give me some hint as to what this is about."

Stacy keeps her eyes on those girls, who look so glum they may as well be gathering firewood with the weary settlers in the mural behind them. "You really want me to discuss our personal life right here in front of other people?"

"I guess not," Melissa says.

"Then come on. Walk down here with me."

Begrudgingly, Melissa follows, though she makes a point to walk beside Stacy, rather than being led by the hand. They pass more of those murals—one of a blacksmith hammering a piece of metal, another of a stiff-looking man with a beard speaking at a podium in the town square, another of a group of women all wearing kerchiefs and preparing a feast. "I am getting a serious case of mural-itis," Missy says. "Somebody save me."

Still, her sister doesn't smile. She hangs a right down a dimly lit hallway where the murals come to an end and the carpeted floor slopes for wheelchairs. Here, the walls are wallpapered with hundreds of miniature horse-and-buggy silhouettes. The sight of them, raining down all around Melissa and Stacy, reminds her of the day trips to Amish country they take every summer with their parents. Compared to those families—dressed in unadorned black, living without electricity, never having a drop of alcohol or caffeine, quilting and farming their lives away—her parents actually seem normal for a change. "Have you been here before?" Missy asks as Stacy stops outside a door that is slightly ajar, then peeks inside. "You seem to know this place awfully well."

"Just guessing. Come on. Let's go in here."

"Stacy, this is ridiculous. We can talk in the hallway."

"I don't want any of those waiters interrupting us."

Melissa cradles her elbows in her hands, her heavy purse slung over her shoulder. "Fine. But I'm only going in there if you promise to make this fast. Ronnie and Chaz are probably back by now and wondering where we disappeared to."

Stacy doesn't offer any such promise, but Melissa steps inside the minuscule room anyway. The only light comes from a small rectangular window overlooking the parking lot. As her sister runs a hand along the wall in search of a switch, Melissa goes to the window and pulls back the tattered blue curtain to stare out at the caravan of limousines in the lot. There are easily fifty parked out there, most of them white, all of them with the same black glass and studs of light lining the doors. Melissa wonders if they look the same on the inside too. She wouldn't know since the only limo she has ever ridden in was the one tonight. Stacy, Chaz, and Ronnie loved every moment of it. They kept hopping from seat to seat as they sipped their champagne, propped up their feet, and made announcements like "This is the life!" (Ronnie) or "We are seriously stylin', my friends!" (Chaz) or "I could so get used to this!" (Stacy). The whole while, Melissa smiled and pretended to enjoy herself too, but the truth was, she hated the experience. There was something claustrophobic about the way the ceiling pressed down, sealing them inside, except for the small rectangle of that sunroof. The thing Melissa found most disconcerting of all was not being able to see out the front window as they drove. So as the rest of them blathered on about how great it was and how they wished they could have taken a limousine to school every day for the last four years, Melissa sat there sipping her champagne and feeling sick. She didn't say a word about it, though, since it was obvious they wouldn't understand.

"Found it," Stacy says.

A bare bulb in the center of the ceiling comes to life, shining down on the stacks of Executive Choice toilet paper, blank receipt rolls, fuzzy white dish towels, milk crates filled with glass ashtrays and salt and pepper shakers, empty Corona Light, Heineken, and Rolling Rock cases, and countless unmarked white tubs of who knows what. The small space reminds Melissa of the darkroom at school, only without the red glow and pungent odor of the developing chemicals. Through the wall, she hears the bass of the band, beating and beating and beating as the singer belts out "La Vida Loca."

"Okay, Stacy. Now that we're safely sealed inside this isolation chamber, would you mind telling me what's so urgent that you had to interrupt the entire evening?"

Stacy takes a step closer to Melissa, her dyed green heels clicking against the peeling linoleum floor, her dress more garish than ever beneath the unforgiving glare of the bare bulb. She puts both hands on Melissa's shoulders, and Melissa thinks briefly of a game they used to play when they were little that they called Mirror. They'd sit face-to-face and imitate each other's movements, pretending to brush their teeth, put on lipstick, comb their hair, and a dozen other motions. The one who fell out of sync first lost—that person was almost always Melissa.

"Stacy," Missy says when her sister takes another step closer. "If you're going to kiss me, I think I should inform you that I already have a date tonight. And if you want to play Mirror, I think we're a little old for that."

"Ha, ha. Missy, this is serious. You are going to get mad at me when I say this. But I love you and I'm going to tell you anyway."

"What? What? What?" Melissa shouts, stomping both her heels against the floor. "Come on! Spit it out!"

"You can't go."

Melissa shakes her sister's hands off her shoulders and pulls her purse closer. "Go where?"

"You know what I am taking about, Missy. Chaz told me what you and Ronnie are planning. And you can't go through with it. I won't let you. Mom and Dad will make your life a living hell. Not to mention mine."

Melissa has one thought: I am going to kill Chaz. Then she thinks, No,

I am going to kill Ronnie. Why did he open his big mouth when he promised he wouldn't? This was supposed to be a secret. Our secret. She considers denying the whole thing, but it's obvious Stacy knows, so that would be pointless. Instead, she says, "Think what you want, but I'm going."

"Missy, you have your whole life ahead of you. You have so much to look forward to down the road—"

"Thank you, Oprah Winfrey, for your empowering message. You're an inspiration to us all."

"I'm serious, Miss. Why would you want to spoil your last summer before college, especially when you'll have all the time you want with Ronnie at Penn in the fall? Think about it."

"I *have* thought about it, Stacy. As a matter of fact, it's pretty much all I've thought about for the last month. I am so sick of Mom and Dad and their stupid rules. Most girls our age have been screwing their boyfriends for years. I want to have sex with Ronnie. No. I want more than that. I want to fuck his brains out. And I don't want to do it here in Radnor. I want to go away. I want it to be special."

"Well, I think you should wait," Stacy tells her.

"Wait to go away? Or wait to have sex?"

"Both."

It used to be that Melissa and her sister talked about everything. But over the last year Missy had imposed a distance between them, because she wanted to be her own person for once in her life without dragging a stunt double along for the ride. As a result, what little she knows about her sister's sex life comes from the things Chaz has told Ronnie, and Ronnie has told her. "You mean to tell me that you and Chaz have never done it?"

"Not officially," Stacy says.

"What do you mean, 'not officially'? Either you have or you haven't. Besides, that's not what I hear from Ronnie. Chaz tells him that you guys do it all the time. The two of you are like friggin' rabbits."

"Well, you heard wrong, Missy. And if you didn't shut yourself off to me this last year, I might have told you what we do."

With her sister standing so close still, Melissa has another flash of that Mirror game. She sees a younger Stacy pretending to put on a pair of earrings, open a tube of lipstick, and spread it on her lips. Back then, so much of their make-believe had to do with pretending they were grown women—best friends who lived next door, teachers at the same school, cashiers at the same grocery store, secretaries in the same office, saleswomen in the same department store. Now here we are, Melissa thinks, all grown-up and arguing with each other in a storage closet on prom night. "What do you mean, 'what we do'?" she asks.

"Never mind. It's none of your business."

"Come on. Tell me. What?"

Stacy's eyes dart around the room, from those unlabeled white tubs to the milk crates full of glass ashtrays and salt and pepper shakers to that bare bulb, which casts slashes of shadows in all the wrong places on her face. Finally, she says, "I let Chaz do it to me another way, you know, so I am still technically a virgin. You know what I mean."

"You keep saying 'you know.' And actually, Stacy, I don't know. What are you talking about?"

Her sister uses her thumb and index fingers to spruce the petals of the gruesome green flowers on the corsage Chaz gave her. Without looking up, she says, "I'm sure you can guess."

"In the mouth?" Melissa asks.

"Well, yeah. But that's not all. I mean, that's not the main thing."

"In the—" Melissa stops when she realizes what her sister is saying. "Eww! You are sick. That is the grossest thing I've ever heard."

"All right, Mom. Lots of girls do it that way. So don't be shocked."

"Like who? Who's 'lots of girls'?"

"Seneca, for one."

"Well, that doesn't surprise me. I'm sure she charges extra for that service too."

"There are plenty of other people, Missy. Laura Mills and Eva Talbot."

"Those girls are all sluts. I'm surprised they even care about being technical virgins, or whatever you called it. I mean, if you're going to do that, you may as well just go all the way." Melissa stops and leans against the wall. The steady throb of music vibrates her body as the band howls to the end of that Ricky Martin song. Melissa tells herself to forget this bizarre, unexpected tangent and get back to the reason they came here in the first place. "Stacy, I can't talk about this right now. It is just too strange. It's freaking me out."

Her sister stays silent, still picking at those green petals on her corsage.

Melissa goes to the window and thinks about what to do next. As she stares out over the parking lot, she spots a group of drivers standing around one of the white limousines, huddled together, talking and laughing, flicking the ashes of their cigarettes to the ground. She scans the group in search of their driver—a rail-thin Asian man who'd been polite, though oddly quiet as he held the door when they got in and out of the car—but she doesn't see him among the others. This is what Melissa decides: first, she is going to find Ronnie and give him hell for telling Chaz. Then, they are going tonight. No matter what, they are still following through with their plans. The limo will take them to Ronnie's house, where they will get into his Mercedes and drive to Rehoboth, Delaware. By midnight, they'll be checking into the room they reserved in his name. Even more than having sex for the first time, the thing Melissa has been looking forward to is sleeping beside Ronnie, cuddling close to his warm body all weekend long. Once she has settled the matter in her mind, Melissa turns back to her sister and repeats an abbreviated version of the plan. "I am going to find Ronnie. And when the prom is over, we are leaving. Tonight, we are going to have sex, the way normal people do."

When Melissa steps past her sister toward the door, Stacy blurts, "Missy, if you go I'll tell Mom and Dad exactly where you're staying."

Melissa spins around and stares at her sister—at the mirror image of her moss green eyes, her shiny blond hair, her delicate nose—and she wants nothing more than to shatter that reflection once and for all. She wouldn't do it, Missy thinks. She is just bluffing. Besides, she probably doesn't know where we are staying. Maybe she knows the name of the town, but Ronnie wouldn't have told Chaz the name of the inn. Why would he?

Stacy must read the doubt on her face, because the next things she says is, "You have a reservation for three nights at the Archer Inn in Rehoboth, Delaware. And in addition to calling Mom and Dad, I'll also call the inn and cancel the reservation before you even have time to get there. Now do you believe me?"

With that, Melissa erupts into a litany of questions. "Why are you doing this to me? Why are you being such a major bitch? What is wrong with you? Don't you have enough going on in your own life, you have to butt into mine?"

In a calm, even voice, Stacy says, "It's *our* life, Missy."

"No, it's not, Stacy. You are my sister, but you are not *me*. We are two separate people. Get that through your head. It's *my* life, and I get to make *my* own decisions."

Now it is Stacy who steps toward the door. "Like I told you before, I am doing this because I love you. Because you're my sister. And because I know how completely miserable Mom and Dad will be to both of us if you do this. So even though you think we are two separate people, and you've done everything to prove that you don't need me in the last year, our parents still treat us like a single unit. If they punish you, it is bound to affect my life too. And personally, I want to enjoy my last summer before college. So like I said, you're not going. Even though you're mad at me now, I feel pretty certain you'll thank me later."

When she is finished, Stacy steps out into the hallway and heads back toward the reception room even as Melissa screams after her, "You're two minutes older than me! Not twenty years! Why are you acting like you're my mother?"

Stacy keeps going without looking back.

Melissa is so angry that she slams the door and stands dead center in the confines of that room, clutching her purse and fuming. What the hell was Ronnie thinking, running off at the mouth to Chaz? she wonders as that drumbeat on the other side of the wall grows louder. It feels as though the sound is seeping under her skin and filling her with rage. Melissa thinks of that paperback she picked up at one of the church fund-raiser book sales, *Carrie*. She imagines her own fury taking supernatural form—bolting doors, bursting pipes, flooding the place, electrocuting every single person dancing on the other side of that wall. When she feels ready to explode from the sheer intensity of her disappointment and disgust with this evening—an evening she has looked forward to for months—Melissa plops down on one of those unmarked tubs and starts to cry.

I hate this prom, she thinks as a list of all the people and things she despises at the moment unfurls in her mind: I hate my dress. I hate wearing this corsage. I hate this stupid closet. I hate this ugly inn. I hate those depressing murals on the walls. I hate Ronnie. I hate, hate, *hate* Chaz. I hate my parents. And most of all, I hate my sister.

When she can't think of anyone or anything else to hate, Melissa's thoughts go back to her parents. They are the root of this problem, after all. If it weren't for their stupid rules, Stacy wouldn't feel the need to get in the way of her plans tonight. Melissa thinks of all the restrictions she's had to abide by all these years while the rest of the people her age were out having fun:

No phone calls after eight.
No cable TV.
No profanity.
Two hours of flute practice a night.
Three hours of homework.
Church on Sunday.
Prayer group on Tuesday.
Family visits to sick people whenever her father damn well decides he's in the mood.

Melissa can't stand it anymore. She simply cannot stand it.

As angry as she is at Ronnie for telling Chaz, her thoughts go to his family next. When the limousine stopped at his house earlier tonight, Ronnie's mother came out on the front lawn, all smiles and laughter. She snapped her way through three rolls of film and bantered back and forth with Ronnie, who was trying to tell her how to take a better picture while posing at the same time. Mrs. Chase talked about *normal* things, like a *normal* parent. She told them she was hosting a big-deal author reading at the library tonight. She told them how much she loved dressing up for special occasions. Even Ronnie's dad, who was on his way to work at the hospital, came outside and acted like a *normal* father too. Instead of lecturing them about curfews and drinking, he told a funny story about going to a dance in high school and getting kicked out for making out on the dance floor with his girlfriend, another about his watch getting caught in Mrs. Chase's veil at the altar during their wedding. As he got ready to leave, they even gave each other a little kiss right there in front of everybody. Melissa can't even remember seeing her parents kiss. Ever. Finally, Ronnie's brother came outside to see them before leaving for his job at the Olive Garden. Melissa had never met Philip before, but back when she was a freshman, she came across an oversize dictionary in the high school library, where someone had brushed globs of Wite-Out next to the words, *loser, faggot, sucker, homosexual, odorous, ugly,* and dozens of others. In blue pen, where the definitions should be, the person wrote: *See also: Philip Chase, Class of '95.* Despite all that, Melissa thought Philip seemed *normal* too. He told them they looked nice and to have a good time, then he got in his car and drove away, minding his own business—unlike her sister.

It is as though thinking of Ronnie's family somehow summons Ronnie himself, because the next thing Melissa hears is his rushed, energetic voice calling her name down the hall. "Missy! Melissa!"

She doesn't answer, because she is too pissed off to talk to him right now. But he pushes open the door and finds her anyway. "Stacy said you were down here. What's—" Ronnie stops when he realizes she is crying. He steps inside, closes the door behind him, and sits beside her on one of the tubs. "What is it?" he asks, wrapping his solid arms around her. "What's the matter?"

"You ruined it with your big mouth," she says into the bulk of his shoulder.

"Ruined what?"

Melissa pulls away and punches him as hard as she can in the chest. "Don't play dumb with me, you moron! You ruined our plans for tonight and this weekend!"

Ronnie stares at her, his head tilted to one side, confused.

"Do I have to spell it out for you? You told Chaz. Chaz told my sister. My evil sister who doesn't want us to go."

Ronnie straightens his head in a way that indicates he gets what she is talking about. His tongue washes over his lips, and he releases a heavy sigh. "I'm sorry, Melissa."

"Well, why did you tell him? You promised. You know he has a big mouth. This whole trip was supposed to be a secret. Our secret."

"I know. But Chaz told me he wouldn't say anything. Then he slipped in front of Stacy tonight. It was an honest mistake on his part. He didn't mean to."

"Well, I still don't understand why you told him in the first place."

Ronnie reminds her of the sports awards banquet this Saturday night, the one he and Melissa agreed he would miss to go to Rehoboth instead. "Chaz kept bugging me about driving there together, and he wanted to hang out afterward. There's a kegger at somebody's house, and he wanted us to go. He was like a nagging old lady about it, Miss. Finally, I had to tell him I wasn't going to be around just to get him off my back. Come on, Missy. Don't be pissed. I didn't mean to mess up our plans."

Melissa doesn't want to forgive him so easily. She doesn't want to admit that she understands. Knowing Chaz, though, the story makes sense. "But why did you have to tell him the name of the inn?"

Ronnie shrugs. "I don't know. He thought what we were doing was pretty cool. So I guess I was kind of bragging about it, telling him how nice everything was going to be. I felt like I had something over him. It was the first thing in a long time that shut him up about his shot put record."

Melissa doesn't know what else to say. She reaches over to grab one of those Executive Choice toilet paper rolls so she can dry her eyes. When Ronnie sees what she is doing, he tells her to wait, then he puts his hand in the front pocket of his tuxedo and pulls out a white handkerchief with the initials *RC*. "Normally, I'd only be able to offer you a scrap of note-book paper from my pocket. But my dad gave this to me tonight to complete my look. It's one of his. Luckily, we have the same initials." Ronnie holds the silk cloth up to Melissa's face and gently presses it to her cheeks. "Don't worry," he tells her. "I haven't blown my nose in it or anything. It's clean."

"Thank God for one good thing tonight," she says, then asks if her mascara ran.

"A little. But it's gone now."

"You know, Ronnie, we can't go anymore. Chaz ended up telling my sister the name of the inn and everything. Now she is threatening to tell my parents where we're staying."

Neither of them speak for a moment as Melissa reaches down and scratches her wrist, adjusting the lace band of her corsage. Through the wall, she hears the muffled words to a Mariah Carey song start up as the drumbeat slows down. Finally Melissa says, "Maybe we can go somewhere else. Another beach. Another hotel. It's not like the Archer Inn is the only place in the world."

Ronnie licks his lips again and sighs. "Missy, there's another problem."

What more could possibly go wrong? she thinks. "What now?"

"I asked my dad to give me my credit card back, and he refused. I asked him for some cash instead, and he said no to that as well. My parents are still punishing me for the Mercedes. So I'm broke. When we stopped at the house tonight, I even asked Philip if I could use his card."

"And what did he say?"

"You'd have to know my brother to really understand. He got all snippy the way he usually does. He told me if I quit wasting my time playing sports and got a job, then I'd have money in my pocket. Like I want to waste my life working at the Olive Garden like him."

"Fine," Melissa says. "Then it's official: our trip is canceled."

Ronnie gets off the tub and kneels on the cracked linoleum floor before her. He takes Melissa's hands in his and kisses both of them on the knuckles, then reaches up and strokes her hair. "I'm sorry," he tells her. "I'm so, so sorry."

As disappointed as Melissa feels, she has to admit that it comes with a growing sense of relief. She would never confess as much to Stacy, but her sister was right about one thing: their parents would have made both their lives miserable. Still, even though Melissa won't have to suffer through the entire summer, she can't help but think of those photographs in the Archer Inn brochure that Ronnie sent away for. All the rooms have a perfect view of the ocean. Each one is named after the color of the walls inside. There is a blue room, a green room, a yellow room, a peach room. She and Ronnie reserved the yellow room, because they liked the look of the king-size canopy bed covered with pillows. Now Melissa imagines that bed staying empty all weekend, or worse, being given to some random, boring couple who might show up without a reservation. She thinks of the boardwalk they wanted to stroll, a restaurant called Ashby's Oyster House where they wanted to eat, a little bookstore called Browseabout Books that they might have stopped in. "I just wanted everything to be perfect," she says under her breath.

"It is perfect," Ronnie tells her, stroking her hair some more. "I don't care if we're sitting in this closet together. I just like being with you."

Melissa looks at him, kneeling before her still. His bow tie has gone crooked, so she straightens it. "Where did you hear that cornball line?"

"I mean it, Melissa. I think this last year together has proven how I feel about you. It's not exactly like we've been able to go on normal dates with all your parents' rules. It would have been a hell of a lot easier for me to date someone else. But I want to be with you."

Melissa doesn't know what to say, so she tells him, "I want to be with you too."

"In a few more months, everything will be different. We'll be living at college. We'll be right across campus from each other."

"Yeah. Except I'll be slaving away in the cafeteria or whatever crappy work-study position the financial aid office assigns me just so I can afford to be there."

Ronnie brushes back a strand of hair that has slipped out of her bobby pins. He presses his soft, full lips to the very center of her forehead and tells her in a low voice, "Well, if you're on dish duty, I'll help you scrub."

"Is that a promise?"

"It's a promise."

Ronnie moves down to kiss her lips as his hand slides around the back of her neck. His fingers do a little dance there, tracing their way from ear to ear, then to the top knob of her spine. Ronnie's kisses always start off as nothing more than tender brushes against her mouth. Soon he begins pressing into her, parting his lips, so they become wetter, hotter. As his tongue pushes inside of her, filling Melissa's mouth, she closes her eyes and leans her head back. Ronnie moves his body closer, then pulls his lips away from hers and presses them to the nape of her neck. His breath feels warm and moist against her skin as he moves closer to her ear. Melissa rubs her hands over the bulky mass of his shoulders and down his back. Something about the motion makes him breathe even harder. And when he reaches her ear, she thinks he is whispering something to her. She listens closer, though, and realizes that there are no words. It is simply the rush of his breath. Finally, he slips his head down near her breasts and buries his face into the lace of her dress. "I feel like I'm kissing a table-cloth," he says, laughing.

Melissa stares at the messy part in his blond hair. "I thought you told me I looked beautiful in this dress."

Ronnie gazes up at her with those blue eyes she loves so much. She feels a stab of regret and sadness that she'll have to wait to find out what it's like to sleep beside him, breathing in the smell of his skin, waking up and seeing his face in the morning. "You do look beautiful in it," he tells her. "But I bet you'd look even more beautiful out of it."

"Too bad you lost your chance tonight," Melissa says.

He plants a kiss between her breasts then slips one hand down to her ankle and beneath the dress. In slow, circling motions, he moves upward along her ankle, her calf, her knee, the inside of her thigh, and higher still. When his fingers reach her panties, the material is already wet just from the touch of him. As he strokes along the seam, gently at first, then pressing harder into her so that Melissa's breath quickens, Ronnie asks, "Says who?"

"Says me," Melissa tells him, forcing herself to push his hand away and bring her knees together. "Ronnie, we can't do this here."

"Why not?"

"We have to go back to the prom."

"Fuck the prom. You think I care about anyone out there? I only care about you."

"But I told you a million times. I want our first time to be special."

"And I told you, it is special. Wherever we are."

Melissa stares at him a long while, thinking of all the turns this evening took before she ended up sitting with Ronnie in this storage room. Practically everyone they know is dancing on the other side of the wall, and he wants to have sex with her. Here. Now. She considers those other girls her age — Seneca Lawson, Laura Mills, Eva Talbot, and even her very own sister, Stacy Moody. Compared to what she learned about them tonight, being in this closet with Ronnie seems perfectly normal. "Want to see something?" she asks Ronnie.

He nods, and Melissa tells him to grab her purse on the floor. When he hands it to her, she unclasps the top and pulls out that tight bundle of clothing. Slowly, carefully, she unrolls the pants and T-shirt, as though performing a kind of surgery, until extracting the glass heart of that red bulb.

"Were you planning on developing pictures while we were in Rehoboth?" Ronnie asks.

"No. I was going to put it into the lamp by the bed in our room. A little surprise to make us feel more at home."

"I have a better idea." He takes it from her and stands, then puts his hand to the bare bulb hanging from the ceiling. It's so hot that he has to grab a dishrag from the shelf. After he unscrews it, there is nothing but the blue light of the parking lot to see by until Ronnie puts in the red bulb. *"Voilà!"* he says when the familiar crimson glow fills the room. "Instant darkroom."

As Melissa looks up at Ronnie's square handsome face, his smile with that slight underbite, she thinks of how tired she is of waiting, how tired she is of saying no. Finally, she stands and locks the door. She pushes a few of those heavy tubs in front of it just in case, then pulls the tattered blue curtains shut. This is not how she wanted the first time to be. It is not how she wanted it at all. But Melissa decides that Ronnie is right. As long as they are together, it doesn't matter where. So at long last, she surrenders to the moment, letting go of the plan, but salvaging this much at least— the part that matters most. Ronnie pulls off his tuxedo jacket and lays it on the peeling linoleum floor beside him. He pats it with his hand and says, "Care to join me?"

Melissa lies down next to him and buries her face into the tender warmth of his chest as his fingers move down her back, slowly, clumsily undoing the buttons of her lacy white dress.

"You know I love you," Ronnie whispers in her ear. "Right?"

"I know," Melissa whispers back. "And I love you too."

chapter 8

ON THE SNOW-COVERED LAWN IN FRONT OF THE RADNOR MEMO-
rial Library sits the crumpled, charred-black shell of a BMW, its doors
punched in, its hood ripped off, its windows long since shattered. The giant block letters on the sign draped across one side read THIS IS WHAT HAP-
PENS WHEN YOU DRINK AND DRIVE. The car—or rather, what used to be the
car—is on display as part of a public service campaign that uses actual
wrecks from alcohol-related accidents in order to bring home the point.
Charlene remembers reading in the town paper that this particular wreck
had been brought here from a deadly pileup at a Pittsburgh tollbooth this
past New Year's Eve. Every time she sees its buckled frame and crushed
roof, Charlene has the same thought: don't we have enough tragedies
around this place without having to drag someone else's leftovers into
town? One look at it makes most people slow down, but Charlene steps on
the gas and speeds up to get past it on her way into the library parking lot.

When she finds a vacant spot and turns off the engine, a fluttery, first-
day-of-school feeling fills her stomach. It has been almost five years since
she has stepped inside this place, almost five years since that wretched

Pilia used Charlene's tragedy as an opportunity to pole-vault into the position of head librarian. Since she cannot bring herself to go inside just yet and let Pilia and the other librarians see what has become of her, Charlene reaches over for the plastic Genuardi's bag on the passenger seat and pulls out the loaf of Wonder Bread she bought on the way here. Ever since she hung up the phone with Richard a few hours before, two things have happened. First, she has become convinced that he is hiding something. No matter how much Richard denied it, Charlene knows—the way a woman who was married to a man for almost thirty years knows—that his cagey, fumbling response to her questions can only mean one thing: he is keeping a secret from her. The second thing to happen is that Charlene has been seized by an inexplicable craving for a taste of the plain white bread she used to make sandwiches with back when Philip and Ronnie were in elementary school.

As she sits in the dusty, overheated interior of her green Lexus, trying to muster up the courage to go inside, Charlene opens the package of bread, takes out the heel, and tosses it on the floor. Next, she pulls out a regular slice and peels off the crust the way Ronnie and Philip used to ask her to do. When there is nothing in her hand but a floppy, crooked white square, Charlene folds it in half and shoves the bread into her mouth. There is something about the spongy texture and tasteless flavor that works wonders to soothe her.

Wonder Bread, Charlene thinks, maybe that's how it got its name.

She chews and swallows, then removes another slice from the bag, regretting ever having switched to those trendy double-seeded/nine-grain/whole wheat/sesame/oat bran concoctions, since none of them could ever come close to bringing her the comfort of happier times the way this bread is doing. As she peels off the crust and stuffs another slice in her mouth, she finds herself thinking back to when she was a young mother, making peanut butter and jelly sandwiches and tucking them in Philip's Scooby-Doo and Ronnie's Ninja Turtles lunch boxes along with an apple, a yogurt, and a box of Juicy Juice. Charlene takes out another slice, peels off the crust, tosses it on the floor, folds the bread in half, and sticks it in her mouth. She chews, swallows, and repeats the process again and again as she thinks back to when she was a young librarian and how good she used to be at keeping things in perfect order—sorting, stacking, shelving, alphabetizing, alphanumerizing, categorizing, discarding, filing, dusting, always dusting—and all of it done with a smile on her face.

When the fog of memories of happier times finally lifts, Charlene looks down at the floor, which is littered with crusts, around her damp beige boots. On the passenger seat, the package is just about empty. She has eaten almost the entire loaf. A big part of Charlene is disgusted with herself, the way she is whenever she surrenders to her cravings. A few nights before, she had given in to an urgent, unrelenting desire for pea soup. After she rushed to the store and loaded up her carriage with dozens of boxes of Birds Eye frozen peas, two ham hocks from the butcher, and a twelve-ounce container of Morton's salt, Charlene went home and cooked up a batch big enough to feed a soup kitchen. As she lay upstairs in her bed, eating bowl after bowl after bowl, Charlene lost herself in the same sort of nostalgic recollection. She was thinking of the days when she and Richard lived in that cramped apartment on Spruce Street in Philadelphia. Philip was still a baby, and they gave him the bedroom while they slept on a mattress on the floor in the living room. (If Philip only knew how spoiled he was as a child, Charlene had thought, maybe he would forgive her for the way she acted later.) Richard was still finishing his residency at Penn at the time, so they didn't have a lot of money. To stretch the budget, Charlene used to make a big pot of pea soup on cold winter days, and it would feed them for most of the week. In the evenings, they'd finish eating and put Philip in his crib, then she and Richard would have sex—passionate, breathless sex, not the predictable routine they fell into later—right there on the lumpy mattress on the floor. Afterward Charlene would lie there, pressed to Richard's warm, naked body, and dream of how perfect their life was going to be once they had a real house outside the city with lots of bedrooms, money in their pockets, two cars in the driveway, another child on the way. . . .

Now, as Charlene sits in her fancy car staring at that deflated bread bag and the discarded crusts by her boots, she would give anything to have those days in that shabby apartment back again. She lets out a sigh and turns toward the gray face of the library, telling herself there's no use hoping for something that will never happen.

All that bread seems to be expanding in her stomach, leaving Charlene with the same bloated gassiness she had after devouring the pea soup. At least, she decides, this cramping is better than the fluttery, first-day-of-school feeling she had before. And now that her nervousness has subsided ever so slightly, she thinks, What the hell do I care if Pilia or any of the librarians see me looking like this? So I've put on a few pounds. So I've let myself go. I doubt any of them look like Miss America — or in Pilia's case, Miss Poland.

With that thought, Charlene crams the remaining three slices of bread into her purse, next to her cell phone and collection of ballpoint pens, just in case she has a craving while inside. She snaps the purse shut, slings it over her shoulder, and gets out of the car. As she walks up the salt-dotted sidewalk, Charlene tightens her black wool cloak against the chill. She passes the overnight return drop on the side of the building, the plaque that says RADNOR MEMORIAL LIBRARY FOUNDED IN 1872, then pulls the handle on one of the glass double doors. The instant Charlene steps inside the lobby, she is overcome by one simple thing: the smell of books. The warm, familiar scent has been absent from her life for so long (excluding those stinky biographies of bad poets that Philip is always reading) that Charlene has to close her eyes and let the aroma envelop her as the door clangs shut. In the darkness behind her lids, she tries to imagine for just a moment what her life would be like had she never left this place . . . what it would be like if there wasn't such a drastic distinction between the life she had dreamed of those nights on the lumpy mattress beside Richard and the one she is leading now. But she can't seem to conjure up any sort of clear picture, so she opens her eyes again.

That's when Charlene spots a handmade poster on the wall that reads: "Get to Know the Great Crime Writers." The sight of the neatly sketched magnifying glass and Sherlock Holmes cap — probably drawn by Pilia — reminds Charlene of all the posters she herself used to make. There was the one of Charlotte in her web, another of James sitting atop his giant peach, both promoting the children's story hour she used to host. Then there was the very last poster she drew of a smiling sun surrounded by the names of the authors in the summer reading series she organized, which kicked off on her final night here. Thinking of those posters, Charlene has the impulse to pull more of that bread from her purse and stuff it in her mouth.

But she resists the temptation and steps inside the main room of the library.

As it turns out, the smell of books and the sight of that poster in the lobby are pretty much the only details that are going to be familiar to Charlene today, because everything else has changed. The red rug speckled with tiny gold stars has been replaced with a flat, starless carpet the same cheerless brown color as a UPS truck. The door that used to say MICROFICHE on its cloudy glass window now says INTERNET. Where there had once been a large card catalog and three computers on the far wall, there is now nothing but computers. Ten of them, in fact, all lined up in a row. Where there had once been a reading area with cushioned chairs, newspapers, and magazines, there are now shelves of videos and DVDs, marked New Releases, Thrillers, Romantic Comedies, Horror, Documentaries, Musicals, and Classics.

What is this, Charlene thinks, a library or Blockbuster Video?

In all this time, it had never once occurred to her that the library would look any different than the night she left it. As a result, all these unexpected alterations leave Charlene feeling as though she had sold her home—given away the deed to someone she didn't quite like in the first place—only to stop by for a visit years later and be horrified to find that the new owner had chopped down the climbing rosebush she loved so much, let a garden of weeds sprout up between the cracks of her flagstone patio, and drained the swimming pool and filled it with cement.

Just about the only thing that is still the same is the small table by the entrance where people leave brochures and flyers for various events around town. Charlene stares down at a pamphlet for an M.S. Walkathon that must have already happened, since the date at the top is November 19, 2003, and today is February 4, 2004. If I were still the head librarian, she thinks, there would not be outdated materials lying around. Out of the corner of her eye, she studies two women behind the circulation desk whom she has never seen before. There is a young lady who can't be more than thirty, with a blond bob, shiny skin, and a simple string of pearls. There is another woman who is much older, with dyed red hair and the kind of skin that looks so white it could be bleached except for the faint brown spots crawling up her veiny arms.

Pilia is nowhere in sight.

Charlene wonders if, in the midst of transforming this place, the staff finally realized the extent of her deviousness. Maybe they ganged up and ran the old hag out of town. Now *that* would be a welcome change. But it is probably just wishful thinking on her part, she decides. After all these years spent fantasizing about telling Pilia off or sticking a pin in her giant breasts, the thought that she might round a corner and bump into her at any moment causes her stomach to cramp. She releases a silent fart and wonders if she should simply turn and leave. No matter how desperately she wants to look up information about the likelihood of a woman getting pregnant with sperm from a deceased man, she decides that coming here was a bad idea. For all of her imagined bravado and that P.I.L.T.R.A.N.A. list in her head, now that she is outside of her bedroom and here in the very real world of her past, she feels awkward and unsure of herself. Besides, there are plenty of other places where she can go to find the information she needs. It's not like the Radnor Memorial Library is the only library in the world.

But when Charlene glances over at the circulation desk again, she notices a familiar face at long last. It is slow-moving, bovine Adele Blumenthal, with her lackluster helmet hair and thick glasses, wearing a short-sleeve dress the colors of a leaf pile. Charlene had trained Adele just a few months before leaving the library. In that short period of time, they had become quite chatty. Charlene had even begun to think of her as a friend. Then again, she had thought of most of the women here as her friends. After their initial condolences, cards, and flowers though, not one of them reached out to her or tried to stay in touch. And Charlene soon realized that they were not her friends at all.

As she stands there, pretending to study that outdated brochure while discreetly watching Adele slug through a stack of returned books, Charlene thinks of that afternoon just three weeks after Ronnie died when Pilia made her move. Charlene was lying on the floor of her bedroom, staring up at the skylight, when the telephone rang. Richard was down the hall in his office, probably making secret calls on his work line to some floozy even then. Philip was off writing in his notebook, watching television, or both. Since Charlene could not bring herself to erase all the messages from the police department, the funeral home, and the church on the answering machine, it was so full that it did not pick up. When the phone reached its sixth shrill ring, it was clear that neither Richard nor Philip was going to stop what they were doing to answer it. Reluctantly, she sat up and lifted the phone off the hook. After Charlene said a quiet, hesitant hello, Pilia began speaking. In that rushed, clunky accent that broke sentences in all the wrong places, she told Charlene that she was calling to inquire about her plans to return to the library.

"Iunderstandifyouneed," Pilia said, "moretime. Butifyou'renotplanning. oncomingbackatall. there'saverynice. youngladywhorecentlygraduated. fromTempleUniversity. withadegree. inlibrarystudies. Shewouldbea perfectreplacement."

"You want to give my position to someone who just got out of school?" Charlene asked in a groggy, confused voice as she leaned her back against the wall just below one of the bedroom windows and picked at her big toe.

"No," Pilia said, slowing down her words for just a moment. "I would take your slot. Then we would give her my slot."

Charlene could still recall how infuriated she had been by Pilia's use of that word: *slot*. She made it sound as though Charlene was nothing more than a book on a shelf. Take one out, she thought, put another one in its place. It had not even been a month, and already she was being treated like one of the titles nobody checked out anymore, dumped on the giveaway table, one step from the trash. Charlene was about to tell Pilia that she'd be back first thing in the morning. But as the curtain rustled above her head and the breeze moved through the gray roots that were already pushing up through her dyed brown hair, she realized that her position at the library didn't seem so important anymore. She wondered if anything would ever feel that important again.

"Charleneareyouthere?" Pilia asked.

"I'm here all right. And let me tell you what you can do—" She stopped. Charlene felt something shift inside of her. For the first time, her polite, cheery self peeled away like the skin of a snake, revealing a bitter, angrier version of herself beneath. When she started speaking again, she burst forth with such resentment and hostility that her words didn't quite make sense. "You go ahead and give her your slot, then you take my slot. That way all you sluts will be in your slots by September! Understood?"

"Excuse me?" Pilia said. "Idon'tunderstand."

"Yeah, well, understand this." Charlene slammed down the phone.

Now, as she watches Adele's fleshy arms jiggle while she works her way to the bottom of the return pile at a snail's pace, Charlene does her best to put that conversation with Pilia out of her mind. She takes a breath and tries to regain her courage, then turns from that tiny table of brochures and walks into the library on her way to wherever the microfiche room is located these days. As she passes the circulation desk, Charlene braces herself for Adele to look up and see her. She can already hear her phony fussing and carrying on about how long it's been since they've seen each other. As much as Charlene tells herself that she dreads an exchange of that sort, she can't help but clear her throat—loudly—so that Adele lifts her head.

But there is no phony fussing and carrying on to follow.

Adele simply gives Charlene a once-over then goes back to her work.

At first, Charlene assumes she is being snubbed, which riles her so much she makes two fists out of her hands and knocks them against her hips as she continues walking. But when she replays the moment in her mind, she realizes by the blank look on Adele's dopey face that she simply did not recognize her. Certainly, Charlene had put on a fair share of weight over the years and let her hair go gray and curly, but she wonders if she really looks so different that a woman she once considered a friend, albeit mistakenly, does not even know who she is.

Let it go, Charlene tells herself, slowly uncurling those fists. It's not like I came here to make small talk anyway.

In the very center of the library, flanked by two new copy machines, is a narrow metal information desk. Behind it sits a man with the kind of jet-black Elvis hair that looks like it comes from a bottle. Charlene knows it is prejudiced of her, but she can never help but feel put off by the male volunteers at the library. There is something unnatural about their presence. She pegs this one as a retiree whose wife went in the ground sooner than expected. Now he's got too much time on his hands, so he spends it dyeing his hair at home or doling out information here.

When she says excuse me, he lifts his gaze from the thick book in his hands and looks at her. Around his neck hangs a black string with four silver keys. Keys Charlene still has copies of on the wooden key rack in her kitchen. As she stares at his placid face, his small white teeth, and his god-awful shoe-polish hair, she waits for him to ask if he can help her. But he doesn't. She supposes that his looking up is meant to be her signal to start speaking, so she asks, "Where is your microfiche room these days?"

"Microfiche?" He repeats the word twice like a question, as though Charlene had approached the desk and inquired about a car part. *Manifold? Muffler?* "Microfiche? Well, let's see. That would be—" He pauses and puts an index finger to his chin. "Do you mind if I ask what you need it for?"

Yes, I mind, Charlene thinks, then says, "Do you mind if I ask why you need to ask what I need it for?"

His pasty face goes blank as he deciphers what Charlene just said. "I'm asking because no one ever uses that stuff anymore."

Charlene doesn't like his condescending tone. She doesn't like it one bit, so she tells him, "Well, I use the stuff. In fact, I can't get enough of it. I'm a microfiche junkie."

He gives her a wary smile. "You should know that there are far better ways to do research now."

Charlene has been waiting a long time for a moment like this, to put some jerk in his place. She sets aside any prior nervousness about being back here again, plants both hands on the desk, and leans closer to his face. Close enough that she bets he can smell the Wonder Bread on her breath when she says in the soft librarian voice she used to use on a daily basis, "And you should know, Mr. Presley, that I don't give one rat's ass if there are better ways to do research. If I want to use microfiche, I will use microfiche. And for that matter, if I want to wrap myself up like a mummy in the stuff and do the Hokey Pokey, my tax dollars have certainly paid for that privilege over the years. So tell me where it is. Now."

When she is finished, Charlene watches his milky blue eyes dart around the library like he might scream for help. She imagines Pilia returning from wherever she is to come to his rescue. Good, she thinks, because I'm warmed up and ready to give it to her now. Instead of calling for reinforcements, though, he changes his tone. In the gentlest possible voice, he says, "I'm sorry. I didn't mean to make you upset."

Now that's more like it, Charlene thinks.

"I'll be happy to show you where the microfiche shelves are."

"Shelves? What, they don't get their own room anymore?"

"Actually, no. Like I said, for most kinds of research these days, it's quicker and easier to use the computer. I know you don't want to hear it, but you'll have far better luck finding whatever it is you need."

Charlene glances over her shoulder at the cloudy glass window on the door of the old microfiche room. She reads that word again—INTERNET. When she turns back to him, she says, "I'd rather not."

Still using that temperate voice, he asks, "Is that because you've never used the Internet before?"

She lifts her hands from the desk and adjusts the edge of her cloak, which is catching on her thin gold watch. Back in her days here, the library had a handful of computers to access the Web. Charlene was always so busy with her other responsibilities that she never took the time to learn how. "No," she admits, keeping her eyes on her watch. It is two-fifteen. "I have not."

"Well, I'd be happy to show you."

He rises from his chair, and Charlene sees that he is much taller than she thought when he was sitting down, as tall as Philip, in fact, and just as skinny. Looking at him, she thinks of Philip back at home. When she left a short while before, he was still lying on the sofa bed, reading that dreadful Anne Sexton biography while the movie *Fargo* blasted on some godforsaken cable channel in the background. Charlene wishes he'd just finish the damn book already and be done with it.

"So can I show you?" the man behind the desk asks.

She reconsiders and decides that maybe he is right, maybe she will have better luck finding the information she needs on the computer. "Fine," Charlene says. "Show me."

Inside the Internet room, the study carrels, bookshelves, metal drawers, and viewing machines have been replaced with one long table that has at least a dozen computers on it. The man from the information desk, who introduces himself as Edward on the way over, leads Charlene past all the people clicking away on their keyboards. When they reach an available computer, he pulls out a chair and tells Charlene to have a seat. It has been so long since anyone has fussed over her that she takes her time peeling off her cloak and draping it over the chair along with her purse, relishing the attention. Before sitting down, Charlene glances around for Pilia again. She is still nowhere in sight. Once she's seated, Edward's pale, nimble fingers type something into the keyboard. He hits the Enter key and a bright white screen appears with the word GOOGLE splashed across the top in blue, red, gold, and green.

"Now don't be afraid," Edward says.

"I didn't say I was afraid," Charlene tells him. "I said I've never used it before."

"Sorry. I just meant that most people find the Internet scary the first time they use it."

"Well, I'm not most people."

Edward smiles that wary smile again. "So I've gathered."

Charlene is about to ask him what the hell that's supposed to mean, but he takes a breath and launches into a five-minute computer and Internet lesson. In the middle of it all, he mentions something that appalls her: if any old Joe Blow were to type in her telephone number, he would be given a map leading straight to her house.

"Stop right there," she says. "Hasn't this Mr. Google person ever heard of something called privacy? I mean, how would he like it if I stood on a street corner handing out maps to his house? What if I had a stalker I was trying to hide from?"

Elvis—or rather, Edward—just laughs.

"Well, I'm glad one of us is amused," Charlene says.

Thankfully, he tells her that she can remove her information from the system. After he helps her to do that, he winds up the minitutorial by repeating a few of the basics. "So like I said, it's really quite simple. All you have to do is type in the key words of your search and press Enter. Google will look up any sites on the Web where those words appear together." As an afterthought, he adds that if she wants to search newspapers and magazines that aren't on the Web, there is a computer on the other side of the table with something called Nexis. For that, she'll have to pay a small amount at the front desk to get a thirty-minute pass.

Charlene doesn't want to have to deal with the chance that the bright light of recognition might finally permeate Adele's thick skull, so she tells Edward no thanks. "Google is good for me," she says. The words feel so ridiculous rolling off her tongue that she can't help but wonder whatever happened to the simple things in life, like the *Reader's Guide to Periodical Literature*.

"Well, good luck then. Let me know if you need more help."

As Charlene watches his tall, thin frame slip out the door, she thinks of Philip again. His words from their conversation this morning echo in her mind: *There's a small, very small, possibility that what she said is true. . . .*

With that, she turns back toward the computer, holds her fingers over the keyboard, and types four words: sperm, birth, after death. When she presses Enter, a cluttered list appears before her.

Ethical and Legal Aspects of **Sperm** Retrieval **After Death** or . . .

. . . and Legal Aspects of **Sperm** Retrieval **After Death** or Persistent . . . the first report of pregnancy and **birth** following postmortem **sperm** retrieval appeared . . .

www.aslme.org/pub_jlme/27.4h.php—6k—Cached—Similar pages

Commentary: Posthumous Harvesting of Gametes—A Physician's . . .

. . . conception but before the resulting birth of a . . . the posthumous disposition of the **sperm** or embryos . . . for disposition of these reproductive tissues **after death**. . . .

www.aslme.org/pub_jlme/27.4g.php—8k—Cached—Similar pages

Life before **birth** and **after death**

. . . I repeated the question, expecting he would disclose his place of **birth** or his residence prior to the . . . Was he not a drop of **sperm** emitted (in lowly form)? . . .

www.mostmerciful.com/life-before-and-after-death.htm—35k—Cached—Similar pages

Charlene scans the page, wondering what to make of such mumbo jumbo, since Edward neglected to warn her about anything of the sort. Finally, she gets the idea to move the mouse around and click on a random cluster of words. This is what pops up next:

JOURNEY OF OUR SOULS
BEFORE BIRTH AND AFTER DEATH:
WILL YOU *BURN* IN SATAN'S FIRE
WITH OTHER SINNERS
OR
BE ALLOWED TO ENTER THE KINGDOM?

In the Bible, the Lord said, we shall reap what we sow. (In other words, we get what we deserve, good and bad!!!) In my Monday morning Bible studies at the Allegheny Baptist Church, I speak about this and that it means that we people (humans) get back from the world what we give. And depending on the extent of our tragedies (very bad stuff) and our hardships, there is no blessing (the good) that HE, CHRIST ALMIGHTY, will not give. So you must ask yourself, where you will go when that bolt of thunder flashes in the sky and Christ comes down on the giant escalator from the clouds. Will you burn in the pit of hell with the other sinners? Or will . . .

Charlene feels as though she has just been accosted by one of those crazy people on the streets of Philadelphia. Exhausted by this whole lousy business of the Internet already, she considers giving up and going to find the microfiche, as she originally intended. Another part of her considers giving up her search altogether and simply leaving the library. But then she thinks of Melissa's words last night: *This baby inside me belongs to him. . . .* Of Philip telling her, *I'm just saying that it's a remote possibility. . . .* Of Richard shouting into the phone from Palm Beach, *Well, then, it's yes, Charlene. Yes. It is possible. Are you happy?*

These bits of conversation come together in her mind and stoke that small, persistent flicker of hope that burns inside of Charlene. More than anything now, she wants to believe that what the girl said is true. So she stays right where she is and continues searching, clicking on site after site, until at long last she finds an article that interests her:

FIANCÉE RENEWS BABY HOPE

A Brisbane woman may have hope of having her dead fiancé's baby. Marvin Tilt studied at the University of New Castle, and may have donated sperm there 10 years ago, according to grieving fiancée Patricia Ducret. "They had a campaign where you could donate sperm and get money for it," Ms. Ducret said. She checked with the university after a friend mentioned that her fiancé may have been a sperm donor. Mr. Tilt, 29, slipped and fell to his death while visiting a waterfall in a national park in far north Queensland.

After still more clicking, Charlene finds yet another article:

CONCEIVING A BABY AFTER HUSBAND'S DEATH

In America a dead man's sperm has been used to fertilize an egg for the first time. Albert Barish died in Chicago following a lethal reaction to prescription drugs. Although his wife stated that they had been planning a family, he had not given permission for his sperm to be used. The man had been dead for 24 hours when his sperm was removed and used to fertilize an egg. Dr. Myron Waite, a Chicago urologist who pioneered postmortem sperm extraction, says that extraction takes around 15 minutes and that sperm can be taken from men who have been dead for up to 38 hours. In the U.S., extracting sperm from corpses is increasingly common. A survey of 250 American fertility clinics by Dr. Gerald Casale, a urology specialist at the University of Pennsylvania, found that 18 admitted to taking sperm from a man postmortem. . . .

And after still more clicking, Charlene finds a total of fifteen articles on the subject. By the time she is finished reading all of them, she looks at her watch and sees that it's three-thirty. Bleary-eyed from so much time spent staring at the screen, she glances around at the other people in the room, who are just as mesmerized by the computer in front of them as she has been for the last hour. Reading these articles has sent a kind of numbness through Charlene. She would have thought that finding such an abundance of stories about women getting pregnant this way would sway her toward believing the girl. But there is still so much doubt lingering inside of her. Mainly, Charlene realizes, because if she gives herself over to this idea of having a part of her son back again, of having a grandchild after she'd long since given up on the notion, she doesn't think she will be able to survive the heartbreak and disappointment if it turns out not to be true.

Charlene has had far too much of that already.

Sitting there, however, she can't help but try to piece together what she knows of her son's life with the information she just read on the computer. Of the many things Charlene came across, the two details she latched on to above all others were the mention of that doctor from Penn and the notion that a student could donate his sperm on a college campus. She attempts to make all sorts of tenuous connections between these pieces of information. In one scenario, she imagines that Ronnie donated sperm for cash when he went to visit Penn after his acceptance. It was just the sort of impulsive thing he might do, and he did need the cash, since Charlene and Richard had taken away his credit card. Perhaps Ronnie told Melissa what he'd done, or maybe she was with him at the time, and after his death she found a way to track it down. In another scenario, that Dr. Casale from Penn who was mentioned in one of the articles happened to be on campus the day Ronnie visited. Or maybe he was at the hospital the night Ronnie died. Perhaps Richard knew him, the way all doctors in this state seem to know one another, and that's the secret he is keeping from her. . . .

In the end, after Charlene is done spinning out all of these far-fetched scenarios, she is no closer to believing the girl than before. And the more she thinks about it, the more she remembers that the way Melissa delivered the news did not make it sound as though this was some sort of medical miracle at all, but rather a miracle from above.

I made the decision to stay away from doctors, because I know they won't understand either. That's why I was hoping Mr. Chase—

Again, Charlene wonders why she kept asking to see Richard. Yes, it could have simply been because he was the only doctor she was willing to trust. But something tells Charlene there is more to it than that. For the first time, she regrets having yelled so much last night and storming off instead of staying in the car with Philip to get the details.

Since she is not going to find any real answers sitting here, she stands and grabs her cloak and purse. When she steps out of the Internet room, Edward looks up from his thick book and asks if she found what she needed.

"Sort of," she says. Charlene feels on the verge of tears suddenly, though she does her best to fight them back. Her nose is running, and she wishes she had a Kleenex in her purse instead of that bread.

Edward notices her sniffling and pulls a tissue from his desk. Charlene thanks him, then gives a loud goose honk into it, disrupting the tranquil quiet of the library. When he returns to his reading, her eyes linger on his bony shoulders and slim frame a moment longer as she thinks of Philip again, at home reading too.

That's when she gets an idea.

In the very back of the library is a cluster of waist-high shelves where the poetry books used to be kept. Much to Charlene's surprise, when she walks to the section, they are still there. It takes her a few seconds to scan the authors—from Maya Angelou to Elizabeth Bishop to Emily Dickinson—before she spots the author she is looking for: Robert Frost. Charlene pulls the book of his collected works from the shelf, intent on taking it home to Philip in hopes that he'll finally stop reading about that madwoman of suburbia's personal brand of suicide-obsessed rubbish. She decides that the book will serve as a kind of peace offering, that maybe it will help them stop bickering with each other so that he might stay a while longer once he gets better.

But there is one small glitch in her plan: Charlene's library card has long since expired. The last thing she wants is to draw attention to herself by going through all the rigmarole of renewing it, so she comes up with a Plan B. After checking to make sure no one is watching, Charlene tucks the book into the folds of her wool cloak and walks toward the emergency exit over by the Science and Technology shelves. Back when Charlene was head librarian, some of the other librarians liked to step outside and smoke. Since she didn't want them puffing away by the front entrance, Charlene left the alarm off on this door so they could slip out for a cigarette without anyone noticing. The ALARM WILL SOUND sign above the push-bar always deterred patrons from going anywhere near it.

Charlene puts one hand on that bar, figuring that if something has changed and the alarm *does* sound, she will have to make a mad dash around the corner of the building to her car. After all, it's not like dopey Adele or that smarty-pants Edward fellow is going to have the energy to get up off their rumps and chase her down. One last time, Charlene looks around to make sure no one is watching. In the distance, she sees Edward slumped in his chair, reading. Just beyond, she sees Adele and that ancient red-haired woman at the front desk, searching through a box of index cards together.

She is about to turn back toward the door when she spots something that makes her stop: there, in a nook between two shelves, are the metal drawers that house the microfiche, along with a lone viewing machine beneath a plastic dust cover. Charlene puts her escape plan on hold and goes to those drawers, scanning the dates on each one until she spots the week of June 18, 1999. Without planning it, she tugs open the drawer and pulls out the canister. A moment later, she yanks the dust cover off the machine. It's not plugged in, so she has to undo the cord in the back and find the nearest outlet. Once it is up and running, Charlene loads the film into the cartridge and takes a seat, keeping that Robert Frost book tucked beneath her wool cloak the entire time. As she cranks the Forward knob and all those headlines whiz by her in a blur of gray and white, Charlene thinks back to what she was doing the night of the accident.

It was the first author event of the summer, and she had managed to book an author whose book had been selected by Oprah. Even though they were guaranteed to draw a crowd, Charlene requested that all the librarians invite as many friends as possible so they would have the biggest turnout ever. She also made a point to warn them against asking what Oprah was like, since she thought the writer must get that question an awful lot. But late in the evening, after the author had finished reading and the floor was opened for questions, Pilia (who brought no friends, probably because she didn't have any, Charlene surmised) raised her hand and asked, "Sowhat'sOprahreallylike?"

Charlene wanted to slug her, but Adele tapped her on the shoulder and said, "There's a phone call for you."

"Can you take a message?" she said.

"But it's someone from the Radnor Police Department. And she says it's an emergency."

As those old headlines speed by on the smudged and fingerprinted screen of the viewing machine, Charlene has the vague impression of looking out a car window, only instead of trees and houses whipping past, she glimpses headlines from stories that were big news on the Main Line at the time. "Fare Increase Has Commuters in a Funk" . . . "Fellman Drops Charges Against Radnor Police Officer" . . . "Developer to Demolish Farm and Build Home Depot" . . . And then, finally, Charlene sees the headline she has been looking for: "Radnor H.S. Student Dies in Limo Accident." Beneath those words is a black-and-white photo of the limousine crushed into a tree. All these years had gone by and never once has Charlene allowed herself to look at this article. But for whatever reason—maybe it is being back in this place where she first got the news of what happened that horrible night—Charlene takes a breath and reads:

> Four students from Radnor High School were being driven home in a limousine from the prom at Fairbanks Inn on Friday, June 18, when the driver of the vehicle, Albert Chang, 38, of Philadelphia, lost control and struck a tree on Blatts Farm Hill. The driver and all four passengers were taken by ambulance to Bryn Mawr Hospital. Both Mr. Chang and Ronald Charles Chase, 18, were pronounced dead on arrival. The three remaining passengers, Stacy Moody, 17, Melissa Moody, 17, and Charles Gimble, 18, suffered a multitude of injuries but remain in stable condition at the hospital. A preliminary blood test on Mr. Chang's body showed high levels of blood alcohol. Complete results will be released from the coroner's office by midweek. Principal Randolph Hulp of Radnor High School said, "We deeply mourn the loss of Ronnie Chase. He was truly one of the finest students ever to pass through these halls. He touched our lives in ways none of us will soon forget." Ronald is survived by two parents, Dr. Richard and Charlene Chase of Turnber Lane, and a brother, Philip, 22. Services will be held at the Miner Funeral Home on South Wayne Avenue, Tuesday, June 22, 4–7 and Wednesday, June 23, 4–7. Burial Services: Thursday, June 24, 1 P.M. at Meadow Rest Cemetery, 22 Feldoma Road, following a noon mass at St. Martin's Episcopal Church on Glen Mary Road.

When Charlene is finished reading, the plain facts of the article—of her life—have her breathing fast and hard. She rewinds the tape so she can put it back in the canister, then back in the drawer, then get the hell out of here. Returning to this library had been a mistake, she realizes. It brought her no closer to believing what Melissa said was true; all it had done was churn up too many bad memories. And now she wants out. But the damn microfiche gets caught in the machine. Charlene cranks the knob to the Stop position. Her fingers are shaking when she reaches in to fix it, but the film won't go where it is supposed to go. Finally, in a fit of frustration, she rips the tape from the reel with such force that it flings out around her, then comes to rest on her shoulders. Charlene leaves it there, picks up the Robert Frost book, which dropped to the floor during the commotion, then marches right through the emergency exit without bothering to hide it in her cloak.

Outside, in the cold winter air, she realizes she is crying because the tears feel hot against her face. She opens her purse and takes out a piece of bread to dab her cheeks as she walks toward her car.

"Charlene?"

The alarm did not sound but someone just called her name. Without even turning around, she knows who that someone is. She would know that voice anywhere. Charlene does her best to stop crying, then turns to see Pilia leaning against the brick wall of the building, wearing an unzipped, baby blue ski parka and expensive-looking black pants, smoking a cigarette. Charlene studies her face and sees that somehow the woman has managed to defy aging. She still has smooth, uncreased skin, those two dramatic blond curls rising up from the top of her forehead, long thin legs. Just about everything at the library has changed except Pilia.

The woman probably bathes in formaldehyde every night, Charlene thinks, so I shouldn't be surprised. "Hello," she says.

"IthoughtthatwasyouintheInternetroom."

"It's me, all right." Charlene stares down at the piece of bread in her hand, which is the slightest bit damp from her tears. She waits for Pilia to ask why she is using the emergency exit, why she is helping herself to a volume of poetry, why she is wearing a strip of microfiche around her neck like a boa, and why she is holding that piece of bread.

All she says is, "It'sbeenhowlong? Sixyears? SinceI'veseenyou."

"Five," Charlene corrects her, neglecting to add the *Since you stole my job* part.

"Howhaveyoubeen?"

"Just dandy," Charlene tells her. "Every day is another blessing. Life just gets better and better. How about you?"

Pilia takes a drag of her cigarette. "OkayIguess."

It's then, as Charlene watches her blow smoke from her nose, that she realizes there *is* something different about Pilia. It takes her a moment to pinpoint exactly what that something is, but once she does, Charlene drops the bread to the pavement and finds herself stepping forward. Her hand, seemingly on its own, reaches out and lifts away the front of Pilia's baby-blue parka to get a glimpse beneath. Oddly, Pilia remains unfazed by this. She stays perfectly still, staring down at her chest, as though she expected Charlene to look there all along. When she confirms her suspicions, Charlene says, "My God, Pilia. What happened?"

Pilia shrugs. She stubs her cigarette against the brick wall. "Breast-cancer. Ihadtohave. Adoublemastectomy."

Charlene lets go of Pilia's jacket and puts her hand to her open mouth. Any sense of schadenfreude she might have imagined feeling at Pilia's misfortune does not come to her. Instead, she finds herself free-falling into a bottomless feeling of guilt for all the time she spent wishing Pilia ill over the years. "I'm so, so sorry, Pilia."

"Metoo," she says, putting half of her unsmoked cigarette back in her small leather purse. "Iwas. Goingtowear. Artificialones. ButthenIjust. Gaveup."

Charlene doesn't say anything for a long moment, then she asks, "Isn't that dangerous? The cigarette, I mean. What if it sparks something inside?"

Pilia looks at her purse and shakes her head. "Idoitallthetime. IfIknow. Ihaveahalfofone. Inside. Itkeepsmefromsmokingmore. Crazyrationale-butitworks. It'sfunnythetricks. Youcanplayonyourmind."

"Funny," Charlene says.

A silence falls in the chilly air between them then, and Charlene's breath clouds before her when she says, "Well, I better go."

"Niceseeingyou, Charlene," Pilia says and smiles.

"You too," she tells her and turns toward her car.

As she walks across the lot, Charlene still feels herself dropping into that bottomless well of guilt. At the same time, there is something else happening inside of her. For the last five years, she has spent so much of her time hating people and wishing terrible things upon them, but after seeing Pilia just now, she doesn't think she can do it anymore. And with this realization comes a strange sense of loss, because she is unsure of what her life will be like without all that hatred churning inside of her day in and day out.

When Charlene reaches her car, she puts her hand into her open purse for the keys and pulls out the remaining slices of bread. Then she opens the door and bends to gather all those discarded crusts on the floor before turning and throwing them on the lawn. After she gets inside and starts the engine, Charlene backs up and catches one last glimpse of Pilia's baby blue parka as she steps inside the library and the emergency exit door closes behind her. She thinks of what Pilia just said about the tricks people play on their minds, and this leads her to thinking of Melissa again, as Charlene shifts into drive and moves forward. She wonders if in the midst of her grief all these years, Melissa had tricked herself too. That thought brings even more guilt to Charlene, because of the way she treated her last night. Even if she can't bring herself to believe the girl just yet, the least she can do is reach out to her and try to help somehow. She decides to start by going to her house and apologizing, giving her a chance to speak.

At the end of the parking lot, Charlene stops the car and takes out her cell phone to call Information. Since she had interrupted Melissa last night before she could say where she lived, Charlene needs to get her address. First, though, she calls home to tell Philip what she is about to do. It takes her a moment to figure out which button to press in order to turn on the phone, since she only got the thing for emergencies and has rarely ever used it. Once she punches in the number, the phone rings and rings until the answering machine picks up and the mechanical, recorded voice tells her to leave a message after the beep. Charlene doesn't know where he could possibly be, but she begins speaking anyway.

"Philip. It's me. Are you there? Pick up." She waits for his voice to come on the line, but it doesn't. "Okay, well, I just want you to know that I'm on my way to Melissa's house. I plan to settle this whole thing once and for all." Again, she stops and waits for him to pick up. During the pause between her words, she even considers blurting out an apology for that hideous thing she said to him so many years ago. But it doesn't seem like the right time, so she waits, promising herself that she will do it as soon as she sees him again. Charlene ends the call by telling him, "By the way, I got you a book from the library. I think you might like it. Well, okay. Bye now. See you when I get home."

Charlene presses the Off button then pulls out onto West Wayne Avenue, forgetting to dial Information. Behind her, a few stray birds have gathered on the lawn of the library to feed on those crusts of bread scattered there. Not far away, the sign draped over that wreck from a tollbooth accident outside of Pittsburgh rustles in the wind, warning everyone who sees it that THIS IS WHAT HAPPENS WHEN YOU DRINK AND DRIVE.

chapter 9

FOR GAIL ERWIN, IT BEGINS AND ENDS WITH A SOCK.

Late on the afternoon of February 3, 2004, exactly thirteen hours before she writes the letter evicting Melissa Moody without warning, Gail
can be found downstairs in the dim, low-ceilinged basement of her cozy,
well-kept home, folding a week's worth of laundry. First, she tackles the
flannel sheets and pillowcases, next she deals with the towels, then two
pairs of crisp, unfaded Wrangler jeans, a worn-out sweatshirt with a frayed
Police Athletic League patch over the heart, numerous pit-stained Fruit of
the Loom T-shirts, her size eight flowery nightgown, and Bill's extra-large
pajama bottoms and boxer shorts covered with miniature trout, swordfish,
whales, and sharks. Finally, Gail begins balling socks as her thoughts wander the way most people's do when they are balling socks.

Today, she is thinking of how different her life turned out than she had
expected. She is happy, most days anyway, but if someone had shown her
a picture years before, say it was a snapshot of herself at this very moment,
standing in a spiderwebbed basement folding laundry in the small town of
Radnor, Pennsylvania, Gail would have said, *No, that couldn't possibly be*

me. But three husbands, two divorces, five states, and a dozen jobs later, here she is nonetheless. At least now, at the age of fifty-seven—with her hair gone white and her skin papery and creased with soft wrinkles—she has the benefit of the world treating her more kindly than when she was younger. She supposes that's because people look at her and see the beginnings of a little old lady rather than the troubled drifter she used to be. Sometimes when Gail looks in the mirror and that old woman's face stares back, even she can be fooled into momentarily forgetting the person she once was.

When the socks are lined up in a neat row on top of the plastic laundry basket, Gail is left holding one of Bill's size 10–12, black Gold Toes. It's not the first time this has happened. In fact, their socks go missing so often in this dryer that Gail is convinced there is an unmarked Swallow cycle on the dial, right between Rinse and Spin. This time around, it irks her more than usual, because she just bought these socks for Bill last Christmas. She lifts the wicker laundry basket and searches beneath. She opens the dryer and bends to stick her head inside, giving it a little spin. The same with the washer. Finally, she leans as far over the machines as possible to look behind them. The only thing back there is a dusty Bounce sheet and a mousetrap loaded with peanut butter, ready to snap.

Common sense tells her to give up. It's only a lousy sock, after all. Gail can buy a whole pack at Target for less than ten bucks. But if there's one thing she hates, it's wasting money. That's become especially true in the five years since Bill was forced to retire from the police department and she left her job as a dispatcher right along with him. Money is tight, and with Melissa Moody defaulting on her rent ever since last summer, it's even tighter. For that reason, Gail gets down on her hands and knees on the cold gray cement floor of the basement and peers beneath the washer and dryer in search of that damn sock. But it's too dark down there to see anything.

What she needs, Gail realizes, is a flashlight. There's one upstairs in the junk drawer by the kitchen sink, but Lord only knows if it has working batteries in it. No matter how many times Gail picks up a new pack at Genuardi's and replaces them, they're dead whenever the lights go out and she needs a flashlight. There's only one way to find out, though, so

Gail puts her hand on the nearest of the many wooden support columns Bill installed down here when the floor upstairs felt dangerously close to collapsing. She uses it to help her stand, careful not to prick her hand on the numerous nails that jut out from the sides, then walks toward the stairs. As she's about to put her slippered foot on the bottom step, Gail glances through that forest of columns at Bill's work area over by the cellar's lone window. Since the flashlight upstairs is probably not going to work, Gail decides she might have better luck finding one down here.

She walks to the far corner of the basement and yanks the fishing wire tied to the light above Bill's workbench, which is really just a sheet of plywood laid across two sawhorses. On the surface, there is a wide-open, gunmetal gray toolbox exploding with screwdrivers, cement nails, wrenches of all different sizes, and dozens of other odds and ends. When she pushes those aside and lifts the tray beneath, Gail sees a spool of metal wire, a spool of twine, a chisel, more screwdrivers, a greasy adjustable wrench, garden shears, a hammer handle with no head, another box of cement nails, three shiny green fishing lures . . .

Everything but a flashlight.

She thinks of Bill at this moment, walking up and down the canyonlike aisles of Home Depot, hands plunged deep in the pockets of his navy blue Dickies, whistling that same old Johnny Cash or Merle Haggard tune. An inch of snow fell earlier today, and he left the house to buy a new shovel since the old one was bent to hell. No doubt he'll return with a bag of assorted junk the way he always does, Gail thinks, despite the fact that he's got plenty down here already. Even though Bill will be home any minute, and even though this area of the house is supposed to be off-limits to her cleaning, she can't help but organize things for him a bit. Gail gathers up the nails and puts them in their box. She collects the screwdrivers, separating the funny round tips from the flat wedgelike ones, then tucks them in separate compartments in the toolbox. She tosses that useless hammer handle into the trash can and winds up the loose spool of twine that Bill uses for his tomato plants in the summer.

It is exactly this sort of compulsive need to organize the world (a need that came late in life to Gail) that served her so well at the police station. Her job description only called for her to answer the switchboard and direct officers over the CB. But the place was so disorganized that she used her downtime to steadily work through the files of fingerprints and criminal records, putting things in proper order. It was a small town police station, after all, so it wasn't like there was a tragedy a minute. Gail had time on her hands and then some. Time enough to flirt with Bill, who she can still remember standing by her desk the very first time she saw him, wearing his dark uniform and holding a Styrofoam cup of coffee in one of his large hands.

A flashlight.

Gail spots one, the same cheery grass green color as the fishing lures, buried beneath a pile of unidentifiable metal parts. When she reaches her small hand out for it, her eye catches sight of something glinting at the very back of the pile. She leaves the flashlight where it is for the time being, pushes aside a rusted triangle, and plucks out that glinting object, which turns out to be a square glass ashtray with a pack of American Spirit cigarettes resting inside, along with a Bic lighter. So Bill hasn't quit smoking after all, Gail thinks. She shakes her head and makes a tsk sound, remembering all the pity she paid him this last year while he carried on about how hard it had been to kick the habit and how sick he was of wearing the patch during those early months. Little did she know that between those Oscar-worthy performances, he was sneaking off down here to puff away.

As annoying and hypocritical as it is, Gail tells herself that there's no use getting on him about it, considering all the other worries in their life. Instead, she tucks the cigarettes, lighter, and ashtray back beneath the metal triangle, then picks up the flashlight. It is so weightless that there are obviously no batteries inside. When she puts it down, Gail hears something shifting around in the tube. Again, she picks it up, this time giving it a little shake. Again, there is that sound. Something loose, scratching against the interior as it slides from top to bottom to top again.

Maybe it's the discovery of those cigarettes that has her curious; whatever the reason, Gail wraps her hand around the head of the flashlight and twists. The top is fastened so tightly that it won't budge. She tries and tries and tries, until finally she uses her irritation about that damn missing sock to fuel her strength and twists as hard as she can. Her face grimaces. A labored grunt escapes her mouth. Then off it comes. When she tilts the plastic tube of the flashlight upside down, this is what falls into the palm of her hand: a curled foil pack of twelve white, circular pills, all but four of them popped out.

Gail doesn't know what she was expecting to find, but it certainly wasn't this. As she stands beneath the shadowy yellow light above the workbench, a few stray rays of winter sunshine casting upon her face through the tiny cellar window, she stares at the pills behind the plastic and wonders what in the world they're doing here. Without her glasses, it's difficult to make out the letters on the face of each one. But this much she can tell: they do not say Benadryl or Tylenol or any of the other names she might recognize. In the blur of her vision, she sees an *H* and an *E*.

Even though there must be a perfectly logical explanation as to what these pills are and why they are sealed away in a flashlight in the corner of the basement, Gail doesn't like the feeling she is getting. She doesn't like it at all. The moment reminds her too much of all those times in her past when she caught the men in her life up to no good. She can still see herself, the way most of us can, in the vivid distortion of life's most painful memories. She is a twenty-seven-year-old woman married to a man she met at a local pub in her hometown of Lake Falls, Ohio. She is opening the glove compartment in his pickup with the simple goal of replacing the expired Allstate insurance card with the new one that came in the mail. She pulls out the old card and an envelope falls to the floor. When she picks it up and looks inside, there is a MasterCard bill in her husband's name with his work address beneath. As she stares down at the long list of motel charges, tears spring to her eyes. A year later, she is a divorced woman with all of her belongings packed inside her Volkswagen Rabbit, telling herself she will start over again, that one day in the not too distant future, she will be okay.

For Gail Erwin, who hasn't had the easiest of lives, there are more of those sorts of memories than she'd care to count. And now all of them press down upon her, coalescing in a solid, deadening feeling of dread. It is a feeling she thought was behind her. A feeling she thought was one of the trappings of that woman she used to be.

She shakes her head and tells herself to relax.

It has been eight years since she first saw Bill standing in front of her desk with that steaming cup of coffee, seven since they got married in a civil ceremony in Philadelphia, five since he was asked to leave his job at the station, and she chose to go right along with him. Despite the uncertain circumstances of his retirement, Bill has never once behaved in any way that is suspicious to her. And when he arrives home from the hardware store, she will casually tell him about her search for the sock, which led to her search for the flashlight, which led to her finding these strange pills. Then he will offer up a perfectly plausible explanation as to what they are and why they're hidden down here. As she backs slowly away from his workbench, carrying the foil pack with her toward the stairs, Gail can already hear his low, crackling voice offering up an explanation.

Oh, those. They're just pills I took for an allergy once. I tucked them inside the flashlight on a fishing trip so they wouldn't get wet. . . .

Or perhaps, *That old flashlight? I bought it at a tag sale and could never get the lousy top off because it was screwed on so tight. It's good to know my wife is stronger than I am. . . .*

Just the thought of those imagined explanations helps corral Gail's feelings of dread as she weaves through those support columns and up the stairs. Inside the living room, the fire in the gray stone fireplace has died, leaving the drafty room in a chill. Gail has never been very good at reigniting the blaze once it has gone out. But she spends a few minutes futilely stabbing at the coals with the poker and tossing wad after wad of crinkled newspaper inside, only to watch it rise up in a sudden flame and quickly burn out. They have lived with this fireplace for five winters, and still she can't master the art of it—a fact Bill loves to tease her about. At last she gives up and leans the poker against the stone.

That's when she turns her attention back to the pills. Gail lifts the foil pack to the light of the picture window and plays a sort of Hangman game with the letters, trying to fill in the blanks. This time, she sees an O and an H. Finally, she decides to get it over with and hunt down her glasses. It takes her a few minutes, and she begins to wonder if the glasses have gone missing as well, but then she spots her gold wire-rims on the back of the toilet, where she put them before her shower this morning. Once they are on, she can see that there are five letters: *R-O-C-H-E*. With a small encircled number 2 beneath and two lines on the back. Other than the occasional Benadryl or Tylenol, the only pills Gail and Bill take are Lipitor for her cholesterol and Zyrtec for his sinuses. She has never heard or seen anything with this name before. So for a long time, she stays just like that, transfixed by those letters until finally Gail can't stand staring dumbly at them any longer.

She goes to the kitchen and picks up the telephone. She dials Janet Pornack's number. Grumpy old Janet is Gail's one friend left from those years at the station, since she was the only other person who stuck by Bill when it got so terribly ugly in his final days. Gail's reason for calling Janet is simple: the woman takes buckets of medicines for her various ailments, from arthritis to bursitis to high blood pressure to diabetes to an unpronounceable fungal disease that sounds vaguely like the name of a noodle to Gail: Aspergillili or something like that anyway. She figures that if anyone might know what these pills are for, it's Janet. As the phone begins to ring, Gail stretches the coiled wire back to the living room and looks out the picture window at the swath of white over their front yard, then at the driveway to make sure Bill has not pulled up in his red pickup yet. All she sees out there is Melissa Moody's Toyota parked by the side of the road, covered with snow. The phone is on its third ring when Gail realizes she better come up with a story that will keep Janet from getting suspicious. She decides to tell her that she found an odd pill mixed in with her usual prescription. Gail runs the lie through her mind, silently practicing the words like a script: *the darndest thing just happened. I was about to take my Lipitor when I found a funny-looking pill mixed in with the others. It says* R-O-C-H-E 2 *on the front. Do you have any idea what it's for?*

Unfortunately, a machine picks up, so Gail puts down the phone without getting a chance to ask that question. For lack of a better option, she returns to the living room and holds the foil pack to the light a second time. She is standing there, telling herself that she is wasting time, that this sort of behavior is nothing but residual superstition left over from the many disappointments of her past, when a door slams outside. Amid the chilly, clock-ticking quiet of the living room, the sudden noise sends a nervous jolt through Gail's small body, causing her insides to seize up. She lets out a gasp and flinches, dropping the pills. Before bending down to pick them up, she stares out the window. The driveway is still empty, but Melissa Moody has just stepped out of her cottage and is walking across the snowy lawn toward her car. Even on such a bitterly cold day, she is wearing nothing but an Indian-print shirt and army green cargo pants. Gail has never had any children of her own, but she can't help but open the door and call out something motherly to the girl.

"Honey, shouldn't you put a coat on? It's freezing out there."

Melissa looks up and shakes her head. "I'm all right."

No matter how many times Gail sees Melissa's face, she is always troubled by those horrible scars. They look especially bad in the dying light of this winter afternoon. Imprinted on her left cheek is that grisly patchwork of lines. Above her right eye is that mangled patch of skin, which looks as though a rabid animal clawed her there, leaving her with only half an eyebrow. When Melissa speaks, there is that black void at the front of her mouth. Over the years, they've had so many intimate conversations about her accident, about that boy who died in the wreck and left her heart broken, but never once has Gail pushed Melissa on the sad topic of her appearance. Still, she wonders why the girl doesn't go to a doctor or a dentist to see about having those things fixed. Surely, there is something they could do. "Where are you off to?" she asks as Melissa scrapes a patch of snow and ice from the window of her car, concentrating on the area directly in front of the driver's seat and nothing more.

"I have an appointment in Philadelphia with that woman, Chantrel. I told Mr. Erwin about her the other day."

That's right, Gail thinks. Bill had said something about another one of Melissa's visits to a psychic when he came back from bringing her a bundle of wood the other morning. "Well, do you really think you should be driving like this?" By "like this," Gail is referring to both her pregnant state and the weather.

"I'll be fine," Melissa tells her and smiles a wan, close-lipped smile.

"Okay," she says. As concerned as Gail feels, Bill is forever reminding her that Melissa is not their daughter. He can bring her wood, Gail can bring her food, they can dole out subtle bits of advice and let her slide on the rent, but they cannot run her life. "Just go slow. And be careful."

Melissa says she will, but after she gets in her car and starts the engine, a puff of white smoke spews from the muffler and she does a U-turn, driving away far too quickly, considering the state of the roads.

She's not our daughter, Bill's voice echoes in her wake.

When Gail closes the front door and bends to pick up that foil pack off the braided rug, a dull yellow glow shines up at her from the basement stairs. She left the light on down there, and she thinks of the laundry basket on the cold cement floor by the machines, of those balled-up socks in a neat pile. All but one anyway. A big part of her wants nothing more than to forget this nonsense and go back to what she was doing. But as she walks across the soft, incessantly creaking floor toward the stairs to the basement, an idea comes to her. There is a very simple way to find out what these pills are. She goes to kitchen, picks up her Lipitor container, and dials the number on the front.

A young woman answers. "CVS Pharmacy."

"Uh, hello. This is Gail Erwin calling. I was wondering if I could please speak with the head pharmacist."

"David's not available at the moment," the woman says, sounding harried. "Can I help you with something?"

"I was just wondering—"

She cuts Gail off. "Hold on a second."

As the woman muffles the phone to speak with someone else, Gail feels grateful for the interruption. Lying always seems so easy when she considers the prospect in her mind, but the execution never fails to make her nervous—even when it comes to a small lie like this one. She needs a moment to gather her thoughts. And when the young woman comes back on the line and tells her to go ahead, Gail swallows and says, "I get my cholesterol pills from your pharmacy, and I have a question about my recent refill."

"And what's that?"

Gail can tell she is impatient for her to get on with it. She hears another phone ringing in the background, and she can picture the line in front of the counter that's almost always there. "I picked up my Lipitor last week. And I was about to take one just now when I found a pill inside the container that doesn't match the others. Instead of the tiny oblong things with the number ten, this one is white and round and has the letters

R-O-C-H-E on the front with an encircled number two beneath and two lines on the back. I'm not sure if I'm supposed to take it."

"Well, I definitely wouldn't take it if it doesn't match the others. But I will give David the message, and he'll call you back as soon as he can." She asks Gail to repeat exactly what's on the pill, then for her phone number. After writing it down, she rushes Gail off before there is time to say anything more.

According to the clock on the stove, it is ten to five. Gail wonders what is taking Bill so long, though she knows better, since the man can make a day out of a simple trip to Home Depot. Considering the eternal lines, too-high shelves, and crowds of people, she can't understand why he likes that place so much. Gail much prefers Leonard's Hardware, where they'd gone for years before Home Depot opened. There is never a line, and the owner knows both Bill and her by name. So what if he doesn't have every screwdriver ever made in stock?

Gail stares at their backyard through the paned window in the kitchen door. The wind gusts, sending a spray of snow from the bare tree branches into the air. For a moment, the yard turns as white as a shaken snow globe, then the wind dies down and the flakes drift to the ground. Those large black birds, the ones that are forever perching in one place or another around Monk's Hill Road, are gathered on the floor of the woods back there, pecking at the frozen earth. Just beyond is the run-down cottage, yet to be winterized because they ran out of money. When Gail and Bill first bought this property, their plan had been to fix up all three houses, live in this one and rent the others for income. But still, that eyesore sits back there with its sagging roof, smashed windows, graffiti-splattered walls, and caved-in floor—a daily reminder of their failed plan. At the very least, Bill finally got around to cleaning up the squashed beer cans and other trash left behind by the teenagers who used to party back there years ago. Now Gail watches as another gust of wind rises up, causing the plastic he taped over the vacant windows to flap violently, making that snap-snap-snap sound she hears from their bed late at night when she cannot sleep.

Without warning, those large black birds spread their wings and take to the air, disappearing into the twisted branches of the trees. Something about their sudden flight breaks the trance of the previous moment, and Gail forces herself to stop staring out the window. She turns and pulls open the junk drawer by the sink, where she wishes she had looked in the first place. Inside is the sleek black policeman's flashlight that she lifted from the station when she packed up her desk in a hurry that last day. She takes it out and slides the button to the On position.

Well, what do you know? Gail thinks when a beam of light shines up at her. The batteries work after all.

She carries it, along with the foil pack of pills, back down the stairs and through the maze of makeshift support columns to Bill's work area. As Gail stares at the neat spool of twine, the nails gathered in their proper box, the sorted and separated screwdrivers, she considers messing everything up again so Bill will never know she's been here. But just then, the front door opens. Gail cocks her head up at the slats of wood above her and hears the unmistakable squeak of hinges, the slow scrape of the door's bottom brushing across the braided rug, followed by the solid thud of Bill's workboots against the rotting floor, which they don't have money to fix either. He is whistling one of his usual songs until coming to an abrupt stop. In his deep, crackling voice, he calls out, "Gail?"

Gail puts the top back on the empty plastic flashlight and buries it beneath those metal tools again. Then she reaches over and yanks the wire, killing the dull yellow bulb over his workbench. The only illumination comes from the sleek black policeman's flashlight, the small window near the ceiling, and the humming fluorescent tube by the washer and dryer. "Down here," she says and walks toward the laundry basket.

"What are you doing?"

"Laundry."

"Still? You were doing it when I left."

"Yeah, well, we had a casualty again."

"Another mouse in one of the traps?"

"No," she calls up. "Another one of your socks is missing in action."

Bill laughs. The hardy, familiar sound comforts Gail. It makes her realize how ridiculous she has been acting, giving in to those feelings of dread and suspicion. From the top of the stairs, he asks, "Well, are you going to join the land of the living or stay down there forever?"

Gail puts the flashlight on the floor by the dryer, then tucks the foil pack into the pocket of her sweater. When she turns and looks up at his large frame in the doorway, all she can see is his silhouette—a paper cutout of a six-foot-tall, barrel-chested man with broad shoulders and thick limbs. "On my way, dear," she tells him as she picks up the basket and carries it upstairs.

In the living room, Bill unloads a bright orange bag from Home Depot. He pulls out a brand-new screwdriver, of all things, and sets in on the wagon-wheel coffee table in front of the couch. More junk, Gail thinks, just as I predicted. Somehow, though, his predictability brings comfort instead of frustration. Looking at him, in his worn-out John Deere cap and oldest flannel shirt, with missing buttons and a tear in the sleeve, along with his faded Dickies, he looks to her like a farmer who has just returned from the fields—overworked, exhausted, underappreciated. And as she gazes at the familiar wrinkles in his wide forehead, the drooping lines beneath his dark eyes, she feels a momentary stab of pity, thinking of all the trouble he's been through. "Good news," Gail tells him. "Your shirts are clean, so you can stop wearing that raggedy old thing."

Bill smiles, flashing his large yellow teeth. He pinches the material by his chest and looks down. "It's not like I'm out to impress anyone at Home Depot."

"I don't know about that. I've seen the way those cashiers flirt with you," she tells him as he pulls a new hammer from the bag. Seeing it in his hand, along with the screwdriver on the table, causes Gail's pity to fade away. She can't help but take a new tone with him. "I thought you went to get a shovel."

"I did. I left them outside by the front door."

"Them?"

"The store had a two-for-one special, so I got a garden shovel for the spring too."

More money we don't have, Gail thinks as she sits in the cushioned rocker by the bookshelf, which is loaded with those books of unusual trivia and real-life oddities that Bill loves so much. He has every volume of *The Darwin Awards,* an annual anthology of truly bizarre deaths, along with every volume of *Uncle John's Bathroom Reader,* a compendium of quirky facts, and *Weird News from Around the World,* which is exactly what the title says. There are also baskets of old *Field & Stream* magazines, as well as Gail's dated copies of *Good Housekeeping, Redbook, Family Circle,* and *Ladies' Home Journal.* Gail runs a finger along the shelf that contains her collection of Mary Higgins Clark novels, to check for dust. There is none. When she turns back to Bill, a voice inside her head—maybe it is the voice of that woman she used to be—rises up in her mind and says, *Tell him what you found. Ask him what they are and why they were hidden in the basement.*

But Gail's mouth will not move.

Instead, she reaches down to the laundry basket at her feet and grabs the Police Athletic League sweatshirt, unfolds and refolds it. As she watches him unload still more junk onto the table, Gail is thinking of that girl from Bryn Mawr College, the one who filed the complaint about him all those years ago after he pulled her over for speeding.

Tell him what you found, the voice says again.

Finally, Bill reaches the bottom of the bag. He puts his hand deep inside, the way a magician might reach into a hat, and says, "I brought you a surprise. Now close your eyes."

Gail does as he says, though she can't help but peek as he pulls out two long, rectangular boxes. He puts one on the coffee table, the other in her hands. When he tells her to open up, Gail sees the words GUARANTEED TO LIGHT ON ANY SURFACE on the boxes.

"They're matches," Bill says. "To help you get the fire going. They're the kind that strike on anything."

Gail looks past her husband's hulking frame at the cold, dark cavity of the fireplace, then back at his weathered face. She does her best to force a jovial voice. "You sure know how to romance a girl."

Bill smiles again and takes the box from her hands. He lifts the top and extracts a long match. One quick swipe against the hard gray stone of the fireplace and it lights instantly. "Pretty nifty, huh?"

"I'll say," Gail tells him.

Instead of holding the match to the fire, he brings the flame in front of her face and tells her to make a wish and blow it out. She goes along with the joke, still forcing that jovial voice. "I wish . . . I wish that the next time you buy me a gift, it comes from Wayne Jewelers instead."

The moment she blows out the flame, a thin line of smoke threads in the air between them and the telephone rings. The sound startles Gail the same way the slam of the door from Melissa's cottage did earlier. Bill walks toward the kitchen to answer it, but Gail springs up from the rocking chair and steps in front of him. "I'm expecting a call," she says and picks up the phone. "Hello."

"Gail?"

"Yes?"

"It's Janet. Your number is on my caller ID, but you didn't leave a message."

Gail doesn't go in for most of the newfangled extras like caller ID and *79, or whatever it is. Neither does Bill. They both believe it's just one more way for the phone company to power-vac money out of people's pockets. But clearly Janet Pornack goes in for them. "Oh, sorry about that. I figured you weren't home."

"I wasn't." She is eating something crunchy, talking between bites. "I was at physical therapy for my herniated disk." She makes a gulping sound and smacks her lips. "But that's what I have a machine for. I just hate when people call and don't leave a message. I find it really irritating."

"Sorry," Gail says again, remembering why she doesn't call Janet very often.

The only extra phone function that Gail and Bill do have is call waiting, and right then she hears the disruptive beep telling her that she has another call. She asks Janet to hold on a second, then clicks over, feeling a flashback to her dispatcher days of juggling phone lines at the station. "Hello."

A man's voice says, "Gail Erwin, please."

"Speaking."

"This is David Burnbaum from CVS Pharmacy."

Gail's eyes go to her husband, who is watching her from the living room with a curious expression on his face. "Hold on," she says into the phone. Then to Bill, "It's just the pharmacist. They made a mistake with my Lipitor refill."

"Oh," Bill says and takes out another match. He strikes it against the wooden floorboards at the edge of braided rug and mouths, "Tada."

Gail winks and gives him a thumbs-up. Much to her relief, he turns his attention to the fireplace to see about getting it started again. Quickly, she clicks over to tell Janet she'll have to call her later, but Janet has already hung up. When Gail comes back on the line, she says, "Sorry to make you wait, David."

"That's okay. Listen, I'm calling about the message you left. It must have been taken down incorrectly."

As he reads back the exact description of the pill, Gail steps deeper into the kitchen. She keeps her gaze on Bill, who bends in front of the fireplace and rearranges the logs so that there is air beneath them, the way he always instructs her to do. "That's right," she says.

"Are you sure this pill was mixed in with your prescription? I just don't see how that's possible. We don't have pills like that here at this pharmacy."

"I'm sure. What kind is it anyway?"

Gail is trying hard not to be too specific, because she doesn't want Bill to hear. But David asks, "What kind is what?"

"What kind is that one, you know, the thing that I found? I mean, what is it for?"

"Mrs. Erwin, it sounds to me like that thing you found, the pill, is Ro-hypnol."

"And what's that?"

"It's a sedative you can't get legally in this country because it's most commonly used as a date rape drug. Mrs. Erwin, have you ever heard of something called Roofies?"

As Bill lights another match and puts it to the paper, she says, "Yes. Yes, I have."

"Well, I checked the computer and I'm certain that's what you found. If you'd taken that pill by mistake, you wouldn't have known what happened to you, especially if you were drinking. But it just doesn't make sense how it could possibly turn up in your Lipitor prescription. I'd like you to bring it down to me the first chance you get so I can see it for myself."

"I'll do that," Gail says, then rushes him off the phone the way that woman had rushed her off earlier.

When she hangs up, Bill is still kneeling in front of the fireplace, flames rising up where that dark cavity of coals had been moments before. Gail's feeling of dread has returned full force now. Her mind feels muddled and confused by this new information. She thinks of that girl from Bryn Mawr. Donna Fellman was her name. She agreed to drop all charges on the condition that Bill leave the force. At the time, Gail tried to convince him to fight her in court, but he insisted that he didn't want to be part of a public spectacle, even though he was innocent. Maybe it was laziness on her part, maybe she was tired of starting over again, maybe she simply took his word as truth because that's what love was supposed to be about, after all, trusting the person you cared for most—whatever the reason, Gail chose to believe Bill.

And now this, she thinks.

Still, none of what that college girl accused him of had anything to do with pills—inappropriate conduct, yes, but pills, no. Even if he did use these on someone else, Gail wonders when and on whom, since other than his trips to Home Depot, the man spends just about every second of his time puttering around the house with her.

Without looking up from the fire, Bill asks, "Everything okay?"

Gail feels as though she has swallowed one of those screwdrivers, maybe even the hammer too, when she speaks. "Oh, fine. It was just an insurance mix-up. We've been using that same pharmacy for years. You'd think they'd get it right by now."

"You'd think," Bill says, his face lit by the glow of the lapping flames. He stands and hands her the box again. "Anyway, my dear, here are your matches."

Gail looks at the extra box on the table. "Who are those for?"

"Melissa," he says. "Poor thing has the same problem as you. Every time I go over there, the fire is out. One time I even found her with the windows wide open. I don't know how she lives with the place so cold all the time."

Once, years ago, when Gail was between husbands, she spent the summer living with her sister in Daytona Beach. On the Fourth of July, they went to see a fireworks show near the ocean. Since her sister was dating one of the men who worked for the fireworks company, they got to lay their blanket on the ground only twenty feet or so from the cannonlike contraption that launched the fireworks. As Gail stared up at the bursts of color in the sky that night, her chest vibrated with each explosion until it ached. That is how she feels now, staring at this man she has been married to for seven years, this man she chose to believe despite the rumors at the station. It is not enough to say that Gail's heart is beating quickly, or thudding, or galloping, or even pounding in her chest, because at the moment, her heart feels insignificant. It feels not much bigger than a bird's, pumping inside of her. On the outside is where Gail feels the steady succession of crushing blasts, quaking through her body and causing her pain.

Bill's mention of Melissa and the discovery of the pills have come together in her mind at long last. She thinks of his constant visits to the girl's cottage to fix this thing or that, to bring her wood in the winter, tomatoes in the summer, and now those matches guaranteed to light on any surface. She thinks of all the times he lingered over there until late in the evening, talking with Melissa, drinking wine and smoking cigarettes, before he claimed to quit and she became pregnant. Never once, not one single time, had Gail's suspicion been raised, because—well, frankly, because of Melissa's horribly disfigured face. And because, even though Bill was always saying that they were not her parents, she used to get the feeling that he liked being a sort of father figure to the girl.

And now this, she thinks again.

Gail's mind calls up the story Melissa told them about a boy she was seeing who wanted nothing to do with her when she announced that she was pregnant. It always seemed slightly odd—a thought that lived at the edge of Gail's mind, though she never took the time to fully develop it— because in all the years Melissa has been their tenant, not one boy had ever pulled up in front of her house or knocked on her door.

"Are you okay?" Bill is asking. "You don't look well."

"I'm fine," she manages in a weak voice. "Just tired. That's all."

"Are you sure?"

Bill reaches out his large hand for her shoulder, and Gail takes a step back, almost falling into the rocking chair before steadying herself at the last second.

"Gail," he says, "are you all right?"

She does something then, though she doesn't know how. Gail shakes her head and clears her throat of that blocked feeling. She uses her fingers to curl a loose strand of snowy white hair over one ear. The phrase "Don't make any sudden moves" pops into her mind. "Yes, I'm sure. I just need to get dinner started. You must be hungry."

Bill is staring at her, his brown eyes even wider than usual, his top teeth biting into his bottom lip. "I am hungry. But maybe I should help you in the kitchen."

Again Gail doesn't know how she manages it, but she forces a smile and says, "Now that's a first. You better be careful or they might list us in the next volume of *The Darwin Awards*. I can just see it: 'Bill Erwin, a man who never once used the kitchen to so much as microwave a hot dog, gives his wife a heart attack by offering to help cook dinner.'"

He laughs, producing the same warm, hardy sound as before. This time, it does nothing to soothe her. "Well, I like to keep you guessing. Are you sure you don't want some help?"

Gail reassures him that she'll be fine then disappears into the comfort of her kitchen with its white appliances, white painted cabinets filled with stacks of mismatched plates and bowls, and the white Formica counter with a wide-mouthed toaster, a mug tree, and an old bread box on top. There is something oddly meditative about the next hour. While Bill heads outside to shovel the driveway, and the woods behind the three small houses grow dark, and the wind blows, and those black birds go wherever they go in the last light of the day, Gail pulls a pack of pork chops from the freezer and defrosts them in the microwave. Next, she gets out a box of Shake 'n Bake, pours the mixture into a Ziploc bag along with the meat, and shakes it over the sink. As she stares down at the bread crumbs and spices clinging to the dewy white flesh inside, her thoughts swirl around her mind, coming together and breaking apart as she tries to complete a time line of events of these last nine months, as well as come up with a plan. But her sense of dismay and confusion is still too fresh and overpowering. It gets in the way of clarity or decision. So as Bill's new snow shovel makes a haphazard scraping sound outside, and the pork chops bake, and the beans and potatoes boil, Gail sets the table, lost in her thoughts. And once everything is ready, she does what seems like an impossible task: she goes to the front door and opens it to see Bill outside whistling a Johnny Cash tune as he shovels the spot on the side of the road where Melissa always parks her car. Gail asks him to come inside and wash up for dinner.

The moment he joins her at the table, the strange, meditative quality of the last hour evaporates in the air between them. In its place remains a thick, unyielding tension. They begin by making their ordinary brand of supper time small talk—discussing first how good the meal is, then how much better Bill finds his new shovel as compared to the old one, then how much more snow they've been hit with this winter than last. The whole while they carry on with this banal, listless banter, Gail pushes her food around her plate, occasionally staring up at her husband to watch him lift the fork to his mouth and chew a piece of pork, a bite of potato, a string bean. When he is just about finished, he gives up on the fork and picks up the bone with his hands to gnaw at the most tender meat. They fall into a long silence then, and the only sound is Bill's chewing until Gail takes a breath and speaks up. "That was nice of you to buy Missy those matches."

"Yeah, well, you know. The poor girl."

Gail has not planned what she is going to say. She simply begins talking, circling around the topic the way she imagines those black birds outside might circle their prey. "The poor girl, that's right. Let's just keep buying her presents and letting her live here for free while we go broke. Poor *us*, is more like it. Because at the rate we're going, the bank is going to seize the property. I've had that happen before, and believe me, it's no fun at all."

Bill lowers the bone from his mouth so that he is holding it a foot or so above his plate. A stray bit of meat is stuck to the corner of his lip. Normally, Gail would point it out, but she says nothing. "Hey, hey, hey," he tells her. "Where is this coming from all of a sudden? So I bought her some matches. They cost me a grand total of two dollars."

"Yeah, well, her rent is a lot more than that, and her inability to pay it all these months is the reason we don't have any money."

"Gail, we've talked about this before. Once she has her baby, she will be able to start working again and pay us back."

"And who is going to watch this baby while she goes to work? Tell me that, huh?"

Bill shrugs. "I haven't thought about it. She's our tenant, not our daughter. There's only so much we can get involved."

"You've said that hundreds of time over the years!" Gail raises her voice so that she is all but shouting, then deepens it in order to do a crude imitation of him: "She's not our daughter and we shouldn't get involved!" When she's done mimicking him, Gail stops circling and swoops swiftly toward the center of the discussion. "I think you know it's a little late for that. We are involved in her life whether we like it or not."

Gail studies his face to gauge a reaction. Bill says nothing, and his expression does not change. It is as though her words washed right over him. As a result, Gail feels a moment of doubt, but she presses on nonetheless. "We are renting a cottage, not running a home for wayward girls. I mean, has she even mentioned the father of this baby to you?"

Bill drops the bone on his plate and wipes his mouth with a napkin. "Gail, you were there when she told us what happened. He was some guy she was dating. She got pregnant and he took off. It's no different than what happens to hundreds of young girls every year."

This is different and you know it, Gail thinks but does not say, because she has decided to halt the conversation right there. Her head is spinning, and she needs to think. She doesn't want to say anything more until she can come up with a plan of action.

Bill pushes back from the table, stands, and comes around to her side. He puts his hands on her shoulders and begins rubbing. Usually, his touch makes all her tension melt away, but her body remains stiff, resistant. In a quiet voice, he says, "I'm sorry. I know it's been hard. But we've gone this far, and it's not like we can kick her out when she's so close to having the baby."

That last word conjures the hideous thought in her mind more clearly than ever before—it is *his* baby she is carrying. Gail feels as though she might vomit. She moves her shoulders from side to side in a way that makes him stop touching her. As she stands to clear the dishes, she says in an unconvincing voice, "You're right. We'll get through this. It will all be fine. I'm sorry too."

Bill lets the discussion go as well and even offers to help her clean up. Gail runs the faucet, scrapes the food she didn't eat off her plate into the trash can, and tells him she'll be fine. More than anything, she wants to be alone right now. To gather her thoughts. To figure out how this happened. To come up with a plan. But Bill sits at the table and reads out loud from the paper, the way he has every night after dinner for years.

"Listen to this one," he says, quoting from his favorite column, "Strange but True." "Utility workers in Montgomery, Alabama, mistakenly hooked up the water-supply lines of ten homes to the city's treated waste-water from toilets instead of the purified drinking system. 'We regretfully admit that a mistake was made,' said the red-faced mayor. But the home-owners aren't so forgiving. 'I'm furious,' roared Don Randel, who's been getting the dirty water since May."

"Funny" is all Gail can say as she sponges the tines of his fork and sub-merges it in the sudsy water. Normally these stories help pass the time while she tidies up after dinner. Tonight, though, they slow everything down to an agonizing pace. They make her want to scream. They make her want to pull the fork from the water and plunge it into his chest.

"How about this one?" he says, then clears his throat and reads: "A Russian man claims to be in possession of Hitler's penis. Victor Vupodroz says his father was among the first troops to storm the evil dictator's Nazi command bunker. Vupodroz said his dad snatched up the penis as a sou-venir after they stripped the body of clothing, then punched and kicked it before cutting it up. He said the penis is just over two inches long. Vupo-droz plans to put it on the block for twenty-two thousand dollars."

"Gruesome," Gail says in a flat, emotionless voice.

Thankfully, Bill does not read any more to her tonight. As soon as she finishes drying the last dish and returns it to the cabinet, Bill closes the newspaper and they retire to the living room to watch television. This has been their ritual for years, though for obvious reasons, Gail cannot focus tonight on the evening news, or *The Odd Couple* rerun, or the TV movie about a mother sent to prison in a case of mistaken identity. As she sits in her rocking chair and Bill stretches out on the lumpy plaid sofa, she looks away from the TV and stares vacantly at those wicker baskets filled with magazines on the shelf.

After a long while of puzzling and contemplating the mess of her life, Gail finds herself thinking of a quiz she took years ago in one those maga-zines, How Well Do You Know Your Husband? She remembers answering every single question about Bill's favorite meals, his favorite television shows, his favorite books, as well as the way he might act in various hypo-thetical situations. When she checked her answers against his, it turned out she had scored in the top category. According to the magazine, she was a woman who knew her husband inside and out. At the time, Gail actually felt proud. All these years later, she feels stupid for allowing herself to be comforted by something so positively inane. After all, she thinks, you could know what a person likes to eat, to read, to watch on TV, you could accurately predict the way he might act at a formal party or a casual get-together, and still you could never really know the true him. Life had taught her that much at least. Though the lesson came at the expense of so many tears and regrets.

When the door to a prison cell clangs shut on the television and the movie cuts to a commercial, Gail glances over at Bill, who is sound asleep on the sofa. His lips are parted, his eyebrows raised, as though he is in the middle of a conversation. Normally, she'd wake him and they'd go off to bed. But the thought of lying next to him makes her hold back. She considers standing up, fetching her purse and car keys, walking out the door into the cold night, and driving away from all of this. She has done it before, and she can do it again. But this time someone else is involved. As much as Gail wants to simply flee, she cannot leave before figuring out Melissa Moody's place in all of this and without making sure she will be okay. So rather than making any sudden moves, or any moves at all for that matter, Gail sits motionless in the blue light of the living room as the prison movie comes back on. She watches a grim-faced guard lead a skinny actress down a hall to a visiting room, where an equally grim-faced lawyer awaits.

"I've got some bad news, Gina," he says, his voice muffled through the glass. "Your appeal has been denied."

Dramatic music rises up, and Gail looks away from those pretend people and their pretend problems to the bookshelf again. Though she cannot say why, she begins thinking of those odd deaths in the pages of *The Darwin Awards* that Bill has read to her over the years. His fascination with those sorts of strange stories used to seem peculiar to her in the early stages of their relationship, but like everything else, she had gotten used to it over time. She recalls one story he read to her about a sailor named Dudley something or other, who survived thirty-seven days lost at sea before being rescued, only to fall asleep in his bathtub at home a week later and drown. She recalls another about an elephant trainer in India who survived being trampled by a herd, only to get hit by a Vespa outside an open-air market and die instantly.

When she is done thinking about all those deaths, Gail rises from her chair and turns off the TV. The only light comes from the slow-burning log in the fireplace, which casts shifting shadows on the walls. The sudden absence of the TV, along with the squeak of her slippered feet on the floor, rouses Bill out of his sleep. He lifts his head from the crocheted throw pillow and squints at her. "Time for bed?"

Because there seems to be no other choice at the moment, Gail looks down at him and says, "Afraid so."

He takes his time sitting up, yawning, stretching, scratching his belly. Meanwhile, Gail lifts the laundry basket from the floor and carries it to the bedroom. Before he can catch up with her, she turns on the lamp beside their bed, pulls out her nightgown, then goes to the bathroom. Beneath the vanity, there is an old TWA overnight kit that Gail got years ago when she missed a flight and was forced to sleep in an airport motel in Lexington, Kentucky. She pulls the foil pack from the pocket of her sweater and tucks it inside, where she plans to leave it until she can decide what to do. Once the pills are safely hidden away, she stands before the mirror and sees that old lady's face staring back at her.

How did it happen? Gail wonders. How did that girl from Lake Falls, Ohio, end up here?

"Did you drown in there?" Bill asks, rapping his fist against the thin door.

"I'll be out in a second," Gail says as she quickly sets about brushing her teeth, washing and moisturizing her face.

When she opens the door, she finds him standing right outside in the flannel pajama bottoms and the pit-stained Fruit of the Loom T-shirt she washed for him today. If this were any other time, she might step up on her toes and give him a kiss or a playful squeeze on his butt. But Gail can't bring herself to do any such thing. And neither does he. Instead, the two walk silently past each other in the narrow hallway—Gail on the way to the bedroom, Bill on the way to the bathroom—as a chill crawls over her body, where it will remain for hours to come.

Back in the bedroom, Gail begins turning down the sheets but stops when she hears a car pull up out front. She goes to the window and peeks through the curtains to see Melissa Moody sitting outside in her Toyota. The snow that had been on her hood, roof, and trunk when she left this afternoon to visit that psychic in Philadelphia is gone. The longer Melissa sits there, the more questions come to Gail's mind. She has the urge to run outside and ask her if she really thinks this baby belongs to that boy she claimed to have been dating early last summer. She has the urge to run outside and ask her if she remembers anything about those nights Bill lingered at her cottage. She has the urge to run outside and tell her to drive away from this place and never come back.

But she does none of those things.

When Bill's footsteps come padding down the hall, Gail leaves the window and returns to the task of turning down the bed. As she folds the top sheet over the comforter, then fluffs the pillows, that pharmacist's voice rings in her head, *If you'd taken that pill by mistake, you wouldn't have known what happened to you, especially if you were drinking.* Once the sheets and comforter are in place and the pillows are fluffed against the oak headboard, Gail hears Melissa's car door creak open and close outside. Her footsteps move across the yard toward her house. If Bill hears her too, he doesn't mention it. They simply climb into bed together.

Before turning out the light, he leans over and kisses her. The touch of his thick, chapped lips against hers breaks her heart, because she senses— no, it is more than that, she knows somehow—that this will be the last time they kiss. And the tinge of sadness Gail feels makes her hate herself all the more for mourning someone capable of doing something so despicable.

"Sweet dreams, my dear," Bill says.

Gail stares at the deep lines in his forehead to avoid looking in his eyes. "Good night."

After he switches off the bedside lamp and the room falls into darkness, Gail listens to his breath slowing down and the sound of that plastic over the windows on the vacant house snap-snap-snapping in the wind. Soon, he falls into a fitful sleep beside her. She lies there with her hair fanned out on the pillow, thinking of the way she spent her day, doing laundry, then cleaning Bill's cluttered work area, only to turn up such an unexpected mess. Her mind moves over and under and around the details once more, touching on each and every one of them—the sock, the flashlight, the pills, the call from the pharmacy. She becomes something like a blind woman making her way around an unfamiliar room, trying to get an exact picture of it all.

The whole while she works toward this more clear understanding, the world moves quietly around Gail. Bill begins to snore. The refrigerator hums on and off in the kitchen, releasing the same pings and ticks as the engine of Melissa's car cooling in the makeshift driveway beside the road. Next door, Melissa stretches her body out on the ratty sofa and rests a picture of Ronnie facedown on her swollen stomach. As her eyes flutter shut, she talks to him the way she often does late at night to help herself fall asleep.

"Remember that day at the library? We went for diesel money. There was that woman at the front desk with the funny accent. I thought she was your mother, Ronnie, but then she pointed to the stacks . . ."

As her words wind down to an incomprehensible mumbling, outside the wind dies off, leaving the woods around the three small houses in a perfect hush.

Across town, five miles away in an apartment on Grant's Passing, Janet Pornack takes her last pill of the day and gulps it down with a glass of ginger ale. As it slides slowly, painfully, down her throat, Janet glances at the telephone by the bed and wonders why Gail Erwin did not call back today. No one ever calls her anymore, and the sight of the silent phone fills her with loneliness. Finally, she gives up thinking about it or waiting for it to ring, and she lies back on the mattress, closing her eyes for sleep.

Still farther across town, at the Chases' large gray-stone colonial at 12 Turnber Lane, Philip is tossing and turning on the foldout sofa in the family room while his mother sleeps soundly upstairs with the help of the pills she swallowed before bed. Philip replays the recent turn of events concerning Melissa Moody and her baby, over and over in his mind. You already know that, eventually, he sits up and turns on the light. And you already know that he opens his musty Anne Sexton biography to a random page and looks down to see the lines of a poem scratched in black pen, like a message in the margin:

The woman wonders why he murdered their love
But the killer in him has gotten loose
She knows she should run while there is still time
But she pauses here
Soon to be dragged into darkness

Since the words have no particular resonance to him, Philip turns to another section and begins reading a chapter he's read before about the death of Anne's parents. After twenty minutes, he finds himself lingering over a single passage of a poem:

I refuse to remember the dead.
And the dead are bored with the whole thing.
But you—you go ahead,
go on, go on back down
into the graveyard,
lie down where you think their faces are;
talk back to your old bad dreams.

His thoughts go back to his brother and then to Missy. Again he mulls over all that happened tonight until finally, he is just too tired to think or read anymore. His arms droop like the branches of the trees outside, and the book comes to rest on his chest. His eyes shut.

As the night passes, the starless winter sky over the small Main Line township of Radnor turns to an inky, fathomless black. The roads become empty, drained of all life. Even the highway on the outskirts of town is soundless, except for the occasional whoosh of a tractor trailer barreling past the exit ramp that leads to Radnor. And when it seems that it can't get any darker or quieter, the first bits of sunlight break on the horizon. The light comes slowly at first, then more quickly.

You know what's coming next, but you don't know all of it.

Inside the Erwins' small house, Gail lies awake in bed. Not once through the entire night did she come close to sleep. But with her insomnia brought the clarity she had been after, as well as this decision: she is not going to call the police and get herself or the girl tangled in an endless legal mess. No. Instead, Gail is going to see to it that Melissa moves away as soon as possible, then she will leave too.

With that thought paramount in her mind, she rises from bed. As Bill goes on sleeping, Gail walks to the living room, where she finds a piece of plain white paper and a pen. She has had hours to draft and redraft this letter in her mind, so it comes out in one fluid rush from the second she puts the pen to the page. She tells Melissa that she is sorry, but as of the first of the month she is seven months behind on her rent. She tells her that they have been very patient and understanding due to her condition, however they cannot allow her to occupy the cottage any longer if she is not going to pay the amount agreed upon. Finally, she tells her that they have no choice but to ask her to kindly vacate the premises as soon as possible. And in closing, she tells her that they—or the truth is, Gail—regrets this more than Melissa knows.

When she is done, Gail does not bother to read over the letter. She simply slips it in an envelope, then puts on her quilted down coat and boots before stepping outside. Her breath mists in front of her face in the early morning air as she walks toward Melissa's cottage. Those dreadful birds, which look as large as pheasants to Gail, are perched on the dented gutters, pecking at their oily wings. The sound of her approaching footsteps sends them into the trees in a rush of flapping and squawking. When Gail reaches Melissa's door, she bends and slides the envelope in the gap beneath before quickly turning toward home.

Back inside, Gail tugs off her coat and boots. She walks down the hallway and is about to return to the bedroom when she catches sight of the lump of her husband's body under the covers. She cannot bring herself to climb in there and lie beside him another second. Not one more second. Instead, Gail goes to the kitchen and puts on a pot of coffee. As the machine brews and the aroma fills the air, she stands by the paned window in the kitchen door and stares out at that vacant house, then over at Melissa's cottage, wondering how the girl will react when she finds the letter. Gail has yet to figure out exactly what she will tell Bill when Melissa inquires about it, but she trusts that the right words will come to her when the moment arises. Perhaps she will simply tell him that she decided to take charge of the matter once and for all in order to get their finances sorted out. And most important, as soon as Melissa is gone, Gail will leave too.

When the coffee is ready, she lifts a mug from the mug tree and fills it. Gail is stirring in milk when a dull, scraping sound comes from another part of the house. She carries the coffee with her to the living room and stops short when she sees the basement door open and that yellow glow shining up at her. With one hand on her chest, Gail walks quietly to the bedroom and peers inside. The covers are pulled back. Bill is no longer there.

That clogged feeling returns to her throat as she calls out, "Bill? Bill, where are you?"

From the basement comes his low, crackling voice, "Down here."

Slowly, Gail walks to the top of the stairs, one hand still holding the steaming coffee, the other pressed to her fluttering chest. Down below, she sees his shadow, stretched and distorted on the cement floor. In a wobbly, uneven voice, she asks, "What are you doing up so early?"

"I couldn't sleep."

"Well, I made some coffee. Why don't you come up and have some?"

"No thanks." Gail sees his shadow shift and reshape before he says, "It looks like you've been busy down here."

"I cleaned a little," Gail tells him. She takes one step into the basement to try and see him better. "What are you doing?"

"I am waiting for you to come down here."

"Why?"

He does not answer. His shadow vanishes, and Gail hears the rumble of the storm doors opening. "Bill?" She takes another step lower, but a moment later a noise comes from behind her. Gail turns to see the front door opening. Bill steps into the house, holding the bottom of that grass green flashlight in one hand, the top in the other. "How did you—" Before she finishes the question, Gail realizes that he went outside and came around. That's when she blurts, "Did you rape that girl? Did you get her pregnant?"

And this is her only answer: Bill drops the flashlight and lifts his hands to push her backward into the basement. But Gail is too fast for him. She splashes her hot coffee in his face. As his arms shoot up to shield his eyes, she cracks the mug against his skull, then turns and runs down the steps. Behind her, Bill lets out a groan. When she reaches the bottom, Gail's chest is heaving, her breath coming in shallow rasps. As fast as she can, Gail weaves between those makeshift support columns, slamming into two of them as she moves toward the open storm doors that lead out into the daylight. Two at a time, she lunges up the cracked cement stairs, but the moment she reaches the top, Bill is standing there. He is holding the garden shovel he bought yesterday and he raises it up and swings, sending Gail toppling backward down the stairs.

Her head whacks against the cold concrete floor.

Her limbs come to rest in twisted, unnatural positions.

Blood pools around her small body.

Bill stands at the top of the cellar stairs, gripping the handle of the shovel and looking at his wife below. Before going down, he turns to be sure no one has seen what just happened. The only witnesses are those beady-eyed crows and the blank face of that vacant hunting cottage with the plastic over the windows. He turns back toward the basement and lowers himself down the stairs, dragging that shovel and stopping to close the storm doors behind him. In the dull yellow light of his workbench, he sees Gail's eyes flickering open and closed, her chest rising and falling in fast, uneven motions. She is still alive, he thinks as he wipes the sweat and coffee from his brow. Sweet Jesus, she is still alive.

And then the crying begins. This is a man who has made grave mistakes before, but never one as grave as this. And the reality of what his sudden rage and fear has produced this time brings an onslaught of strangled sobs. Between each and every gasp for breath, he repeats one single question: "What have I done? What have I done? What have I done?"

The only thing that stops this crying is the warm feeling of more blood pooling around his bare feet. Bill turns and searches for something to stop it, and that's when he finds the lint-covered sock that went missing, dropped behind a black flashlight on the floor and a box of Tide. He picks it up and presses the scratchy material to the wound on Gail's head. In seconds it is soaked through, and the blood keeps coming. Bill is about to look for something more substantial when a banging noise comes from the top of the stairs. He stares up at the rotting floorboards, the same way Gail did yesterday, and hears the sound again.

Someone is at the door.

Without thinking, Bill yanks off his T-shirt and tries his best to make a tourniquet around his wife's head. Even though he did this to her, he wants to save her. That is all he wants right now. But whoever it is up there keeps banging, and Bill is afraid that it might be someone who saw what happened. And that person might go to the police. So he leaves Gail and climbs the stairs, then rushes down the hall to the bedroom, where he wipes the coffee from his brow, the blood from his hands and feet with a towel from the laundry basket. When he throws on another shirt, Bill goes to the living room and opens the door.

Melissa Moody is standing on the stoop—one hand on her stomach, the other clenching a piece of paper, tears streaming down her face.

"What is it?" Bill asks in a breathless voice. If she witnessed what happened from the windows of her cottage, and this is the reason for her tears, he doesn't know what he will do.

Melissa holds out the letter she found beneath her door. When he takes it from her, her voice croaks out the words, "This note . . . from your wife . . . I can't . . . I don't have anyplace to go."

As Bill stares down and reads Gail's graceful handwriting with all its slopes and curls, his hands begin to shake. So this is what she was doing when he woke up this morning and found the bed empty. This is what she was doing when it finally dawned on him that she must know something. And when she came back inside and went to the kitchen to make coffee, Bill got the idea to go downstairs, push those tools aside, and see if the flashlight had been touched. Still, he had not planned on losing control, the way he had so many times in his life. He had not planned on something so horrible and irreversible to occur.

Once he is finished with the letter, Bill crumples it in his hands and takes Melissa nervously, tentatively, in his arms. Her soft, tender body feels familiar and foreign all at once, because he has never held her this way before. Not like this. The touch of her skin so close to his sends the shame he has felt all these months spreading through him like a poison. The two of them stand there just like that, shaking, clinging to each other, while down below in the damp darkness of the basement, Gail struggles for her every breath.

"You go back to your cottage," Bill tells Melissa after hugging her against his chest for what seems like hours. "You have nothing to worry about. This has all been a terrible mistake. You are like a daughter to us now. Gail and I would never turn you away."

chapter 10

THE MAN ON THE PHONE SAID THAT HIS BUZZER WAS BROKEN, SO
he instructed Philip to shout up from the street when he arrived. The plan
sounded simple enough until Philip reached the slim brick building on
Sixth Street, just off Avenue A in the East Village. Given the steady stream
of foot traffic and customers pouring in and out of the health food store on
the first floor, he feels ridiculous screaming a name that sounds like it is
straight from the pages of a Dr. Seuss book. Philip stands on the sidewalk
in the middle of this brisk October afternoon, listening to bits and pieces
of passing conversations as he waits for the right moment to start yelling
for Donnelly Fiume.

"The manager promised that the flaxseed was finally supposed to be in
on Tuesday, so where the hell was it? This is beginning to get abusive," a
gaunt man says to an equally gaunt woman as they step out of the store
and walk down the street, leaving a whiff of BO in their wake.

Why is it always the health nuts who look so sickly, smell so funky, and
are *forever* in a crabby mood? Philip wonders as he thinks of the no-butter-
no-cream-no-oil freaks who come into the Olive Garden. Over the years,
there were so many times when Philip wanted to scream in their faces,

"You are in an Italian restaurant! What the hell do you want us to serve you, a rice cake?"

But of course he never did anything of the sort, since he had to suck it up in hopes of getting a decent tip. Whenever Deb Shishimanian was in one of her good moods, she and Philip used to joke that the restaurant's slogan should be changed from "When you're here, you're family" to "If you're here, you're an asshole." Thankfully, Philip doesn't have to worry about that place any longer. It has been almost twenty-four hours since he walked out during his shift, and he has not missed the job even once. Last night, he parked his car in the garage at the Marriott Marquis in Times Square, checked into a suite overlooking Broadway, and ordered a turkey club from room service—all courtesy of his father, since Philip finally christened the emergency credit card.

When the door to Nature's Melody Health Foods swings open a moment later, out steps a woman so sweaty she looks as though she has just finished running a marathon. Beneath her arm, she is carrying a tightly rolled purple mat. At first, Philip thinks she is talking to herself until he sees the cell phone wire dangling from her ear. "The thing about Bikram is that it's a lot like growing up in Texas," she says. "Every summer was so damn hot, it was like a three-month Bikram session. I swear that's why I adjust so easily. Plus, I was sick of Pilates. All that rolling like a ball and clapping like a seal. I just don't see how that was helping to downsize my ass."

As Philip watches her tight, slender body stroll away on the sidewalk, it occurs to him that he has only a vague idea what flaxseed, Bikram, and Pilates even are. Still, he looks up at the two windows on the fourth floor and decides that he has a good feeling about living over this store. So what if the glass on the apartment windows has a thick yellow film on it? So what if the sills are cluttered with an assortment of sickly looking plants that remind him of the ones in his high school science classroom? There is something about this place he likes. And when there is finally a break in foot traffic, Philip lifts his hands to his mouth and shouts, "Donnelly! Donnelly Fiume!"

His eyes stay fixed on the dirty windows, but no Donnelly Fiume appears. As he waits for some sign of life, Philip glances down at the bright pink flyer in his hands:

Sublet Available
Immediately
Furnished and *Pristine*
Studio Apartment
Fourth-Floor Walk-up
Prime East Village Location
Must *be able and willing to care for my*
loving pets *while I am out of town*
$1,000 a month plus utilities

If the windows are any indication, this Donnelly guy had exaggerated about the pristine condition of the place, but it was nothing Philip couldn't fix with a bottle of Windex and a few rolls of paper towels. As far as the pets are concerned, the more Philip thinks about it, the more he likes the idea of having cuddly, loving animals around to care for and keep him company. After all, he doesn't know a soul in the city, so life is bound to be lonely at first. Besides, after wandering into two different real estate agencies today, Philip had been left with the impression that the best he could hope for would be a short-term lease on a cardboard box some-where in Queens—*if* he was lucky. Both brokers told him the same thing: he'd need his last three pay stubs, a security deposit, first and last month's rent, as well as a letter of reference from his most recent landlord if he hoped to secure an apartment. Even if Philip did have the pay stubs, most of the money he made at the restaurant was in undeclared tips, so his checks would not impress anyone. As for a letter of reference, his most re-cent and only landlord was his mother. He doubted they'd accept a letter from her, not that she'd write a very nice one after what she had said to him yesterday.

Luckily, as Philip wandered along St. Mark's Place—where it seemed to him that a person could get anything he wanted, from acupuncture to tattoos to pizza to Thai food, all in a single stretch—he spotted the pink flyer taped to a street lamp. At the bottom, there were several small slits cut into the paper so people could tear off Donnelly's name and number. But Philip ripped down the entire sign and three more like it down the street, because he had already figured out just how competitive this apartment-hunting business was.

"Donnelly!" he shouts again when a full two minutes pass and no one appears in the windows. "It's me, Philip Chase! The guy who called about the apartment!"

This time a woman with a bright, multicolored scarf tied over her head appears. She waves to Philip then drops a balled-up towel down to the street. Philip extends his hands to catch it but chickens out at the last second, the way he used to during Little League games when the coach stuck him in right field. After the towel smacks against the sidewalk Philip picks it up and finds a gold key inside. He walks to the front door and lets himself into the small vestibule that leads to the stairs. The interior of the building smells like a church meeting room—a combination of weak coffee and old perfume, as well as a hardy dash of carpet deodorizer thrown into the mix. The slanted wooden staircase is covered with a threadbare, burgundy rug. The Pepto-Bismol pink paint is peeling off the walls in large, plate-size slivers. If I want lead poisoning, Philip thinks as he begins clomping up the stairs, I know where to come.

When he reaches the fourth floor, he hears what sounds like Judy Garland's voice singing about a trolley going *clang, clang, clang,* and a bell going *ding, ding, ding.* From somewhere else in the building—up one more flight perhaps—there is a faint chirping sound, though it doesn't quite register with Philip, since he is distracted by the music.

The door is open the slightest bit but he knocks anyway.

"Come in," Donnelly's thin voice calls over the music. "I'm on the phone, dear. I will be with you in two shakes."

Philip steps inside the cramped, cluttered apartment as Donnelly continues his conversation behind an Asian-style dressing screen with an assortment of scarves draped over the top. Other than that screen, the first thing Philip notices is the wall opposite the front door. It is plastered with row upon row of framed black-and-white head shots, like the kind Philip saw when he stopped in a deli at lunchtime to buy a bottle of water and a sandwich. He had recognized a few of the people in those photos—Tom Selleck, Martin Scorsese, Connie Chung. But the faces before him now

don't look the least bit familiar, though every single one is personally au-
tographed to Donnelly:

For my pal, Donnelly—Love always, Gaylord Mason
To the world's best backstage dresser! xoxo Sylvia Gassell
Thanks for making me look so damn good out there, Donnelly . . .
*   Kisses, Polly Bergen*

Beneath the photos is a marble fireplace that must not work since the
inside is filled with a hodgepodge of half-melted candles, the wax pooled
and hardened on the floor around them. A few feet away, there is a dusty
wooden bureau with a martini set and a record player on top, playing that
Judy Garland song. To the left is a large suitcase, the hard vinyl kind nobody uses anymore. Just beyond is a minuscule kitchen with two stools
tucked beneath a small counter, shelves instead of cabinets, an old gas
stove, and a squat refrigerator with a large silver handle. Philip puts down
the towel, then turns to close the door. There is a hinged piece of wood attached to the back, painted with a mural of New York City. Once closed,
the door blends with the scene on the rest of the wall—taxicabs, hot dog
vendors, fire hydrants, and all the rest. There is a Murphy bed, he realizes,
folded up and concealed by the mural too. As cluttered and small as the
studio is, this detail makes Philip smile. The place is far from perfect, but
he is already planning on how he can make it more livable—washing the
windows, bringing the plants back to life, dusting the furniture, shaking
out the Oriental rug.

"Due to some unfortunate and unforeseen events in my sister's life," he
hears Donnelly say into the telephone behind that screen, "I need to sublet the place immediately."

There is something distinguished about the way he talks. Philip noticed it on the phone earlier as well. Donnelly enunciates almost every
consonant and vowel that comes from his mouth in a way most people
don't anymore. It makes him sound regal and dramatic, as though he
just stepped out of an old black-and-white movie. The way Philip imagines the people in those photos on the wall might sound if they started
talking.

"No time for references," he hears Donnelly say. "I'll know when I see you if I trust you or not. No, you mustn't come tomorrow. You have to see the place today or it will be gone. As a matter of fact, I have someone standing here right now, and I have five others lined up for later this afternoon."

All this, and everything else he goes on to say, is verbatim what he told Philip on the phone: he is in a rush to find someone to take the apartment, because he needs to leave town and care for his ailing sister. He doesn't know if he will be gone only a few months or much, much longer. He has a lot of people coming to see the place. And finally, he wants two months rent up front in cash. Because of that last detail, Philip went to Citibank on the way here and took an advance of two thousand and change on the emergency credit card. He figured that if he liked the apartment he would need to act fast. Now he's glad he did. At least, that's what he thinks until he hears Donnelly say, "We will discuss the pets when you arrive."

The pets.

Philip glances around the room, expecting to see a dog or a cat he hadn't noticed before, curled up on the floor asleep. But he doesn't see any such thing. At that very moment, Judy Garland stops clang-clang-clanging and the trolley song comes to an abrupt end. Automatically, the needle lifts from the record and goes back to the beginning. In the silence before the song starts up again, Philip hears the chirping sound—louder than before. He looks at a closed door against the back wall of the kitchen and realizes that it is not coming from upstairs as he had thought earlier. It is coming from in there.

Philip doesn't like this new development at all. Ever since he was a kid, he has been afraid of birds. He can trace the phobia back to one of his mother's anniversaries at the library. Her coworkers had a party for her, and among the many gifts she received was a small green parakeet in a cheap metal cage from that Polish woman his mother used to complain about. Nobody—not his father, not his brother, and certainly not his mother—liked the thing very much. But Philip detested the creature more than any of them.

He couldn't stand the sound of its scaly feet flitting around the cage.

He despised the way it screeched without warning.

He hated the commotion it made while flapping its wings.

Worst of all, Philip dreaded the times when it managed to bend the flimsy bars with its beak and get loose. The bird (no one ever bothered to give it a name) flew around the house, swooping and soaring, sending the entire family into a tizzy. His mother would gather Ronnie and Philip, and they'd hide in the bathroom beneath the stairs. Meanwhile, his father attempted to catch it by tossing a towel over its body when it flew by in a green blur. And if his father happened to be at the hospital when there was a jailbreak? Philip was sent to do the job. The best day of his life was when the bird flew out an open window and kept going. He can still see his mother slamming that window shut and saying, "Good riddance."

"I need to go now," Donnelly tells the person on the phone. "I will see you in an hour. I'll certainly try to hold the place, but I must warn you, it is going to be tough."

After he hears the sound of the telephone being set back in its cradle, Philip turns to see the woman with the multicolored scarf over her head step out from behind the screen. She smiles at Philip then goes to the record player and turns it down. Philip is confused a moment until he realizes that it is not a woman at all. It is Donnelly Fiume. He is a short, slender man with skinny wrists and long fingers cluttered with colorful jewelry. As far as Philip can tell, he is not a transvestite exactly, or even a drag queen. Donnelly is just an older man whose features are unusually feminine, his clothing too. Spidery lashes frame his wide eyes; he has a slender nose, slightly bulbous at the tip, plump lips, and a narrow chin. He is wearing tight white pants and a shirt made to look paint splattered, as though Jackson Pollack had a go at it. Something about the scarf over his head gives him the appearance of someone getting ready to step onstage, or who has just come off. Philip has never been very good at guessing people's ages but he puts him at somewhere around seventy.

"All right, cupcake," Donnelly says in that thin, overly articulate voice as he brings one hand to his cheek. "Let's have a look at you."

Philip stands still, feeling self-conscious because he is wearing the same black jeans and denim shirt as yesterday. He figured finding a place to live ranked higher on his list of priorities than buying a new wardrobe.

"My, my," Donnelly says after his eyes finish roaming up and down Philip's lanky body. "Aren't you the picture of the new kid off the bus? Where did you say you were from? Kansas?"

"Pennsylvania," Philip tells him.

"Forgive me. I can't keep track of what everyone tells me when they call. So am I right?"

"Right about what?"

"That you just got off the bus."

"Half right," Philip tells him. "I moved here last night." The word *moved* sounds strange coming from Philip's mouth—*escaped* would be more appropriate. "But in a car, not a bus," he adds.

"Bingo," Donnelly says. "I knew it. Tell me. Have you been to New York before?"

"A couple of times with my family at Christmas, and once on a school trip."

"Well, you haven't experienced New York until you've lived here, dear. Edward used to have a saying." Donnelly stops and stares down at the Oriental carpet, tapping his white deck shoe against the gray fringe at the edge. "What was it? Oh, yes. It was: New York is a nice place to live, but I wouldn't want to visit."

"Huh," Philip says and smiles, turning the statement over in his mind. He doesn't bother inquiring about who Edward is, since he plans to leave once he confirms his suspicions about what's on the other side of that door.

"Tell me the cross streets where you first stepped foot on the sidewalk here in town," Donnelly says.

Philip doesn't know why the old guy wants this information, but he tries to remember anyway. Last night he parked in the garage at the Marriott, and this morning he got in his car out of sheer habit, and drove down to the Village since he'd heard Deb Shishimanian talk about it so often. "St. Mark's and First Avenue."

Donnelly cups one side of his white face. "That has a nice ring to it. You see, I think it is crucial to remember these things in life. Someday when you look back, you can say, My New York story all started on St. Mark's and First."

"Where did yours start?" Philip asks.

"Ah. It all began for me when I stepped out of a taxi onto Bank Street and Waverly. And what a wonderful beginning it was." Donnelly looks toward the ceiling and seems to lose himself in thought for a moment before clearing his throat and getting back to business. "So what do you think of the place?"

"New York?"

"The apartment. Does it appeal to your refined Kansas taste?"

"Pennsylvania."

"That's right. My apologies."

"I like it. But I have a question about the—"

Before Philip can say the word *pets*, Donelly starts talking again. "This was my very first apartment when I came to New York from Commerce, Georgia, some fifty years ago. Just off the bus like you."

Philip ignores the bus comment. "You're from Georgia? But you don't have an accent."

"Honey," Donnelly says, "the first thing I lost when I arrived in this town was my virginity. The second was my accent."

Philip smiles. "I need to ask—"

"I have a lot of memories here, so whomever I select as my sublet has to be trustworthy. Are you trustworthy, Philip?"

"I guess," Philips says. "But about the—"

"You guess?"

"No, I mean, yes. Yes, I am."

"Good. I thought so. Now, listen. I know I may have embellished a tad about the place being pristine. But there's no harm in employing a little hyperbole when one is trying to sell one's wares. So what do you think?"

"It's cozy. I like the pictures on the wall. I like the mural. But what about the pets?"

"Oh, yes," Donnelly says. "Sweetie and Baby. Let's go pay them a visit, shall we?"

He steps into the kitchen on the way to that door and Philip asks, "Sweetie and Baby wouldn't happen to be birds, would they?"

The question causes Donnelly to stop and turn around. His womanly face takes on a pinched expression, as though he has been through this before. In a resigned tone of voice, he answers, "Sweetie is a mynah bird."

"And what about Baby?"

"She's a snake."

"A snake?"

"A snake. A darling one. But nonetheless, a snake."

Hasn't this guy ever heard of a dog or a goldfish? Philip thinks. "Listen," he says. "I really like your home and all. But I don't want to waste your time, especially since you have all these people coming to see the place. I have to be honest with you. I can't live here because I am afraid of birds."

"Nonsense," says Donnelly. "Sweetie is not a pterodactyl for goodness sake. She is a loving little black bird who will sing and talk to you and keep you company. Do you remember the birds in *Snow White* who flew around her when she sang?"

"Vaguely," Philip says.

"Well, Sweetie is that sort of a bird."

"A cartoon one?"

"No, silly. She is a nice one. I'm telling you, no one could be afraid of her."

"Trust me," Philip says. "I could be. In fact, I already am."

"No, you're not," Donnelly says.

"Yes, I am."

"No, you're not."

Philip feels as though he is back at home, having one of his trademark discussions with his mother. "Yes. I am."

"Did you ever see the movie *The Birds*?" Donnelly asks.

"I have," Philip tells him. "And it validates my fear."

Donnelly taps his white deck shoe against the checkered kitchen floor. More to himself than to Philip, he says, "No one ever made a movie about my biggest fear in life. If there was one, I'm not sure I would be brave enough to watch it."

"What are you afraid of?" Philip asks.

He clasps his jewelry-cluttered hands together and looks up at Philip. "Oh, I don't want to get into all that sad business right now. Listen, why not just take one little look-see? I guarantee you'll fall in love with her."

"I guarantee I won't," Philip says.

But against his better judgment, he follows Donnelly through that door into a long narrow bathroom. The birdcage hangs from a metal wire that's hooked to a vent on the ceiling, directly above the toilet and next to an open window. The snake tank sits on the floor beside the grimy bathtub, a heating bulb glowing inside. Philip can't bring himself to focus on the pets right away so he looks around at all the bottles of dandruff shampoo—Head & Shoulders, Selsun Blue, and a few medicated brands he has never heard of. He wonders if Donnelly wears that colorful scarf over his head simply to prevent a blizzard of his flakes inside the apartment.

"Why do you keep your pets in the bathroom?" he asks.

"Sweetie loves to flirt with the pigeons who land on the fire escape. And I leave Baby in here so the two of them can be together."

As Donnelly presses his fingers to the cage, Philip looks out the window at the crumbling fire escape. Down below, he sees a narrow alley with a stained mattress and a rusted shopping cart turned upside down. Someone spray painted the words *Suck My Cock* on the brick wall of the neighboring building. When he looks back, Philip allows himself a quick peek at the bird. Its feathers are shiny and black. There is a splash of orange nears its dot eyes. It lets out a whistle and claws at the bars, rubbing its beak against the stones in Donnelly's rings.

"She thinks my jewelry is fruit," he says. "Don't you, precious? But you've already eaten your fruit today so don't be greedy."

Not that he had any doubts before, but after seeing the bird Philip is convinced that he cannot do this. And when Donnelly reaches his hand toward the door of the cage, Philip says, "Please don't open it."

"But how will you get to know her if she's behind bars?"

"That's my point. I don't want to get to know her. I have to go."

"Go where?" Donnelly asks, pulling his hand away from the cage door.

Philip doesn't have an answer. But he wonders why this guy is so determined to make him stay. He is about to ask that very question when the birds squeals, "Make me a martini."

Donnelly laughs. So does Philip, despite himself.

"Edward taught him that phrase. One summer we set up a tape recorder that played those words over and over until she finally got it through her bird brain."

Again, Philip doesn't ask who Edward is. He is used to people introducing new players into the conversation without explanation. Shish used to do it all the time. If Philip interrupted to question who was who, she became annoyed and told him just to forget it. Now he asks Donnelly, "What else does the bird say?"

"Oh, lots of things. She's in the bathroom, so as you might imagine, she can mimic all sorts of foul noises. But she didn't learn them all from my fanny, mind you. She picks up her most disgusting sounds through the echoes in the ceiling vent that leads to the neighbors' bathroom. Stay away from those people up there, Philip. They're the real animals in this building. You'll see for yourself if this sublet works out."

"Listen," Philip says, glancing down at the snake tank on the floor. The creature must be hiding in the little box inside, either that or it has escaped, because he doesn't see it anywhere. "I just don't think this is a good fit because I don't like—"

"Shh." Donnelly holds a finger over his mouth then motions toward the cage. "Let's adjourn to the parlor and discuss the matter further. I don't want to hurt a certain someone's feelings with all this antibird talk."

Once they are back in "the parlor," Philip glances behind the dressing screen in the corner, where he sees an antique desk in front of one of the windows. On top there is a large computer. The sight of it surprises him, seeing as the guy still owns a record player. For a brief moment, Philip pictures himself sitting there working on his poetry, staring out the window as he searches for the perfect word. He has not decided much about the details of his new life in New York, but he has made up his mind to keep writing his poems and to submit his work to the journals Dr. Conorton suggested. The list of names and addresses, along with his portfolio, is under the driver's seat of his Subaru parked on St. Mark's Place.

"Would you like a cup of coffee?" Donnelly asks.

Philip turns and sees him holding a container of Taster's Choice instant coffee and a small white teacup. "No thanks," he says.

"Cigarette?"

"No thanks again. I really should get going."

"You young people are no fun these days," Donnelly says as he puts a pot of water on the stove, then uses a match to light the burner as well as his cigarette. When he's done, he sits on a wooden stool next to the counter, takes a drag, and blows the smoke through his nostrils. "Never underestimate the power of coffee and a cigarette, Philip. I'm telling you, it's pure magic." He pauses. "You're not one of those health nuts like the people downstairs, are you?"

Philip shakes his head. "I—"

"Good. Because let me give you some advice. Stay away from that restaurant."

"Restaurant? I thought it was a store."

"It's both. And Lord knows what else they do in the back. Uterine massages or some such nonsense."

"Uterine what?"

"Massages."

"What is that?"

"I don't know." Donnelly inhales his cigarette again and blows more smoke through his nose. "And I certainly don't want to find out. I saw it on a flyer on the front door one day. If you ask me the people who go into that store need to eat some red meat and get laid. I know that sounds extremely Republican of me, and I am not a Republican mind you, but it is the truth as I see it."

"Listen," Philip says, determined not to be interrupted by his rambling any longer. "Once and for all, I need to get going. I'm sorry again that this didn't work out. I'm sure one of the other people coming to see the place will be happy to sublet it from you."

Philip steps toward the door but it takes him a moment to locate the knob, which is painted to look like a hubcap on one of the taxicabs in the mural. The instant he puts his hand on it, Donnelly blurts, "There are no others."

"Excuse me?" Philip says, turning to look at him, but keeping his hand on that hubcap-doorknob.

"The last three people I had lined up to sublet the place backed out. One young lady canceled just this morning. I am supposed to be on a bus right now to Georgia. I printed up a half dozen signs on my computer and went around the neighborhood hanging them up. Believe me, at my age, that is no small feat."

Philip thinks of the selfish way he shredded and tossed those pink pieces of paper into various garbage cans on the street. As he watches

Donnelly's skinny arm stretch to the counter, where he sets his cigarette in a green ceramic ashtray, Philip feels guilty for interfering. "What about that person you were talking to on the phone when I came in? The one coming here in an hour."

Donnelly's thin voice lilts when he confesses, "I was just playacting."

"What do you mean *playacting*?"

"I wasn't really on the phone. I was just trying to make the place seem more desirable to make you want it. People only want something in life if they think they might not be able to get it. You must know that by now."

Philip lets out a breath and takes his hand off the doorknob. "I don't understand. Why did the last three people back out?"

"Two words: Sweetie and Baby."

"I thought they were loving."

"*I* think so. But most people, like yourself, don't seem to agree. Nobody much likes the idea of feeding Baby a mouse once a week. And sometimes Sweetie can—"

"Can what?"

"Peck you if she's in a bad mood. She pecked the girl this morning when I was showing her how to clean the cage. It was only a little wound on her forehead for goodness sake. Hardly any blood at all. But of course, she ran out of here crying. That's another thing about your generation— you people love high drama. You can't relax and have fun, but you certainly know how to howl and carry on about all the wrongs that have been done to you. Next thing I know I'll be getting a letter from her attorney."

Philip waves his hand at the photos on the wall. "Can't one of your glamorous friends do it while you're gone?"

Donnelly stands and goes to the stove. He turns off the burner but doesn't bother making coffee. "Honey, most of those people up there are dead. When you get to be my age, friends drop off like flies. The ones who are still alive are in no shape to climb these stairs. I can barely get up them anymore. You'll see. You'll be old yourself one day. People think it's a happy stage in life, and it is for about a year and a half. Then it becomes absolute drudgery. A slow march to the grave."

"Why don't you board the pets?" Philip asks, trying his best to stick to the subject.

Donnelly raises his scant, almost nonexistent eyebrows. "We are talking about a bird and a snake here. Not Lassie. Besides, it would cost money and I'm on a fixed income."

"Well then why don't you take them with you?"

"To my sister's? Ha! Fauncine's a bitch when she's healthy. I can only imagine how miserable she is going to be in her dying days. Do you have any brothers or sisters, Philip?"

Philip has yet to figure out the appropriate answer to this question. He doesn't like to say no, since that would deny the fact of Ronnie's existence. But answering yes always leads to the inevitable follow-up questions like *How old is he?* and *Where does he live?* Philip settles on telling Donnelly that he has one younger brother, figuring he'll evade any further questions if pressed for details.

"Well, be nice to him," is all Donnelly says, "because you never know if you'll need him to take care of you when you're on your deathbed."

Philip lets out a breath and rubs his eyes. The cigarette is still lit in the ashtray, and the smoke is bothering him. Behind the bathroom door, the bird squeals then makes a sound like a toilet flushing then asks for a martini.

"Even if Fauncine wasn't such a shrew," Donnelly says, "Sweetie and Baby have lived all their lives in that bathroom. I can't move them now. Snakes are very sensitive to their environment. A change like that could be very traumatic. She might not make it. And I promised Edward I would take care of her. Believe me, I'd rather own a poodle or maybe a nice dachshund hound. I've always been partial to small dogs of that sort. But when you make a promise to someone who has passed on, you need to keep it for your own peace of mind—whether or not you believe they are up there watching. Does that make sense?"

"I suppose," Philip says. "Listen. I wish I could help you, but I can't."

This time, when he puts his hand to the doorknob, Donnelly blurts out one long breathless sentence: "This is a rent-controlled apartment and I only pay two hundred and eleven dollars a month, but I am willing to give it to you for five hundred if you take care of my pets."

Philip stops. He turns around and asks Donnelly to repeat himself. When he does, Philip finds himself actually considering the offer. Five hundred dollars a month is far, far less than what those real estate agents had quoted him today for a place in another borough. As much as Philip dreads the idea of feeding mice to a snake and caring for a nattering, peck-happy bird, a rent that low would mean he wouldn't have to work while he was here. He has enough money saved from his days at the Olive Garden to survive years at that price. And so long as his father didn't cut off the emergency credit card, he could get by for ages without ever having to get a job at all.

"Three hundred," Philip tells him without turning around.

"Four-fifty."

"Four hundred."

"Deal," Donnelly says and slips his warm, limp hand into Philip's. "Bless you, young man. I guarantee you are going to be very happy here."

When he lets go, Donnelly goes to his desk and riffles around until he finds a crinkled Greyhound schedule. He dons a pair of enormous glasses to see about catching a bus tomorrow. When he grows flustered and confused by the crowd of numbers and tiny print, Philip takes it from him and determines that there is a bus leaving at nine-thirty in the morning. Then he sees that there is also one leaving at six o'clock tonight for D.C. From there, Donnelly can connect to an overnight bus headed to Athens, Georgia. Philip double-checks the schedule by calling the 800 number. When he confirms that the information is correct, he presents Donnelly with his options.

Without pausing to consider it, Donnelly says, "The midnight bus to Georgia, you say? Well, this is Fauncine's swan song after all. I shouldn't deprive her of any extra time to make me miserable, seeing as it's been her life's work and all. It's settled then. I'll leave in a few hours. Why put off till tomorrow what you can cross off your to-do list today?"

Philip tries to picture this little old man, who looks like a little old woman, getting on a bus and going all that way. "Are you sure about this?" he asks. "It seems like an awful long distance to travel by bus."

But Donnelly tells him that he doesn't like to fly. Ever since reading about all those train derailments, he stays away from Amtrak too. "The bus is my preferred mode of transportation," he says in that overly articulate voice. "I will make my grand exit from the city the same way I made my grand entrance so many years ago. And above all, I will keep my dignity intact."

With that, he launches into an explanation of the various quirks of the apartment—and there are plenty. The radiator leaks, so it is necessary to keep a pan beneath it at all times. If Philip neglects to empty it once a week, the water will run down to the neighbor's apartment. In the kitchen, there is a similar pan beneath the refrigerator that needs emptying on a regular basis as well. Next, Donnelly tells him that he cannot run the computer and the record player at the same time or a fuse will blow. If he forgets and it does blow, there are extras in the desk drawer. The fuse box is concealed in the mural, painted to look like the hot dog vendor's cart. Donnelly opens it and demonstrates how to replace one. Then he shows him how to take the phone wire and plug it into the back of the computer in order to use the Internet, since he will be checking his e-mail from his sister's in case Philip has questions.

"*You* have an e-mail address?" Philip says in a surprised voice.

"Of course," Donnelly tells him. "What do you think I am, a dinosaur?"

Finally, he gets around to explaining the care involved with the pets. Every morning, Sweetie gets a bowl of mashed fruit. Once a week, Baby gets a mouse from a store called Happy Pet on First Avenue—or if Philip is "lucky" there will be a "fresh kill" in the traps beneath the sink. As Donnelly goes over all those details and others, like what to do with the mail, where to send the rent check, what to say if he runs into the landlord, since sublets are forbidden, Philip gets the feeling that he is making a tremendous mistake. But then he looks over at the desk by the window and imagines sitting there, writing his poetry, instead of going to work, and that makes him feel better. Besides, he tells himself that the old guy will probably be back in a few months even though he insists it could be much, much longer.

"Knowing Fauncine," he says, "she'll drag this final act out until they have to put me in the ground right along with her."

When he is done with all the explaining, Donnelly announces that he is going to make himself a martini for the road. He pours one for Philip as well. At first Philip resists, but when Donnelly blasts him about how dull his generation is, he buckles. After only a few sips and a bite of one large vodka-soaked olive, Philip can feel his body relaxing for the first time since the argument with his mother yesterday. The more he drinks, the better he feels. Donnelly turns up the Judy Garland record again and pours them each another. Before Philip knows it, they are plopped down on the Oriental rug, and he is telling the story about Walter and Shish and what happened at the restaurant. When he gets to the part about the tray spilling and all those people clapping, Donnelly glances up at the gold starburst of a clock on the wall and says, "I hate to interrupt when you are on such a roll, dear, but I really should be off."

Philip is disappointed that he won't get to tell the part where he walks out the door and keeps going. But his mind feels so wonderful and woozy that he doesn't care. He asks Donnelly, "Are you sure you want to leave a complete stranger to take care of your pets?"

Donnelly reaches over and pinches Philip's cheek. "Cupcake," he says. "I have always lived life by trusting my instinct. And right now my instinct is telling me that you are a very special and honest young man. Now help me with my suitcase."

It takes them a few minutes to get downstairs. But once they are out on the street, a cab pulls up right away. As Donnelly climbs in, wearing a jacket he pulled from the closet that says *Sugar Babies* on the back, Philip puts the hard, bulky suitcase into the trunk and slams it shut. He comes around to the open window and asks Donnelly how he will manage getting his bag into the bus station. Donnelly tells him not to worry, that there will probably be a porter waiting to help him. Philip doubts as much, but what does he know about these things? The booze has him feeling melancholy suddenly, and he is sorry to see him go.

"Good-bye," he says.

"Farewell." Donnelly reaches his jeweled hand out the window and squeezes Philip's arm. "By the way, the answer to your question is dying."

"What?" Philip asks.

"Earlier you wanted to know what I was afraid of. I have always been afraid of dying, which is not such a good thing when you are my age."

Philip doesn't know what to say so he stays quiet.

"It's a smart idea for you to face your fears, Philip. That's why taking care of a bird is not such a bad situation for you to be in. You'll see. And if you're afraid of death like me, I suggest you come to terms with it too. Because it's going to happen to all of us eventually."

With that, he tells the cabdriver to step on it already because he has a bus to catch. As the car rolls forward, Donnelly blows a big movie-star kiss from the window. Philip stands in the street watching the taillights round the corner until they are gone.

Once he is alone, Philip takes a breath and stares up at the dark windows on the fourth floor as the streetlight comes on in front of the building. Free from the whirlwind of the last few hours, his sense of melancholy grows stronger. It is always this way with drinking, he remembers now—a surge of happiness followed by a dip of sadness—which is why he doesn't do it very often. Instead of feeling glad that he has just secured his first apartment for very little money, he feels down about the prospect of caring for that bird and snake. Part of him thinks about going to the store and getting some Windex and paper towels, but he decides the cleaning spree can wait until tomorrow when he is sober. Instead, Philip heads over to St. Mark's Place, where he parked his car. He opens the door and takes out his poetry portfolio and Madonna tapes from beneath the seat, then locks the car again. Before walking away, he glances up at a sign that tells him he'll have to move the vehicle before eight o'clock tomorrow morning or else it will be towed. Since there aren't any spots on the other side of the street, he leaves the car where it is for the time being and returns to the studio.

Inside, the bird is quiet behind the bathroom door since Donnelly draped one of his scarves over the cage before he left. Judy Garland is still singing about all the sounds the trolley and the bell make. Philip turns off the record. He sets his Madonna tapes down, wondering why he bothered, since there is not a tape player in the place. As he stands in the middle of the room, or the parlor as Donnelly called it, Philip reviews the events of the past two days that led him here. He thinks of everyone at the Olive Garden in Wayne right now, where the dinner shift is getting under way. He thinks of his father somewhere in Palm Beach, probably playing golf or tennis with Holly at this moment.

Then he thinks of his mother at home by herself.

The thought makes Philip go to the phone and dial the number in Pennsylvania. It rings three times before she picks up. "Hello."

"Mom, it's Philip."

There is a long pause. Outside, on Sixth Street, a police car whizzes by with its lights flashing and sirens wailing. She asks, "Where are you?"

"New York City."

"What? But I thought you were working at the Olive Garden last night, and then, I don't know, you didn't come home."

"I was, Ma. But I hate that place. I hate my life in Pennsylvania. I hate living with you and fighting all the time. You're just too mean now. That's why . . . that's why I'm not coming back."

He waits for her to say something, but she doesn't. The only thing Philip hears is a click. At first, he cannot believe what she did. He stands there so long holding the phone to his ear that the recording comes on the line saying, "There appears to be a receiver off the hook. . . ." After that, Philip puts down the phone and steps away from it, telling himself not to give into the sadness rising up in him.

Philip wants that happy feeling he had on the floor with Donnelly back again. He pours himself another martini—without olives or vermouth this time—but it is in the funny-shaped glass, so he considers it a martini just the same. After only a few sips, though, he gives up on the drink because it is not working anymore. He goes to the desk instead. As best he can in his fuzzy mental state, Philip looks over his work in the portfolio. But he does not try writing anything new tonight. Mainly because he still feels drunk and he knows the words won't come. But also, because sitting here is more or less a kind of rehearsal for him. Philip is practicing what it will be like to live this new life as a poet in the city—away from all the sadness of the past. Finally, he looks up at the desk and sees a stack of envelopes and a roll of stamps beside the computer.

Why put off till tomorrow what you can cross off your to-do list today?

Philip turns on the computer, opens a blank file, and retypes his "Sharp Crossing" poem, making a few minor improvements. Next, he types a separate cover letter addressed to each of the journals on Conorton's list. After all the pages are printed and sorted, the envelopes stuffed and stamped, Philip stops short of licking the seals because he wants to check for typos when he has a clear head in the morning.

At the moment, there doesn't seem to be anything left to do. And since he has to get up early to move the car, Philip stands and pulls down the Murphy bed the way Donnelly instructed. Next, he finds an extra set of sheets in the closet and changes them. He considers using the bathroom to pee and wash up. But even though Donnelly said it would be a good idea for him to face his fears, Philip is not ready to face them at the moment.

He turns out the light and climbs into bed.

With only the street lamp shining in through the window and the glow of the computer screen to see by, Philip lies there, repeating a mantra to himself that he must wake up at seven-forty-five. He has always been good at making himself get up this way, but it takes concentration, and he cannot seem to concentrate at all tonight. His thoughts keep shifting and moving, but what he comes back to again and again is the way Donnelly asked if Philip had a brother, and what he said about being nice to him. Then Philip thinks of that last time he saw Ronnie, standing on the front lawn with his girlfriend and her sister and Chaz. Their mother snapped pictures and their father told a story Philip had heard a thousand times before about his watch getting stuck in his mother's veil at their wedding. Philip remembers that he felt an incredible sense of isolation and loneliness as he drove away in his Subaru toward the restaurant, leaving them all on the front lawn. It seemed to him then that everyone had someone: Ronnie had Melissa, Chaz had Stacy, his parents had each other. Even though that is not true any longer, the same feeling hollows out a part of Philip's heart right now.

When the ache becomes too much, he gives up on sleep. Philip gets out of bed and goes to the desk again, where he reaches around to unplug the phone cord and hook it to the back of the computer. Next, he logs onto the Internet the way Donnelly showed him. Philip has never done this sort of thing before, but he knows all about it from Deb Shishimanian and her stories about the various women she has met this way over the years. And tonight, for the first time, Philip wanders into a chat room the way some lonely soul might wander into a bar in any other time and place. It doesn't take long for him to learn the strange language of this place.

lol . . .
brb . . .
what ru in2?
stats?
brwn, brwn, 6', 165, 22

And it is only a few nights later that he works up the courage to invite someone over. As he waits, Philip sits by the window with a cup of coffee in his hands, staring out at the tall brick buildings of the housing development across the street. When he hears an unfamiliar voice call a made-up name from the street, he looks down at the stranger in the shadows and wonders one last time if he should go through with this. Finally, Philip wraps the key in the same towel Donnelly had used. He reaches his hand out the window and lets go. Soon, he hears the clomp-clomp-clomp of shoes on the crooked old stairway.

The closer they get, the faster the beating of Philip's heart.

chapter 11

BECAUSE OF THE DIFFICULTIES HIS CAST AND CRUTCH PRESENT, IT takes Philip a good five minutes to get into the bathroom, drop his pajama bottoms, and do his business. So when the telephone rings, he is not about to jump up and go running to answer it. As he sits on the toilet in the small bathroom beneath the staircase, Philip listens to the answering machine pick up on the extension in the kitchen. After the mechanical, recorded voice instructs whoever is calling to please leave a message, his mother's voice echoes through the house. "Philip. It's me. Are you there? Pick up." Filtered through the machine, she sounds softer than usual, stripped of her harshness. He might actually mistake her for a sane, decent person with manners if he didn't know better. Then she says, "Okay, well, I just want you to know that I'm on my way to Melissa's house. I plan to settle this whole thing once and for all. By the way, I got you a book from the library. I think you might like it. Well, okay. Bye now. See you when I get home."

Philip tilts his head back and looks at the ceiling. Even though he doesn't believe in God, he shouts a frustrated question up to the heavens, "Why can't she just leave the poor girl alone?"

After he flushes and washes his hands, he hobbles to the kitchen with the help of his crutch, picks up the telephone, and punches in *69. "M," Philip says when the call rings through to voice mail. "It's me. I don't know how you even found out where Melissa lives. But please don't drive over there and rail on her about last night. Call me back when you get this. Or better yet, just come home."

He hangs up and sits in one of the stiff ladder-back chairs at the kitchen table, exhausted from what little sleep he had the night before and jittery from all the coffee he drank today. Ten cups was a lot, even for him. After his mother woke him this morning then went upstairs to her room following their lovely mother-son talk, Philip tried to focus on reading his book or writing in his journal between watching the occasional scene from whatever old movie happened to be on television. It was then that he began to feel utterly stir-crazy for the first time since he came home. A feeling that returns to him now. Since he didn't exactly make contingency plans for his life beyond that night on the fire escape, the question of what to do next has slowly begun to creep up on him. He can't envision himself staying in Radnor forever, or even a few more weeks for that matter. Likewise, he can't imagine going back to New York—not after the way things ended there.

Five minutes pass.

Five minutes during which Philip sits at the table doing not much of anything except ponder his lack of options. And still, his mother has yet to call back. Finally, he stands and picks up the phone, hits *69 again. Voice mail. He repeats an abbreviated version of the message he left last time, telling her not to bother Melissa, that she should call him or simply come home. After he hangs up, Philip considers putting on another pot of coffee. Then he thinks better of it and goes to the sink to see about cleaning those pots and bowls that have been there for days.

Back in the city, Philip never would have dared to leave out a dirty dish even for a second because of the mice problem. Between those mice and cockroaches, plus that bird and snake, Philip lived a life that was something akin to a zookeeper's. With the exception of those strangers who came clomping up the staircase late at night to ease his loneliness, those rodents and pets—if you could call them that—were his only company.

Four and a half years of living in the city and Philip had spent almost every single day alone. In the mornings, he sometimes went to Aggie's Diner on Houston Street, not far from where he lived, and treated himself to breakfast on his father's credit card. As he sat at the counter, sipping his coffee and picking at his oatmeal with a spoon, Philip often spotted a guy about his age sitting at a booth with a blond woman and her baby. There was something about the three of them that drew Philip in. Throughout the years, he eavesdropped on their conversations so often that he knew the details of their lives. She was a novelist and he was her student. She taught a writing class at NYU and he taught one at a Senior Citizens Center. They had traveled to California and Key West together. Like Philip, they had each lost a sibling. While they talked and laughed and gave each other advice on everything from their writing to where to get the best Tarot card reading, the baby—a beautiful blond boy with bright blue eyes—fussed in his seat. Sooner or later, one of them would sweep him up and lift him over the table until he was laughing and giggling too. Meanwhile, Philip looked on and wished for a friendship like theirs to save him from his loneliness. On so many of those mornings, he envisioned getting up from his stool and introducing himself, but he could never go through with it. If his mother's personality had exploded in the aftermath of Ronnie's death, Philip's had *imp*loded. There in the city, among all those millions of people, any of whom might have become his friend, he grew more isolated than ever.

After he hunts down a stray S.O.S. pad beneath the sink, Philip begins the insufferable task of scrubbing the dried green gunk from all the pots and bowls. The residue from his mother's pea soup concoction is attached so firmly that Philip may as well be scraping barnacles off the hull of a ship. As he scours away, it dawns on him that even if his mother gets his messages (an iffy proposition at best, considering she's not the most technologically savvy person around) there is no way in hell that she is going to listen to what he said. In fact, Philip would be willing to bet money that at this very moment she is defying his every word. He can just see her fat fist knocking on Melissa's door, her big mouth opening as she lays into her the way she did last night.

When will it be enough? Philip wonders as he gives up this business of scrubbing pots already and tosses the S.O.S. pad into the sink. When will she have yelled and screamed herself all out so that there is no anger left?

He turns off the water, dries his hands on his pajama bottoms, then goes to the phone again. This time, he picks it up and calls 4-1-1. When the automated operator comes on the line, he asks for the number of Melissa Moody on Monk's Hill Road. But the only listing for a Moody in Radnor is under the names Joseph and Margaret on Church Street. Her parents, Philip figures, and hangs up. Standing there in the middle of the dirty kitchen, he feels an acute sense of restlessness once more.

His eyes go to the wooden key rack on the kitchen wall.

Dangling from one hook is a slim silver key with a black grip attached to Ronnie's bottle-opener key chain. Philip steps closer to the rack and stares at the tiny Mercedes symbol, a pie split three ways, etched into the silver. Before lifting the key from the hook, he waits a half minute more, willing the phone to ring, willing his mother's Lexus to pull in the driveway. When neither of those things happen, he resigns himself to the obvious fact that she is not going to call back or come home of her own volition. And since God only knows what his mother is capable of, Philip decides to take the Mercedes, whether she likes it or not, and drive over there before she can do any more damage.

He removes the skinny key from the hook and cups it in his palm, then makes his way to the family room where he begins searching for his wallet, which contains his driver's license. Not since his first week in New York has Philip been behind the wheel of a car. He realized pretty quickly that the alternate-side-of-the-street-parking game was nothing but a royal pain in the ass that served to ruin a big chunk of each day. And since he didn't need a car in the city anyway, he decided to get rid of it. Philip dialed up the Olive Garden and did his best to disguise his voice when that imbecile Walter answered. He asked to speak with Gumaro, and when his old pal came on the line, he said, "*Oye, maricón. Es* Philip. *Come estás?*"

Gumaro laughed. "*Bien, pendejo. Donde estás?* Miami? Las Vegas?"

"*Nueve York.*"

"Ah, you are finally living the good life, my friend."

Philip remembers looking around the studio then at Donnelly Fiume's dusty antique furniture and the mote of glue traps he strategically positioned around the Murphy bed on his second night there. The good life, he thought. If Gumaro only knew . . . Just then, Walter began grumbling in the background, and since Philip didn't want to get Gumaro in trouble for staying on the phone too long, he came right to the point and asked if he wanted the car. *"Te gustaria tener un auto nuevo? Mi* Subaru?"

"Quante costo?" Gumaro asked.

"Nada."

"Nada?"

"Sí. It's yours for free if you want it."

"En serio?"

"I'm serious, Gumaro."

A few days later they met and made the exchange, taking care of the necessary paperwork. And when Gumaro drove off a happy man down St. Mark's Place, Philip felt freed from one more vestige of his life in Pennsylvania.

Now, as he sorts through the mess of his belongings on and around the foldout bed, he wonders if he'll be able to manage maneuvering his brother's car with his leg in a cast. Since there is only one way to find out, Philip keeps searching until he spots his black leather wallet shoved inside one of his black leather shoes on the floor. He plucks out his driver's license then slips off his pajama bottoms and tugs on the clothes he wears once a week for his trips to Dr. Kulvilkin's office—a pair of jeans cut on one side so they fit over his cast and a giant wool sock that slides right over his toes. Then Philip pulls on the turtleneck he wore the night before, finger-combs his hair and heads out of the room. On the way, he glances up at that antique schoolhouse clock on the wall. The hands point to five-thirty, even though it's somewhere around four. For an entire month now, the ceaseless ticking of this defective piece of junk has driven him crazy. Philip finally decides to do something about it. He pulls open the hinged wooden and glass face, reaches inside and grabs hold of the small pendulum, as though choking its neck, until the thing stops moving.

The room is silent behind him when Philip leaves. He considers making one last stop in the bathroom, since all that coffee is going right through him. But he makes up his mind to hold it and keeps walking to the door that leads down to the garage. The biggest problem with wearing the cast is that he cannot bend his leg. For that reason, descending a simple set of stairs becomes an Olympic sport for Philip—never mind driving. He persists nonetheless, taking step after awkward step until he has lowered himself into the bowels of the house. From here, he moves quickly, limping through the narrow hallway cluttered with Ronnie's and his forgotten ten-speeds, a collection of tennis rackets, a volleyball, an old Weber grill, as well as a long-deflated alligator raft they used to float on in the pool out back when they weren't playing Marco Polo.

When Philip reaches the garage, he runs his hand along the wall until he locates the switch inside. The bulb must be blown because nothing happens when he flicks it on. He tries a few more times before giving up. With only the hall light to see by, Philip steps inside and looks around at the snug canvas cover his mother must have bought to keep over the Mercedes. The other two bays are empty except for the Rorschach-style oil stains on the floor, a few dented paint cans, and a box marked CHRISTMAS DECORATIONS.

He peels back the cover on the car and tosses it in the corner. As Philip sticks the key inside the door, he thinks of how ridiculous it is that his mother keeps it locked in the first place, just like Ronnie's room upstairs. Once it is open, he puts his crutch in the back then gets situated in the driver's seat. It takes some effort, but he finds a way to position his legs so that his right is stretched to the passenger side, while his left (the one free of the cast) is poised to man the gas and brake pedals. It is not an ideal setup, not even close, but he tells himself that Monk's Hill Road is only so far away and he'll just have to make do.

Before pressing the button on the garage-door opener that's clipped to the visor, Philip sits a moment longer inside that dark, sealed garage. He is thinking of a section in the biography he's been reading, the part that came last, though he read it first. *At the age of forty-five, after two unsuccessful suicide attempts, Anne Sexton finally succumbed to her demons. After pouring herself a glass of vodka, she went into the garage of her house at 14 Black Oak Road, started her red Cougar, turned up the radio, and listened as the exhaust fumes took her life.* As Philip wonders what kind of courage, foolishness, and instability it must have taken to successfully follow through with an act like that, a few scattered lines from one of Anne's poems drift back to him:

Of course guitars will not play!
The snakes will certainly not notice.
New York City will not mind.

Philip is sure that somewhere, some stuffy erudite scholar has a lofty interpretation of those lines, but he takes them to mean that she did not expect there to be a heaven and that the world would go on without her. It is much the same way he feels when he contemplates his own death and his brother's too, though when it comes to an afterlife, Philip wishes he felt otherwise. He used to assume that atheists were comfortable, even smugly defiant, in their disbelief. Now that he is one, he realizes it is quite the contrary. In Philip's case anyway, he wants to believe. He wants desperately to regain the wholehearted, unquestioning faith he had as a child. But after suffering from his own demons all these years as he carried the memory of his mother's words wishing him dead, and after facing so many other cruelties and disappointments of the world, Philip has lost something he cannot get back. That something is his faith.

Finally he forces himself to stop thinking about the last chapter in Anne Sexton's story and all the related tangents to his own. Philip reaches up and presses his thumb against the button of the remote control. Above him, the belted contraption lets out a cough then a low rumbling begins. The door lifts and sunlight streams inside. It comes gradually, like a time-lapse of daybreak, until the entire garage is filled with light.

He starts the engine, shifts the car into reverse, and backs into the driveway. He pulls onto Turnber Lane, adjusting and readjusting his position in the seat as he tries to get used to working the pedals with his left foot. It is not unlike attempting to write with his opposite hand. Things go relatively smoothly until he encounters the first stop sign on the corner. Philip presses down on the brake with much more force than he intends to, and the Mercedes bucks and skids to a sudden stop. His body jerks forward into the steering wheel, then slams back into his seat. He looks around to be sure no one is watching. As usual, the lawns and sidewalks in front of the large houses in this neighborhood are deserted. For a fleeting moment, he considers simply turning around and going home. Making another pot of coffee. Switching on the TV. Opening his book to the very beginning, since that's just about the only section he has left. But he has come this far, and there is still the prospect of his mother unleashing one of her trademark tirades on Melissa right now. So, however clumsily, Philip puts his foot to the gas pedal and keeps going.

As he heads across town, moving well below the speed limit, the steering wheel feels too large in his hands. The tires seem to sway the slightest bit beneath him. The Mercedes is only a 1979 model, but it feels like a relic, especially compared to his mother's Lexus. He has ridden in her car quite a bit these last four weeks as she begrudgingly shuttled him back and forth to Doctor Kulvilkin's office, repeating ad nauseam that she didn't like him, all because his name sounded like you know who's.

At the intersection of Matson Ford and Unkman Avenue, Philip makes the same mistake and puts too much pressure on the brakes. The car bucks to a quick stop again, and after he flies forward into the steering wheel then back in his seat, he decides to put on his seat belt. As he does, Philip looks in the rearview mirror to make sure the driver in the car behind him isn't suffering from whiplash or giving him the finger. That's when he notices a police car, two vehicles back, behind a station wagon and a minivan.

"Shit," he says as all that coffee he consumed splashes around his stomach.

The light turns green. If Philip wants to take the most direct route, he should hang a right onto Unkman. But the sight of the police car has him nervous about messing up the turn, so he keeps going straight. This proves to be a mistake. The station wagon and minivan quickly weed themselves out, turning off one after another, until the cop car is directly behind him. Philip stares ahead and keeps going well past any direct route to Melissa's house. When he finally reaches the intersection of Matson Ford and King of Prussia Road, he works up the courage and signals, then presses his foot to the brake as gently as possible. He is so careful not to apply too much pressure that he ends up taking the turn too fast. The police officer turns too.

"Shit," Philip says again.

No lights come on and there is no signal for Philip to pull over, so he keeps driving. He cuts onto Blatts Farm Hill, doing his absolute best to navigate the hills and curves of this windy road. As he passes the stretch where his brother's accident occurred, Philip doesn't even glance out the window to see if that stump is still there or if the town finally had it ripped from the ground and taken away. Instead, he keeps his eyes focused straight ahead. When he arrives at Monk's Hill Road, Melissa's Corolla is parked up ahead; his mother's Lexus is nowhere. Since the only driveway has a red truck parked in it, Philip signals and pulls to one side behind Melissa's car, hoping the police officer will keep going. No such luck. The lights begin flashing. The car comes to a stop directly behind him.

"Shit," he says a third time.

As he waits for the officer to get out and come to his window, Philip releases a breath and glances over at Melissa's small house with the number 32 on the door. Beside her place is a slightly bigger house. And there in the back, at the edge of the woods, Philip notices a third. Together, they remind him of those roadside motel cabins he remembers seeing on their trip to Cape Cod with his grandparents so many years ago. He and Ronnie had begged to stay in one of those cabins instead of the inn, but his grandmother argued that they were too depressing. At the time they couldn't understand what she meant, but now he gets it. When Philip looks in the side-view mirror, he sees the officer—a stocky black woman with aviator sunglasses—coming toward him. He rolls down the window and turns his head so that he is eye level with her swollen belly when she reaches the car. She's pregnant, Philip realizes.

"Did I do something wrong, officer?" he asks, mustering his most innocent voice.

She lowers her sunglasses to the tip of her nose and tilts her long neck to one side in order to look at his crutch in the backseat. Then she leans forward to get a view of his broken leg stretched to passenger-side floor. "Driver's license and registration, please."

Philip hands her his license immediately. But it takes some serious stretching to get into the glove compartment. When he finally manages it, he pulls out an envelope and flips through the forms inside. "I'm not sure which one it is," he says.

"The yellow one," she tells him in a brusque, all-business tone.

Philip hands her the paper. As she stares down at it, he puts on that innocent, friendly voice again and says, "Just like *Fargo*, huh?"

The officer looks up at him over her sunglasses. "Excuse me?"

"You're pregnant. Just like that movie with the pregnant cop. It was on cable this morning. I watched some of it."

Her brown eyes stay fixed on him an extended moment. Finally, she says, "We've got a number of problems here, sir. First, you've been driving erratically ever since I spotted you back on Matson Ford. Second, your license expired two years ago. And third, probably your biggest offense of all, I'm not pregnant."

Philip's eyes drop to her belly again. "Shit," he says for the final time today.

"That's right. Now, why don't you tell me what someone in your condition is doing operating a vehicle when it looks to me like you should be convalescing in bed?"

He knows it is completely shameless of him, but Philip decides to play the pity card in a last-ditch effort to dig himself out of this mess. "I'm sorry," he tells her. "It's just that this is my brother's old car. He died about five years ago in an accident back on Blatts Farm Hill." Philip watches her face for some sign of recognition or softening but it stays as cold and blank as ever. He continues, "I'm home for the first time in years because I fell from a fourth-floor fire escape in New York City." Still no reaction. "Anyway, I guess I found myself missing my brother. I thought being in this car again would make me feel closer to him."

"And you couldn't feel closer to him parked in your driveway?"

Philip doesn't know what to say to that, and since she doesn't seem willing to join his pity party, he tells her, "No. I couldn't."

"Why did you pull over just now?"

He glances at Melissa's motel cabin of a house and the two others clustered nearby, then at the cop's stern face again. "My brother's old girlfriend lives here. She was in the accident with him. I was coming by to see her."

The officer lifts her neck and squints at the three houses. Philip finds himself peeking over at her large stomach, wondering how he could have possibly made such a stupid mistake, when she asks, "Isn't this Bill Erwin's place?"

"Who?"

"Bill Erwin."

"I don't think so."

She is quiet as she continues squinting at the cottages.

"Unless he lives in one of those others," Philip adds.

He waits for her to look back at him, but she keeps her eyes on those ramshackle houses, so different from the others here in Radnor. Finally, she stops staring and turns her attention to Philip once more. "Look. I can't let you drive like this. Do you think whoever you said you're coming to visit can give you a ride home afterward?"

"Yes. Definitely."

"You answered that question awfully fast. I just hope you are telling me the truth, because if I catch you driving, I'm not going to be so nice next time."

Philip isn't aware that she is being so nice *this* time. "I promise," he says, wondering where his mother could possibly be if her car is not here. "I'll be sure to get a ride."

When she sticks out his license and the registration, he lifts his hand through the window to retrieve them. But she doesn't let go right away. Once she has his attention, the officer looks him squarely in the eyes and says, "Let me give you two pieces of advice, Mr. Chase. Number one: get your license renewed. Number two: never, as long as you live, ask or imply that a woman is pregnant. I don't care if she's in labor and you can see the baby's head peeking out between her legs, the rule is: Do. Not. Ask. Get it?"

"Got it."

"Good."

With that, she releases the license and registration and walks back to her car. Philip returns the yellow paper to the envelope and tosses it on the seat. Before making another move, he waits for her to drive away, but she sits inside her car a while, looking as though she is doing some sort of paperwork as those lights on her roof continue flashing. He glances over at the houses again, surprised that neither Melissa nor her neighbors have come to their doors to see what it going on. At long last, the officer turns off her lights and drives away down the road. Philip gives a friendly wave as she goes, but she does not wave back.

Once her car is out of sight, he runs his hand along the rim of his turtleneck, feeling the wound beneath. According to Dr. Kulvilkin's orders, Philip is supposed to put the bandages back on every morning after letting the wound breathe all night. But he is so tired of dealing with ointments and gauze and medical tape that he didn't bother today. As best he can, Philip tries to put his faux pas with the police officer out of his mind so he can concentrate on what to do next. If his mother isn't here, he doesn't particularly want to go to the door. But he can't drive home, now that old Jelly Belly is likely to be waiting around every turn. He takes out his cell and calls his mother's number again. It goes straight to voice mail. He tries her at home too. The machine picks up. Since there doesn't seem to be any other alternative, Philip surrenders to the moment and makes up his mind to knock on Melissa's door. Who knows? Maybe she will tell him that his mother has already come and gone. After all, it has been almost an hour since she called, and it's not like they would have passed each other on the roads, seeing as he traveled the most indirect route possible.

Outside the car, the air smells of burning wood. A squawking sound comes from the trees. When Philip gets a firm footing on the ground, he looks up to see a flock of large black birds perched in the bare branches above him. Over the years, while cleaning that nasty mynah bird's cage in New York, Philip had been pecked in the face no less than six times—so much for facing his fears as Donnelly advised. If Philip had a slight phobia of birds to begin with, those experiences leave him filled with terror whenever he comes remotely close to the creatures. This time is no exception.

Philip looks away from those demons in the trees and retrieves his crutch from the backseat. He maneuvers up the shoveled walkway as quickly as possible while paying careful attention not to slip. When he reaches the cement stoop, he knocks on the metal storm door and waits for Melissa to open up. The birds stop squawking, and the yard grows silent except for a steady snapping sound that Philip can't identify. He stares over at the neighboring house, just forty or fifty feet away. On the front door, there is a quilted decoration with pinecones and ribbons below the word *Welcome*. The place doesn't appear the least bit welcoming, though. All the curtains are drawn, and the only sign of life is a trail of white smoke rising out of the stone chimney. Philip looks more closely at the third house by the edge of woods. The roof is sagging so much that he would not be surprised if it collapsed from the weight of the snow before his eyes. Every one of the windows is covered with plastic, which rustles in the wind—the source of the snapping, he realizes.

Not a single sound has come from inside Melissa's house. Philip knocks again, harder this time. He figures he'll give it another minute then try her neighbor and ask if anyone has seen a green Lexus pull up in the last hour. But then he hears footsteps and the creak of floorboards behind the door. Melissa's muffled voice says, "Just a second."

A moment later, she opens up. Philip peers through the smudged glass of the storm door at her scar-ridden face and long, greasy hair. She is wearing an oversize, wrinkled white button-down and has removed the silver studs and hoops from her ears so that there is nothing but a cluster of small holes dotting her lobes. Her eyes look red from crying. Before he can even get out a hello, Melissa says, "I knew you would come. I knew you would change your mind."

He is about to tell her that he has not changed his mind at all when he looks at the odd, close-lipped smile on her face and realizes what sort of response that is likely to bring about. The fact is, he is just too fatigued to handle that sort of discussion right now. So he allows her to believe whatever she wants for the time being, as he skips over her comment and asks, "Missy, by any chance has my mother come by here?"

Melissa opens her mouth to answer but is distracted by something behind him. Her gaze shifts over his shoulder. Philip turns, expecting that he might see his mother's Lexus pulling up, but nothing is there. Only those birds watching from the trees.

"You drove Ronnie's car here," she says, her voice weighted with longing, just as it had sounded last night when she inquired about the car then too.

Philip turns to her and nods, but Melissa keeps her eyes on the old cream-colored Mercedes. "We were supposed to take that car to the prom instead of renting a limo."

"I know," Philip tells her. "You mentioned that yesterday."

Melissa stops staring out at the street and brings her gaze to him again. "I did? Oh, that's right, I did. I just woke up from a nap, and I've had a pretty rough day, so I'm not thinking straight. Would you like to come inside?"

Philip doesn't see another choice just yet so he steps into the confines of her cold, dark house. Inside, the chilled air smells less like chimney smoke and more like stale cigarette smoke, the same as her car. The thought of her puffing away during her pregnancy squelches any pity Philip had been feeling for her ever since they separated last night. In its place, a sense of doubt and apprehension returns, along with a distinct feeling of disgust.

"Do you want to sit down?" Melissa asks, adjusting the sagging cushions on her tattered sofa and smiling that eerie, closed-lip smile.

Reluctantly, Philip puts aside his crutch and takes a seat, crossing his arms in front of himself. He cannot help but feel bothered by how happy she is to see him. He knows he should tell her this instant that he has not changed his mind. He knows he should ask about his mother again and make sure to get an answer this time. But as his eyes adjust to the dim light, and he begins to take in the details of his surroundings, Philip is startled into speechlessness. Before him on the coffee table is a messy pile of newspapers, at least twenty of them, all from the day after his brother died with the photo of that crushed limousine on the cover. Over on the mantel of the fireplace are more pictures of Ronnie—two of them duplicates of the ones taped to her dashboard. Philip's eyes go to the bookshelves next, and he scans the titles: *Visits from the After-Life*, *To the Other Side and Back*, *Blessings from Beyond*, *Conversations with the Dearly Departed*, *The Dead Are Always Watching*, *The Language of the Deceased*, *Breaking Through to the Fourth Dimension*, and countless others. He spots just one lonely title that is not like the rest: *Your A to Z Guide to Pregnancy*.

Maybe she should look under C, he thinks, and read up on the effects of cigarette smoking on fetuses.

"Philip," Melissa says. "Did you hear me?"

"I'm sorry, what?"

"I asked if you wanted something to drink."

His gaze moves past her to a row of empty wine bottles on the floor of the kitchenette. This girl has lost her mind, Philip tells himself. What other explanation can there be except that she has lost her mind?

Melissa must sense what he is thinking, because she says, "Those bottles are really old. Obviously, I don't drink any alcohol right now because of the baby."

"Obviously," Philip says, more confused than ever.

"I just have cranberry juice or water to offer you."

He tells her water is fine while silently urging himself to ask about his mother. But he feels nauseated now. Not just from the ten cups of coffee roiling in his stomach, but also from being thrust into this shrine dedicated to his brother's memory. Philip has to pee as well. "Can I use your bathroom?"

Melissa glances at the closed white door at the end of the short hallway. "Sure," she says. "No one but me and my cat ever goes in there, though. So it's a bit of a mess."

"That's okay," Philip tells her and forces a smile. "You saw the way our kitchen looked last night."

He uses his crutch to stand and makes his way down the hall as her cat darts out of nowhere and runs behind the sofa. Once he is inside the tiny bathroom, Philip takes a deep breath and unzips his jeans. As he stands over the toilet, looking around at the mildewed shower curtain beside him and the dirty Kitty Litter box on the floor, he wonders how this could have happened. How could a girl who once seemed so normal wind up as this damaged young woman living in this creepy house, surrounded by memories of her dead boyfriend and believing that the baby inside her is his?

Yes, the accident was terrible.

Yes, she obviously loved Ronnie.

But it has been nearly five years—long enough for most anyone to move on.

By the time Philip finishes peeing, he is no closer to an answer. He flushes, zips his jeans, then turns around to use the sink. That's when he catches sight of something he hadn't noticed in his rush to get to the toilet. There, on the back of the bathroom door, hangs Melissa's prom dress. The sleeves torn. The lace shredded. The bloodstains dried to a murky black color on the yellowed material. The sight of it, a ghost rising up before him, causes Philip's mouth to drop open once more. His stomach twists into a tight knot that won't loosen. He yanks open the door and hobbles down the hallway to find Missy sitting on the sofa, two glasses of water before her on the coffee table, that black and white cat beside her now. She runs her hand from the V-shaped fur between its ears all the way down to its spotted tail, shaking out the loose hair between her fingers.

Philip tells himself that he should get the hell out of here. Cop or no cop back on the roads waiting for him, he should leave. Now. He wants no part in this insanity any longer. In the end, though, he does not heed his own advice. Caught up in his dismay, disgust, and confusion, Philip finds his mouth moving, and he does to Melissa exactly what he came to prevent his mother from doing. At first, his words come out in clumped, disconnected phrases. "That dress on the back of the door . . . All of these books . . . So many copies of the newspaper." Philip stops and puts his hand to his cheek, then gathers his thoughts and presses on. "Melissa, this is what I was talking about last night. There is something terribly wrong with you."

Missy stops petting the cat as the last bits of loose fur float in the air around her. The tight-lipped smile she had worn since she first opened the door and saw Philip fades from her face.

"I'm sorry, Melissa. But there is no other way to say it. You have a serious problem. It's like you're stuck on my brother. And no matter what miracle you think has happened with this pregnancy, the fact is he is dead. Ronnie is dead. You have to stop pining and obsessing over someone who is no longer here. Even if he was still alive, the truth is, most high school relationships don't last anyway. The two of you probably wouldn't even be together anymore."

The words keep coming, and though he doesn't realize it, the sense of urgency Philip feels causes his voice to climb higher and higher until he is shouting at her. The cat leaps from the sofa and scurries down the hall. Melissa presses her hands together in the shape of a tight little prayer over her stomach. Only twice does she interrupt. First, when Philip tells her that she should not be smoking, and she says that she has not had a single cigarette since the day she realized she was pregnant. Second, when Philip points to those wine bottles on the floor, and she insists once more that they are from a long time ago. Philip plows right over her denials, though. He keeps rambling on and on until finally returning to the horrible, undeniable fact of that dress on the back of the door.

"Why on earth would you keep something like that around to look at every day? I just don't understand, Melissa. Why?"

When he is finished, she does not burst into tears the way she did last night after his mother yelled. In fact, she does not say another word. Her

198 • JOHN SEARLES

hands stay pressed together in that prayer position over the mound of her stomach as she rocks gently back and forth on the couch. Behind her, through a split in the curtains over the picture window, Philip can see the neighbor's house and that stone chimney with the smoke rising up from it.

"Well?" he says.

Melissa looks at him with her scarred, motionless face. She does not respond.

"Well?" Philip says again.

Finally, she opens her mouth. In an angry voice, charged with conviction, she tells him, "I am not crazy. You believe what you want, but I know what is happening to me. I know. And I don't have to explain myself to you. Because you have no idea what I've been through."

"Melissa, we all went through it. Maybe you were in the accident with Ronnie. But we all lost him that night."

"I'm not talking about the accident!" she shouts. "I'm talking about what happened that summer after!"

"I don't understand," Philip says. "What happened?"

"Why don't you ask your father? Or go find mine and ask him."

He is about to ask what she means when there is a heavy knock on the door. My mother, Philip thinks. He cannot remember the last time he felt this grateful for her presence. But when Melissa rises from the sofa and opens the door, Philip sees that it is not his mother after all. A tall, lumberjack of a man steps inside the house, wearing a faded John Deere cap, a flannel shirt with the sleeves rolled up, and a gold Timex ticking on his thick, hairy wrist.

"I heard shouting," he says in a deep, gravelly voice as his gaze travels to Melissa then to Philip, then back. "Is everything okay?"

"Everything is fine, Mr. Erwin. Thank you."

Philip remembers that police officer's question when she squinted at the cluster of houses: *Isn't this Bill Erwin's place?* He studies the man's face, which looks so haggard and weathered that he may as well be scarred too. His size and height leave Philip feeling dwarfed in his presence. It is the way he used to feel back in high school when Jedd Kusam cornered him in the hallway. The way he felt that last night in Donnelly Fiume's studio when he opened the door to see that tall, muscular stranger standing there.

"You were the one the cops stopped out front a while ago," Bill says.

"Cops?" Melissa says. "What cops?"

So someone had been watching after all, Philip thinks. "It was just one cop. And it was nothing really. No big deal."

Bill Erwin won't let it go. "What was the problem?"

"The officer wanted me to—" Philip stops before saying that she wanted him to get a ride home, since he doesn't want this man to offer one. There is something about him that Philip doesn't like. As he tries to determine exactly what that something is, he notices a rectangular bulge in the front pocket of his flannel shirt, pressing against the raggedy material. "I was driving too fast. The cop gave me a warning. That's all."

The answer seems to satisfy him, because he softens his tone when he speaks next. "We all know you have to be careful on these roads."

After that, he asks Melissa once more if everything is okay. When she tells him that everything is fine, he turns to go without so much as saying good-bye to Philip. Melissa closes the door behind him, and Philip steps closer to the window by the sofa and pulls back the curtain. Outside, the sky is growing dark. Bill Erwin is almost a silhouette as he moves across the lawn then stops at the front door to pull a cigarette from his shirt pocket and light it. He takes a long drag then stomps his boots on the mat and steps inside.

Philip keeps watching but cannot see, of course, as Bill closes the door behind him and walks inside the living room of his and Gail's house. He cannot see, of course, as Bill stands on the braided rug by the basement door, fidgeting with that cigarette as he listens to the sound of Gail moaning in the basement. Somehow, he had managed to stop the bleeding. Somehow, by some strange miracle, she is still alive down there. For this, Bill is grateful, though he does not know what to do next. If he takes her to the hospital, she is certain to tell the first person she can about how this happened to her. Eventually, she will speak up about Melissa and those pills, which will lead the police to believe that the things Donna Fellman said years ago were true. Eventually, that will lead them to suspect Bill of those other women over the years, which could lead them to that vacant house in the back. So instead of taking her to the hospital, Bill dragged the comforter and quilts from their bed down to the basement. He arranged them on the floor, lifted her body, and placed her on top of them. He gave her water. He put ice packs on her ankles, which have ballooned to impossible sizes.

But her moaning won't stop.

Bill opens the door just a crack and tells her, "Please be quiet, dear. Please. I'm thinking about what I should do. I need quiet so I can figure out what we should do next."

It seems that all through their marriage he has been waiting for something like this to happen. He thinks of all the nights he sat at the table while Gail cooked dinner. Bill would look up at the large knife in her hand as she pulled it out of a drawer to slice a roast, and the same questions would flash though his mind: *What if I lost control the way I did with those other women? What if something in me rose up and I grabbed that knife from her?*

He does not want to think about that now. Until he can figure out what to do next, he goes about making another check of the front and back windows the way he has done compulsively since this morning. Then he takes down one of the books from the shelf, *Weird News from Around the World*, to calm his nerves. He reads a story about a man in New York City who spent his days begging on the streets, then took all the money he made back to his six-bedroom house in New Jersey. Another about a family in Switzerland who was stuck on a faulty ski lift for thirteen hours in bitter cold and winds, but survived. Bill keeps on reading as Gail moans beneath him, and outside those birds stay perched on the branches, and next door, Melissa and Philip argue back and forth.

Finally, Melissa says, "Look, I don't want to fight with you anymore."

Philip is about to look away from the window when he notices something glinting in the corner of his vision. He stretches his neck to see what it was or where it came from. But whatever it was is gone, so he turns back to her. "What did you mean before about my father?"

"Forget it," she tells him and waves her hand in the air. "I was angry. I wasn't making sense. Like I said, I've had a rough day. But I'm not sure why you even came over here if all you wanted to do was tell me again how crazy I am. I think I got the point from you people last night."

"That's not why I'm here. I came because my mother left a message saying she was on her way to see you."

"Well, she hasn't been here. I can tell you that much."

"Are you sure?" Philip asks.

"Don't you think I would remember a visit from her?"

There it is again. In the corner of his vision, Philip sees something glinting outside the window. But when he looks, there is nothing there. He lets out a breath and tells himself that he should go home and get into bed. Clearly, he is exhausted and drained by this experience. He will just have to drive himself back and hope that the officer is bothering someone else by now. For all Philip knows his mother might have changed her mind about coming here. That would be just like her. Maybe she was struck by some sudden craving, and at this very moment, she is standing in the checkout line at the Genuardi's, laying the ingredients to rice pudding or a tuna casserole on the conveyor belt. Maybe Philip will arrive home and find her cooking something up. The thought actually makes him miss her. He feels sorry about giving her such a hard time this morning when she wanted to talk—so many other times too.

"I better get going," he says.

Melissa steps toward the door and puts her hand on the knob. "Do me a favor, Philip. Don't come here again unless you've changed your mind."

He tells her that he won't be back. "But if my mother shows up, will you please have her call me?"

"I don't have a phone," Melissa says. "It got disconnected months ago. I couldn't keep up with the bills."

Philip wonders briefly, the way he did last night, if all this really is part of some scheme she came up with for money, but he decides against it. "Then how did you call our house yesterday?"

"From a pay phone on my way back from Philadelphia."

He remembers then the sound of cars speeding by her in the background when he first answered the phone last night. "Well, my mother has a cell, so she can call me on that."

Melissa pulls open the door. With the help of his crutch, Philip steps past her onto the stoop. It is just about dark now. He looks up into the trees to see if those birds are still there, but it's difficult to tell in the dying light. Philip is about to walk away when he glances over at Bill Erwin's house and thinks of that rectangular bulge in his shirt pocket, the way he pulled out a cigarette before going inside.

Cigarettes, he thinks.

He turns back to Melissa. "You really haven't smoked in all these months, have you?"

She shakes her head no. "Of course not."

"I believe you," he says. "I know that sounds strange. I'm sorry I didn't before."

"What about the rest?" she asks, pressing her hand against her stomach. "Do you believe me about the baby too?"

Philip sighs. As he stands there in the darkness, he tries to imagine the possibility—beyond the medical scenarios from the newspapers he mentioned to his mother this morning, since those are clearly not the case. But try as he might, Philip cannot make himself believe in miracles any more than he can make himself believe in God again. He tells Melissa, "I want to believe you. Probably more than you will ever know. But there is something inside me that won't allow myself. I'm sorry."

There really is nothing left to say then except good night. Melissa closes the door and Philip begins maneuvering up the walkway to his brother's car. He stops just once and pretends to be fussing with his cast while staring over at Bill Erwin's house, thinking of those cigarettes in his pocket again. Though he is a long way from figuring out the truth, Philip's initial dislike of the man has turned to suspicion now, bringing him that much closer.

Since he doesn't want to call attention to himself standing there any longer, Philip keeps going until he reaches the Mercedes. Once he is seated in that awkward position and the engine is started, he steps carefully on the gas pedal. As he is pulling away, Philip turns back for one last look at the houses. The curtains are still drawn at Bill Erwin's place, and nothing but the dimmest of lights shines from Melissa's windows. Philip stares toward the third house and notices that glinting once more. This time, he gets a good enough look to see that it is a light, turning on and off. He is wary of slamming on the brakes, though, so he continues moving forward while craning his neck to determine exactly where it is coming from. As far as he can tell, it must be from that house with the plastic over the windows.

Before he makes the mistake of veering off the road, Philip forces himself to look ahead. After he rounds the first sharp turn, he realizes that this stretch of Monk's Hill Road has hooked around in such a way to place him on the other side of the woods near that third house. He pulls the car over. For a long while, Philip sits and stares out the window into all those trees, trying to get a glimpse of that flashing light again. It is not possible to see it from here, though. Briefly, he considers turning back and driving by the front of the houses. But if Bill Erwin had been watching from his window when Philip arrived today, he could very well be watching now. Still, something won't let him leave. He has a suspicious feeling about that man, a worried feeling about his mother's whereabouts as well.

Philip turns off the engine, opens the door and climbs out of the car. Armed with only his crutch and cell phone, he stands perfectly still at the edge of the woods. Breathing in the frigid winter air. Listening. Just on the other side of those trees, he can hear the sound of plastic snapping in the breeze. He figures that the house cannot be very far away. Without wasting another second to debate the matter, Philip steps into the woods. The hardest part is making it over that first mound of snow left behind by the plows. Once he is inside, it is not so terribly deep, and the large wool sock over his toes does the job of keeping his toes warm. Each time Philip begins to slip, he pitches his crutch in the snow and shifts his weight onto it in order to keep his balance. Even though it difficult to see at first beneath the canopy of tangled branches, he soon figures out that if he stares down at the white floor of the woods, the reflection of the moonlight illuminates a makeshift path toward the house.

The closer he gets, the louder the sound of that plastic snapping in the wind. Before long, Philip sees the boxy, black silhouette of the vacant house, rising up at the edge of the woods. Somehow, he manages to make it the whole way without falling. Philip touches his hand to the back wall and pauses there to catch his breath. Finally, he tightens his grip on his crutch and steps around the corner to the side of the building. When the light blinks on and off again, he realizes that it is not coming from this house at all.

It is coming from a window in Bill Erwin's basement.

Philip watches as a single beam of light spills out over the snowy lawn before going dark again. For a good five minutes, he stands in the shadows, watching it go from dark to light to dark again. He glances down at the glowing green face of the cell phone in his hand and has the sudden urge to call the police. But what exactly is he going to tell them? That there is a light blinking in someone's basement? And that he happened to see it while trespassing? Or worse, while driving by in a car he was told not to drive?

Philip does not make the call.

But he does not turn around and leave either.

Even though some part of him is working on the notion that the flickering light is nothing more than the product of faulty wiring or a dying bulb getting ready to blow, he cannot help the overwhelming feeling that there is something more to it than that. And once his suspicion has completely taken hold, Philip steps away from that vacant house and moves as quickly as possible across the lawn before making a final, clumsy dash toward the basement window. Since he is unable to bend one of his legs, Philip leans forward as far as he can and hangs his head down in order to see inside. The light is off now, but he waits. When it comes on a moment later, Philip peers inside. He sees nothing but a bunch of wooden columns, and then everything turns black. Once more, he waits. And when it comes on this time, Philip looks more closely and can tell that it is a flashlight shining across the room.

Behind him, there is a noise.

Philip jerks his head around to look, though he doesn't see anything. There is only the sound of that plastic rustling in the wind. He turns to face the window again just as the light comes on. It sweeps along the wall like those searchlights he used to see some nights over the sky in New York. Philip looks to the right of that table with the tools and glimpses what is unmistakably a woman on the floor holding the flashlight. She turns it off before he can make out anything more. The sight startles Philip so much that he falls backward from that awkward, leaning position. But he does not let go of his cell phone. He sits in the cold snow and brings it in front of his face, making up his mind to dial 9-1-1. His hands are shaking. His fingers feel big and unwieldy against the tiny buttons. He presses 6 instead of 9, then hits Clear and tries again. He hits the 9 correctly, but presses 2 instead of 1. Again, Philip hits Clear.

When the light flashes on in the window again, he flinches and drops the phone into the snow. Philip reaches down to try and find it, then hears a noise behind him again. He tells himself that it is just the plastic rustling in the wind, that he should ignore it and focus on locating the phone. Still, he can't help but look. And when he turns, Philip sees a figure looming in the darkness and coming closer. The light flashes on in the basement window once more. It has an effect like lightning, illuminating everything around him for just a few seconds—long enough for Philip to glimpse the image of Bill Erwin, holding a shovel in his hands and raising it high above his head.

chapter 12

IN THE WEEKS FOLLOWING RONNIE'S DEATH, MELISSA'S PERIOD
stops coming. At first, she tells herself that it is simply the trauma of it all.
She does nothing but lie upstairs in bed, her face covered in bandages, as
she watches the thirty-three-inch wide-screen Toshiba television set that
her parents bought and set up in her room. It is fully loaded with every cable channel she could ever want—MTV, VH1, HBO, Cinemax, Show-
time, Comedy Central, A&E, Bravo, CNN, MSNBC, public access, and
dozens more—a consolation prize, Melissa thinks, that is supposed to
make up for the fact that her boyfriend is dead.

For days on end, she leaves it on the Discovery Channel as show after
show comes and goes, detailing all sorts of unusual facts about animals
and insects and outer space that Melissa never knew before. She learns
that the average spider can weave a web in thirty to sixty minutes. She
learns that centuries ago people believed the appearance of a comet in the
sky was a sign of evil, which foretold plague, famine, and death. She learns
that beavers can hold their breath for up to forty-five minutes. That the
planet Venus spins in the opposite direction of all the other planets in the
solar system. That the longest sustained flight of a chicken on record is

thirteen seconds. That emus and kangaroos cannot walk backward. That birds can see in color, while dogs and cats only see in shades of black and white. That male anglerfish attach themselves to their female counterparts and never let go, since their vascular systems unite and the male becomes entirely dependent on the female's blood for nutrition.

Melissa takes in all this information, though the truth is, she could be watching anything, or nothing at all. The only reason she keeps the TV on is so that her parents won't continually come in the room to check on her and pray together the way they do if she turns it off. Let them bother Stacy instead, she thinks. Her sister was fortunate enough to survive the wreck with nothing more than a broken arm. Even though her face will not be scarred the way the doctors at the hospital said Melissa's will be, even though her boyfriend is alive and well, all she does is complain. While her parents fuss and tend to Stacy's every need, Melissa stares at the television and replays that scene in the storage closet with Ronnie again and again.

He packed condoms for their trip.

Of course, he packed condoms.

But he did not have any with him in the closet, since they were tucked inside his duffel bag in the trunk of the old Mercedes. They'd both had plenty to drink by then, but Melissa refuses to blame what they did on alcohol. If she wasn't going to get the opportunity to go away with Ronnie—to have sex in that canopy bed at the Archer Inn, to wake up in his arms—then she certainly wasn't going to stop what they were doing on that floor all because of a stupid condom. And now she is glad she went through with it, because as it turns out, that was her final chance to be with him.

As it turns out, she might very well be carrying his child.

But as much as Melissa wants and wishes and prays for that to be true—if for no other reason than to keep some part of Ronnie alive—she tells herself that just because her period has not come does not mean she is pregnant. She has been late before. It is probably just the shock of it all. And the chance is highly unlikely, considering they had sex just a single time. That is what she keeps repeating in her mind as one week passes, then another. Finally, on a sweltering summer afternoon, seventeen days after the accident, fourteen days after her period was due, Melissa turns off the television. When her mother walks in the room around one o'clock, holding a tray of gazpacho soup and a soft roll (the only kind of food

Melissa can eat because of the trouble with her missing teeth and sore gums), she says, "Mom, I need you to take me to CVS."

Melissa has her driver's license, but her parents barely let her take the car before the accident, never mind now. Her mother sets the tray on the nightstand and sits on the bed. Around them, there are dozens of cards, several wilted flower arrangements, and a number of Mylar balloons floating by the ceiling with *Get Well Soon* messages on the front—all sent from church parishioners, Principal Hulp, various teachers and people at school. As she waits for a response, Melissa looks at her mother, who keeps her eyes cast downward. Even in such hot weather, she is wearing a knit top and cream-colored pants instead of a T-shirt and shorts like Missy. The bright sunlight streaming in from the window lends a waxy sheen to her smooth skin. In that melodic voice of hers, she says, "Your father and I can go there for you. What is it that you need?"

"I want to get a card to send to Ronnie's family, so I'd rather go myself."

"We'll get the card for you, Missy. You shouldn't have to worry about that now."

She reaches out to stroke her daughter's hair but pulls away when she brushes one of the large bandages on Melissa's face. There is a gauzy white strip above her right eye that stretches over her forehead, another covering her left cheek. Every two days, they go to the doctor's office to have them changed, since it is too complicated to do on their own.

"Mom," Melissa says in the same monotone voice the narrators use on the Discovery Channel to describe the awesome power of a black hole, the great speed of a bobcat, or any number of unthinkable facts about the universe. In Melissa's case, the unthinkable facts are this: "I was cheated out of the funeral, I was cheated out of the wake, I was even cheated out of the memorial service at school, all because I was stuck in the hospital. Everyone else got to pay their last respects to my boyfriend except *me*. So the least you can do is let me get his family one lousy fucking card."

Normally, her mother would scold her for using such language. Normally, she'd threaten her father's wrath. But ever since the accident, her parents act nervous and unsure of themselves in Melissa's presence, as though their daughter has been taken away and they're not certain how to handle this wild, injured one left in her place. Neither of them can bring themselves to look at her for more than a few seconds at a time, never mind yell at her for using the *F* word. Instead of offering up any sort of reprimand, her mother runs her hand over her own stiff yellow hair and looks at one of the wilted flower arrangements. "Fine then," she says. "As soon as you finish your soup, I'll take you to CVS."

When they pull into the crowded parking lot almost an hour later, every space is occupied. Around and around, her mother circles, letting one car after another cut in front of them and steal the next available spot. In the flat, emotionless voice Melissa used back at home, she tells her to pull into the handicap zone.

Her mother grips the steering wheel and brakes. "But we don't have a permit."

Melissa turns to face her in the driver's seat. "Look at me, Mother." She does, but only for a second. Melissa goes on anyway, "I look like the walking dead. I dare a cop to even try and give me a ticket."

After that, Melissa can tell her mother is more nervous around this new daughter of hers than ever before. She pulls in front of the blue sign with the wheelchair symbol, cuts the engine, and asks, "Are you sure you don't want me to go in with you?"

On the way here, Melissa made it clear that she wants to do this alone. Once more, she tells her, "I'm sure. But I need money."

Her mother removes her wallet from her purse in a tentative, uneasy manner, the way she might if she was being robbed. She produces a five-dollar bill and gives it to Melissa.

"I need more than that."

"For a card?"

"Yes. I might get a bunch. One for his brother, one for his father, and one for his mother."

"I think a single card for the entire family will do just fine," she says, but Melissa doesn't retract her hand, so her mother gives her a twenty-dollar bill as well.

Inside the store, Melissa walks slowly up and down the aisles, her flip-flops slapping against her heels as she listens to a dreary, Muzak rendition of a Taylor Dayne song piped in from somewhere in the spongy white ceiling. She passes shelves full of toothpaste, mouthwash, dental floss, shampoos and conditioners, then rounds the corner and heads through the candy section. As she works up the courage to go and pull a pregnancy test from the shelf and throw it in her basket, Melissa thinks of when she came here a few weeks before to buy the red lightbulb for her trip with Ronnie. After they were done in the storage closet, he unscrewed it and Melissa put it back inside her purse. Now she wonders whatever happened to her purse, her dress, and her corsage. She makes a mental note to ask her mother, then rounds the corner and spots a shelf full of Trojans and Ramses not far from the pregnancy tests. Melissa remembers laughing as Ronnie told her about coming here as well to buy a box of condoms — condoms they never used.

I was freaking out, Missy. But I finally had the balls to do it.

As she stands there staring over at the pregnancy tests, the words on the packages seem to shout at her: First Response!, 99% accurate! e.pt.!, Early Detection! Melissa looks around to be sure no one is watching. Other than a line of old ladies over by the pharmacy and a woman with a stroller studying a Children's Tylenol container, there isn't anyone in the immediate vicinity who might see what she is about to do. In two quick movements, Melissa thrusts out her hand, swipes a pink and white box off the shelf, and drops it in her basket. Before going to the register, she gets the idea to pick up a few random items so the pregnancy test will not stand out as much at the counter. She grabs a bag of fish licorice, a copy of the local newspaper, a flimsy pair of $3.99 sunglasses, plus those three cards for Ronnie's family. Even though Melissa plans to pay the Chases a visit sometime soon, she figures she will mail these cards first with a note telling them how sorry she is for their loss.

Their loss.

That's how her parents make her feel anyway. Like this is a terrible tragedy for the Chase family, but a mere inconvenient blip in the grand scheme of Melissa's life. When they come into her room to pray with her, they say things about moving on, putting "this incident" behind her, preparing to take the next step toward her future with God on her side. There have been so many times when Melissa wanted to scream at them to shut up, to tell them that they don't understand how she feels and never will. But she stays silent. She keeps her face as still and motionless as possible, because it hurts to make even the slightest of expressions.

After she selects a card for each of the Chases—one with a purple lilac for Mrs. Chase, another with a burning sunset for Mr. Chase, and a third with a field of red poppies for Philip—Melissa takes a breath and approaches the register. She doesn't know any of the women behind the counter or anybody waiting in line, and for that she is grateful. When it's her turn, a lady with a butterfly barrette in her frizzy black hair rings up the items. She glances at Melissa's face, then promptly looks away. It is exactly what her parents do—exactly what Melissa used to do too whenever she saw a handicapped person, because she thought it was rude to stare. Now she realizes how rude that deliberate looking away is. The woman puts the kit in the bag along with the rest of Melissa's purchases. With her eyes still focused on the counter, she tells her that the total is twenty-four dollars and eighty-seven cents. Melissa shoves the twenty and the five into her hand, grabs the bag, and walks out of the store without waiting for change.

Back in the car, her mother has popped a classical music tape into the stereo and pumped up the air conditioner. The tinkling piano clashes with the Taylor Dayne song still echoing in Melissa's mind. The cold air blowing against her bare legs makes her all the more uncomfortable. Her mother starts the engine and says, "It looks like you got more than a few cards in there."

Melissa shoves the bag against the passenger door in case the pink and white box is visible through the cloudy white plastic. She says nothing.

"You'll be glad to hear that the cops didn't come around to bother me," her mother tells her.

"I didn't think they would," Melissa says and slouches in her seat.

As they pull out of the handicap spot, she stares up at the blue sign with the wheelchair symbol. Her thoughts linger on that woman with the butterfly barrette at the register, the way she looked away from her face— just like her parents. I am a freak, she thinks, sliding her hand into the CVS bag and fishing around for the sunglasses. No matter what anyone says, I will never be the same again.

Once she locates the glasses, Melissa attempts to put them on, but the bandages are so bulky they get in the way. Her mother sees what she is trying to do and says, "Don't worry. Once your wounds heal, your father and I are going to take you to a plastic surgeon like Dr. Patel suggested. He gave us a list of almost a dozen names, and we are going to find the very best one. It is all going to be fine. You'll see."

Again, Melissa says nothing. For weeks, she has been hearing about this magical list of plastic surgeons and all the miracles they are going to perform. But she has seen her face with the bandages off. Even though Dr. Patel did not want her to look, Melissa caught a glimpse of herself in the reflection of a silver towel rack while the bandages were being changed, so she knows full well how impossible it will be to make her look like her old self. Thinking of that reflection now, Melissa rolls down the window and tosses the sunglasses outside. She watches in the side-view mirror as they clank and bounce off the curb before snapping against the pavement.

"What did you do that for?" her mother asks.

"They don't fit," is all she can say. Then she remembers the red lightbulb and asks, "Whatever happened to my purse and my dress and all the rest of my stuff from the prom?"

"I—" Her mother stops speaking a moment. "Why do you want to know?"

"Because it's my stuff, Mother. I want to keep it so I can remember that night."

"Why on earth would you want to remember something so horrible?"

Melissa looks out the passenger window. They are driving along a stretch of road where the tree branches arch overhead. The resulting shade makes it possible to see the faintest of reflections in the glass. Because it is all I have, Melissa thinks as she stares at her bandaged face, remembering how ugly and disfigured she is beneath, Because even if I wanted to love someone else, which I don't, who is going to want me now? No one, that's who. Not like this anyway. To her mother, she simply says, "I just do. That's all."

"Well, we got your dress and shoes back from the hospital and your purse back from the police station. As far as I know, your father put all of it in the garage. But I suggest you leave it there. It will be too painful for you to look at right now."

After that, they ride along with only the sound of the tinkling piano between them. Melissa's reflection is gone, and she stares out the window at the lush, leafy summer woods blowing by. She wonders what her first step will be if the pregnancy test turns out to be positive the way she hopes. She wonders exactly how her parents will react if she has to tell them that she is going to have a baby—Ronnie's baby. Then Melissa thinks of a documentary she watched the other day about a rhino, or maybe an octopus, or a rare species of bird, she cannot recall exactly. Whatever it was, she remembers that the creature sought seclusion before giving birth. Maybe she will do the same, Melissa thinks. Maybe she will move away somewhere and have the baby without telling a soul.

Her mother turns the car onto Church Street. They pass the white clapboard church where Melissa has gone to services every Sunday for as long as she can remember. She thinks of the repetitious cycle of sermons her father has given over the years. There is the one about faith, during which he quotes a passage from the Bible where Jesus shouts up at God from the cross, "Why hast Thou forsaken me?" There is another about miracles, during which he quotes the passage where Jesus turns water into wine. And then there is that one about the importance of praying to Christ and Christ alone in times of need, since he does not believe in praying to saints or to the Virgin Mary the way Catholics do. As Melissa recounts her father's greatest hits in her mind, they drive past the wooden board and stones on the side of the road, which made up the jump Wendy Dugas and those girls were attempting to Rollerblade over only a few weeks before. The sight of it fills Melissa with deep sadness because she remembers how excited and hopeful she had felt about her trip with Ronnie as she watched them from the window.

"Now that you seem to be feeling a little better," her mother says, breaking the silence as she pulls the car into the driveway, "your father and I think it would be a good idea if we took you to a dentist sometime soon as well. You'll want to get your teeth fixed before starting college in the fall."

College in the fall.

Not once since the accident has Melissa thought of Penn, or September, or classes, or schoolbooks, or any of the other details she might be mulling over if things hadn't gone so horribly awry. No matter what the pregnancy test shows, one thing is certain: Melissa cannot—she *will not*—go off to Penn now that Ronnie won't be going with her. How can she when every single day will be a reminder of the life they planned?

If you're on dish duty, I'll help you scrub. . . .

"Did you hear what I said?" her mother asks as the car comes to a stop.

Melissa stares at the closed garage door and wonders about her dress and purse inside, that red lightbulb, which must be shattered into hundreds of tiny shards. "I heard," she says.

"And?"

"And what?"

Her mother turns off the engine and lets out a long breath. "And—I don't know. When would you like us to make the appointment?"

Melissa looks away from the garage door at her mother—her poor hapless mother who has never been good at handling small tragedies, like when the toaster catches on fire or when the sump pump in the basement breaks and the downstairs floods. She is far better at tackling the minor problems life serves up, like a tear in a sweater that needs sewing, or a stuck zipper on a winter coat that needs fixing. The way she treats Melissa is just like one of those minor problems, as though her daughter can be easily fixed—sewn up, zipped up, made as good as new. Melissa opens her mouth and tells her, "Make the appointment for whenever you want. I really don't care."

"What do you mean, you don't care? These are your teeth we're talking about. Your smile."

Melissa pushes open the car door and steps out into the hot summer air. She hears some sort of banging sound, like a faint series of gunshots or perhaps a muffler backfiring far off in the distance. "Mom," she says, ignoring the sound and looking into the car. "Even if I had something to smile about, which I obviously do not, it hurts to move my face. Do you understand that? It hurts to smile or frown or smirk or even talk to you right now. So like I said, I don't care when you make the appointment. I don't care."

With that, Melissa slams the door, storms into the house, and marches up the stairs, clenching that CVS bag in her hands the whole way. When she passes her sister's room, Stacy is inside, stretched out on her bed, yammering away on the telephone. Ever since the accident, all phone restrictions have been lifted. Their parents did not make any sort of official decree, but Stacy is on it at all hours, and neither of them has told her to get off the way they normally would.

"Chaz called me twice from the base already," Melissa hears her say to the person on the other end of the line. (Probably Seneca Lawson, she guesses, or another one of Stacy's fellow "technical virgins.") "I think he is still in shock. In a way it's a blessing that he had to leave so soon afterward." She pauses. "I need to call Rutgers about registering for my fall classes, but I haven't felt up to it yet. Hold on a sec—" Stacy puts her hand to the receiver and calls out, "Hey, Miss."

Without uttering a word in response, Melissa keeps going down the hall. They have not spoken since the accident, and she isn't about to start now. Not only did Stacy ruin a big part of that last night with Ronnie, but while Missy was stuck in intensive care for more than a week, Stacy and Chaz were released from the hospital after only three days.

They went to the memorial service.

They went to the wake.

They went to the funeral.

They got to say good-bye.

On top of everything else her sister has done, those facts make Melissa hate her all the more. She walks into the bathroom and shuts the door. After double-checking to be sure it's locked, Melissa leans against the wall and says a prayer to God that the test will turn out the way she hopes. In the mirror of the medicine cabinet, she catches another glimpse of her face. The same thoughts that have been haunting her for weeks wash over her once more: Who is going to want me now? Who is ever going to hold me, or kiss me, or love me again? No one, that's who. Not like this anyway. It is all the more reason why Melissa wants to be carrying Ronnie's baby—not just to keep some part of him alive, but also to keep some part of her old self alive as well. She sees this as her last chance at the life she might have lived. Finally, she pulls the e.p.t. kit from the bag, trying her best to keep quiet despite the crinkling plastic. She tears open the box and reads the instructions:

After removing the plastic top, hold the tip in the urine flow for a minimum of five seconds. The test must be kept on a flat surface while developing. Wait three minutes for a result. If a single pink line appears in the windows you are not pregnant. If two pink lines appear in the windows you are pregnant. . . .

Melissa pulls the wand from the foil packet, which looks vaguely like a toothbrush. She tugs down her shorts and sits on the toilet, holding the tip between her legs for five seconds. When she is finished, she sets it on the edge of the vanity. Since she is not wearing a watch, Melissa stares at the tiny windows and silently counts, One thousand one, one thousand two, one thousand three. . . . When she gets to one thousand fifty, there is a knock at the door. Melissa sucks in a nervous breath and holds it.

"Missy," her father says in his Sunday sermon drawl. "Are you okay in there?"

"I'm fine."

After his footsteps recede down the hall, she looks at the windows again. There are no pink lines yet, and now she has lost count. For what seems like an eternity, she waits, forcing herself to look away in order to make the time go faster. Melissa stares up at the ceiling, then back at the windows. She stares down at the white linoleum floor, then back at the windows. She even stares in the mirror again, holding her gaze the way no one else will, then back at the windows.

Still, no lines.

Finally, she picks up the instructions and searches the fine print for some scrap of information about what to do if nothing appears at all. The only thing she finds is an explanation of something called human chorionic gonadotropin, which goes on forever. When Melissa can't stand reading anymore, she tosses the paper on the floor and stares at the windows one last time. And that's when she sees it: a single pink line before her eyes.

I am not pregnant, she thinks. I am not pregnant after all.

Even though it hurts to cry, Melissa's face crumples and the tears begins. She puts a finger to her mouth to keep her lip from quivering as she wonders if the test could be wrong. It even says right there on the box that these things are only 99 percent accurate. Doesn't that mean there is a 1 percent chance? And if she isn't pregnant, then why has her period not come? Melissa thinks again of that sermon her father used to give about the importance of praying to Jesus Christ and Jesus Christ alone. But where has that ever gotten her? For the first time in her life, she defies that stupid rule and prays to whomever she damn well pleases.

Melissa prays to Ronnie.

"I love you," she whispers. "I love you, and if you can hear me, I want to have your baby."

There is so much more Melissa wants to say to him, but she realizes that it is best not to say it in this house where her father, her mother, or her sister might hear. Melissa gathers up the contents of the kit as well as the plastic bag and the instructions from the floor. She takes one last look around to be sure she has left nothing behind before stepping out of the bathroom. Down the hall, she hears Stacy whining about her broken arm. Melissa tucks the CVS bag beneath her T-shirt then rushes past her room and down the stairs.

"Missy," her mother calls from the living room. "Where are you going?"

The screen door slaps shut behind Melissa and she hurries across the yard. Her mother comes to the front porch and calls out to her again, but she doesn't follow any farther. At the corner, near Wendy Dugas's dismantled jump, Melissa stops and takes off her flip-flops so she can move more quickly. The pavement feels hot and gritty against her bare feet, a feeling that reminds her of childhood as she continues on past the church. She takes a left onto Runnymede Avenue, then a right onto Hashen Street, heading in the direction of the cemetery on Faldoma Road. Melissa has been there before, but not since Ronnie was laid to rest. Years ago, the place was an airfield, and on summer days like this one, her parents sometimes took Melissa and her sister to watch the biplanes do loop-de-loops and the wing walkers perform midair stunts. After too many fiery crashes, though, the place was shut down. It went unused for ages—the grass grew tall, the metal hangar rusted and collapsed—until last summer, when it was announced that the field would be turned into a cemetery.

On her way there, Melissa cuts through the town park, which is more crowded than usual. People are laying blankets all around as though they are getting ready for a game. She walks by a young mother sitting on a bench holding a book in front of her child's face. "Blue," she says. "This is the color blue. Can you say it? Blue. Blue. Blue." The child says nothing so the mother turns the page. "Red. This is the color red. Can you say it? Red. Red. Red." Melissa keeps going past the tennis courts, where two women dressed in white are hitting the ball back and forth over the sagging net, grunting each time they swing and make contact. When one of them finally misses, the other lets out a throaty heckle and shouts, "Yes! I got you! I finally got you! It's about time I got you!"

In the distance, Melissa hears the same banging sound as earlier. She ignores it and continues walking. In bare feet still, she cuts back onto the road and heads through another series of streets. Nearly forty minutes later, she reaches the entrance to the cemetery. Sweaty and breathless,

Melissa stops at the mouth of the unpaved driveway, looking over the field before entering. Since her father drags the family to every single funeral of an old person from church who has no loved ones alive to attend, Melissa has been to her fair share of cemeteries. But this place feels different from the others. Those are usually cluttered with headstones, as well as the occasional statue of a lamb or angel, its eyes and mouths worn away from years of rain and snow. Here, there are no statues at all—only a small cluster of a half-dozen or so stones in the far end of the field where the hangar used to be, since not many people have been buried here yet. There are no fancy wrought-iron gates either—just the old chain-link fence that used to be here way back when she came to see those air shows. Most of the field is still covered by tall grass, burned brown by the sun so that it resembles a wheat field.

Melissa spots a single stone with a small heap of flowers in front. She figures it must be Ronnie's and begins walking up the dirt road and across the grass, talking to him once again. Melissa tells him how lonely she is without him. She tells him how desperately she wants the test to be wrong. She tells him that she is not going to go to Penn now that he is gone. She tells him how awful her parents and Stacy have been acting toward her. And when she gets to the smooth gray stone engraved with his full name—RONALD CHARLES CHASE—along with the dates that bookend his life—MARCH 17, 1981 to JUNE 18, 1999—Melissa grows silent. She does not want to cry anymore today, so she fights back her tears and sits beside those flowers, which are wilting like the ones in her bedroom.

As the hot summer sun beats down upon her, Melissa stares at those letters and numbers on the stone, then up at the blue sky. A memory comes back to her then, not of Ronnie, but of herself as a little girl. She remembers looking up at a wing walker and feeling so afraid that he might fall that she let out a shriek and buried her face in her father's side. She remembers too that her father picked her up in his arms and told her that everything would be okay. Staring up at that same sky above her now, Melissa wishes that her father, or someone else, anyone else, could offer her that kind of comfort today.

Missy pulls the pregnancy kit from the CVS bag again, hoping that by some miracle there will be two lines in the windows. But there is still just one. Even if she is not going to have Ronnie's baby, Melissa makes the decision right then and there that she is still going to move out of her parents' house. She wants to find a secluded place, like whatever animal she saw in that documentary, so she can be alone in her grief. With this in mind, she removes the newspaper from the bag and turns to the Classifieds. Melissa scans the listings, which include all sorts of large, expensive homes that she cannot afford. Then she spots an ad at the very bottom of a column:

Partially Renovated Cottage
One Bedroom with Kitchenette
Rent: $600 per month plus utilities
Available: August 1
Contact: Gail or Bill Erwin at . . .

Melissa reads and rereads those words, wondering how she can get her hands on that kind of money, which is so much less than the others, but still a lot for her. That's when she hears a sound in the distance. It is not the sharp, sudden banging she heard earlier, but a low rumbling that causes her to lift her head. A silver Range Rover is coming up the drive, raising a cloud of dust as it approaches. Melissa stretches her neck forward and sees that it's Ronnie's father behind the wheel. Embarrassed to be plopped down so casually beside his son's grave, she closes the newspaper and stuffs it back inside the CVS bag along with the pregnancy kit, the fish licorice, and the cards. She stands and lifts her hand to wave. Dr. Chase waves back, and she can tell by the look on his face that he is surprised to see her.

After he comes to a stop and steps outside, Melissa notices how much he resembles Ronnie—something she never realized before. Certainly, his graying hair, the wrinkles around his eyes behind his silver, wire-rimmed glasses, and his slight belly pushing against his blue Polo shirt are not the same. But there is a similarity to his darker complexion, his tall frame set off by bulky shoulders. He is wearing khaki shorts and loafers without socks. His legs are long, lean, and hairy, just like Ronnie's. There is a plastic ID card strung around his neck that Melissa remembers all the doctors and nurses wearing at the hospital. When he walks to the grave,

Dr. Chase looks Melissa in the eye and does not look away. He is the first person—the very first person—to hold her gaze since the accident, and it leaves her feeling unsettled. "How are you?" he asks.

"I'm okay," Melissa says in the smallest of voices. Her mind flashes on another long-ago memory of her parents snapping a picture of her and Stacy beside the wing walker after he came down from the sky. Melissa can still remember how shy she felt around that man, not unlike the way she feels now. "I used to come here when I was little," she says out loud without planning to. "I mean, with my family, to see those old daredevil shows."

He looks around the field, and she can tell that he is seeing the place as it used to be, rather than what it is now, then turns to face Melissa again. "So did we. The stunts were too scary for Philip. He used to wait in the car with my wife. But Ronnie loved them."

"I bet he did," Melissa says, then stops and stares down at the mound of dying flowers between them, at Ronnie's name and those dates etched into the stone. She imagines that years from now, his name will be worn away like the features on those statues in the other cemeteries she's been to.

"We were going to bury him at St. John's," Ronnie's father says, as though he knows what she is thinking. "But this cemetery is so much closer to our house. It makes it easier to come by every day on my way home from the hospital."

Melissa looks up at him again and their eyes meet. He does not look away. "I like this place because it doesn't feel like a cemetery," she tells him. And then, once more, she speaks without planning to. "I lied before."

"What do you mean? About what?"

"When you asked how I am, and I told you that I'm okay. The truth is, I'm not. Actually, I'm terrible."

Dr. Chase puts his hands deep into the pockets of his khaki shorts. He runs the tip of his brown leather shoe along the edge of the grass where it meets the flowers. "Me too. We're all pretty terrible right now." He takes a breath and tells her, "But this must be particularly hard for you. You're so young, and it is all so unexpected. This is supposed to be a happy time in your life."

For weeks, Melissa has been waiting for her parents to acknowledge that what's happened is difficult for her—that it's more than a matter of fixing her face and teeth so she can go off to college and put "this incident" behind her. But they have yet to acknowledge anything of the sort. Hearing Ronnie's father, of all people, speak those words is enough to make Melissa want to weep. She holds back her tears and opens her mouth to thank him for saying what he just did. When she realizes how incredibly ugly her missing teeth must look, she presses her lips together and stays quiet.

Who will ever want me now? The question comes and goes along with the same answer, *No one, that's who. Not like this anyway.*

Somewhere in the distance, Melissa hears the banging sound she's been hearing all day. She holds the CVS bag close to her body and finds a way to speak without moving her mouth very much at all. "I'm sorry I missed the funeral. I was stuck in the hospital so I couldn't go."

"I know," he tells her, absently tugging on the ID that hangs from his neck. His picture on the front is only slightly bigger than a postage stamp, but Melissa can see that in it, he is wearing one of those green hospital shirts doctors always wear. There is a grim, mug-shot expression on his face. "I meant to come by after that first night. But I just—I just couldn't."

"That's okay," Melissa says. "What was it like? The funeral, I mean."

He lets out a sigh and pushes his hands back inside the pockets of his shorts. "To tell you the truth, Melissa, it was all a big blur. My son read a poem. Apparently he likes to write poetry. Go figure." He shrugs. "I never knew that before. Anyway, other than that, it was just an endless stream of cards and flowers, relatives and friends."

"I bought you a card too." As though she needs to prove it, Melissa finds the card inside the bag and hands it to him. "I haven't filled it out yet, so I don't know why I am even showing you now. I guess—I guess I just want you and your family to know that I have been thinking of all of you too. Even though I couldn't be there."

Dr. Chase looks at the burning sunset on the front. He opens it and stares at the blank white space inside. He doesn't seem to know what to do next, so Melissa takes the card back from him and returns it to the bag. "I'll still write something in it and mail it to you. I got one for Philip and your wife as well."

He tells her that's very kind of her, then asks, "Was Ronnie happy that night? He seemed it when you all stopped by the house. But you would know better than me. Was he *really* happy?"

So many moments from that evening flash through Melissa's mind. She thinks of Stacy dragging her down the hall to the storage closet. She thinks of Ronnie coming to find her. She thinks of him pulling out the handkerchief with the initials *RC* on it—his father's handkerchief. She thinks of them popping their heads out of the sunroof and laughing, howling into the night. She thinks of Ronnie kissing her and saying that he loved her no matter what. That is the last thing she remembers. "Yes," she answers. "He was happy. We both were."

"Well, it makes me feel a little better knowing that. For whatever it's worth."

"Dr. Chase—"

"Richard. You can call me Richard."

Melissa begins again. Even though it feels awkward calling him by his first name, she says, "Richard. Can I tell you something?"

"Of course."

She doesn't know why she is about to confess what she's been going through. Maybe it's because she has no one else to talk to. Maybe it's because Dr. Chase, or Richard as he asked to be called, is the only person who has shown any sign of understanding or caring about the way she feels. "You're a doctor," she says in a hesitant voice. "I know it's strange for me to be talking to you about this, since you're Ronnie's father. But, well, I guess there is no other way to say this than to just say it. My period has not come. I am two weeks late today. I've been late before but hardly ever. I thought that maybe I was pregnant so I took an e.p.t. test." Here she pauses to reach in the bag and pull out that plastic wand with the single pink stripe in the tiny windows. "It says that I am not. But—"

Before Melissa can say anything more, Richard begins to stutter. "I—" He stops and looks at the test in her hands. "Did you—" Again, he stops. This time he takes one hand from his pocket and strokes his chin. "Were you and Ronnie having unprotected sex?"

Melissa nods. "Just once. On the night he died."

He lifts his gaze from the test to look at her face. Behind his glasses, she notices, his eyes are almost the same blue as Ronnie's, only slightly faded. "You poor girl," he says.

"Could it be wrong?"

"It's doubtful, Melissa. Those tests are highly accurate, as long as you followed the instructions properly."

"I did," Melissa says, relinquishing any last bit of hope.

"I know you say you're rarely late. But you've just gone through quite an ordeal. I'm sure that when your body regulates itself again, you'll get your period. Who is your doctor?"

"Dr. Patel."

"Have you mentioned this to him?"

"No."

"How about your parents?"

Melissa lets out a sarcastic laugh, thinking of the way they might handle an announcement of that sort. Just then, the mix of disappointment, sadness, frustration, anger, and so many other emotions rises up in her, catching her off guard and turning the laughter into tears. From the other side of those wilted flowers, Ronnie's father says the same words her own father said to her so many years ago in this very field, "It's okay. Everything will be okay."

The message does nothing to comfort her the way it did when she was a child. In fact, the words sound so hollow and hopeless that she finds herself crying harder. Richard steps around the pile of flowers and takes her in his arms. She buries her ruined face in his shoulder—a shoulder that feels different from Ronnie's but similar, a similarity that only brings more tears.

"It's okay to cry," he whispers, stroking her hair. "I know how much you cared for him. I know how hard this must be. In time, things will get better. You'll see."

That's when the first of those questions come pouring out of her. "Even if I wanted to love someone else, which I don't, who is ever going to want me now?"

"Don't talk that way."

"But it's true," she says, her voice muffled against his T-shirt. "No one is ever going to hold me or look at me again."

Richard does not say anything for a long while after that, because he must realize there is no arguing against her on this matter. Instead, he keeps hugging her and stroking her hair. It's then, as they stand so close together beside Ronnie's grave, that something shifts inside Melissa. She has the image of her heartbeat, the way it appeared for so many days on that monitor at the hospital as a steady succession of peaks and dips. Now she imagines that neon green line going flat on the screen for a long, long moment. And then there is a sudden blip again. Then another. And another. Melissa allows herself to take comfort in the arms of Ronnie's father. No, it is not the kind of heated, sexual feeling she had with Ronnie. It is not like that at all. What Melissa feels is warmth and safety, a solace no one else has offered her in the days since the accident. The feeling is enough to bring her crying to an end. Finally, Richard lets go and takes a step backward. He looks down at his watch and says that it's almost dinnertime and he really should get going. "How did you get here?" he asks.

"I walked."

"Well, let me give you a ride home. Where do you live?"

Since Melissa feels too tired to go all that way on foot again, and since she wants to be near him just a little longer, she accepts the offer and tells him that she lives over on Church Street, not far from the library. They both say their silent good-byes to Ronnie then climb into the Range Rover. With its black leather seats and complicated dashboard, Melissa feels out of place inside. The warmth she experienced in his arms is fading fast, and she wants him to hold her again, if only for a few minutes more, before leaving this place. Of course, she cannot bring herself to ask for that, so Melissa slouches in her seat and stares out the window the way she did when her mother was driving earlier today. As they roll out of the long dirt driveway, raising another cloud of dust, she hears that banging sound in the distance and finally asks what it is.

"Fireworks," Richard tells her. "Even though the fire department is having their usual show tonight at the park, people insist on messing around with their own at home. Someone always gets hurt. It happens every Fourth of July."

As Richard goes on about the dangers of roman candles and M-80s, Melissa asks herself how she could have lost track of the holiday in the midst of counting the days since her period was due. The realization leaves her with an odd sort of feeling, as though the world has left her behind, as though everyone and everything has gone on without her.

She is not sure she wants to catch up.

After the fireworks discussion, Richard stays quiet as they make their way across town. Melissa wonders if he feels the least bit awkward about their long hug beside Ronnie's grave. She wonders too if he felt the same sort of solace and comfort that she did. Since she cannot think of the right way to ask him she stays quiet. The closer they get to her house, the more she dreads going home. The last thing she wants right now is to get back in her bed, to turn on the Discovery Channel, to be served another bland meal on a tray, to listen to Stacy whine on the telephone down the hall, to recite those same prayers with her mother and father, day in and day out. That's when Melissa recalls that ad in the newspaper for the cottage. She tries to come up with some sort of plan as to how she can get that kind of money and move away. By the time they reach Church Street, she has yet to work out a solution—she has yet to consider asking Richard.

"You can let me off at the corner," Melissa tells him. "Otherwise, my parents will want to know why we're together. And I can't deal with their questions right now."

Richard signals and pulls over, coming to a stop directly in front of the church. "I don't understand," he says. "Why would your parents mind if you were with me?"

Melissa shrugs and glances at that grim photo of him hanging from his neck, then she looks up at his face, which appears so much kinder in real life. He is staring into her eyes again. "I don't know. But trust me, they would."

He mulls that over, then lets it go. From a compartment between the seats, he pulls out a business card and gives it to her. "Well, if you ever need anything, don't hesitate to call. You have our home number. But the number of my service and my cell are on there as well."

Melissa takes the card from him and glances down at the Bryn Mawr Hospital logo with its ivy-covered torch and the clutter of phone numbers beneath. "Thank you," she says, then asks, "so you go to the cemetery every day on your way home?"

"Every day," Richard tells her.

"Maybe I'll see you there again."

"Maybe," he says. "That would be nice."

Before opening the door, Melissa pauses in case he is going to hug her again. She craves that last bit of warmth, a small something she can carry with her back inside her house. It does not happen, though, so she pulls on the handle and steps outside.

"Good-bye, Richard," she says, practicing the way it feels to call him by his first name.

"Good-bye, Melissa."

She stands there in front of the church as his Range Rover disappears around the corner onto Hashen Street. After he is gone, Missy turns toward home, holding his card tight in her hand, being extra careful not to bend it. When she reaches the giant evergreen at the edge of the front yard, which smells incongruously like Christmas, Melissa stops and looks toward the garage. She remembers what her mother said about her belongings being inside, then decides to take a detour. As quietly as she can, Melissa lifts the door, figuring she should retrieve her things before her parents throw them away. It is dark enough inside that she has to turn on the light in order to see. Just as she suspected, everything is in a heap next to the garbage cans, all of it in clear plastic bags of varying sizes. Behind the plastic, Melissa sees her blood-splattered dress, sliced unevenly up the back, since the doctors had to cut her out of it. She sees her shoes in another bag, her purse in another, even her corsage.

Melissa gathers up those bags, the dress draped across her arms, the rest balanced on top, then carries them out of the garage and inside the house. At the bottom of the stairs, she pauses to eavesdrop on her family eating dinner in the kitchen. It is well after five now, and the din of her sister and mother conversing as their forks clank against their plates gives Melissa the same odd feeling that the world has gone on without her. She thinks of Venus spinning backward while all the other planets in the solar system move forward. Melissa doesn't hear her father's voice, so she figures that he must not be with them. As a result, the conversation is more relaxed, the way it always is when he is not around, since their mother never stands up to him. Melissa listens as Stacy talks about how much she misses Chaz. Then she hears her usual list of complaints about how itchy her arm is beneath her cast. Then they talk about Stacy's plans to call Rutgers in the morning and deal with her fall class schedule. Finally, their mother interrupts to say something that pertains to Melissa.

"There is an old woman from church who is going into a nursing home. She has a cat that needs a new home. Your father and I thought we'd give it to Missy. She has always wanted one. And even though she is going off to college in the fall too, I figure we can take care of it for her and she can see it when she comes home."

"Mom," Stacy says. "I think Melissa would rather have a kitten than some old lady's recycled fleabag cat."

"It is not a fleabag cat, Stacy. I've seen Mumu, and she's precious."

"Hold on a second. What's the thing's name?"

"The *thing* is a cat," her mother says. "And its name is Mumu."

Stacy snorts. "What kind of a stupid name is that?"

"Don't be so rude. Besides, Melissa can change its name if she wants to."

"Mom. How can you just change its name? The thing is probably used to being called Mumu. I mean, what if people decided to stop calling you Margaret?"

"Well, that's ridiculous. It's clearly not the same."

"Okay, Nancy."

"Nancy?"

"Yeah," Stacy says. "I just changed your name. I hope you don't mind."

With that, Melissa stops listening and steps gently up the stairs. She should feel touched that her parents have finally agreed to get her a pet, but it does nothing to soften her feelings toward them. Inside her bedroom, she lays her dress and all the things from her prom on the floor beside her bed, then pushes them into the darkness beneath. She is too tired to look at that shattered red lightbulb and the rest of the keepsakes from that night, but tomorrow she will. When she stands, Melissa notices a present on her pillow, wrapped in paper that's covered with drawings of bumblebees. She picks it up and tears off the paper. Beneath all those smiling bees, she finds a black leather diary with her name emblazoned in gold on the cover. Melissa opens the book and reads the inscription: *For*

my sister and best friend, Although it doesn't seem like it now, you will start
over, and you will be happy again one day. I promise. Love, Stacy.

Melissa puts the diary on her nightstand along with Richard's card.
Her sister is right. She will start over again. But not in the way anyone expects. She digs the newspaper out of the CVS bag and dials the number in
the ad.

In the middle of the second ring, a woman answers. "Hello."

"Hi," Melissa says, talking softly so no one downstairs will hear. "Is Mr.
or Mrs. Erwin at home?"

"This is Gail Erwin," the woman says in a cheery voice.

"My name is Melissa. I'm calling about the cottage that's for rent beginning in August. If it's still available, I was wondering if I could come
see it."

"It's still available," Gail tells her. "We are just finishing up some small
renovations on the place. But of course you can come by. When would be
good for you?"

"How about tomorrow?"

"Tomorrow is fine. My husband and I will be here all day."

They agree to meet around noon, and Melissa hangs up the telephone.
Even though she has yet to work out how she will get the money, she feels
hopeful about the prospect of leaving home. Melissa goes to the window
and sits on the cushioned seat, staring out at the street the way she did so
many nights before when she was waiting for that white limousine to
round the corner. This time, she whispers a prayer to Ronnie, asking him
to help her find a way to get the cash she needs. Melissa keeps on talking
to him until she feels so drained from her first day out of bed in weeks that
she stretches out on the window seat and drifts off to sleep.

It is not until hours later that she wakes to the sound of the fire department's fireworks exploding in the dark summer sky over Radnor. Melissa
opens her eyes, and the first thing she sees is a burst of purple and green
shimmering above the treetops. It's then that the idea finally comes to her,
and it is as simple as this: after visiting the Erwins' cottage tomorrow, she
will go to the cemetery and wait for Ronnie's father to arrive. Maybe not
right away, but eventually, she will ask him for the money. If she can work
up the nerve, she will ask him to hold her again too. Once that is settled in

her mind, Melissa lies back on the pillows as a spray of gold rises up in the sky outside the window, then rains down behind the silhouette of trees, just like the comets she learned about in that documentary on TV, the ones people used to believe were a sign of plague, famine, and death.

A sign of all sorts of horrible things to come.

chapter 13

BY THE TIME CHARLENE REALIZES THAT SHE FORGOT TO CALL IN-
formation, she has already pulled out of the library parking lot and into traffic. She reaches over to the passenger seat and picks up her cell phone again. It's too difficult to dial and drive, though, so she turns on the emergency flashers and comes to a sudden stop by the side of the road. The driver of a Lexus, which happens to be the same make and color as her own, lays on the horn and flips her off while zipping past, sending a spray of icy slush splattering against her window. For an instant, a familiar rage rises up inside of Charlene. She has the urge to floor the gas pedal, chase down the car, and give the driver a piece of her mind—maybe even take out a few windows with the help of the crowbar in her trunk while she's at it. But then something strange happens: Charlene thinks of Pilia's flattened chest beneath her baby blue ski parka, and the thought is enough to make her anger shrivel up and vanish.

She releases a breath, punches in 4-1-1, and asks for the address of Melissa Moody in Radnor, Pennsylvania. As it turns out, there is just one listing, under Joseph and Margaret on Church Street. Charlene remembers seeing her parents' names on some of the legal documents surrounding the lawsuit against the limousine company. Now that she thinks about it, she also remembers that Melissa's father is a minister at the Lutheran church, so the address makes sense. From here, all she has to do is take a few lefts, then a right onto Runnymede and another left, before she is driving slowly down Church Street, squinting at the numbers on the houses.

Once she spots their small white cape with two dormer windows jutting out from the roof and a tall evergreen looming on the corner of the snow-covered lawn, she pulls into the driveway and cuts the engine. Melissa's battered blue Corolla is nowhere in sight, but Charlene tells herself that it could be parked inside the garage—either that, or the girl doesn't live here anymore. Since there is only one way to find out, she steps outside and heads up the shoveled walkway. The instant Charlene presses her thumb against the doorbell, and a staccato chiming comes from inside the house, her cell phone rings in the pocket of her wool cloak. It must be Philip returning her call, since no one ever uses this line to contact her. But just as Charlene pulls out the phone to answer it, the door swings open.

A balding man stares out at her, dressed in a burgundy cardigan and neatly pressed corduroys. He has a pale complexion, a delicate nose, and full lips—traits that once made Melissa so pretty but give him a slightly sinister look. Judging from the resemblance, Charlene assumes this is Melissa's father. "Hello," he says.

Her phone releases another shrill ring and she presses a bunch of different buttons, hoping to make the call go to voice mail, so as not to be rude. Whatever she does works because the sound stops. "Sorry about that. You know how cell phones are. Always ringing at the wrong moment."

He smiles a placid, artificial smile. "Actually I don't have one. So I wouldn't know."

The way his arid voice dips at the end of each word hints at a faded southern accent. Charlene tries to picture him standing at an altar giving a sermon, but all she comes up with is the image of him checking into a run-down motel with a prostitute, like Jimmy Swaggart and the rest of those hypocrites she cannot stand. "I don't either," she says, trying to focus on the conversation. "I mean, obviously, I have a cell phone. But I don't usually know how they are, since I only use mine for emergencies."

He takes a moment to make sense of what she just said. "Do you mean that call was an emergency?"

"No—" Charlene stops. How she had managed to get off to such an awkward start she is not sure, but she does her best to smooth things out. "It was just my son calling. There's no emergency. He's fine. Or almost fine anyway. What I mean is that I'll call him back later."

He seems to have had enough of this cell phone discussion too, because he asks, "So what can I do for you?"

"I'm wondering if Melissa is at home." It occurs to Charlene then that she has yet to introduce herself. "Forgive me," she says and extends her hand. "I'm Charlene Chase. Ronnie Chase's mother. My son was Melissa's—"

"I know who you are," he says, cutting her off as the smile fades from his face.

Charlene keeps her hand extended, though he does not reach out to shake it. Finally, she gives up and puts her hand back in the pocket of her wool cloak, nervously fiddling with the buttons on her phone. "I take it you're Mr. Moody, or rather, Reverend Moody."

"Joseph," is all he says.

If he is trying to make her feel unwelcome, it's working. Charlene opens her mouth to inquire about Melissa when she hears footsteps from somewhere inside the house. A moment later, a woman appears in the doorway with the same smooth skin and pale complexion. Missy's mother, Charlene figures. She is wearing a flowery apron and has the kind of tall slender build and neat yellow hair that make her look like a housewife in one of those commercials for a kitchen floor cleaner. Charlene can just see her mopping away, while her husband is climbing into bed with a prostitute. "Who is it?" she asks Joseph as she looks out at Charlene.

"It's Richard Chase's wife."

"Ex-wife," Charlene blurts out then considers how odd it is that he described her in relation to Richard instead of Ronnie. "Am I missing something here?"

"You're not missing anything," Joseph tells her.

"Well, then." Charlene clears her throat. "Is your daughter at home?"

"Melissa no longer lives here. You of all people should know that."

"Me of all people?" Charlene says.

And then, much to her dismay, he tells her good-bye and begins to close the door. At the last second, Margaret speaks up. "Joseph, wait." She pulls open the door, takes a nervous breath, and asks why Charlene wants to see Melissa after all this time.

Charlene is unsure where to begin. She starts by saying, "Your daughter came by my house late last night." She lets out a sigh. "To be honest, I didn't treat her very kindly. And, well, something happened just a little while ago that made me realize it was wrong of me. I decided I should talk to her. That I should hear her side of the story about her baby—"

"Baby," they both say, their voices overlapping so it creates a sound like *Bababyby*.

"Baby," Charlene says.

No one says anything after that. All three of them stand there— Melissa's parents with their hands on the door, Charlene still fiddling with the buttons on the phone in her pocket. It's clear to her that they have not spoken to their daughter in quite some time, and since Charlene does not want to be the one to fill them in on the developments in Melissa's life, she says, "Listen, I don't want to start trouble. So if you wouldn't mind telling me where she lives, I'll be on my way."

"Is she okay?" Melissa's mother asks. "Tell me that. Is she okay?"

Charlene shrugs. "I really don't know."

"But I don't understand," Margaret says, stumbling over her words as she tries to come up with which question to ask next. "I— What— Whose baby is it? And why would she come to see you?"

"I don't know that either." It is the most honest answer Charlene can offer without going into the details Missy gave them the night before.

"Well, I think we've heard enough," Joseph says and begins to close the door again.

This time, when Margaret stops him, she does so with more force than before. "But I haven't heard enough." She is not yelling exactly, but her voice is taut and unyielding. She grabs his hand and repeats herself. "I haven't heard enough, Joe. She is still our daughter and I want to know whatever there is to know about her."

Charlene gets the feeling that if it weren't for her presence, he might burst into a tirade or even strike. As it is, he just stares at his wife a long moment, his jaw clenched, his upper lip curled in until finally, he shakes off her hand and says, "Fine, then. Do whatever you want."

When he storms off into the house, Margaret looks at Charlene and asks if she'd like to come inside. In the background, Charlene sees Joseph climbing the stairs to the second floor. She cannot help but feel that she is indeed missing something here, and for that reason, she steps into the house. Something about the place—the small size perhaps, or the way everything is so neatly arranged—reminds her of a doll's house. The wooden floors are perfectly polished, and just about every surface, from the backs of chairs to the tops of tables, is draped with a white doily. What Charlene finds most unusual is the utter silence. Even when her house is quiet, there is always the sound of that faulty antique clock ticking in the family room, or the ice maker in the freezer occasionally clunking away. Even the quiet at the library this afternoon had been punctuated by the clicking of keyboards and the murmur of hushed voices. But here it is so soundless that every inhalation, every exhalation, every footstep Charlene takes as she follows Margaret into the pale green living room feels amplified.

"Can I take your coat?" Margaret asks in a voice so perfectly polite it sends the signal that they are going to take this visit from the top and act more civilly this time around.

Charlene does not plan on staying long so she tells her no thanks. But when Margaret offers her a drink, she is still so parched from all the bread she gorged on earlier at the library that Charlene accepts.

"What would you like? We have water, grape juice, or milk."

Any of those choices would be fine, Charlene thinks, if I were a first-grader. She wonders if she is going to offer her animal crackers too. "Do you have any Diet Coke?"

Margaret presses her hands flat against her flowery apron. "Sorry. But we don't keep carbonated beverages in the house."

That's pretty much the *only* kind of beverage Charlene keeps in her house. "I'll just have water. Thanks."

When Margaret goes to the kitchen, the first thing Charlene does is turn and stare at the white brick fireplace, which she remembers seeing in the background of the snapshots taped to Missy's dashboard. She steps over to the mantel and stares at the row of framed pictures—all of Melissa in a wedding dress. She is smiling and happy. What's more, she does not have a single scar on her face. Charlene picks up one of the photos and examines it more closely, trying to figure out when it could have been taken and who the red-haired young man is standing beside her.

"That's our other daughter, Stacy," Margaret says when she returns to the room with two tall, skinny glasses of water on a tray. She sets them down on the doily-covered coffee table next to the sofa, a doily over the back of that too.

Charlene had been so preoccupied thinking about Melissa that she'd forgotten the girl had a twin. Now her mind fills with the memory of Stacy standing on the front lawn in that bright green prom dress with Chaz. Then her thoughts rush forward, like those newspaper articles on the screen of the microfiche machine, stopping on a memory of the day Chaz came to visit when he was home from the air force, a year or so after Ronnie died. Philip and Richard had moved out by then, so she was the only one at home. Charlene still remembers when she heard a car door slam outside and peeked though her bedroom window to see him coming up the walkway, dressed in a dark blue uniform, his head shaved completely bald. She remembers how much she dreaded his impromptu visit. But after he came inside and they began talking at the kitchen table, that feeling left her and she found herself feeling grateful that he stopped by. Finally, she recalls what he told her about the reason he and Ronnie had set out to date the Moody girls. Charlene had never divulged that secret to anyone, though she'd come close when she was standing at the front door with Philip last night.

You don't know everything.

What don't I know?

I just told you. Everything.

"Stacy got married last spring," Margaret says. "She met a wonderful young man at Rutgers. They still live in New Jersey."

"Good for her," Charlene says, realizing that it's been quite some time since she has had one of these parent-to-parent conversations. "What does she do now?"

"Stacy is a systems analyst at an insurance company. Ted, her husband, is a controller at a technology firm."

At one time in her life, Charlene used to read the wedding section of the local paper every week without fail. It seemed to her then that just about everyone in that column had a job with that sort of title, though Charlene didn't have the foggiest idea what those jobs were. "What does that mean exactly?" she asks Margaret, figuring she'll go along with the chitchat a while longer before focusing on Melissa. "I mean, what does a systems analyst or a controller do when they arrive at work in the morning and sit down at their desk?"

"Well, I—" Margaret stops. "I never thought about it. I suppose that Stacy analyzes systems of some sort. And Ted, well, he must control . . . things."

"I see," Charlene says, though she doesn't see at all. She puts the photo back on the mantel and gives up on the discussion.

Margaret offers her a seat on the humpbacked sofa, and they both make themselves as comfortable as possible, though the cushions are thin and hard. Charlene picks up her water glass from the tray on the coffee table. As she takes a sip, Margaret asks, "You have another son, don't you?"

Charlene thinks of Philip at home on the foldout bed, reading that biography as the television blares in the background. "Yes. My son Philip. He's unemployed." She laughs. "I guess that's an easy job to explain. He doesn't analyze or control a damn thing all day long. Not counting the remote control."

Margaret smiles warily.

"That's a joke," Charlene tells her. "Kind of a joke anyway."

"Oh," Margaret says, and produces an unconvincing chuckle.

There is an awkward moment of silence between them then. Charlene senses that Margaret wants to get back to the topic of Melissa, but she finds herself thinking of Philip and his poetry. Charlene had never been very encouraging, which is the opposite of what one might think, seeing as she was a librarian. But Charlene had met too many poets at the library during National Poetry Month every April. Almost all of them had the same dazed look, and they seemed so full of regret and sadness. Frankly, she didn't want that sort of life for Philip. What she wished for him was a career with some semblance of security, which didn't seem to matter much in youth, though Charlene knew damn well it became important later. Now, though, she wonders if it had been a mistake to discourage him, because look how his life had turned out anyway. And who was to say those poets were any less happy than the thousands of systems analysts and controllers roaming the world?

The sound of Joseph's footsteps creak on the second floor. Charlene glances up at the ceiling, and just then, she feels something vibrate in her pocket. The motion startles her until she realizes that she must have switched the cell phone to vibrate while playing with the buttons.

"Is something the matter?" Margaret asks.

"No," Charlene says, letting the call go to voice mail again. She is surprised Philip called her back at all, never mind twice. Still, she doesn't want to be rude and answer it, like those mothers who are always yapping away in line at the Genuardi's.

"So can you tell me what you know about Melissa?" Margaret asks in a quiet voice.

Charlene takes another sip of water. "How long has it been since you've seen her?"

"Years. It's not that I haven't tried. I have. Not in a long while, but when she first left, I used to try all the time. I'd send cards and gifts. But she never responded. She just shut us out after what happened with— Well, after what happened that summer."

"I'm sorry," Charlene says and means it, since she knows full well how it feels to be cut off from your children.

"Does she still look the same?"

"If you mean, does she still have all those scars, I'm sorry to tell you that yes, she does."

Margaret stares down at the carpet, where her feet are arranged side by side in flimsy, heel-less black shoes. She looks as though she is about to cry. "Missy was such a pretty girl, and I knew the scars bothered her. I would have done whatever it took to make her look better. Joseph and I have the money from the suit. We've had it for years now, but she refused it long ago."

"You have the money?" Charlene asks.

"We settled out of court. Didn't you?"

"No. The lawyers tried to get me to do that. But I'll never settle."

"Well, we just wanted the whole ugly business behind us," Margaret says, her eyes still on the floor.

For Charlene, it's just the opposite. All these years, she has been holding out for her day in court, just waiting for the moment when she could get up in front of a courtroom and give her side of the story. Sometimes she even dreamed about it, and when she looked out into the courtroom in that dream, she saw the faces of everyone she knew: Philip, Richard, Holly, Pilia, even her parents, who were long since dead, had come back from the beyond to hear her side of the story.

"Tell me about the baby. Is it a boy or a girl?" Margaret asks. "And what's its name?"

Charlene realizes that she had not made herself clear earlier. "Oh, Melissa hasn't had the child yet. She's still pregnant. Nine months, actually."

Margaret pauses to think that over, then asks, "Why did she come to see you last night? Did it have to do with your husband?"

"Ex-husband," Charlene says as something coalesces in her mind. She thinks of Richard's caginess on the phone earlier, of the way Joseph described her in relation to Richard instead of Ronnie, of Melissa looking up the stairs last night and asking, *Is Mr. Chase home?* "Why do you keep saying that?"

"Saying what?"

"Before at the door, Joseph referred to me as Richard's wife. And just now, you brought him up again. Why?"

All Margaret says is, "You know."

"No," Charlene tells her, growing more suspicious by the second. "I don't know."

Above them, the ceiling creaks again. Margaret lowers her voice so she is all but whispering. "Richard never told you?"

"Told me what?"

"That Joseph caught them together."

"Caught who together?"

"Your husband—ex-husband, rather—and our daughter. Melissa."

"What do you mean, 'caught them together'?"

"I don't know the specifics," Margaret says, "because Joe would never talk about it. All I know is that they started meeting at the cemetery that summer after the accident. My husband began following her to see where she was going and who she was with."

"And she was with Richard?"

Margaret nods. "Apparently."

Charlene puts her hand to her forehead. She wishes she'd taken off her cloak because she is sweating beneath. "Are you saying they had an affair? An affair that took place at the cemetery?"

"Please," Margaret says, pointing toward the ceiling. "Keep your voice down."

Charlene hadn't realized that she raised her voice at all. In an exaggerated whisper, she asks, "Are you telling me they had an affair?"

"I don't know if that's the right word. Melissa denied that's what it was. She said they had a friendship. A close friendship. But that wasn't the way my husband saw things."

"So what happened?"

"Your ex-husband gave her the money to rent a house and buy a car. Then she left us."

Now Charlene understands the reason for Richard's fumbling behavior on the phone this morning. Now she understands why Melissa kept asking about him last night. All day long, Charlene had been trying to make a connection between Richard's medical expertise and her pregnancy. But that wasn't the case at all. Charlene had been around long enough to know that when a man gave a woman money for a house and a car it could only mean one thing. That's when an odd thought occurs to her: she wonders if the child could be Richard's. Just the thought of it, just the thought of the two of them together, causes her to sweat even more. All the bread she had eaten in the parking lot of the library feels as though it has hardened into a cement ball inside of her.

"Is there anything else you can tell me about Missy?" Margaret asks, her soft voice breaking through the haze of Charlene's thoughts.

Charlene blinks. She wants to tell her that she should go to her daughter, that the girl is obviously troubled and needs her help, that she should find a way to make up with her and stop their fighting. But that would be hypocritical, considering the way she treated Philip all these years. And even though it might seem that Charlene's instinct would lead her to call Richard right now, that is not what she wants to do at all. What she wants is to go home and give Philip that Robert Frost book, to sit in the family room and watch TV together, to have a conversation without bickering, and to let him get the last word if they do. She rises from the couch and says to Melissa's mother, "I've told you everything I know. And now I need to go. My son is waiting for me at home."

"I'm sorry if I upset you," she says, standing too.

Margaret trails Charlene to the door, where they say a rushed good-bye. "If you see my daughter, will you please tell her that I miss her?"

Charlene promises that she will, then steps outside, where the sky is just beginning to grow dark. On the way to her car, she fishes through her pockets for her keys and pulls out the cell phone as well. On the glowing green screen, the words TWO MESSAGES blink beside a digital image of a mailbox. Charlene starts pressing buttons again in an attempt to retrieve Philip's messages, but she cannot figure out how to access the damn things. Finally, she gives up and gets in her car, tossing the phone on the seat next to that strip of microfiche and the Robert Frost book.

Once she pulls out of the driveway and heads off down the street, Charlene allows herself to think of what she just learned about Richard. Yes, she knew he ran around with women like Holly after Ronnie died. But she never would have imagined that he would be so completely devoid of morals as to have an affair with his dead son's girlfriend. And yes, there is a part of her that wants to get on the highway and drive straight to Palm Beach. But what good would that do now?

Instead, Charlene keeps going toward home.

When she pulls in the driveway ten minutes later, she comes to a stop outside the garage door and presses the remote control on the visor. Slowly, the door lifts and she begins to ease the car forward until she notices something that causes her to let out a small gasp: the Mercedes is gone. Charlene slams on the brakes and shifts into park. Only the nose of the Lexus is in the garage, but she leaves it right where it is. Without bothering to shut off the engine, she gets out and walks to the spot where Ronnie's car has been parked for years. There in the corner, among the shadows, she sees the canvas cover she bought long ago to protect it.

Charlene doesn't know why but she picks up the edge of that cover and holds it in her hands. For a long while, she stands there listening to the sound of the engine running, breathing in the cold, oily garage air, and wondering what Philip has done and where he has gone. Finally, she decides there is no way he could have possibly driven the car with his leg in the cast. With this thought in mind, she goes back to the Lexus and turns off the ignition, not bothering to pull the car the rest of the way into the garage. She cuts through the basement hallway, past Philip's and Ronnie's old ten-speeds and tennis rackets and that dusty, deflated alligator raft, and up the stairs.

The first thing Charlene notices when she opens the door is that the house is quieter than usual—eerily quiet in fact, just like the Moodys' place. She doesn't hear the television set. She doesn't hear the papery scrape of Philip turning pages. She doesn't even hear the ticking of that antique clock. "Philip!" she calls out, heading straight for the family room. "Philip!"

But Philip does not answer, and she finds the room empty.

At first, Charlene thinks that he must have gone back to New York just as she knew he would eventually. But then she notices that all of his belonging are still scattered around the bed. His duffel bag on the floor. His miniature reading light on the foldout sofa. His musty Anne Sexton book facedown on a pillow.

But where is he? Charlene wonders.

Had someone described this scenario to her one month before, she would have said that she'd be more bothered about him taking the car. At the moment, though, she only feels upset about the prospect of Philip leaving. Admittedly, she has her selfish reasons: Charlene dreads the thought of going back to living in this house alone. But there is also the fact that she still wants the chance to make amends with him.

After doing a complete check of the house, Charlene finds herself standing at the foot of the sofa bed, staring blankly at the rumpled sheets and wondering where he is. Finally, she sits on the mattress the way she did this morning after she woke him and before he turned on Judge Judy. Charlene picks up that Anne Sexton book and reads a passage, as though it might hold some clue as to where he is right now.

While it is obvious that Anne Sexton drew the worship of readers with a prurient interest in her suicidal tendencies, her psychotic breakdown, her

numerous hospitalizations, it must be acknowledged that her forthrightness
comforted the people who looked upon her poems as the Holy Grail. . . .

Charlene puts down the book and shakes her head. How he could stand
to read such nonsense she didn't know. That's when she looks up and sees
the clock stopped on five-thirty—the reason the house is silent. Charlene
had just wound the thing a few days before, since it was one of the few
household chores she actually kept up with, so it shouldn't have stopped already. She wonders if it should tell her something about where Philip has
gone. When no correlation comes to her, Charlene reaches down and
picks up his duffel bag. She knows he would be furious at her for looking
inside, but she can't help herself. And when she finds a packet of stapled
pages inside among his clothes, Charlene takes them out and reads:

FROM: *Dfiume34@mstc.com*
TO: PhlpChse@ mstc.com
DATE: April 16, 2000

Dear Philip,
First things first: You must gently open Baby's mouth to see if there is
any white mucus resembling cottage cheese in the back of her throat. If
so, I'm afraid this could be an indication of mouth rot, which is not
good. You see, my dear Philip, snakes have a slower metabolism, so
they are often more sick than they appear on the surface. (The former is
true of many overweight people who cannot help their size; the latter is
true of almost all people, but we can ruminate on those tangents on
another occasion.) As far as Baby is concerned, she is no spring
chicken, or spring snake as the case may be, so we should not be surprised. Even Elizabeth Taylor has grown old on us and lost her luminous
beauty, although that did not seem possible at one time. I digress. If you
investigate Baby's oral cavity and fail to discover any of that dreadful
cottage cheese festering in there, then the symptoms you described in
your last missive could simply mean that she is shedding. DO NOT—I
repeat—DO NOT try to help her shed by picking and peeling away at
the dead skin. Snakes need to shed in their own due time. No one can

rush the process, and in fact, it is dangerous to try. (Again, the similarity to humans does not escape me.) Speaking of which, I imagine you are going through your own shedding, now that you have officially been a New Yorker for six months. In your missives, you tell me all about the loud neighbors and the pets and the progress of your poetry, but you say nothing of your own personal life. How are you? Where do you like to go? What do you do with your free time? Have you made any colorful new friends? Do tell. I trust that even your most boring tale will be vastly more interesting than Fauncine's incessant deathbed howls. On that note, I must sign off now. It is time to administer her meds and she refuses to let the visiting health aide do it. (Yesterday she clocked her in the face when she was helping to change the sheets.) Enjoy your youth, my dear Philip. I am telling you, it's fleeting.

Yours,

Donnelly

FROM: PhlpChse@ mstc.com
  TO: *Dfiume34@mstc.com*
DATE: April 17, 2000

Dear Donnelly,

I wish I could tell you that I do much more than take care of the pets, read books, watch television, and write my poetry. The truth is, I have made no new friends. It is not that I don't want to, I do. But I am not very good at it. The whole thing seems so easy for other people. I can make conversation, of course, but somehow I am never sure how to bridge that into friendship. The same was true when I worked at the restaurant. And the same was definitely true back in high school. I guess I am what people call a loner. But the thing about being a loner is, it's lonely. There's a guy about my age and a woman only slightly older who I always see at Aggie's Diner where I go sometimes for coffee and oat-meal on Houston Street. I have listened to their conversations so often that I feel as though I know them. She is a novelist and he is working on his first book with her guidance. I gather that he babysits for her child while she teaches. Anyway, they seem like people I would like to become friends with. On so many occasions, I have wanted to go over and say hello and sit with them and talk and laugh, but something always stops me. I just don't know how to go about it. Sorry to be rambling. I guess what you really want to know about is Baby. I tried to work up the courage to brave her oral cavity but could not. So instead, I put her in a pillowcase and brought her to a vet on First Avenue, a few blocks from Happy Pet where I get her mice. You'll be glad to know there was no cottage cheese. Just a small amount of clear saliva, which the vet said is good. However, her eyes are cloudy, which the vet said is not good. It is an indication that Baby is about to shed. Apparently, shedding is very stressful to snakes so I need to take extra good care of her. Don't worry, Donnelly, I am on the case.

Sincerely,

Philip

FROM:　　*Dfiume34@mstc.com*

　TO:　　PhlpChse@ mstc.com

DATE:　　April 18, 2000

Dear Philip,

Just a short note because Frankenswine is ready for her feeding and I need to tend to her trough. (By the by, I would not hold your breath for me to return to the grand castle on Sixth Street anytime soon. My stubborn sister seems to be getting stronger every day instead of weaker, though the doctor insists her condition is terminal.) More importantly, what wonderful news about Baby! Thank you for taking her to the vet. You can deduct the bill off next month's rent.

Yours,

Donnelly

P.S.

Next time you're at Aggie's, why not send over a couple of martinis to your potential writer friends? Alcohol always helped grease the wheels for me. In fact, it's how I met Edward.

FROM: *Dfiume34@mstc.com*
  TO: PhlpChse@ mstc.com
DATE: April 19, 2000

Dear Donnelly,
It is a diner, and I see them there at breakfast, often with a young child.
So I don't think martinis would be appropriate. I am glad you are happy
about Baby. Sweetie is fine too.
Sincerely,
Philip

FROM: *Dfiume34@mstc.com*
  TO: PhlpChse@ mstc.com
DATE: April 20, 2000

Dear Philip,
Good point. I'll keep brainstorming on the matter.
Yours,
Donnelly

After that, there is a break in the dates. Before going onto the next
e-mail, which is dated more than a year later, Charlene pauses to consider
what she just read. Even though she is well aware of the answer, she cannot help but wonder how she had let a child she had raised, a child she
loves, become such a stranger to her? She knew none of this business
about snakes and mice and Donnelly Fiume and his ailing sister, never
mind Philip's loneliness. All these years, she had the image of him leading
a busy life in New York full of friends and parties while she was rattling
around in this big old house alone. Maybe she deserved such a lonely fate.
After all, she had lived her life and had her share of good times early on.
But it didn't seem fair that Philip shouldn't have his turn. Sitting there,

Charlene is filled with a sense of sorrow at the thought of him alone in the city, lacking such confidence that he cannot even make a friend. Again, she takes a breath and begins reading:

FROM: PhlpChse@mstc.com
TO: *Dfiume34@mstc.com*
DATE: November 17, 2002

Dear Donnelly,

I know you have been asking for a while, but the reason I have not sent you any of my poems is that I am very shy about showing people my work. In fact, after my first round of rejection letters, I have made the decision that I don't ever actually want to publish anything. I just like to write for myself. I know that may sound strange, but it is the truth. However, since you have insisted for so long, I will send you this one poem I have been working on. Although I would never admit this to anyone but you, I actually think I may be improving after all these years. It is a poem about my mother, who I might have mentioned in these e-mails I have been estranged from now for quite some time. I was thinking a while back about the way she always seemed to rush life when I was growing up. Anyway, it is not really her in the end, but I used that idea and my disconnected relationship with her as a jumping-off point. Well, I'll spoil it if I say much more, so you will just have to read below. If you hate it, you don't have to ever mention it again. I won't ask. I promise. Here goes:

"Hurry" by Philip Chase

You were always in such a rush, Mother
On Labor Day, you spoke of Christmas coming
In spring, you spoke of uncovering the pool
Living your life like the displays in the department stores
Where you escaped to on Saturday afternoons
To push a shaky-wheeled carriage up and down the aisles
And dream of all that you would have someday
I tried to slow you down, Mother

I told you to come look outside the window with me
At the leaves raining from the orange sky
Their bursts of color like paper money from faraway countries
Valuable to others, but not you
Because today was worthless in your eyes
It was tomorrow—the sweet glittery gold of tomorrow—that held promise
Now all but a handful of your tomorrows have arrived, Mother
I have not seen you but I imagine
Your hair is streaked with gray
Your bones are growing brittle beneath the creased sack of your skin
One of your children, my brother, took his last breath too soon
And I am a stranger to you now
Do you see that the promise you believed in,
the promise I tried to caution you against,
was as empty as the windowless coffins that wait for us too?

FROM: PhlpChse@mstc.com
  TO: *Dfiume34@mstc.com*
DATE: November 20, 2002

Dear Donnelly,
You have not written since I sent you my poem. I know I said I wouldn't ask, but, well, I lied. Does that mean you hate it?
Philip

FROM: *Dfiume34@mstc.com*
  TO: PhlpChse@mstc.com
DATE: November 24, 2002

Dear Philip,
This is Donnelly's baby sister Fauncine writing. I am sorry to deliver this sad news over the computer, however, my dear brother, and your dear friend, Donnelly, passed away two days ago. Forgive me for not writing sooner, but as you can imagine, I have been in a bit of a state. Even

though Donnelly has been struggling with cancer for a number of years, and we all knew his time with us was limited, it does not take away the sadness I feel. I hope you don't mind, but I have read over many of the e-mails the two of you have exchanged. I see that Donnelly created quite a colorful story around his sickness at my expense, which is just like my brother, since he always had a flair for drama and he never liked to talk about his failing health. I assure you I am not the monster he painted me to be. In fact, we have always been very close and that's why he came here so I could care for him in his dying days, rather than face those indignities on his own in the city. I guess we are all guilty of telling lies to ourselves and to the world in order to make the truth, however sad, scary, or strange, more palatable. You should know that Donnelly spoke very highly of you. He believed in you as a poet and a friend. He left the name of a literary agent who was an acquaintance of Edward's. Her name is Jean Pittelman, and her office is on Greenwich Avenue should you ever be in need of her services, although I read about your desire not to publish. Finally, Donnelly also requested that you be allowed to keep the studio as long as you like. You can continue to send the rent money to me here and I will forward it on one of Donnelly's checks, since it is doubtful the landlord will read the death notice in the Commerce paper and evict you. If life ever brings me up to New York, I would love it if we could meet for tea, and if perhaps I could come by and see Donnelly's old studio. Until then . . .
Fondly,
Fauncine Fiume

That is the last page of e-mails. Charlene reads the poem about herself a second time, then puts the packet back inside the duffel bag. She stands and goes to the kitchen, mulling over what she just read—especially that poem. What an odd detail of my personality for Philip to focus on, she thinks. Certainly, Charlene had looked forward to the holidays and the changing seasons, but she didn't consider herself any more guilty of rushing through her time in this world than anyone else.

In the kitchen, Charlene finds that a few of the pots and bowls from the pea soup have finally been scrubbed. She wonders if this is another clue that might tell her something about what Philip was thinking before he left, though it does not help her at all. She walks to the telephone with the thought of calling him on his cell. And that's when she sees the number 5 blinking on the answering machine. When she presses the button, her recorded voice plays back, "Philip. It's me. Are you there? Pick up. Okay, well—" Charlene hits Erase and the next voice to come through the machine is Richard's. "Charlene. It's me. I need to talk to you. If you get—" Again, she hits Erase. The next voice is a young woman's. "This is Jennifer from Dr. Kulvilkin's office. We are calling to remind you that Philip has an appointment tomorrow morning at nine A.M. Please let us know if he has to cancel for any reason. Thank you." After that, there are two more messages from Richard, which is odd to say the least. Charlene erases them both without listening.

The bastard, she thinks, then pushes the thought of him out of her mind and looks up Philip's cell phone number in her address book. When she calls, his voice mail answers. Charlene leaves a message, trying to sound unconcerned about where he is and why he has taken the car. After she hangs up, she hunts around for the directions to her cell so she can figure out how to retrieve those messages he left. But she cannot find them anywhere, so at last she gives up and decides to simply sit tight and wait for him to return. She grabs a Diet Coke from the fridge and goes back to the family room, settling into the bed where he has slept this last month. Charlene doesn't know why exactly, but she has a terrible feeling of dread that she cannot shake. She tells herself it is just that news about Richard and Melissa still haunting her, but she can't help feel that it is something more than that. She is worried about Philip out there on those slick winter roads with that old car. She is worried about his abrupt departure. For a moment, she considers taking a sleeping pill to put her mind at ease. But Charlene wants to be wide-awake when he returns.

It is only a short while later that she hears a car pull into the driveway. Philip, Charlene thinks and gets out of bed. She goes to the foyer, where she presses her face to the glass just as she had the night before. Outside, she does not see Ronnie's old car, but a taxi stopped at the edge of the driveway. Whoever it is pays the driver then gets out. When the dark figure comes closer up the walkway toward the house, Charlene recalls a scrap of conversation with Richard on the phone this morning:

Do you want me to come there? Is that what you want?

No, I don't want you to come here!

Whether she wanted him here or not, she sees that it is Richard outside right now. He has come home after all.

chapter 14

BEFORE RICHARD CAN EVEN RING THE BELL, THE FRONT DOOR swings open. Charlene is standing before him dressed in beige pants and a cowl-neck sweater. Even though he saw her at St. Vincent's hospital in New York City just one month ago when they were visiting Philip, he cannot help but be freshly taken aback by all the weight she has put on over the years, not to mention the way she has let her hair go gray and frizzy. Looking at her, though, it is still possible to see through to the pretty, smart-mouthed girl he first met at a party back in college when one of his drunken friends spilled a glass of wine on her and Richard went over to apologize.

Let me get you a towel . . .

Thanks, but I'd prefer a new outfit instead. . . .

"Hello, Charlene," Richard says now as he stands in the center of the moonlit porch and braces himself for her to begin screaming.

Much to his surprise, she keeps her voice perfectly composed when she asks, "What are you doing here?"

Ever since Holly dropped him off at the airport in West Palm Beach this afternoon, he has been rehearsing the multitude of answers to that question. He considers telling her that after seeing Philip lying in that hospital bed he has not been able to focus on his life in Florida, because it made him realize how much he had failed his family. He considers telling her that all these years he has carried around the unshakable feeling that he fled the scene of a crime when he left his life in Pennsylvania behind. Most of all, he considers telling her that after her phone call this morning he made up his mind to come here and explain what went on that summer between him and Melissa, before someone else did. Despite all the time Richard spent constructing those responses in his mind, he finds himself abandoning every last one and saying just three words, "I don't know."

"What do you mean, you don't know?"

"Just what I said. I don't know."

"That doesn't make any sense, Richard. You haven't been here in ages, and suddenly you show up unannounced. You must have a good reason."

"It's not unannounced. I asked you this morning if you wanted me to come here."

"And I told you no."

"Well, I left you all those messages saying that I was coming anyway."

That statement causes Charlene to drop the more modulated tone she's been using. In a rushed voice, she asks, "Did you leave any messages on my cell phone or just here at home?"

"Here at home," Richard tells her. "Why?"

She looks past him toward the driveway, where her Lexus is parked half-in and half-out of the garage. Richard tries to guess what she is thinking, but it's no use. Finally, she looks back at him. "Sorry to disappoint you, but I didn't bother listening to your messages. In fact, I erased them just a short while ago. So you'll have to tell me again why you're here."

"You erased them without even listening?" He shouldn't be surprised, nevertheless, he is.

"That's right." She sounds proud of the fact. "So get to the point."

A heavy wind gusts across the yard then, stinging Richard's face. All these years in Florida have left him sensitive to the cold. It doesn't help that he is wearing nothing more than a windbreaker, jeans and a T-shirt. He crosses his arms and tries one of the other answers he rehearsed. "Haven't you ever done something just because you felt like you had to?"

Charlene removes her hand from the doorknob and cups her chin in an exaggerated *I'm thinking* pose. In an equally exaggerated voice, she says, "Hmm. Let's see now. Oh, wait. I know." And here, at last, her voice escalates to an angry pitch. "I divorced you because I felt like I had to. And because you were a dishonest, cheating jerk of a husband. Little did I know I should have added 'pedophile' to the list too."

"Pedophile? What are you talking about?"

"Last time I checked that's what they call men who mess around with underaged girls."

Now he knows what she is getting at. So what I was afraid of has already happened, Richard thinks. She knows. "Charlene, I'm not sure what Melissa told you, but—"

"Melissa didn't tell me anything. I happened to pay a visit to Joseph and Margaret this afternoon."

"Joseph and Margaret who?"

"Moody!" Charlene shouts. "Melissa's parents!"

The wind blows harder still, and Richard shivers against it. His mind fills with the memory of that final afternoon at the cemetery when he held Melissa in his arms, the way he did so many afternoons as she cried, and sometimes he cried too. He remembers looking up to see a car coming toward them on the dirt driveway, which was unusual, because there was never anyone else there since the place had so few graves for people to visit. When the car stopped, Melissa's father got out. He didn't bother to close the door, and as he walked toward them, the vehicle released a steady succession of chimes, reminding Richard of the tonal emergency codes over the loudspeaker at the hospital. Even though he and Melissa had broken their embrace, it was too late. He knew what her father was thinking: they were doing something they shouldn't be.

"Dad," Melissa said over that incessant chiming.

"Shut up," her father told her. "Shut your mouth, young lady, and get in the car."

Richard shakes that memory from his mind the way he has dozens of times today, hundreds of times over the years. A shiver moves through his entire body. "Can I at least come inside so we can talk about this?"

Charlene stares at him, blinking, biting her bottom lip, as she debates the question. Finally, she steps aside and lets him in. After Richard walks through the door and closes it behind him, he glances up the staircase at the same pictures that hung on the wall when he lived here. There is Ronnie and Philip with both sets of grandparents at Pat's King of Steaks in Philly. There is Charlene and Richard standing in a white gazebo at their wedding. There is Philip, wearing a cap and gown at his high school graduation, a forced smile on his face. "Is Philip home?" Richard asks, realizing suddenly how quiet the house is, as quiet as it was that summer after Ronnie died, when they each retreated to separate areas of the house and shut down any semblance of family life.

Charlene does not answer him. "I was nice enough to let you inside. Now let's finish the conversation."

"Can't we go into the family room? Do we have to do this here in the foyer?"

"I'd prefer to stay right where we are. That way it will be easier to kick you out once you're done lying to me. So go ahead. I'm waiting. Let the bullshit begin."

"It's not bullshit, Charlene."

"Call it whatever you want, Richard. Just tell me what went on with that girl."

"I—" He stops. For all his planning on the two-and-a-half-hour flight up from Florida, Richard never did come up with the right way to explain the brief, unexpected attachment he formed with Melissa Moody all those years ago. As he tries to figure out a way now, he hears a replay of his voice attempting to make Holly understand this morning. *It was more than a friendship, but it was not an affair. I never so much as kissed the girl, Holly. Still, I knew meeting at the cemetery all those afternoons blurred the lines of what was appropriate. But everything was so complicated that summer that I let it continue—even though Melissa got worse instead of better, talking endlessly about her desire to have Ronnie's child long after she'd gotten her period. . . .*

"Since you seem to be at a loss for words," Charlene says, interrupting his thoughts, "let me help you. You know something, Richard, I knew you were a fucker but I had no idea how big a fucker you were. I mean, the girl was a child when this happened. For Christ's sakes, it was your son's girl-friend! Your *dead* son's girlfriend! No wonder she lost her mind! Ronnie's death didn't make her go crazy, *you* did!"

"Keep it down," Richard says. "I don't want Philip to hear you, because what you're saying is not true. I'd rather tell him myself."

Charlene crosses her arms and sits down on the second-to-last step. "Well, good luck because he isn't here."

Beyond the issue of Melissa, one of the main reasons Richard made such an impulsive decision to come back to Pennsylvania was so that he could lay eyes on his son again. In his time as a doctor, he had seen thousands upon thousands of people recovering in hospital beds with injuries far worse than Philip's. But there was something different when it was his child—a child he had failed so miserably. Richard wants to see him again so he can erase that image of Philip's bruised body and weary eyes from his mind. He hopes to rid himself of those guilty feelings too. "Where is he?"

"I have no idea where he went. Maybe he hopped on a plane to Florida because he suddenly *felt* that he had to see his long-lost father. Or maybe he got sick of this place and went back to New York. That's how he left last time. He walked out the door and didn't come back for almost five years." Charlene's voice cracks suddenly, and Richard realizes she is crying. He watches as she puts her elbows on her knees and her face in her palms. Since he doesn't know what else to say or do, he leans against the banister and places his hand on her shoulder. It is the first time Richard has touched her in years, which is odd in a way, since there was once a time when he couldn't get enough of touching her. "You ruin everything," Charlene says, her voice barely audible as she talks into her hands. "This is all your fault."

Richard tells himself not to take the bait, but he does anyway. "What's all my fault?"

Charlene looks up at him, her face wet with tears. "I saw Pilia today."

It's been ages since he has heard that name. Still, Richard would never forget the way Charlene used to carry on about that woman. "What does Pilia have to do with anything?"

Charlene wipes her eyes with the back of her hands to no avail, because the tears keep coming. "I've been wishing bad things upon her for years. And she's not the only one either. I had an entire list of people in my head. She was right up there at the top. Next to you, as a matter of fact. And when I saw her today, it turned out she had cancer. *Cancer.* She had to have both of her breasts removed." Charlene stops to take a breath as Richard tries to figure out what she is getting at. "Afterward, I got in my car and thought, 'You know what? I am going to make an effort to be nice today. I am not going to scream, and I am not going to yell.' It was like a little promise I made to myself. But today of all days, I have to find out about you and Melissa! Today of all days, you decide to show up and make me break that promise to myself!"

"Why are you blaming me?" Richard says, his hand still on her shoulder.

"Who the hell should I blame?" she screams, brushing him away. "Tell me that. Who?"

"I don't know, Charlene. Maybe there is nobody to blame. Maybe it's not about blame at all."

After that, she grows quiet. She holds her hands out before her, absently inspecting her nail-bitten fingers as Richard walks to the other end of the foyer and leans his back against the wall. Holly had warned him that it was a bad idea to come here. But she hadn't really understood about his relationship with Melissa Moody either. The only thing she did seem to comprehend was how shaken he felt after seeing Philip in that hospital bed. Now Richard tries once more to make Charlene understand. "I swear to you, Charlene. I am telling the truth about that girl. No matter what her parents or anybody else said, I did not have an affair with her. We ran into each other at the cemetery one afternoon and we started a friendship."

Without looking up, she says, "A friendship with a seventeen-year-old girl. That's normal, Richard."

"I never said it was normal. None of it was normal. But her parents were awful to her. She had no one. She needed help. She needed me."

"Well, why didn't you tell me then? Why did you keep it a secret?"

"Think about what you're asking, Charlene. I could barely talk to you that summer. All you did was lie in bed and stare at the ceiling. You wouldn't even have a conversation with me about the way Philip was handling it. Never mind how Melissa felt."

That comment makes her reach for the banister. She pulls herself to a standing position, points a finger at him, and says, "Don't come here and pretend that you were some do-gooder trying to help Philip and Melissa and me. Please. That's what I have to say to that, Richard: *please!* Half the time you were off screwing that slut girlfriend of yours from Vegas and—"

"Do you always have to call her that? Besides, Charlene, she is not my girlfriend anymore. She is my wife."

"Well, good for you." Charlene throws both hands up in the air. "I'm glad you picked one over the age of eighteen this time."

Richard resists the impulse to yell at her. He should be used to these sorts of attacks. At the very least, he should be prepared for them, seeing as he walked right into it. Still, he can't help but be bothered by the things she is saying. In a calmer voice, he tells her, "I don't know how to make you believe me."

"Me neither," Charlene says. "And I don't want to think about it anymore. You better call that cab back. And when it comes, you can show yourself out. Do me a favor too. Next time you decide to make a surprise visit, don't."

With that, she steps into the bathroom beneath the stairs and reappears a moment later holding a box of tissues. She hugs it close to her breasts as she walks off down the hallway toward the kitchen. Richard stands there a long while, wondering what to do next, since he has no intention of leaving so quickly after coming all this way. Somehow, he thinks this would be easier if Philip were here. He glances up at the photo of him in his cap and gown with that forced smile on his face. Then Richard looks at the picture of both his sons in front of Pat's, where they used to go all the time for cheese steaks. Even though he tried not to play favorites while the kids were growing up, he couldn't deny that he got along better with Ronnie than Philip. It was just so much easier with Ronnie, who was almost always cheerful, whereas Philip was so sullen and moody all the time. But as Richard stares up at that photo on the wall, he tells himself he should have tried harder to reach out to Philip—especially in recent years. Yes, he made a point to regularly send checks to him in New York, and yes, he paid for whatever Philip charged on the emergency credit card, which was mostly books and cheap meals but he has the sense that he should have done something more.

258 • JOHN SEARLES

A loud clanging sound comes from the kitchen, and Richard turns his gaze away from those photos. He walks slowly down the hall and finds Charlene standing at the sink, scrubbing a pot. The smell of brewing coffee fills the room. "What are you doing?"

"Making strudel," she says over the sound of running water. "What the hell does it look like I am doing? I thought I told you to leave."

"You did, Charlene. But I've come all this way and I'd like to see my son before I go. I would also like it if we could work this out."

Charlene continues scrubbing. "I don't know what there is to work out, Richard. To tell you the truth, I don't even care anymore. It doesn't matter to me if you and that girl were madly in love or if you just had a friendship. Either way, it won't affect my life after today. It is never going to bring Ronnie back. And it is never going to make that baby she is carrying my grandchild."

"Your grandchild?" In the midst of all this arguing, he had managed to lose sight of Melissa's claim that the baby she is carrying belongs to Ronnie. In Richard's memory, he hears her voice from one of those afternoons at the cemetery, telling him, *I pray to Ronnie all the time. I pray to him and I tell him everything I am feeling. I ask him to come back to me somehow. Miracles like that happen, you know. My father talks about them all the time . . .* "Charlene," Richard says now, "you didn't honestly believe her, did you?"

She finishes cleaning the pot, turns off the water, and grabs a dish towel to wipe it down. On the counter, the coffee maker releases a loud gurgling sound as it brews. Richard wonders why she would put on coffee at this time of night, but he doesn't ask. "Of course I didn't believe her," she says finally.

There is an unconvincing tone in her voice that makes him suspect otherwise. "Good," he says. "Because it's not possible."

"This morning on the phone you told me that it was possible. So which is it?"

"I only said that after you forced me, Charlene. What I meant was that it is feasible in a hypothetical sense. But it is not the case here. Nobody froze Ronnie's sperm. I know that for a fact."

"So I just have to ask. Do you know a Dr. Gerald Casale from Penn?"

"Who?"

"Dr. Casale. He's a fertility doctor who does this sort of thing. I Googled him today at the library."

"What were you doing Googling a fertility doctor?"

"Never mind that. Just tell me, do you know him?"

Richard realizes how much she must want to believe Melissa if she made the effort to actually research specialists in the field. A big part of him feels bad for disappointing her. Still, he has no choice but to tell her the truth—he has never heard of the man before.

His words cause Charlene's face to go slack with resignation. She looks exhausted from it all. Richard watches as she dries her hands with the dish towel, then drapes it over a cabinet handle. "Well, like I said, it's not as though I was stupid enough to believe her anyway." Charlene turns away from him, focusing on something in the corner of the room. When Richard looks, there is nothing but the pale yellow phone on the wall, her address book open on the counter. She lets out a sigh and says, "Listen, it's been a long, trying day and I want to go up to bed."

"I understand," Richard tells her.

"How nice of you. But I'm not looking for your approval. My point is, what are you going to do?"

"I don't know. I guess I'll stay here and wait for Philip."

Charlene cocks her head. "Hold on a second. You weren't planning on sleeping here, were you?"

"Obviously, I wasn't planning much of anything. I came here without really thinking about it."

"Well, maybe you should have," Charlene tells him.

All Richard can think to say is, "It's too late now."

After that, Charlene stares away at the silent telephone again until finally she waves her hands in the air and steps past him into the hallway. Under her breath, she says, "Fine. Do whatever you want. You always do anyway. I'm too tired to fight anymore. You can sleep on the sofa in the family room. It's already pulled out. Have a party if you want to. Just don't turn off the coffee because I made it for Philip in case he comes home."

"Good night," Richard tells her.

Charlene mumbles something else but he cannot make out the words.

Her footsteps pad up the stairs, and the house grows silent again. Richard is so accustomed to the lull of the waves outside the condo in Palm Beach that he'd forgotten how quiet this house can be at night. There is only the sound of the wind rustling through the trees outside. Somewhere in another room, a branch scrapes against a window. Richard pokes around the kitchen, noticing that Charlene's address book is open to the P section, and that Philip's cell phone number is the only one on the page. Then he looks at the sink, where the few remaining bowls are caked in green. Pea soup, he thinks, remembering those days on Spruce Street when Charlene used to make a giant pot to last the week.

He turns and stares at the nicked farmhouse table, surrounded by the stiff, ladder-back chairs he used to find so uncomfortable. Night after night after night, he and Charlene had eaten at that table when the kids were growing up. He thinks of all the conversations that took place during those dinners—about report cards and field trips to the Liberty Bell and the capitol building and the zoo and birthday parties and library events and nice teachers and mean teachers and new doctors at the hospital and retiring doctors at the hospital and who wanted a new bicycle and who needed to study harder for algebra exams and so on and so on and so on. It is not that Richard is unhappy in his present life—no, it is not that at all—but remembering those dinners makes him realize it is a different kind of happiness than what he felt back then. In those days, he carried inside him a certain kind of hopeful buoyancy—a sense that things were as they should be—a feeling that is all but foreign to him now.

Richard rubs his eyes and releases a breath. He has never been the nostalgic type, so he doesn't know why he is giving in to those feelings. To distract himself, he opens a cabinet and takes down a glass. He locates the Brita pitcher in the fridge and pours himself some water. The airplane ride left him dehydrated, and he gulps down three glasses before his thirst is quenched. Afterward, he wanders into the family room, where the sofa bed is unfolded just as Charlene said. The sheets are rumpled. The pillows tossed every which way. There is a small, portable reading light in the center of the bed as well as a book open facedown. On the floor, there is an unzipped duffel bag. Judging from the looks of things, he figures that this must be where Philip has been sleeping, since it is probably too difficult for him to navigate the stairs in his cast. The thought makes him wonder how Philip was able to leave the house at all tonight.

Without bothering to peel back the covers, Richard sits on the bed and leans his head on the pillows. For a long while, he stares up at the ceiling the way Charlene used to do that summer. The longer he waits for Philip to arrive, the more Richard begins to think that Holly was right: it was a bad idea to come here without any sort of planning. And as the wind blows outside, and that branch scrapes against a window in another room, all those reasons he'd had—which had seemed so compelling this morning—fade from his mind. The clock on the wall is stopped at five-thirty, but his watch says that it is almost ten. Normally, Richard wouldn't nod off this early, but he allows himself to close his eyes as he waits for Philip. It is only a matter of time before his breathing slows, his mind drifts, and he is asleep.

As he goes on sleeping, Charlene lies sideways across her bed upstairs, mentally examining the puzzle pieces of the last twenty-four hours—from Melissa Moody showing up at their door, to her discussion with Philip this morning when he first planted the slim possibility in her mind that the girl could be telling the truth, to her odd encounter with Pilia at the library, to her visit to the Moodys' house, to coming home and finding Philip gone, to reading those e-mails in his duffel bag, and now Richard's unexpected return. When it becomes too much to think about, Charlene gets up from bed. She goes to the bathroom and fetches her nightgown on the back of the door, then pulls off her clothes and changes into it. Before climbing into bed again, she walks to the window and parts the curtains, looking out for some sign of Philip. Charlene can't say why exactly, but the feeling of dread she had earlier still plagues her. She tells herself that it is nothing more than the turmoil of recent events. But something has her worried. Down in the driveway, she can see the trunk of her car sticking out of the garage. The sight makes her think of her cell phone, which she'd left inside on the seat, and those messages that she couldn't figure out how to retrieve.

At last, she gives up thinking about them and forces herself to return to bed. Since it will be nearly impossible to sleep tonight with her mind weighed down by so many worries and her ex-husband downstairs, Charlene reaches over to the nightstand for her container of sleeping pills. Instead of uncapping it and swallowing a pill, the way she normally would, she does something different tonight: Charlene simply squeezes the container in her palm for comfort before closing her eyes and trying to give herself over to sleep.

Outside, the wind continues to blow. The stars and the nearly full moon illuminate the black winter sky. Under that same moon, far away from the Chases' house—past the rows of suburban homes and the tangle of wooded streets, along one stretch of highway, then another, then another, past hundreds of green exit signs and lonely rest stops, where waitresses are making watery coffee and janitors are scrubbing urinals and running mops over bathroom floors and truckers are dropping coins into vending machines—across seven state lines to Florida and then to Palm Beach, the ocean crashes against the shore outside the window of Holly and Richard's condominium, just as he was thinking of earlier tonight.

Inside, Holly lies in their king-size bed alone, occupying only a slim portion of the left side, since she is so used to Richard hogging the rest. Like Charlene, Holly is replaying recent events in her mind. In particular, she mulls over her conversation with Richard this morning, dissecting what he told her about his relationship with his son's girlfriend. *It was more than a friendship, but it was not an affair. I never so much as kissed the girl. . . .* For what must be the hundredth time today, Holly wonders why he kept it hidden if, as he claimed, there was nothing to hide. Her thoughts go to the many details of her own past—the men she'd slept with before meeting Richard, the various drugs she'd tried in her early twenties, even the boyfriend of her mother's whom she'd once kissed when she was barely sixteen—none of those things had she ever divulged to Richard. Not that he wouldn't understand, because she figures he would. She supposes that she kept those parts of her past a secret because the woman who did those things is not the woman she is anymore. In the same way, Holly wonders if the man who formed such an unlikely attachment to his son's girlfriend was not the same man he is today.

Something about this thought causes Holly to get out of bed and go to her closet. It takes a few minutes of digging before she locates the shoe box in the very back, behind an old down comforter and a small mountain of heels she never wears anymore. She pulls off the top and sorts through the cassettes inside. When she spots the tape she is looking for, Holly stands and goes to the living room, where she puts it in the stereo. The instant she presses Play, a crackly recording of her voice fills the room. It is of her in Vegas at a medical convention, telling jokes about male gynecologists and their lack of proper "vagina-side manner." Each time she blurts out a punch line, the audience erupts with laughter. But there is one laugh that rises above the others. It is an odd sound—heavy and reckless—the sort of laugh that sounds close to tears. It is Richard's laugh. Holly still remembers how sad that sound had seemed to her then, because it sounded like a man in pain, which is what he was when they first met.

Who he was then, she thinks. Who he is now.

She presses Rewind and plays that same section of the tape again, listening to Richard's uncontrolled bellow rise above the other voices in the crowd. And she begins to wonder if she should have been more sympathetic about his sudden need to return to Pennsylvania. Finally, Holly presses Stop and steps out onto the terrace, where she gazes up at the moon above the ocean. She is not one to pray, but she finds herself saying a silent prayer just then, not just for Richard's happiness, but for Philip's too. And then, despite herself, she even says a few words for Charlene.

Back again—past all those state lines and exit signs and along those miles of highway and beyond those rest stops, where still more weak coffee is being made and bathrooms are being scrubbed, off one exit ramp, then another, then another, past the rows of suburban homes—to the tangle of wooded streets on the far side of town in Radnor, Pennsylvania. Back again to the three small houses on Monk's Hill Road. Inside the largest of the three, Bill Erwin is pacing the rotting floor in his dimly lit living room.

Over and over, he mumbles the question to himself, "What do I do now? What do I do now? What do I do now?"

He has been asking this question for hours, though no answer has come. Beneath him, the basement is quiet. There are no more noises down there tonight. He made sure of it. What's more, he made sure to get the keys to that old Mercedes then pull it down a nearby dead end and off into the woods so the vehicle is hidden from view. While taking care of this necessary precaution, he found a yellow registration slip on the passenger seat, which indicated that the car belonged to Charlene Chase of 12 Turnber Lane. He knows the last name from his many conversations with Melissa about the boy who died in the accident. So he can only assume that the young man who'd been visiting her earlier, the one he dragged down into the basement when he caught him outside, must be the boy's brother. This detail makes him realize yet again that there is no turning back from what he has done. This is not like the other times. Those girls were all anonymous—a hitchhiker he picked up on I-95, a woman he met on a fishing trip, a teenage runaway outside of a bar in Philly.

This time is different, because he has harmed his wife and a friend of Melissa's.

This time is different, because they can be traced back to him.

Sooner or later, Bill knows that someone will begin to wonder what happened to Gail and that young man. When that happens, all signs will point to him, and eventually to that third house in the back. That's why he needs to figure out what to do next. For the time being, though, all he can do is pace and mumble. He walks from one window to another, checking and rechecking to make sure no one else is out there. And when he goes to the bedroom window and peers out at Melissa's house, Bill sees a dull light shining through her plaid curtains. He wonders what she is doing up at this time of night.

What he cannot see, of course, is that behind those flimsy curtains, Melissa is wiping up the sudden rush of water that burst forth from her body. Ever since Philip left the house tonight, her contractions have grown stronger and more frequent. Almost all of the psychics Melissa visited these past nine months told her that she would not have the baby until after the full moon. So she did nothing more than lie on the sofa and wait for them to pass. But now that it has come to this, Melissa knows there is no more waiting. She must get herself to a hospital. First, she goes to the bookshelf and pulls out the book on pregnancy that Gail bought for her as a gift. Her hands flip the pages until she finds the section on labor. She reads that contractions can last up to an average of twelve hours for a first pregnancy, but once the water breaks, things begin to move more quickly. If she thinks back, Melissa suspects that she felt her very first contraction last night while driving home from the Chases' house. She also felt them while she slept on the sofa, and this morning when she woke to find that horrible letter.

Melissa closes the book and takes one last look around her cottage before going to the door. When she pulls it open and steps into the night, the chilly winter air pours over her burning skin. Halfway to the car, another contraction seizes her. Melissa stops to grip her stomach. After the feeling passes, she turns to look at the Erwins' place. For a brief moment, she considers asking Gail and Bill to drive her, as they had offered to do so many times. But the confusion she feels over that eviction letter this morning makes her decide against it. She continues walking to the car and gets inside.

As Melissa navigates the windy roads toward Bryn Mawr Hospital, she tries to calm herself by conjuring the memory of Ronnie's face, though her thoughts keep drifting to Mr. Erwin instead. She thinks of the way he came to her house tonight after he heard Philip yelling. *No matter what miracle you think has happened with this pregnancy, the fact is he is dead. Ronnie is dead. . . .* The memory seems to bring on another contraction, sharper and more painful than any of the previous. Melissa takes her foot off the gas and pulls to the side of the road. She pauses there, unable to think about anything but the pain, as she waits for the feeling to subside. When it does, her mind gravitates back to the memory of Mr. Erwin standing inside her small house earlier this evening. She thinks of his gold Timex watch ticking on his thick wrist. She thinks of the way his John Deere cap caused a dark shadow to fall over his eyes. She thinks of his gaze roaming the room. None of this was so terribly unusual, but Melissa's mind stays locked on the memory anyway.

Finally, Melissa takes a few deep breaths before continuing on. Traveling this way takes longer than it normally would. With all her starting and stopping, thirty minutes pass before she turns into the parking lot of the hospital. Rather than search for a spot, Melissa pulls in front of the Emergency Room, swings open the door, and gets out.

"Ma'am, you can't leave your car there," a parking attendant shouts at her.

Melissa ignores him and keeps walking. The double doors open automatically and she makes her way to the front desk, one hand pressed to her stomach, the other on her lower back, where she feels most of the pain now. When the petite woman with razor-thin lips and teardrop glasses looks up from behind the desk, her eyes go wide at the sight of Melissa's disfigured face. Then she looks away the way everyone does—everyone but Ronnie's father. And Bill Erwin, Melissa thinks as another contraction comes over her.

"Help me," she says, wincing from the pain. "I'm about to have a baby."

As the nurses gather around Melissa, the sky outside the hospital turns from black to gray to blue. The moon and the stars fade away. Very soon, sunlight breaks over the bare treetops. Exactly fourteen miles from the same hospital where Richard Chase once spent most of his days, he is waking to the sound of Charlene calling his name. He squints his eyes and sees her standing at the foot of the sofa bed, wearing a threadbare nightgown with a terry cloth robe pulled over the front to keep it from being completely obscene. "What is it?" he asks.

Charlene holds her cell phone in the air. "I finally figured this out."

"Figured what out?"

"How to retrieve my messages."

He rolls over on his side and rubs his neck, wondering how he managed to sleep through the night fully dressed and in such an uncomfortable position. "So?"

"So Philip left me two messages yesterday afternoon." She presses a button, then thrusts the phone out to him. Richard puts it to his ear and hears Philip's voice say, "M. It's me. I don't know how you even found out where Melissa lives. But please don't drive over there and rail on her about last night. Call me back when you get this. Or better yet, just come home."

"Who is M?" Richard asks when the message is through.

"That's what Philip calls me now."

"Why?"

Charlene shrugs. "I guess it's short for *Mother.*" She tells him that there's another message as well saying basically the same thing—that she shouldn't go to Melissa's house. "It made me realize that he might have gone there to get me, not knowing that I was at her parents' house instead."

"But why wouldn't he come back?"

"I don't know," Charlene says. "But I never asked her parents where she lives, and she's not listed with Information. I just tried again. I also tried the police to make sure there were no accidents reported last night."

"And?"

"None."

Richard thinks back to the day Melissa took him to see the cottage where she wanted to live. He kept telling her that she could find something bigger and nicer, but she liked the place. She also liked the old couple who owned it. "Thirty-two Monk's Hill Road," he says to Charlene.

"What?"

"That's where Melissa lives."

"How do you—" She stops, and Richard figures that she is remembering the detail of the money he had given Melissa. Her parents may not have told Charlene the address, but he can only assume they shared that detail. "Never mind," is all she says. "I'm going over there."

He stares at the clock, still stopped at five-thirty, then looks at his watch. "It is barely seven. Don't you think it's a little early?"

She pulls her robe tighter around the front of her body, then ties the floppy belt attached to the sides. "I don't care how early it is. I want to find out if he was there. Who knows? Maybe he still is."

"But you said yourself that last time he left without any warning. Maybe that's the case again. It seems more likely that he's in New York right now instead of sleeping over at Melissa Moody's house."

Charlene looks down at that Anne Sexton book on the bed, then at Philip's unzipped duffel bag. Richard's eyes follow, and he sees that she is staring at the stack of papers inside. "No," she says in a quiet voice. "I don't think he would have left his things behind this time. Now tell me where Monkey Hill Road is. I've never heard of it."

"That's because it's *Monk's* Hill Road," Richard says as he gets out of bed, rubbing his stiff neck again. "And I may as well go with you."

Much to his surprise, Charlene agrees without a word of protest. She even goes so far as to retrieve an old suede coat of his from the hall closet. It is one he'd forgotten about until now, and the material reeks of mothballs. Since his windbreaker is useless in this weather, it will have to do.

"I'm surprised you didn't burn it," Richard says.

"Me too," Charlene tells him as she goes upstairs to change.

After he uses the bathroom and she comes back down bundled in a baggy wool sweater and thick black pants, they make their way to the garage, where Charlene's car juts outside, a detail he noticed when he arrived last night, though he was too preoccupied to focus on it. When he inquires about it now, Charlene tells him that she left the car there when she saw that Philip had taken Ronnie's Mercedes.

"You let Philip drive with his leg in a cast?" Richard asks, then he blurts another question before she has time to answer the first. "And you still have that car?"

"I didn't *let* Philip do anything," she says. "And of course I still have that car. What, you expected me to get rid of all my memories of Ronnie?"

"That's not what I was suggesting," Richard says and opens the passenger door, letting the conversation die because he doesn't want to argue.

He is about to sit down when he spots a strip of tangled film beside a book of Robert Frost's poetry. Charlene reaches over and makes room for him, then starts the engine as he gets inside. Out on the road, Richard tells her the most direct route to Melissa's house. Then he takes to staring out the window, remembering so many of the winter mornings like this one that he spent driving the short distance to the hospital. As they pass a stretch of land that was once woods but is now a development of homes even larger than the ones on Turnber Lane, Richard takes a stab at normal conversation. "When did they put up those monstrosities?"

Charlene keeps her eyes on the upcoming intersection. "A few years ago. Tell me again. Do I turn right or left here?"

"Right," Richard says. "Build. Build. Build. They won't stop until there's nothing left."

"I guess not," is all she says.

That seems to be the end of the discussion, and Richard decides to leave it at that. He should be grateful, after all, seeing as it is probably the most civil one they've had in years. But then Charlene surprises him by speaking up again. "Remember when we first came to Radnor to look for a house?"

"I remember."

"This town was so different back then." She looks briefly out her side window, as though seeing what it once was, which was more woods and far fewer homes, instead of the overdeveloped area it has become. "The place used to seem so much more quaint."

"That's because it *was* more quaint," Richard tells her.

Charlene lets out the smallest of laughs, and he thinks of that girl he met at a party back in college when his friend spilled a glass of wine on her. Then he recalls their first date, when he gave her a sweater that was almost identical to the one his friend had ruined. Richard had been so embarrassed hunting through the various women's sections of department stores, describing the kind of clingy red sweater with the zigzag design by the collar and sleeves that he was looking for. But it was worth it, because when she opened the box at the restaurant where they met for dinner, she couldn't believe he had found something that was pretty damn close to the original. That sweater became something of a joke throughout their marriage, since Charlene wore it for years afterward, referring to it as the "Sweater That Made Me Fall in Love with You."

"Even though this town has changed," Charlene says now, "I still love the house as much as I did that very first day."

For years, Richard wondered why she didn't sell the place and move somewhere smaller and more manageable—someplace without all those bad memories. But looking at that table last night helped him understand the reason she held onto it. The house on 12 Turnber Lane was all that remained of those days when Ronnie and Philip were young, those days when all of their lives were infused with that feeling of hope. It's then that Richard's mind goes to the memory of what he considers to be the last night of their former lives—the evening Ronnie showed up with Melissa and her sister and Chaz before heading off to the prom. It is a memory he thinks of often, and he asks Charlene if she still thinks of it too.

"Of course I do." She pauses, both hands clenching the steering wheel, and what she says next takes Richard by surprise. "You know, when Ronnie and Chaz started dating the Moody twins, it was all part of a bet."

He turns to look at her in the driver's seat as the pungent mothball odor of his coat fills his nose. "A what?"

"A bet. Ronnie and Chaz placed a wager to see who would sleep with which sister first."

"Why?"

"You were a young single guy once, Richard. You know how they think. Melissa and her sister were the twin daughters of a minister. Plus, they were pretty. The boys saw them as a challenge."

"Well, that's just terrible," Richard says. "How do you know any of this?"

"Chaz came for a visit once when he was home from the air force. He told me. But he also said that once they got to know the girls, Ronnie developed feelings for Melissa. He fell in love with her. So he called off the bet with Chaz. He never wanted Missy to know. So I've never told anyone."

"Why are you telling me this now?" he asks.

A silence fills the car, and Richard glances out at the dirty mounds of snow alongside the road as he awaits an answer. Finally, Charlene says, "To tell you the truth, I had almost forgotten about it until she showed up at our door the other night. I guess remembering that detail made me realize Ronnie wasn't as perfect as I like to think. The fact is, he could be just as cruel as the rest of us."

Richard doesn't know what else to say, so he tells her, "Well, we're all a little cruel sometimes."

The words hang in the air between them, and he expects Charlene to make a dig about the many cruelties he has dished out over the years, but she spares him.

"That's the truth," she says as they round the final turn onto Monk's Hill Road.

Now that they are so close, Richard wonders what it will be like to face Melissa again, since she had been so terribly angry when he told her they shouldn't see each other anymore. Then his thoughts go to Philip, and he wonders whether he will even be at her house at all. As they approach the three small cottages, Richard tells Charlene to slow down. Just a single red pickup truck is parked in the driveway. Ronnie's old Mercedes and Melissa's Corolla are nowhere in sight. Charlene pulls into a small inlet of shoveled snow beside the road and asks which house is Melissa's. Richard points to number 32, and she turns off the engine, then pushes open her door.

"What are you doing?" he asks.

"I think we should knock just in case."

Richard glances at his watch. Seven-thirty. "But the Mercedes isn't here, Charlene. We can't just show up unannounced at this time of day."

"Watch me," she says and steps outside.

At first, Richard tells himself that he is going to do just that: watch her make a fool of herself from the comfort of the passenger seat. But then something makes him open the door. When he catches up with her at the cracked cement stoop, he asks, "Why are we doing this?"

Charlene holds her fist a few inches from the door and says, "Remember how you had a feeling that you should come home yesterday? Well, I have a feeling too. Something isn't right." With that, she gives a few hard raps. They stand in silence, watching their breath fog the air before their faces. When no one comes to the door, Charlene pounds harder.

"Come on," Richard says after there is still no answer. "Let's forget this."

Charlene points to the next house, only fifty feet or so away, and asks who lives there. Richard thinks back to that chipper, snowy-haired woman who showed Melissa and him the place all those years ago. Then he remembers her husband, who struck Richard as the kind of guy you might spot sitting in a pub in any number of seaside towns—strong arms, a gravelly voice, a weatherbeaten face. "The landlords," he says.

"Well, I think we should ask if they saw Philip here yesterday."

Knocking on Melissa's door is one thing, but Richard doesn't want to wake the couple just because Charlene has a feeling. "If you're so concerned, why don't you try calling Philip again?"

"Fine, I will."

She retrieves her cell phone from her pocket, presses the Callback button, and holds it to her ear. That's when something odd happens. Richard hears two faint rings that are not coming from the phone in Charlene's hands. As far as he can tell, the sound is coming from somewhere around the side of the house.

"Do you hear that?" he asks.

"Hear what?"

"The phone. It's ringing."

Charlene shakes her head. "Of course it's ringing, Richard. I just called Philip back."

Instead of trying to explain, he reaches up and takes the phone from Charlene. "Listen."

A moment of silence follows, and Richard begins to wonder if he imagined the sound. But then he hears it again: a single muffled ring from somewhere around the side of Melissa's house. Richard can tell by the puzzled look on Charlene's face that she heard it too. Quickly, they step off the cracked cement stoop and look in the small yard between the two houses. There is nothing to be seen except a trampled patch of snow by the landlord's basement window. Just beyond, that third house sits at the edge of the woods, all its windows covered with cloudy sheets of plastic. They appear to shiver in the breeze. The ringing has ceased, so Richard holds the phone to his ear, where he hears Philip's voice asking him to please leave a message after the beep. He hangs up, intent on calling back right away so he can listen for that sound again. But just as he is about to press the button, another noise comes from that third house in the back. It is the creak and slap of a door opening and closing, followed by heavy footsteps. A moment later, the landlord with the weathered face appears from inside the vacant cottage. He places a shovel against the side of the house, then walks toward them, wiping a thick layer of dirt from his fingers and coming to an abrupt stop at the trampled patch of snow.

"Morning," he says.

Richard holds his thumb to the Callback button but does not press it. "Good morning," he says as Charlene falls silent. She is still holding out her neck, listening for that ringing even though the sound has long since stopped.

"Can I help you?" Bill Erwin asks.

Behind him, the plastic over the windows of that vacant house shivers more violently with a passing gust of wind. Richard notices a number of black birds perched on the sagging roof. He looks away from them and into the deep-set eyes of Melissa's landlord, who is standing with both his unlaced boots planted in the snow. Charlene is keeping her silence, so Richard takes his thumb off the Callback button and says, "I don't know if you remember, but we met years ago. I'm Richard Chase. I came here with Melissa when she first looked at the place."

Bill shifts one of his large dirty boots against the ground. "That's right. Nice to see you again. I must admit that I'm not used to getting visitors this early."

"We're here to see Melissa," Charlene tells him, speaking up at long last.

"Melissa? Well, she's at the hospital. Someone from there called early this morning to tell my wife and me that she had the baby."

At the mention of the baby, Richard sees a residual glimmer of hope flash across Charlene's face. It is quickly replaced by the slack look of disappointment he remembers from the night before. "Is she at Bryn Mawr?"

Bill reaches up to scratch his forehead, accidentally knocking his hat from his head. Richard and Charlene watch as it falls to his feet, seemingly in slow motion, before he stoops down and clumsily drags it across the snow to scoop it up. When he is standing again, the hat squeezed in his two thick hands instead of back on his head, there is a pained expression on his face. "That would be the place," he says and offers a weak smile.

In Richard's memory, this man had been warm and welcoming that summer when they first came to look at the place. He even remembers him talking to Melissa about his garden, telling her that she could help herself to anything he grew there. He told her that in the wintertime she could use the firewood he kept out back as well. At the time, it made Richard feel good that Melissa would have someone watching out for her. Now, though, Bill Erwin seems shifty and nervous, different from that memory. "Is everything all right?" Richard asks. His fingers have grown cold, so he slips the cell phone into the pocket of his old suede coat.

Bill's smile widens. "Everything is fine. Why do you ask?"

Richard decides to let it go. It's early, after all. Besides, the man probably doesn't like the idea of people wandering around his property unannounced. "No reason," Richard says.

"Well, then, I better get back inside. It's cold out here. Good seeing you again."

"Wait," Charlene calls as he turns to go. "By any chance, do you know if Melissa had a guest yesterday?"

Bill stops, then slowly turns back to face her. "A guest?"

"A young guy with his leg in a cast. He was driving an old cream-colored Mercedes." She pauses. "Our son."

Bill wrings his hat in his hands, considering the question. "Can't say that I saw anyone like that around here. Things were pretty quiet, though they won't be for long with the baby and all." After that, he excuses himself once more and disappears inside the largest of the three houses.

When the back door scrapes open and shut, Charlene says in a loud whisper, "What a creep."

Richard agrees, then pulls the cell phone out of his pocket and presses the Callback button. As they wait to hear that muffled ring, Charlene takes a few steps into the side yard, getting closer to that patch of snow where Bill Erwin had just been standing. But there is no ring to be heard anymore. Richard holds the phone to his ear and listens as the call goes through to Philip's voice mail. Again he hangs up and calls back. This time, Richard steps into the side yard too, staring over at that abandoned house, where those birds have congregated on the roof. Bill Erwin's shovel remains propped against the wall just below one of the plastic-covered windows. When there is still no sound, Richard says, "Maybe we imagined it."

"No," Charlene tells him as her eyes scan the yard. "I know what I heard. Try again."

He does try again. As a matter of fact, he tries three, four, five, six more times. And when there is still no ring, even Charlene's certainty begins to fade.

"I could swear I heard it," she says, letting out a sigh. "But it was just that once. Maybe you're right. Maybe we just got carried away."

Richard gazes over at the landlord's house. All the curtains are drawn, but he can't help the feeling that they are being watched.

"What should we do now?" Charlene asks.

"I think we should go to the hospital," Richard tells her, turning away from those windows at long last and staring into her worried eyes. "Maybe Melissa can help us figure out what's happened to Philip."

chapter 15

"HELP ME," SHE SAYS, WINCING FROM THE PAIN. "I'M ABOUT TO have a baby."

The woman behind the desk grabs a telephone, punches in a few numbers, and barks into the receiver, "I need assistance up front, right away." After putting down the phone, she springs from her seat and calls to someone at the other end of the hall. In what seems like seconds, Melissa is surrounded by nurses, who are less organized than she might have imagined. A short one, whose lumpy body is stuffed into her tight white pants and shirt, calls for a wheelchair. When a young male orderly appears and wheels it toward her, they ease Melissa into the seat. Another nurse, who has the same sort of papery skin and snowy hair as Mrs. Erwin, asks Melissa if she has been timing her contractions.

"No," Melissa tells her. "Not really."

"That's okay." The woman holds up her wrist and looks at her slim silver watch. "We are going to start now. You just let me know when you feel the next one coming on. All right?"

"All right."

"Who is your doctor?" she asks.

"I don't have one."

"Do you mean that you don't have one affiliated with this hospital, or you don't have one at all?"

"I don't have any doctor at all," Melissa says, feeling ashamed of this fact for the first time. She thinks of Dr. Patel all those years ago and his list of plastic surgeons. She thinks of Ronnie's father and that ID card he used to wear around his neck, just like the ones hanging from all the nurses' necks right now. "I haven't visited a doctor in a very long time."

The nurse's expression becomes more apprehensive then, causing her faint resemblance to Gail Erwin to fade away. She seems wary of Melissa, far less gentle as she rattles off a list of questions: "How many months has it been since your last period? . . . How long since your water broke? . . . Are you allergic to any medicines?" In the midst of all this chaos, yet another nurse appears with a clipboard in one hand and a chewed black pen in another. In a harsh, nasal voice, she badgers Melissa about insurance information, which she doesn't have. "Okay, let's back up to the beginning. I need you to give me your full name."

"Melissa Ann Moody."

"Do you spell that M-O-O-D-Y?"

"Yes."

"Age?"

"Twenty-three years old."

This begins an endless session of questions and form signing, interrupted only when Melissa feels another contraction coming on. She informs the nurse with the papery skin, who begins timing. After the pain rises up in Melissa and then subsides, the woman with the clipboard resumes her questions. At the same time, the orderly gives a push and the rubber wheels of the chair start to move. Melissa leans her head back and stares up at the white squares of light in the ceiling, blurring into a single streak. Her thoughts grow hazy and white. She finds herself slipping out of the present moment only to be thrust into the clarity of a distant memory. In this memory, she is sitting alone in the living room of her cottage on Monk's Hill Road late one afternoon last spring. She is listening to her Jewel tape while numbing her ear with an ice cube in order to give herself another piercing. Just as she is about to stick the needle into her lobe, there is a knock on the screen door. She looks up to see Mr. Erwin's lined face on the other side.

"Hey," she says and puts down the needle while absently holding the ice cube in one hand.

"How you doing?" he asks, smiling so big and wide that his yellow teeth can be seen through the mesh of the screen.

At the sound of his gravelly voice, Mumu wakes from her catnap and leaps from the sofa, scurrying down the hall the way she always does when Mr. Erwin comes around. On the stereo, Jewel somberly croons about a boy who broke her heart. It used to be one of Melissa's favorite songs, but lately she has grown tired of this album, so she doesn't play it as often as she once did.

"I'm okay," she tells Mr. Erwin and means what she says.

More and more, there are days like this one when the sun is shining, and a breeze moves through the windows of her cottage, and she feels a shift in her spirit. It is the feeling of happiness returning to her life after all this time. It's not that she has forgotten about Ronnie, but Melissa has begun to lose faith in the notion that he might return to her somehow. As a result, those prayers she says by her bed each night are beginning to grow shorter. Some evenings, she finds herself praying for different things altogether, like guidance about what she should do with the rest of her life. She has even started looking in the paper for a job she might like better than washing sheets at that ratty motel in Conshohocken and answering phones for those grouches at the insurance company.

"I brought you flowers from the garden," Mr. Erwin says, and holds them up so she can see the bulbous white tips of a dozen or so tulips through the screen. "If I leave them in the ground, the deer will get to them. So I figured I'd gather some up for you."

Melissa feels a sudden, wintry pinprick against the top of her bare foot. Startled, she looks down and sees that it is nothing more than drops of water from the melting ice cube in her hand. She puts what's left of it into a glass on the coffee table, then goes to the door and pushes it open. Mr. Erwin steps inside, his presence so large and hulking that it never fails to make the cottage feel even smaller. He glances around at the piles of dirty clothes and books and tapes on the floor, the framed pictures of Ronnie that Melissa has only recently considered removing from the mantel. Even though the Erwins have assured her that they don't care how she keeps the place, she sometimes gets the feeling they don't like the clutter—especially Mrs. Erwin, who keeps their house neat and organized. "Sorry about the mess," Melissa says.

"Don't be sorry. It's your place, so you do as you like. Heck, if it wasn't for Gail, I'd be living in a pigsty next door."

Mr. Erwin hands her the tulips, and Melissa sees that his fingers are caked with soil from the garden. She thanks him then goes to the kitchenette to look for something to put them in. Since she doesn't own a vase or anything remotely like one, Melissa settles on a large pasta pot. When she fills it with water and places the flowers inside, the white heads barely peek out over the top. Still, they look pretty to her. If there is one lesson she has learned in recent years, it is to find the beauty in life's imperfections. Melissa sets the pot on the counter beside a bottle of wine she uncorked a short while ago, since she likes to have a glass while doing her piercing. Bill Erwin's gaze lingers on the bottle, so she asks, "Would you like some?"

He glances at the window that looks out onto his and Gail's house. It takes him a long moment to answer, but finally he tells her, "Yes. A glass of wine sounds good to me."

Melissa opens her eyes.

Her thoughts return to the present, where she feels her next contraction coming on. The lanky young orderly is still wheeling her toward the elevator. Two of the nurses still flank her, but the woman with the clipboard is gone. Melissa tells them what's happening, and the lumpy nurse holds her hand as the pain rises up inside of her until it is almost unbearable. When it recedes, they inform Melissa that the contractions are coming less than three minutes apart, so they need to move quickly. At the elevator doors, the woman with the clipboard appears again and says that she forgot to ask Melissa if there is anyone she would like the hospital to notify that she is here. For a fleeting instant, Melissa actually considers giving her parents' phone number. It's been years since she felt even the slightest pang of longing for their presence in her life, but something about the chaos of the present moment has her missing them—especially her mother. But then she thinks of the way they punished her after that day in the cemetery when her father caught her with her arms around Richard Chase. They locked her in her room. They refused to speak to her. They took away her television and phone. All of that was unfair, but none of it was as cruel as what her father did on the ride home from the cemetery. What Melissa cannot and will not ever forgive for as long as she lives was the way he struck her countless times—the back of his hand becoming a sort of frantically spinning windmill that slapped and slapped and slapped against her face, which was already in so much pain.

"You can contact Gail and Bill Erwin," Melissa says when the memory becomes too much to take. Even though some part of her is still angry and confused about that eviction letter Mr. Erwin explained away as a mistake, Melissa gives their phone number instead.

The elevator doors finally part, and they move inside the boxy silver space, large enough to fit a small car. The button for the eighth floor is pressed. The doors close. The squat, lumpy nurse says, "I'm going to talk you through what's about to happen, Melissa. We're taking you up to the maternity ward, where Dr. Halshastic will examine you to determine exactly how dilated your cervix is. If you're dilated more than ten centimeters, then we're going to begin the birthing process. Do you understand?"

Melissa tells her that she does. Then she takes a breath and looks toward the white light on the ceiling. Her thoughts go spinning backwards again to that afternoon last spring.

When she finishes pouring the glass of wine and hands it to him, Melissa asks where Mrs. Erwin is at the moment. Once more, his gaze shifts over her shoulder to the window. "Home cooking dinner, I suppose."

"What's she making?" Melissa asks, simply for something to say. In all the years she has lived in the cottage, never once has she felt nervous around Mr. Erwin. Today, though, she senses an odd tension in the air as he clenches and unclenches one of his soiled hands, and his eyes stay fixed on that window.

"Nothing fancy. Probably just some burgers or fish sticks." At last, he looks toward Melissa. "You're not going to make me drink alone, are you?"

She already had one glass before he arrived, but the tense feeling is enough to make her pour another. "Of course not," she tells him.

"That's more like it," he says, then raises his glass in the air. "To your pretty new flowers."

Melissa raises hers too. "To my pretty new flowers," she says.

He takes a gulp, then another, before making himself comfortable on the sofa. Melissa stands by the counter, feeling awkward still. A warm breeze cuts through the cottage, and the late afternoon light fills the room, casting a brilliant orange glow on everything. It makes her think of the renewed sense of happiness she has felt lately, the sense that she might be okay after all. Melissa recalls an ad she circled in the paper for a job working at a veterinarian's office. She has yet to call, but she thinks the position might suit her, since the animals won't care about the way she looks.

"So what are you doing here?" Mr. Erwin asks, pointing his thick, dirty index finger at the needle on the table. "Surgery?"

Melissa swallows her wine, which tastes bitter in the back of her throat. "I was piercing my ear."

He stares up at all the studs and crosses already cluttering both her ears. "Looks like you've got plenty of holes in you already."

At one time in her life, this sort of comment would not have bothered Melissa. After all, she and Stacy used to insult each other on a regular basis. Now, though, the slightest mention of her appearance leaves her feeling bruised. Mr. Erwin must read the hurt on her face, because the next thing he says is, "I don't mean any offense. They look real nice on you."

Melissa shrugs. "Well, it's just a hobby, I guess. Some people like to garden or go fishing or read those strange but true stories from the newspaper the way you do. Other people cook and clean, like your wife. And I like to—"

"Put holes in yourself," Mr. Erwin says, dropping his voice lower.

Maybe it is the wine, but something about the statement strikes Melissa as funny. She leans her head back and releases a laugh, not bothering to cover her mouth with her hand the way she normally would to hide her missing teeth. Mr. Erwin laughs too. And this begins an unexpected fit of giggles between them. As Melissa stares up at the ceiling, which is blotchy from so many leaks, she says, "That's right. My hobby is putting holes in myself."

The elevator releases a high-pitched ding when it reaches the eighth floor, summoning Melissa back to the present. The doors part and the orderly pushes her out into the hallway. The two nurses follow at her sides still, their rubber-soled shoes squeaking against the speckled floor. As they move through the maternity ward, Melissa smells a flat antiseptic odor in the air as well as a scent that is something akin to boiled corn. Both smells are familiar to this building, though she'd forgotten them until now. She thinks of the bland food and ever-revolving shifts of listless nurses and hurried doctors the last time she was here. The biggest difference Melissa notices is that the maternity ward is quieter than intensive care had been with its beeping machines and the constant clamor of the staff. Here, they pass room after room where the lights are off, and only the occasional television flickers inside.

"The last time I was in this hospital it seemed so noisy," Melissa says out loud without really meaning to.

"Excuse me?" the lumpy nurse says.

"I said, the last time I was here, the place was so noisy."

"When was the last time you were here?"

"Five years ago," Melissa tells her.

"And what was that for?"

"An accident," is all she says.

The discussion is cut short because they have arrived at their destination. The orderly wheels her into a large room where the walls are bright green and a series of blue curtains divide the space. Melissa eyes a cluster of machinery that is similar to what she remembers from intensive care—a heart monitor, an IV rack, and dozens of other pieces of equipment she doesn't know the names of. A nurse she has never seen before approaches as the others cross the room to talk with a bearded man who Melissa guesses is her doctor. This new nurse is a kind-faced black woman, with thick eyebrows and a broad smile. She wheels Melissa behind a curtain to help her change into a hospital gown. It takes some time, though, because of another contraction. This one sends an agonizing spasm into the deepest part of Melissa's body. She feels the urge to push but does her best to hold off. When the feeling finally passes, she returns to the task of slipping on the thin gown. The nurse takes her blood pressure, then taps the veins on Melissa's arm, before hooking up an IV. Just as she is taping the tube to

Melissa's skin, the bearded man appears in green scrubs and one of those familiar plastic ID tags hanging from his neck. Melissa reads his name at the same time the nurse says, "This is Dr. Halshastic."

"Hello, Melissa." He is talking to her but staring at a clipboard in his hands. "How are you feeling?"

"Fine," she says.

This answer causes him to look up. Melissa sees that familiar, startled expression on his face, before his gaze drops to the vicinity of her chin. "Well, I'm happy to hear it. Now listen, we are going to ask you to lie back on this table so we can determine how far along you are in the labor process. Is that okay?"

Melissa nods.

"I'd like it if we could make a deal. I'm going to need you to speak to me when you answer. No nodding. All right?"

"All right," she says.

"Good," he tells her. "If we do this as a team, I'm confident that things will go smoothly."

After the doctor and nurses help Melissa onto the table, she lays her head back on a pillow. They tell her they are going to put a monitor against her stomach to keep track of the fetal heart rate. Then they ask if she would like an epidural for the pain. Melissa declines. She is not afraid of the pain. And besides, she wants to feel this baby coming into the world. The last thing she hears the doctor say before her eyes flutter shut is that her cervix is fully dilated.

That's when Melissa's thoughts travel back again to last spring. Only this time she sees herself waking the morning after Bill Erwin came to her door with those white tulips. As she stretches out on her sagging mattress in her pale yellow bedroom, Melissa realizes that she is dressed in her flannel pajamas—a pair she only wears during the winter months. She cannot remember changing into them, nor can she remember climbing in bed to sleep. The only thing she does recall is Bill Erwin lighting a cigarette and opening another bottle of wine after they'd finished the first. Then she remembers the way they kept giggling about people's hobbies, particularly Melissa's hobby of piercing her ears.

Why had we found that so funny? she wonders for the longest time.

When no answer comes, Melissa gets out of bed and walks to the living room, feeling sluggish and more hung over than ever before. Everything in the place looks the same, though slightly more orderly. The cushions on the sofa have been fluffed. The glasses have been placed side by side in the sink. The empty wine bottles are on the floor by the kitchenette. Thinking of how much they drank, Melissa is filled with worry about how she might have acted in front of Mr. Erwin. Finally, she pushes the thought from her mind and goes to the refrigerator to pour a glass of water, touching one of the silky white flower petals in that pasta pot as she gulps it down. After that, she turns and heads back to bed a while longer before starting her day.

"So here's what we are going to do," Dr. Halshastic is saying when Melissa opens her eyes. "First, we are going to help you regulate your breathing. I want you to hold Barbara's hand and breathe right along with her. Okay?"

"Who's Barbara?" Melissa asks.

The doctor points to the kind-faced black nurse, who is already holding Melissa's hand. "Meet Barbara."

"Hi," Melissa tells her, wondering where the nurses from downstairs have gone.

Barbara smiles and gives her a gentle squeeze, then instructs Melissa to inhale. All throughout her pregnancy it seemed to Melissa that it has been getting harder to breath. Sometimes she even wondered if the baby was slowly suffocating her from the inside. For the first time in months, though, Melissa finds it easier to take deep breaths. When she says this out loud, the nurse tells her, "That's because the baby has dropped, relieving some of the pressure on your diaphragm. So let's take another deep breath and release it. Ready?"

Soon they are working together—inhaling and exhaling, inhaling and exhaling. Finally the doctor says, "Okay, we are going to ask you to begin pushing when you feel the next contraction coming on. Do you think you can push?"

Melissa nods, then remembers their agreement. "Yes," she tells him.

And when the next contraction comes, she takes her deepest breath yet, filling herself up with air before giving a good hard push. Her eyes close, and this time she does not return to that morning last spring. Instead, she simply sees the image of Bill Erwin's wrinkled face, his chapped lips, his silver hair, in the darkness behind her lids.

"You are doing great," Dr. Halshastic tells her. "Now push again."

The whole while Melissa pushes and breathes and pushes and breathes, Mr. Erwin's weathered face remains there. She remembers the sound of their laughter. She remembers taking slow sips of her wine at first, then drinking more quickly. She remembers the way his eyes kept darting over to the window. She remembers the way he came back a week later and they drank and smoked again. The week after that too . . . until soon, it became something of a tradition. She remembers so many mornings when she woke, exhausted and hung over, her limbs aching, wondering why she had allowed herself to get so carried away the night before.

"Keep working with us, Melissa. Come on. Now give us another push."

Melissa sucks in a breath and gives her hardest push so far as the pain racks her body. She feels the baby shift inside, moving through the birth canal. The nurse's hand is soft and warm in hers, and Melissa squeezes it tight. Her eyes close, and she sees herself getting out of bed again that first morning after Mr. Erwin came to visit. She sees herself walking to the living room, where everything looks the same though more orderly. The cushions and pillows on the sofa are fluffed. The glasses placed in the sink. The wine bottles lined up on the floor. And that's when Melissa notices the curtains, which had been open the night before while Mr. Erwin kept looking outside, are now closed.

"You are lucky, Melissa, because this is going very quickly. A few more pushes and we are in business. But we need you to focus."

"Breathe with me," Barbara says and pats a damp, cool cloth against Melissa's forehead. "Stay in the moment."

Melissa wants to go backward again, but the nurse and the doctor keep urging her to focus. Finally, she gives up on those strange memories and forces herself to remain in the present. When she does, Melissa inhales and summons her strength, then pushes with all of her might.

"Very good," the doctor coaches. "Can you give me another?"

Again Melissa inhales. And again she pushes. She continues working just like that and does not let up until she hears the doctor say these words: "You have a boy. A beautiful baby boy."

When the sound of his crying fills the room, tears spring to Melissa's eyes, because it is her baby making that sound. Moments pass, as the nurses clean and weigh the child, then complete a few quick tests, before placing his small body in her arms. Melissa holds the baby carefully, crooking one arm and placing a hand beneath his head, just as Barbara instructs her to do. She stares down at his squeezed-shut eyes, his round, pink face, and his fuzzy scalp with all its bumps and wrinkles as so many emotions tumble through her at once. She feels happier than she can ever remember. Yet, there is also a sense that, while something has been given to her, something else has been taken away. Melissa doesn't allow herself to indulge in the tumult of those emotions, though. She asks the doctor, "Is he okay?"

Dr. Halshastic smiles. "Ten fingers. Ten toes. He looks pretty okay to me."

Melissa counts each and every one of those fingers and toes herself. They seem impossibly small and fragile. She brings the baby closer to her face and kisses his soft, tender forehead. She smells his sweet skin. And this is what Melissa tells herself: that she is not going to force this child to live a life bound by the sort of rules and restrictions that her parents imposed upon her. Rather, she will give him freedom and unconditional love. No matter what, she is going to love this child. That is what Melissa keeps thinking long after the nurses take the baby away to lay him down in the nursery. And that is what she is thinking about when they wheel her to a room with two empty beds and turn out the lights so she can close her eyes and drift off to sleep.

Twice during the night a nurse gently wakes Melissa, so she can feed the baby. The third time, she wakes on her own and looks out the window to see that it is a bright winter morning. The lighthearted chatter of nurses in the hallway makes the place seem livelier than it did before.

"Most people can't wait to get out of here," she hears one of them say. "But I think that lady mistook this place for a hotel. She got used to being waited on hand and foot."

"If it's a hotel," another one says, "then I'm waiting for my tip."

This last comment causes their laughter to rise up. As Melissa lies there in bed—feeling exhausted, but surprisingly clear-minded considering all she's been through—she begins planning her new life with her baby. The first thing she decides is that it's time for her to move out of that cottage and into a place more suitable for a mother and her child. The next thing she makes up her mind about is that she is going to begin looking for a job again. Perhaps she will try for one in a veterinarian's office, the way she wanted to do last spring. And though it will take time for her to save enough money, especially with the hospital bills that are about to be piled upon her, Melissa tells herself that eventually she is going to make an appointment with a dentist and see about having her teeth fixed. In the midst of all this planning, a nurse pops her head in the door and says that there are people in the hall who want to see her.

"Who?" Melissa asks. If it's the Erwins, she does not want to see them.

Before the nurse can answer, the last two people Melissa expects step inside: Charlene and Richard Chase. Unsure of what to make of their presence here, Melissa sits up in bed and stays quiet as they say hello and enter the room. It has been almost five years since she has seen Richard. Five years since that day when he wrote the check for the cottage and the car, then told her that their friendship had to end. After the incident at the cemetery with her father, he said he realized that whatever they had between them was wrong. For years afterward, Melissa hated him for abandoning her. Over time, though, her hatred softened. Mostly, she learned to feel grateful that he had helped her leave her parents' house. That is the way she feels looking at him right now.

"I thought you were in Florida," she says to Richard, while glancing nervously at Charlene, who is standing near the doorway.

"I was," he tells her, stepping to the foot of the bed. "I came up yesterday at the last minute."

Melissa wonders if he came for her, but she doesn't bother to ask. Up close, she sees that Richard has aged over the years. His hair is grayer than it used to be. His blue eyes have faded behind his wire-rimmed glasses; the skin there is crisscrossed with wrinkles. He still bears a resemblance to Ronnie, though it is not what she chooses to see. Melissa is about to inquire about the reason they're here, when Richard asks, "So how are you feeling?"

"Good," she tells him. "A lot lighter."

Still lingering near the doorway, dressed in the same black cloak she wore the other night, Charlene speaks up for the first time. In a muted but pleasant voice, so different from her hysterical outburst two nights before, she says, "I remember what a wonderful feeling that is."

Melissa is overcome by a momentary sense of shame, thinking of the scene she caused at their house. But she forces herself not to dwell on it. Earlier this morning, while she was feeding her baby, she decided once and for all that her prayer had finally been answered. No matter what the circumstances, this child is still a miracle. That is the only truth worth believing. "Did you see my baby in the nursery window?"

"We did," Richard tells her.

"He's beautiful," Charlene says, taking a step closer to the bed.

"Can I ask," she says at last, "what made you come to hospital?"

"Well, we wanted to see you," Charlene tells Melissa. "And I . . . well, I wanted to tell you that I'm sorry for the way I acted the other night."

"It's okay. Why don't we just forget it?"

"It's forgotten," Charlene says.

They are all quiet until Richard puts his hands on the metal footboard of Melissa's bed and clears his throat. "There's something else, Melissa. We also came to talk to you about Philip."

"Philip? What about him?"

"We want to know if he came by your house yesterday."

"Yes," Melissa says. "Why?"

That's when Charlene tells her that he didn't return home afterward. She goes on to ask what time he'd been there, and Melissa says that it was late in the day, around four or five. She also questions her about whether he mentioned where he was going when he left. Melissa thinks a moment, recalling the last words they said to each other as he stood on her stoop in the dying light.

You really haven't smoked in all these months, have you?

Of course not.

I believe you. I know that sounds strange. I'm sorry I didn't before.

She wonders if somehow he had figured out what she could not, or rather, what she didn't allow herself to before. "He didn't say where he was going. But there didn't seem to be anything wrong with him. I mean, other than his leg, so I don't think you should worry."

"Like I said before," Richard tells Charlene. "He probably left for New York."

"Probably," Charlene says in a quiet, resigned tone of voice. She is standing at the end of the bed now too, her hands gripping the metal footboard as well. Melissa watches as her eyes move around the room—from the stripped bed on the other side, to the blank face of the TV near the ceiling, to the wide window overlooking the parking lot where the bright morning sunlight streams inside. When her gaze returns to Melissa, she offers her a limp, melancholy sort of smile. "Now that you're a parent, you're going to see for yourself how hard it is to let go of your child. It's one of the hardest lessons a mother ever has to learn."

Melissa doesn't know what to say so she stays quiet. She scratches the skin around the white tape on her arm and stares up at the clock. In another ten minutes, it will be time for the baby's next feeding. Melissa can hardly wait to hold him again. She can hardly wait for the feeling of peace she has when he is in her arms.

"You know," Charlene says. "If you—Well, never mind."

"What?" Melissa asks.

"I was just going to say that if you need a place to stay—other than your cottage, I mean—until you get back on your feet, I have plenty of extra rooms."

Melissa thinks of how vast and empty their house felt two nights before, how welcoming it used to seem when she visited Ronnie there all those years ago—especially compared to the house where she grew up. Still, Melissa wants to take her time making these sorts of decisions. She has made too many mistakes already. "I'll think about it," she tells her.

Charlene is about to say something more when she stops and points her finger in the air, as though she has just been struck by an idea. "I'll be right back."

After she excuses herself and steps into the hallway, Melissa feels awkward and unsure of what to say now that she is alone with Richard. The intimate rapport of those conversations they shared in the cemetery seems unlikely now. Thankfully, Richard makes an effort at small talk. As he goes on—first about the cold weather, then giving her the names of two doctors he still keeps in touch with at the hospital in case she needs anything—Melissa notices that he is not looking into her eyes the way he used to do. But it no longer matters to her. She watches his gaze go to the blue index card on the side table by her bed. It's the one the nurses gave her, and it lists the baby's birth weight, measurements, and blood type. Melissa reaches over and picks it up. "Can I ask you something?"

Richard lets go of the footboard and puts his hands deep in his coat pockets. "Of course."

"Do you remember your sons' blood types? I mean, since you're a doctor, I figure you might." When Richard tells her that he does, she asks, "So you remember Ronnie's then?"

"Yes. He was type A."

Melissa stares down at the information on the card. She knows her own blood type, because she had asked one of the nurses to look it up on her chart this morning. "Can a type A mother and a type A father make an AB baby?"

"I'd have to check to be sure, since I'm a little rusty," Richard says, "but I don't think so."

Missy folds the card evenly down the middle then slips it beneath her pillow. "Thanks," she tells him. "There's no need to check. I have things pretty much figured out."

Just then Charlene steps back into the room, holding out her cell phone. "There is someone on the line who wants to talk to you."

The previous discussion about Philip leaves her with the feeling that it is going to be him on the other end of the line. But when Melissa takes the phone and says hello, she hears a different voice altogether. "Melissa, honey. It's your mother."

The words bring back the pang of longing she felt for her presence last night. She remembers all the times when her mother tried to contact her over the years and Melissa hung up the phone, ripped up the cards, and refused to answer the door. In the gentlest of voices, she says, "Hi, Mom."

Her mother is silent and Melissa can tell by the sound of her short breaths coming through the receiver that she is crying. "I've missed you so much," she says finally.

"I've missed you too," Melissa tells her. Then she asks, "Would you like to come here?"

"I would like that a lot."

"Me too. But I want you to come alone. Without him."

Her mother doesn't push the issue. She simply tells her that she understands. "I will come by myself. Tell me. Is there anything you need?"

Melissa looks up at the clock again, expecting the nurse to bring the baby in any minute. "There is nothing I need."

"What about the baby? Does the baby need anything?"

"The baby needs everything, Mom. Including a name." All this time, Melissa thought she would name the child after Ronnie if it was a boy, but she no longer thinks it's a good idea. "You can help me pick it out."

"Okay," her mother says. "I will be there before you know it."

After they hang up, Melissa thanks Charlene and hands the phone back to her. When she sees that melancholy smile on her face again, Melissa says, "I'm sorry I couldn't help you figure out where Philip went."

One last time Charlene tries to make her remember. "Are you sure there wasn't anything he said that might have told you something about his plans?"

"No. He just came in the house. He was looking for you because he said you left a message that you were coming by. Then we started arguing. Then my landlord came over—"

"Your landlord?" Charlene and Richard say at the same time.

"Mr. Erwin," Melissa says, reluctantly speaking his name. "He came because he heard us fighting."

"So he saw Philip there yesterday?" Richard asks.

"Yes," Melissa tells them. "Why?"

"Because that's not what he told us when we went there this morning," Charlene says. "He said he never saw anyone at your house at all."

chapter 16

OUTSIDE THE SMALL, RECTANGULAR BASEMENT WINDOW OF THE
Erwins' house, a lone black bird blindly pecks at the trampled patch of
snow where Philip had fallen in the moments before Bill Erwin raised his
shovel and brought it down upon his head. From where he lies on the
cold, damp floor of the cellar, Philip can see it pecking and twitching and
shaking its oily wings. His mouth is gagged with a scratchy wool sock and
covered with duct tape. His legs are bound at the ankles, his arms at the
wrists, both with endless amounts of fishing wire that digs into his skin
with the slightest of movements. There is dried blood on the back of his
neck that itches, driving him mad because he cannot scratch it. Nevertheless, he is breathing. For that, Philip is grateful. As he shivers from the
cold, all the things Gail Erwin explained to him in the short while she was
conscious replay in his mind.

She told him about the pills she found in a flashlight.

She told him how she linked them to her husband's involvement with
Melissa.

She told him that he came after her when he realized that she had dis-
covered his secret.

There is still so much more he wants to know, though it's not possible to find out, since without warning Gail's voice grew faint and she stopped speaking again. The only sounds that punctuate the silence of the dank, shadowy cellar are her erratic breaths as well as the thunder of Bill Erwin's footsteps as he paces the floor above. Philip stares up at the wooden slats as they sag and creak with his every step. During the hours he has spent on this floor, Philip's mind has drifted in all sorts of directions. Those footsteps make him think of the days when his mother used to take him to the library for the story hour she hosted. He remembers the way she would stomp her feet on the red and gold carpet to imitate the monster from *Jack and the Beanstalk* rumbling around up in the clouds.

His mother.

Philip wonders if she has even bothered to take notice of his absence. And if so, has she done anything more than fold up the sofa bed, throw his stuff in the garbage, and wish him good riddance? Since there is no way to know for sure, and since he doesn't think the answer would give him much hope if he did, Philip tries his best to stop thinking about her. He turns his attention toward the basement window again, where a short while before he had seen someone's legs moving. Impossible as it was to call for help with his mouth gagged, he tried. Nonetheless, nobody heard.

Now there is only that lone black bird out there. The sight of it pecking at the ground makes Philip think of Donnelly Fiume's mynah bird in New York City. He recalls that last night in the studio on Sixth Street when he sat by the window, the way he had so many times throughout the years, waiting for whatever made-up name he had used to be called from down below. When the shout finally came, Philip balled up the keys in the very same towel Donnelly first used to throw the set to him, then tossed them to the street. It was only a matter of seconds before he heard the familiar clomp-clomp-clomp on the crooked old stairway. After taking one last sip of coffee, Philip walked to the door and waited for the knock on the other side, wondering what the person would look like when he opened up.

In all the time he had been having strangers over, Philip had come to expect that in person they were and weren't what they described. Yes, one might be six feet tall with black hair and blue eyes as he claimed in their exchanges on the computer. But somehow Philip always filled in the details differently. He neglected to imagine the gray crescents of dirt under one's fingernails, or the smell of too much cologne splashed on to cover up the need for a shower, or the foggy, disconnected feel of another's eyes that made Philip think of a fish gone bad. And there was something else about these visitors that was different in person: once this one or that one was standing inside the small studio or sitting on the edge of the Murphy bed, the easy lingo of those Internet conversations was gone. Sex was easier than talking. The entire time it was happening, Philip told himself it would be the last, though it never was.

At least not until the night when he opened the door and saw that the man on the other side was exactly how he described himself to be and more: six foot four, broad-shouldered, with a buzz cut, a square jaw, and a grim expression. Philip had learned to exaggerate his own appearance over the years, and this time his hyperbole left him worried. "Hi," he said, not liking the way his voice sounded so thin and stretched, the way it did when he was nervous.

"Take your shirt off," the man told him when he stepped inside.

His words came out so slurred and distorted that Philip knew the guy was either drunk or high. The red, watery state of his eyes confirmed it. Normally, there was some sort of preamble to these events—a quick discussion of comfort and approval. The way this one skipped over any of those flimsy formalities left Philip both more excited and more afraid. Philip stared into the square, rugged face of this stranger, thinking how much he resembled Jedd Kusam from high school. In his memory, Philip could still see Jedd pushing his books to the ground, shoving his head into a locker, and saying, "Repeat after me: 'My name is Dickless Fairy.'" He thought of that dictionary in the library, where Jedd and his friends covered all those definitions of words like *faggot, sucker, ugly,* and dozen of others, then put Philip's name beside each one. Why, he wondered, was he attracted to the exact type of person who taunted him all those years ago? It seemed like a cruel joke his mind had played on him, a curse that would never allow him to forget the insufferable humiliations of his past.

"I said, take your shirt off."

Philip had the sense that he should tell him to leave, but he found himself reaching down and tugging his shirt up over his head. Standing there before him, Philip felt as cold and pale as a plucked chicken. He could not remember the name this guy gave—was it Mike, or Joe, or Ted? Either way, he decided it was probably as phony as the names Philip used during these encounters. So for that reason, he switched it in his mind, silently dubbing him Jedd since he looked enough like him. At the sight of Philip without his shirt, this Jedd let out a hideous laugh.

"What?" Philip asked.

"You have a little kid's body. Haven't you ever heard of a place called the gym?"

Philip looked down at his hairless, underdeveloped chest, the small curve of his stomach, his lanky white arms, and was filled with shame. He made the motions to put his shirt back on when Jedd wrenched it out of his hand and threw it on the floor, shouting, "Thanks for wasting my time, asshole!" With that, he lifted off his own shirt, revealing a hard, thick-veined body covered with tattoos. There were so many dragon faces with long curly tongues and flames and wild eyes and cryptic symbols inked into his skin that it didn't look like skin at all. It was more like staring at a strange map of some sort, or an optical illusion, that fascinated and re-volted Philip all at once. Jedd looked him in the eyes and said, "That's what a man's body looks like. Memorize it, you fucking loser."

"Listen, you should just go," Philip told him, hating the sound of his voice still, hating everything about himself and his life at the moment.

But he did not go anywhere. Instead, he craned his neck around and stared at the mural of New York City on the wall. "It's like fucking Alice in Wonderland in here. What the hell kind of freak are you?"

"Just go," Philip said again.

"First I have to piss."

Philip glanced over at the door to the bathroom, thinking of Baby and Sweetie inside. "The toilet doesn't work."

Jedd walked to the door and pushed it open anyway, then stepped in-side and slammed it shut. Philip had invited all kinds of men here, and certainly there had been times when things didn't go as expected, but he had never experienced anything like this. In some distant corner of his mind, he supposed he had been waiting for it to happen all along. He thought back to those early days in the city. He remembered reading in the newspaper about a pianist who was last seen leaving a bar with a man he met there, only to be found by a friend the next day, murdered in his apartment. There had been a black-and-white photograph of the building in the paper, one Philip recognized from the neighborhood. And the same force that compels most of us to gape at the scene of an accident took hold of Philip too. He made a point to walk by the building later that day. When he looked up, Philip saw that the windows of the third-floor apartment were splattered with blood. What more of a cautionary tale could he have asked for? he wondered. Regardless, he went right on engaging in this shameful habit of his—all just to ease his insatiable loneliness for a short while.

Behind the door, the bird squawked. "What are you doing in there?" Philip called.

"This place is a fucking zoo, man."

"Please," he pleaded, standing directly outside the door now, arms crossed in front of his hairless chest. "Please get out of there and go. I'll call the police if you don't leave."

As he waited, Philip retrieved his T-shirt and slipped it back on. When the door opened, Jedd stood before him with his pants unzipped, his penis actually hanging out in front of him. Philip hated himself for looking, but the flick of his gaze was automatic, uncontrollable. Why? he wondered again.

"You like it?"

Philip turned his eyes away. He said nothing.

"I'll be on my way."

He gave Philip a good hard shove as he passed. But Philip was so glad to see the guy leave that he didn't care. He raced to the door and closed it behind him, twisting the dead bolt that was concealed in the street scene of the mural. Never again, he promised himself, leaning his back against the door and releasing a breath. Never again.

That's when he noticed something odd: the apartment was silent.

Philip didn't hear the sound of Sweetie scurrying around her cage or whistling or singing or making flushing or farting sounds or asking for a martini. Nothing. His stomach knotted as he stepped closer to the bathroom and opened the door.

The birdcage was empty.

The snake tank too.

Philip reached inside the tank and lifted the top of Baby's hide-box, but she was not there. His eyes darted around the bathroom until they landed on the gaping black hole of the drain at the bottom of the tub. He always kept that hole plugged just in case, so it could only mean one thing. Philip put his hand to his mouth and stood motionless, a feeling of guilt and remorse sweeping though him. He had been trusted to guard something precious to Donnelly—albeit a silly old pet snake—nevertheless, he had failed. And then the question entered his mind: What about the bird? The instant the words came, Philip felt a cold wind press against his face. He turned toward the open window and looked outside, where Sweetie was perched on the fire escape in the dark.

If you make a promise to someone who has passed on you have to keep it, whether you believe they're watching or not.

As quietly as possible, Philip reached inside the cage. At the bottom of the bird's dish was a small chunk of leftover pineapple, the sides turned brown from sitting there all afternoon and evening. Using the kind of careful precision people normally reserve for a pair of tweezers, Philip plucked out the fruit then went to the window. With one hand outstretched, he called, "Come here, Sweetie."

The bird flapped its wings but did not take off.

"Come here, Sweetie," Philip called again. "I have some nice fruit for you here inside. Pineapple. Your favorite."

"Make me a martini," she squawked. And this time she flapped her wings and flew over to the neighboring fire escape one floor below, where there was a tangle of rusted barbed wire, a collection of smashed terra-cotta pots, and a long-forgotten hibachi grill.

Philip didn't like this at all. But he stepped up on the toilet and slowly lifted one leg, then another through the narrow window. And then the rest of his body. Out on the fire escape, the icy air pricked the skin on his arms. A chill shot down his back. In the distance, he could hear the din of horns

honking. Far away, sirens wailed. Of all the fears that lingered in the re-
cesses of his mind during his years of inviting strangers over, never once
had Philip imagined that this would be the danger he'd find himself in.
He looked below at the alley, which was littered with a lopsided white
stove, an upside-down shopping carriage, and a striped mattress with coils
popping out every which way. In the dim light from the neighboring apartment windows, Philip could make out the words *Suck My Cock* spray-
painted on the brick wall of the building next door. Donnelly's bird had
pecked him so many times that Philip should have felt happy just to just
let the creature go. But he thought of his promise to Donnelly, and Donnelly's promise to Edward, and in a single fluid motion Philip extended
his arm all the way across and down the narrow alley, as far as he could
reach.

"Come here, Sweetie," he called once more.

This time the bird flapped its wings in a great scurry of noise, startling
Philip so much that he lost his balance. The last thing he remembered
was the sting of the barbed wire slicing into the soft skin of his neck as he
looked up to see that bird disappear into the New York City sky before
everything went black.

Now, as he lies on the cold cement floor in the Erwins' basement,
Philip watches as the bird outside continues pecking at the ground. He
looks around at the rows of makeshift support columns and at the shadowy
lump of Gail's body rising and falling with her every breath. He wants to
do something to get them out of here, but what? Even if he could free
himself, which he has been trying unsuccessfully to do for hours, he is far
too afraid to face that monster at the top of the stairs.

He thinks of his mother again and remembers when they used to go to
those daredevil shows at the old town airport where they later buried Ronnie. Watching those men walk out on the wings while the planes flew so
high overhead used to frighten Philip, so she would take him to the car
where they would wait until it was over. He can still recall how happy it
made him to rest his head on her lap, especially when she wore one of her
outfits that he liked best—a knee-length skirt covered with miniature
daisies. To Philip, it was like lying in a field of flowers as he gazed up at
her and she stroked his hair.

"Don't be afraid," she used to tell him on those occasions. "Everything will be okay."

The memory makes Philip think of all the fears he has let hold him back in life. There was the panic he felt when faced with the bullying from Jedd and his friends so long ago. There was the dread about submitting any of his poems after that first round of rejection letters. There was the trepidation about going over and introducing himself to that man and woman with the baby who he used to see at Aggie's Diner. (Philip always told himself he might work up the nerve to do it next time, but then, a little over a year ago, he showed up at the place to find that it was closed for good. He would never see those people again.) Finally, there was the anxiety that consumed him when faced with the prospect of seeking out a relationship. The reason, Philip supposes, is that he doesn't want to be proven unworthy of someone's love the way he had been by his parents.

And now there is the terror of trying to escape.

Don't be afraid, his young mother says in his memory.

It's a smart idea for you to face your fears, Donnelly tells him through the cab window on that very first day in New York.

Philip looks around the basement and decides to attempt something—anything—to get them both out of here. Even if there is only a slim chance that he will make it, he is going to try. Since he heard the rattle of chains on the storm doors last night as Bill Erwin locked it, Philip knows that is not an option. He sees his only choices as the window or the stairs that lead up into the house. When he considers exiting through the window, though, Philip realizes that it is too small and high off the floor for him to get up there and slide through. He settles on the idea that his only hope is to make it up the stairs and past Bill Erwin. The prospect brings a strangled feeling to his throat, but he only allows himself to focus on the first step of this plan: finding a way to free his hands and legs.

Across the room, not far from where Gail lies on the floor, there is the tool bench that Philip had seen from outside the window last night. If he can get over there, he might find something sharp to cut through the fishing wire. Slowly, Philip draws his body over to a wooden support column several feet away. With every push and pull, he is more aware of the battering Bill Erwin has done to his body. His shoulders ache. His arms are stiff. The wound on the back of his neck burns. It takes him a long while, but eventually he manages to stand, using the support post for leverage. A stray nail sticking out of the wood pricks his back, but the pain is slight compared to the agony he feels at the moment. Once he is standing, he shuffles, inch by inch, across the floor, listening to Bill Erwin's footsteps pace back and forth above him. The sound brings the brief memory of Philip's mother again. She is stomping her feet on the red and gold carpet in the library and raising her voice to imitate the monster, "Boom! Boom! Boom!"

Inch by inch, Philip shuffles across the floor, the bottom of his cast scraping against the cement, until he reaches the tool bench at last. It is so dark in this corner of the basement that he has to lean his face as close as possible to the jumbled pile of tools in order to see. He makes out some sort of a handled tray filled with screwdrivers, nails, and wrenches of all sizes. Beside it, there is a toolbox with the lid flipped open. Inside he sees a spool of wire, a spool of twine, a chisel, more screwdrivers, a greasy adjustable wrench, what looks to be a number of shiny fishing lures, and a pair of garden shears.

His eyes lock on the garden shears.

For a long moment, he stares at them, trying to devise a plan as to how he will maneuver the handle in order to cut the fishing wire around his wrists. He is at a loss, so he gives up and continues searching until he spots a small saw. This time Philip reaches out and runs the tangled clump of wire that binds his hands against the serrated edge. It's no use, though. The saw is pushed away every time he applies pressure. He decides to pick it up with his elbows, figuring he might be able to secure it somewhere, then cut the wire. But just as he lifts it from the bench, the saw slips from his grasp. Philip moves to try to catch it, knocking two screwdrivers, those fishing lures, and some nails to the floor in a loud clatter.

Bill Erwin's pacing comes to a sudden stop upstairs.

Only the sound of Gail's ragged breaths fills the basement.

Philip looks up at the wooden slats of the floor above, his heart slamming in his chest as he waits. And then, to his relief, the pacing continues. He swallows, the synthetic taste of that wool sock scratching his dry mouth and throat. More than anything, he wants to free his mouth so that he doesn't have to taste that sock anymore. With that thought, he remembers the nail jutting out from the wooden support beam, the one that pricked his back while he was trying to stand. He doubts it's substantial enough to slice through all the fishing wire, but he wonders if he can at least cut through the duct tape over his mouth.

As quietly as he can, Philip moves back to that post. When he feels around for the nail, he realizes that there are actually several sticking out of the wood. He bends down and pushes the duct tape into one of the points, forming the tiniest opening. He drags the duct tape across the point, back and forth, until the opening begins to tear. Soon, he creates a tear large enough so that he can open his mouth—only slightly at first, but wider as the tape comes apart in the center.

Philip spits out the sock and gasps for breath.

His first instinct is to scream for help, but he holds back, since he doesn't know who will hear him other than Bill Erwin. Instead Philip stands there, taking the chilly air into his lungs until he catches his breath. When he is ready, he returns to the tool bench and looks down at its surface once again. There are those garden shears, but he still has no idea how he can manipulate them, even now that he has the use of his mouth. He is about to try anyway when he spots that saw. This time Philip uses his teeth to pick it up. Clenching it in his mouth, he manages to sit down among those screwdrivers and nails and lures he dropped on the floor. Carefully, he positions the saw between his legs. Once it is secure, Philip runs the fishing wire back and forth against the edge until he feels it loosening.

The instant his hands are free, he reaches up and grabs those garden shears at last. A single snip slices through all the wire around the bottom of his legs. He goes to Gail Erwin and looks down at her blank white face. Her eyes are open, though when Philip speaks to her in the softest of voices, all she does is let out a faint groan. He presses his hand to her forehead and feels the heat of her skin, then glances at her swollen legs. There is no way she will be able to stand and walk out of here. And since

Philip cannot carry her, he decides to try to get out first, then find help. He tells her his plan, then walks to the staircase and looks up at the door. From here, he can see the shadow of Bill Erwin's footsteps in the small crack of light beneath when he passes. Just the sight causes Philip's heart to race harder. His body feels older than its years, too broken to fight Erwin.

Don't be afraid . . .

It's a smart idea for you to face your fears . . .

Philip stands there a long while, feeling the ache of his muscles and the sting of his skin where that wire had bound him. Finally he forces himself to return to the bench in search of a weapon. He locates a hammer and picks it up. He grabs a screwdriver, tucking it into his cast just in case. Even though he is still not certain he believes in God, Philip finds himself saying a prayer for the first time in ages. He prays for his safety. And he prays that if his brother Ronnie is indeed watching from some heaven after all, that he look upon Philip now. Donnelly too.

Once he is finished, Philip moves, one careful and awkward step at a time, up the staircase and toward the closed door. Halfway to the top, he pauses to be certain Bill Erwin hasn't heard him. Philip tries to count the seconds it takes for the man to pace the room. There doesn't seem to be any clear pattern, though, and Philip keeps going. At the top, he listens to the frantic, scattered mumbling on the other side.

". . . Put them with the others . . . Don't think of her as your wife . . . Think of her as the others . . . It will be easier . . . Put them with the others . . . Put them with the others . . ."

Philip knows that there is no more waiting. He also knows that the only thing he has on his side is the element of surprise. He must catch the man off guard then take him quickly, otherwise there is no hope of taking him at all. So the next time the shadow of boots come closer, Philip shoves open the door. The sudden explosion of noise and motion causes Erwin to stumble, and Philip whacks him in the chest with the hammer. The man staggers backward but does not fall. Philip steps into the living room, raises the hammer once more, and swings. But Erwin blocks it with his arm. Again Philip swings, bringing it down in a solid thud on his shoulder this time. A loud moan escapes Erwin's mouth before he lunges forward. He locks his thick arms around Philip's legs, and they both go tumbling across the room. The sheer weight of the man's body causes Philip to collapse on the floor beside the blazing mouth of the fireplace. As he feels the heat of the burning logs near his skin, Philip realizes that he has dropped the hammer. In the seconds before Erwin stands and comes toward him again, Philip glances across the room and sees a faded John Deere cap on the wagon-wheel coffee table. Tucked inside is his cell phone. It is too far away for him to reach, however, and Erwin is standing above him now, holding the fireplace poker in his hands.

"You little prick," he says and raises it above his head.

He's about to bring it down when Philip reaches back and grabs a handful of ashes from the fireplace, throwing them in the man's face. Erwin screams and presses his hands to his eyes, releasing the poker. It falls to the ground with a loud clank and Philip takes hold of it. There is no time for him to stand, so he swings with as much force as he can muster from his position on the floor. The hard iron of the poker cracks against the man's boots, right at the ankles, knocking him off his feet and sending him crashing facedown onto the coffee table. The hat and the phone go flying as the legs of the table buckle. Erwin lands among the pieces of broken wood.

Quickly, Philip stands. He brings the poker down upon the solid mass of the man's back, swinging once, twice, three times against his hulking frame. Each time Erwin releases another loud moan, but soon the moaning stops.

The room grows quiet.

In the sudden stillness, Philip finds it hard to breathe. His hands shake as he steps away from the broken table and Bill Erwin's body on the floor. He limps to the basement door and calls down to Gail. "If you can hear me, I'll be back for you. You're going to be okay. I promise."

Philip grabs his cell phone among the rubble, dropping the poker. He walks unsteadily to the front door and steps out into the glaring light of this winter morning. His eyes have been in darkness for so long that he has to hold one hand to his forehead in order to see. He is not sure what to do next, so he staggers over to Melissa's house. The door is locked, so he bangs on it, still gasping for breath. As Philip waits for her to open up, he reaches down and presses the On button of his cell. His thumb is shaking, but he doesn't miss a single button when he presses 9-1-1.

"Melissa!" he calls, pounding his fist against the door as he waits for the call to go through.

Behind him, a voice says, "There's nobody home."

Slowly, Philip turns and sees him: Bill Erwin standing outside the front door of his house, his shoulders slumped, his gray hair falling down in front of his haggard face, blood streaked across his chin and hands, down near the cuffs of his pants.

"This is the emergency operator, how can I help you?"

Philip's eyes go to the phone. He knows the police won't get here in time to save him, so he makes the impulsive decision to run as fast as he possibly can to the only place he thinks might be safe for a while. Philip goes toward the vacant house at the edge of the woods. When Bill sees where he is headed, he doesn't follow right away. Instead, he waits as Philip steps into the shadowy darkness of that abandoned cabin, slamming the door behind him.

"This is the emergency operator, how can I help you?"

Philip's hands quiver uncontrollably now. It is all he can do not to drop the phone as he lifts it to his ear. His voice is hoarse, his words come out clumped and broken, as he whispers, "I. Am at Thirty-two. Monk's Hill. Road. In Radnor Pennsylvania. Someone is trying to kill me."

The operator says she is notifying the local police department, but she needs him to stay on the line and give her more information. Philip repeats the address. He tells her that someone has already been badly injured. A woman. Gail Erwin. It's her husband who is after Philip now. The operator continues to question him, urging Philip to stay on the line, but he presses the Off button. Philip stands by the door, listening for Erwin's footsteps outside. The only sound to be heard comes from those snapping sheets of plastic. He looks around him and sees that the layout of this house is almost identical to Melissa's. But here the peeling walls are covered with graffiti. The ceiling sags so much that it looks as though it might give way any minute. And there, in the center of the room, he sees an enormous hole in the floor where it must have collapsed.

Philip takes a step closer to the edge of that gaping hole, peering down into the absolute darkness of the crawlspace below. Something about the black void down there sends a violent shudder through his body. Slowly, he steps away. With his back to the window, he waits. Staring at the door. Not knowing what he will do when Erwin steps through it. But just then the wide metal end of a shovel slams through the plastic behind him. In an instant, the room goes from darkness to light. Philip whirls around and sees Bill Erwin on the other side. The man reaches in and swings the shovel like a baseball bat, slicing the air in front of Philip's face. When he swings again, Philip takes a step backward. As he does, the boards by the edge of that crater in the floor give way and he drops three feet into the crawlspace below.

Now that the cabin is filled with light, Philip can see the dirt and rocks around him. And that's when he spots them: two empty holes, the perfect size for human bodies, to each side of where he landed on his back against the cold hard earth.

Put them with the others . . .

Above him, he hears the door creak open. Philip remembers that screwdriver tucked in his cast just in case. He reaches down and grips the ridged plastic handle, staring up at the tattered sheets of plastic hanging by the window, as the footsteps get closer and closer. The instant Erwin's shadow eclipses the hole in the floor Philip hears their voices.

"Philip!"

It is his mother outside.

"Philip!"

Though it cannot be, he thinks he hears his father too.

"I'm down here!" he screams.

And then comes the faintest of sirens. The sounds cause Bill Erwin to drop the shovel. He turns and his footsteps slam through the doorway. As the high-pitched wail grows louder in the distance, so do the voices of Philip's parents. Again Philip calls, "I'm down here!" Instead of waiting for them to find him, he struggles to a standing position, leveraging his aching body against the rotted floorboards and lifting himself out of that hole. A moment later, he limps outside to see his mother and father coming around the back of Melissa's house. "I'm here," he calls out, though his mother has already spotted him. She rushes across the yard and wraps both her arms around Philip with so much force and love that she just about knocks him down again. His father does the same.

"You're alive," Charlene says in a breathless voice into his ear, stroking his hair the way she used to do those long-ago days at the airfield. "I'm so happy you're alive."

As she repeats those words again and again, Philip squeezes both his parents tight. He gazes over their shoulders at a faint but certain trail of blood leading off into the woods. The sirens grow louder still, and Philip turns his eyes upward toward the spindly treetops. The branches are empty. Those birds—those strange dark birds—have all flown away.

Acknowledgments

Before *Boy Still Missing* was published, another novelist told me that he always found it best to begin a new book before the current one came out. I took that advice and started writing immediately. Two years later, the story was nearly done, but it hadn't come together as I had hoped. Then, on a rainy April night, I was riding the subway home from work when the idea for *Strange but True* came to me. The moment I got to my apartment, I began writing in longhand, and in three weeks I produced a very rough draft on twenty-three pads of paper. I spent the rest of the spring, summer, and fall transcribing, rewriting, and revising, telling almost no one what I was up to.

The morning the book was due, I arrived at my editor's office with the manuscript in hand and the feeling that it might have been slightly more professional to let her know sooner that I had put aside the novel I was under contract to write. So at the top of my list of thank-yous is my editor, Carolyn Marino—first for not throwing me out of her office that day; second for responding passionately to this story and caring so deeply for these characters that I sprang on her without warning. Her careful editing of this story helped more than I can ever say. I am also grateful to the rest of the gang at William Morrow/HarperCollins, especially Michael Morrison, Lisa Gallagher, Sharyn Rosenblum, Debbie Stier, Jennifer Civiletto, Jane Friedman, Cathy Hemming, Julia Bannon, Sam Hagerbaumer, and Michele Corallo, who all treat me with such kindness and make the publishing process fun.

I am forever indebted to my incredible agent, Joanna Pulcini, who works tirelessly on my behalf, reads draft after draft of my work with great care, and laughs with me along the way. On the foreign front, I am doubly blessed to have Linda Michaels and Teresa Cavanaugh taking on the world for me. On the film front, I am triply blessed to have the amazing Daryl Roth in my life, plus Matthew Schneider at CAA, and now Ross Katz too.

At *Cosmopolitan*, Kate White is a dear friend and fellow writer who offers me unending encouragement and support.

Alison Kolani read too many drafts of this story to count, and I owe her a gift certificate to every spa in the city.

For the help with Philip's Spanish, I thank all the many dishwashers I've worked with over the years who taught me everything I know. Plus, Ann Luster, who was unfazed by the nasty e-mails I sent her, and John Hansen, who double-checked my dirty work.

There have been so many others who have read, commented, given me a place to write, or simply cheered me on over the years, and I owe each of them a huge heartfelt thanks: Betty Kelly, Susan Segrest, Alysa Wakin, Stacy Sheehan, Elizabeth Barnes, Amy Chiaro, Patricia Burke, Jan Bronson, Linda Chester, Gary Jaffe, Colleen Curtis, Carol Story, Andrea Sachs, Atoosa Rubenstein, Sara Nelson, Alison Brower, Amy Salit, Dawn Raffel, Chris Bohjalian, Wally Lamb, Frank McCourt, Terrence McNally, Adriana Trigiani, Melise Rose, Vivian Shipley, Richard and Linda Warren, Abigail Greene, Michele Promaulaykyo, Isabel Burton, Esther Crain, Jenny Benjamin, Sara Bodnar, Pat Cliff from Blue Heron Books in Key West, Rob Carlson, and the Caruso family—Birute, Mario, Paul, and Yanna—who never mind when I sneak away at family gatherings to write.

And, of course, I need to give my family the biggest thanks of all: my mom, my dad, my sister, Keri, my brother, Raymond, and Grandma Dottie too.

Finally, there are those two friends with the baby at Aggie's so many years ago—they were special to me too.